All Joking Aside

Slippery Slopes

Piper Sheldon

Querque Press

To J.R., always

And to my #VIPeeps

Chapter 1

Miles

I OFTEN FOUND MYSELF MUMBLING OBSCENITIES WHEN rudely awoken. Today was no different.

It took me a second to register the knocking at my door.

How long had I been here, lying face down on this hotel bed?

I rubbed my cheeks back and forth between the two pillows. At least these were nice—soft and high thread count. I hadn't become a pillow aficionado overnight; I'd earned this badge through hundreds—if not thousands now—of nights in various hotels, motels, B and Bs, and everything in between.

A downside to traveling for a living was that there was always that first minute upon waking, where it took a moment to remember where I was. Eventually, the hazy fog of confusion burned away as I recalled the events of the evening prior.

It had been a late flight, followed by a long drive. I'd barely had the cognitive ability to check in before making it to my room to pass out. Late nights and jet lag, even just a time zone or two of difference, hit harder in my thirties.

I groaned as the realization set in.

I was back in Slippery Slopes.

Back in this odd little mountain town in Northern New Mexico, full of strange characters . . . and wasn't there a pest population out of control?

The guinea pigs. Running wild and rampant around town, and nobody seemed to think it was weird at all. While all small towns really were the same, Slippery Slopes was weirder than most. It had an energy that was impossible to describe: part woo-woo, part Midwest charm, part Southern hospitality. Maybe because it was populated with so many transplants looking for their place. Or maybe the local hot springs regularly released some sort of noxious gas that drugged people in small doses. There was a strange energy in the air here . . . like a genuine sense of community and caring for each other.

"Gross." A shudder passed through me.

I sat up and scrubbed my face.

I never planned to be back here a few months after I left the first time. It went against my strict policy of ever returning to the same place twice, lest other people start to form—I shuddered again in the early morning air—*attachments*.

"Mr. Asher?" a tremulous male voice called through the door. "I've got your coffee and breakfast here?"

I jumped slightly in surprise. I'd forgotten the knock that had woken me.

"You can leave it there." I lifted my head to yell in the direction of the door.

See, now this would never happen in a chain hotel. Minimal human interaction was as it should be. Yet here at the Slippery Slopes Inn, someone was trying to talk to me at—I glanced at the clock: nine *a.m.*—unfathomable.

At least when I checked in last night, I appeared to have had the foresight to order breakfast for today.

Yes. I vaguely remembered an overeager college-aged kid at the front desk being all too happy to help as I rolled in sometime after midnight, bleary-eyed and with a pounding headache. What had his name tag said? It had to do with an archangel . . . Michael? Raphael?

"It's Gabriel?" he called.

He was still talking. Why was he still talking? Did he need a response?

"Thank you," I said. Loudly. With a finality.

I dropped my head back to my hands. I needed to get moving. I had a meeting with the esteemed Mayor Sparks today, and then . . . maybe I might call upon Natalie Weatherby.

"Call upon?" I mumbled to myself, shaking my head in disgust. What century was it?

Maybe if I were self-narrating in old-timey talk, the possibility of seeing Natalie again weighed on me more than I thought. Not that much. No more than when the hem of a sock rubbed my foot the wrong way. Forgettable, really. Ignorable. And how I'd left things with the beautiful, friendly, charming blonde? A sidenote. As if I ever thought about her. Maybe once or twice since I landed and drove back up here. Hardly at all in the grand scheme of things.

Sure, we'd worked together a little and hit it off when most people found me to be a pretentious pain in the ass, but it had never meant anything. I had always planned to leave.

I groaned again. I was never meant to be back here . . .

A throat cleared outside my door. "I brought you some extra water bottles," Gabriel called.

I opened my eyes and stared at the door with incredulity.

He was. Still. Here.

"Thank you, Gabriel." I threw out my arms in a silent, *Is that all?*

But it wasn't all. I couldn't see or hear him, but he was there. I could *feel* him. Waiting to say more.

I dropped my shoulders. I sighed before I got up to throw on a shirt and jeans. I opened the door and thrust some cash in the direction of the kid.

"Oh. No." The hotel employee—concierge? Busboy? One-man welcome wagon?—held up his hands and stepped back. He wouldn't look at the proffered cash, as though it was a woman changing clothes. "Thank you, but we can't accept tips."

I frowned but tucked away the cash with an amused shake of my head. I'd just leave extra for him in the housekeeping envelope when I left.

If he wasn't fishing for a tip, why was he still here? My thumb scratched between my eyebrows.

I looked at him expectantly.

He smiled openly. "Hi." Gabriel had to be in his early twenties, friendly-looking, with deep dimples and messy blondish-red hair. He reminded me of those dogs left tied up outside convenience stores with a tongue hanging out and an eager tail wag for every passerby in hopes of being pet. Same energy.

I blinked. "Hi. My food?"

His toothy grin grew as he pushed my tray at me. "I know you said to leave it—" He looked up and down the hall, dropping his voice. "But Mr. Graves is staying here again, and he's been known to, uh, sample things. He thinks if he sees it, then he has access to it."

God, this town was so weird.

I took the tray and turned to set it on the desk. "Good looking out, Gabriel."

"You can call me Gabe. Everybody does."

"Gotcha." I saluted him and returned to the door. He was still there, propping the door open with his foot and holding water bottles that appeared from nowhere.

"Make sure to stay hydrated. It's very dry up here," he said. "And the high altitude can catch people off guard. So take it easy until you're acclimated."

I took the water bottles and set them down just inside the room. "Noted."

Gabe did not leave.

"So, you're back in town?" he asked.

My mouth parted in surprise. I never expected anybody to remember me after I finished a job. Though, to be fair, I'd never tested the theory.

"Yeah," I said.

"More of that film thing? For the town? You're the camera guy?"

I was a videographer and one of the most highly sought-after certified drone pilots in the country. But yeah. Sure. Camera guy was fine.

I nodded, still surprised he remembered me. Still wondering why he was lingering. Also, should I remember him? I must not have been a total ass to him last time if he was still here. But I had a job to do, and the sooner I got to it, the faster I could leave.

"Well, I better get back to it," he said. He did not move. Instead, I watched as he balled his fists and gathered courage in the set of his shoulders. "I, uh, I just wanted to let you know that I did what you said last time you were here. I, uh, did end up going to talk to him." His ears went red as the gaps in my memory filled in, my chin lifting as missing pieces fell into place.

"Right. The bartender?" I vaguely remembered him staring moon-eyed over the tattooed guy behind the bar.

I hadn't done much, just nudged him a little. Assured him that at worst, the guy wouldn't say anything back—he'd gone a little green around the gills at that—but best case, they could talk more and see if they hit it off. Glad to see it was the latter.

"Yeah. Oz. That's his name. We've been, uh, talking," Gabe explained.

"Good for you." I was honestly surprised. I wasn't sure the kid had it in him. The bartender struck me as one of those strong, silent types, taking no shit.

Gabe blushed deeper, shuffling his feet. This could really wrap up any time, and that would be absolutely great. The coffee would be tepid by the time I got to it.

"Yeah. So I just wanted to say thank you." He did an awkward little bow. "Despite what some people say, you're a good guy."

"Wait, who said—"

"And if you need anything at all, I'm here to help."

I pushed off the doorframe as Gabe finally started his retreat.

"Yep. Appreciate it. Thank you." I spun back in his direction. "Wait, actually. Maybe you can help me?"

He was back in front of me before I could finish what I hadn't meant to ask. The prospect of seeing Natalie again discombobulated my pre-coffee brain, and the question had just slipped out.

"Do you know Natalie Weatherby?"

His eyes went all soft, and he smiled. "Of course, who doesn't? Are you going to work with her again?"

"How did you—" I shook my head. Small towns. It didn't matter. The question felt far too complicated to answer, so I just settled on, "Yeah. I need to find her."

"Isn't she so great? She's helping me with my dissertation. I'm doing it on—"

"Yeah, that's great. She's great." Everybody in this whole town is *just so great*. "But, um, any idea where she'll be today? I have to meet with the mayor"—I looked at my watch. *Shit*—"in an hour, but any idea where Natalie might be after lunch?"

Gabe laughed.

I looked side to side, wondering what in that question was funny, but then again, maybe I was naturally hilarious.

"Oh, you're serious?" Gabe asked. "Today's the big day." He lifted his eyebrows meaningfully. "The Governor's Ball?"

At my blank expression, he shook his head with a disbelieving laugh, as though I was the one not to be believed.

"Wow. You really don't know. Okay, well, you're in luck. I don't know if you'll still be here by July, but today's the big drawing for the Governor's Ball in the town square." His eyebrows lifted hopefully.

"There's going to be a Governor's Ball here? In the town square?" I asked.

He laughed heartily. I still hadn't been joking.

"No, no. It's the raffle for the Governor's Ball, which will be held on the Fourth of July in Santa Fe. The drawing is happening today. One lucky winner, two tickets for two nights."

"Ah." I scratched my hand through my hair. They were having a whole town event about this. Very normal and not at all strange.

"Natalie will definitely be there," he said with emphasis. "Did you hear she saved the mayor's son?"

"What?" I asked, trying to follow the kid's excitement.

"Right after you left. There was an incident. She's a big deal around here."

She was already a big deal last time. Now I imagined her lifting a bus off a small child like a superhero as the townspeople threw flower petals at her feet and cheered her name. Great.

It didn't matter. If I ran into her or her gorgeous smile, she would probably not even notice me, surrounded by her adoring fans. I wasn't here for her. I was here for the work.

"Okay, well, thanks again for the coffee. Can we assume this will be a daily thing unless I say otherwise?"

Gabe nodded happily. "You bet!"

I shook my head. "Good kid," I mumbled as I left the doorway to grab my coffee. "Strange, but good."

With drink in hand, I made my way to the blackout curtains and pushed them open. I blinked back at the bright sky, clear blue, and the little park below my window. Sure enough, a podium was being erected in the gazebo that sat in the center of the park.

I could have been anywhere in America. It was all the same, town after town. A guinea pig, followed by a gang of four more, ran across the square.

Okay, maybe not *Anywhere*, USA. But these towns were all the same.

I let out a long sigh.

The view was nice though. The mountains lined the valley, and town was nestled comfortably within, tucked away from the fast-paced real world. It was easy to see what attracted people here.

"Not for me," I said. As soon as I was done, I was headed back to Callie and our life of travel and filming.

After a quick shower, I had just enough time to catch the mayor en route to the big to-do in the town square.

"Mayor Sparks," I said, jogging to catch up with her just outside her office.

The mayor was a well put-together woman, in her mid-sixties, if I had to guess. Flowing down her back, her hair was solid, shining black, save for streaks of gray at her temples.

"Mr. Asher, nice to see you again. I thought you might be late," she said.

"Not for you, Mayor Sparks," I said with a smile that didn't fit naturally on my face.

She smiled in return, but in a way that said she wasn't buying my shit. *Noted.*

"I was sorry to hear about your partner. Send Callie our love and best wishes, will you?"

I cleared my throat. "Of course."

"She made quite an impact on this town in the brief time she was here."

"She always does."

We turned abruptly around a corner to find what must have been half the town, if not more, packed into the town square. The mayor came to a stop and turned to me.

"All this for a dance?" I asked.

The mayor looked over her shoulder at the gathering crowd. "Not just any dance. But I'm sure for someone like you, it's all very pedestrian." She smiled warmly at the gathering people, then looked back at me, eyes neutral but her disdain for me clear in that neutrality.

Had I been so transparent? Had I really rubbed her the wrong way? A wave of guilt passed over me. I shouldn't be here. I wasn't good at people-ing. I cleared my throat and searched the surrounding crowd for something positive to say.

A woman in multiple layers of vividly printed fabric waved crystals in the air. "It's an important day. I can feel it," she said to nobody and everybody, holding the rocks in her palms toward the sun.

"I'm sure it's . . . fun," I tried with another smile.

Mayor Sparks's mouth pinched into a tight purse. Damn, if I'd known I was coming back here, maybe I wouldn't have been such a prick last time.

"It's important to many people," she said.

I nodded, hands in my pockets, feeling chastised.

"I reviewed the footage you sent so far," she said, and I focused on her. This was the reason I was here. "The aerial footage of the mountain and the slope covered in snow is phenomenal."

I nodded. No surprise there. There was a reason I was paid so well.

"I look forward to more footage of the town and the springs with the warmer weather."

"I'm sure it'll be great," I said honestly, already envisioning shots in my head.

"I'm curious what your plan for the interview portion is now, with how things have changed."

"I spoke with Callie about that. She suggested that I take footage of the townspeople on the ground, inside the shops, to get a feel for everything, but maybe cut the interviews."

That wasn't entirely true. Callie suggested we keep the interviews but have me conduct them. Quite possibly the worst idea. Callie was the people person. I was the quiet genius behind the camera. That was our whole schtick. The mayor sought a well-rounded tourism video for the town, and while I didn't see the appeal in talking, apparently that was a crucial aspect. The problem with being a pretentious asshole meant that I wasn't the face guy, I was more like the snarky sidekick.

"Actually." She lifted her chin, searching the crowd for someone. "I had an idea. Ah, yes. I was thinking. You should tap Natalie Weatherby for assistance. You won't find anybody who knows and loves this town more."

Of *course*. The muscles of my jaw flexed as my stomach pitched.

"I'm not sure—"

"I'm going to insist." The mayor gave a curt smile. "She'll be happy to help. She helps everyone."

"I don't know—"

"It's Natalie or nothing, I'm afraid," the mayor said with a smile that belied the threat in her gaze. "She recently saved my son's life, you know?"

"I heard something about that." I scratched the back of my neck.

"I owe her a lot, as you can imagine. You're here for the next eight weeks, correct?" I nodded. "Good. This will give you time to really fall for Slippery Slopes. There is so much to love, I know you will grow to appreciate all it has to offer."

Eight weeks of mild threats from the locals for daring to talk to their queen. I couldn't wait.

"I know this is a long assignment. But there are so many things worth staying for," she said. Her eyes flicked around the crowd and then stilled. Her gaze softened. "There's our girl now."

I followed her line of sight and felt my heart flop over once in my chest.

The spring sunshine seemed to beam like a spotlight right onto Natalie. Her golden hair and her warm smile were like a beacon. She was surrounded by people, but still set apart.

And she was painfully more beautiful than I remembered.

Natalie had a way of standing out no matter where she was, and not only because of the long blond curls trying to escape her tight coil of hair or the ready smile she wore like a welcome badge. It could be the straightforward beauty of hers, the figure that would always draw attention from anybody that she passed, but it was more than that. It was an unspoken draw that not everybody had. An aura of sincerity that made people look to her and trust her.

That thump of my heart must have been from frustration. She was more incredible in person than I remembered. Not that I thought of her a lot. Here and there, at most.

"Also." The mayor gave me her full attention, her tone all business. "Make sure you stay hydrated and be careful—the altitude can sneak up on you."

I should get an award for not rolling my eyes. "Yes. I will be careful."

Was there some sort of commission earned for warning visitors about elevation? Maybe a badge of honor? *We're a great town, even our air is special! It will kill you if you're not careful.*

"Good luck," the mayor said. "We appreciate you making this film."

"Yeah," I mumbled after I realized I'd gone back to staring at Natalie with my mouth parted.

"I have tickets to give out." The mayor was already walking away. "I look forward to hearing your updates, Mr. Asher."

Maybe Natalie would be happy to see me. Maybe we'd even hug. I regretted not giving her a proper hug last time when I left. It had all happened so quickly. Callie got sick, and then we were flying back. Then it didn't matter.

This place was just a job. I'd find Natalie and we'd get done what needed to get done.

Chapter 2

Natalie

The problem with living a lie was that there was no great way to sleep. My brain never stopped replaying all the ways I was a terrible person. Why were the mean voices in my head their loudest in the middle of the night?

Liar. They're all going to find out and kick you out of town. You were never meant to be here in the first place.

"Welp. Time to get up and live another day of lies," I said to my ceiling, which I'd been staring at wide awake since two a.m.

I shot out of bed and took a shower. I brushed my wet curls into a low bun, wincing with the brutal force I used to contain them. This wasn't the curly-hair treatment that they deserved, but I preferred them slicked back, gelled down, and out of my face. If I put in enough product, they mostly stayed put throughout the average day. Before the sun came up, I left my apartment and set off to my Thinking Place.

As always, I detoured a block out of the way to pass my favorite house: a part-time rental for a couple who lived in Florida. I liked to sometimes pretend that I would own it one day.

Maybe when I was a Real Resident of Slippery Slopes. The single-family home was paneled in white, but light purple trimmed the large front windows and the edge of the roof. There was a small porch big enough for two chairs to rock at night, drinking margaritas and watching the sun set behind the surrounding mountains. Most importantly, it had a lush garden that, come summer, would be overflowing with lavender and loads of wildflowers great for the local bee population.

"One day," I said as I passed.

I'd lived in Slippery Slopes for ten years, but the timing still wasn't right for home ownership.

My Thinking Place was a hidden and long-forgotten room along Main Street, past the town square with the Jane Smith statue and the gazebo. It was where I went when I needed to relax my face muscles or take off my bra after a day of tours. Or hide from the people who thought me a savior. I often came here to get ready for the day because it felt more like home than the apartment I lived in.

I got to work once I was settled in the only chair in my Thinking Place. Ignoring my gritty eyes and the heavy weight on my chest, I made plans as Slippery Slopes' resident tour guide. I tweaked some notes to include more fascinating local facts and reviewed Gabe's thesis pages he'd sent me so far.

I could hardly look at myself in the mirror as I finished getting ready for the day's big event. Not even a thick layer of concealer could hide the puffy bags under my eyes or the perpetual crease of worry between my brows. The guilt had begun to manifest physically, and I had to come clean to Deckard Sparks before it ate me alive. The mayor's son deserved the truth. For the last three weeks, I'd been tormented with the guilt of out-of-control bad timing.

"Deckard. I wasn't the one who saved your life that day," I practiced with my reflection. "It was a complete misunderstanding. I was just walking by. I was pissed off at Miles Asher for coming into town and toying with my heart like the pompous jerkwad he is. Even though he had been so nice and we'd gotten along so well . . ." I stopped applying mascara and blinked at myself. "Great job. Talk about another guy while you're asking him out."

I groaned, already losing the nerve. The accusatory voices in my head weren't as loud in the light of day, but I still wanted nothing more than to curl up with a book and hide here. Unfortunately, today was the lottery drawing for the Governor's Ball, and I was expected to be there. I was a bit of a town ambassador at this point.

More guilt pushed on my shoulders until I thought I might sink into the earth. I couldn't go on like this much longer.

I'd tried to talk to Deckard before, tried to tell him the truth, but every time I was near him, I just froze up. There was too much pressure to say the right thing and act in the right way. It didn't make any sense. If I could just get him alone, away from all the prying eyes and listening ears, then maybe it would be easier.

I could ask Deckard out finally and get him alone to come clean. If Deckard and I were dating, then we could put this whole misunderstanding behind us. Nobody was more beloved in town. Therefore, *I* would be beloved in town. And I would never have to leave.

An image of the townsfolk with pitchforks and flaming torches chasing after me, calling me a liar, flashed through my mind.

I needed to find Deckard.

I took a deep breath before leaving my sanctuary.

The bright New Mexico sun filled the center of town with a warm light that was just perfect on this fine spring day. I plastered a smile on my face, set my shoulders back, and slipped into the role I needed to play. I buzzed with urgency as I half walked, half ran my way toward the town square. My eyes found Rochelle right away. My best friend was easy enough to spot because she stood several inches taller than most, and her perfect bone structure and tiny pores always led my gaze, and the gaze of most people around us, right to her. She could have been a model in another life, but she was content here in Slippery Slopes, rocking the lawyer life, married to the only other lawyer in town, and keeping Slippery Slopes equipped for all its lawyer-y type needs. Like property deeds? Honestly, I wasn't sure. I should probably know more about the woman I've called my best friend since I was eighteen.

Spotting Rochelle was one thing, but getting to Rochelle was another story. I had to squeeze my way through the whole town's population, stuffed into the small park in the town square. But this was typical on a day like today. This was typical in general. Slippery Slopes loved an event. Several people smiled and said hello to me, and I returned the gesture like the big fat phony I was. A few even patted me on the back like I was some hero. Each step grew heavier.

"Hey, Ro," I said, winded. When I finally made it to Rochelle, I saw she was husband- and kid-free. "Where are John and Olive?"

"The churro truck is here. And you can't mention anything sugarcoated around Olive without her giving puppy dog eyes."

I nodded in understanding. Olive had turned those bad boys on me more than once, and any and all boundaries went crumbling. Which incidentally was why all sugar was hidden when I babysat.

"Well, good. Not that I don't love those attention hogs, but I have news for grown-up ears only," I said and shimmied my shoulders with excitement. She blinked slowly at me.

"We can play the game where I guess witty things that are

hilarious and not related at all to the truth, or we can skip straight to the point."

I gave my best Olive-inspired pout. "Aw, but guessing wrong answers is half the fun. 'You finally cleaned out your fish tank and found a buried treasure,' for example."

"You don't have a fish tank." She tilted her head. "Just tell me."

"Boo. Lawyers."

"Even in the Land of Mañana, time is still money, baby." She shrugged. "Fine. You are going to rent the house on Cherry Street?"

"Okay, this isn't fun." I shook my head. "No. I've decided today is the day. I can *feel* it. I'm sure of it."

"Does this have anything to do with your sudden fixation on the mayor's son?"

I guffawed with insult. "Sudden? I have always liked Deckard Sparks."

"Sure." She looked me over with narrowed eyes.

Not even Rochelle knew the truth about the fake saving. I had planned to tell her so many times, but ultimately decided Deckard should know first.

I must have gone frozen because she flipped her hand, gesturing for me to go on. "So you're asking Deckard out finally. Is that the big news?" One dark eyebrow arched skeptically. I'd been saying that I wanted to ask Deckard out for weeks. Ever since I saved him. I just hadn't explained why. If I could just get him alone, then I could find my words and come clean.

And I did want to ask Deckard out. He was perfect. Anybody in town would agree.

"Yes. Well. Sort of. I need to find him. Have you seen him?" I asked.

"About time. And no, I haven't seen him yet." Rochelle arched her head to where John and Olive were queued. When she looked back at me, the smile melted from her features. "Oh, God."

"What?"

"You just look all cute and hopeful. You're like a little cartoon chipmunk that found a stash of nuts."

"I am hopeful." I felt my whole face lift with a smile as I said it. *Hopeful to make the right moves for once.*

"But I have to be 'the friend' now—"

"You don't have to use air quotes. We are actually friends, you know."

"—and that means saying truths you might not want to hear."

I felt my mouth turn down as a chill spread through me. "Oh?"

"Stop, you're making it worse. With your sad eyes and cute wittle cheeks." She wiggled my cheek as she pinched it with her thumb and pointer finger.

"You could *not* say it." I rubbed the area she'd squeezed.

"No. I think this is one of those stupid things that I have to stupidly say. Stupid having friendships and relationships. God, being a mother and a wife has made me soft."

I patted her arm reassuringly. "Even something as gentle as water wears the strongest things down. You haven't lost your edge. People are terrified of you all the time."

She smiled with a glint in her eyes. "Thank you for saying that." She lifted her chin and shook back her gleaming locks. All at once, she transformed into lawyer mode. "Which is why I've got to tell you that just because you saved his life doesn't mean you have to date Deckard."

"I know that," I said, surprised and embarrassed.

"Do you?"

"I've always thought we'd be a good match," I said, and it wasn't *un*true.

"A good match? Natalie, this isn't the Regency era. Are you even attracted to him?"

"He's very cute," I said. Relationships were more than just attraction. They were a commitment, and in time, I'd feel those fireworks that love songs and my books talked about. "I just thought he was going to marry Bee Perkins eventually."

"We all did at some point. But now Bee is very clearly with Owen Campbell." We turned in unison to where Bee chatted happily next to a behemoth of a man with his arms crossed and features hard. She was flailing her arms in anger when Owen scooped her up to kiss her head. All at once, the anger melted from her, and she flopped like a rag doll against his chest. Speaking of fireworks, those two had them.

"They work weirdly well together," she said as I nodded.

Then we both turned back to the stage where the mayor (Deckard was the son of a powerful woman—that'll be another green flag, thank you very much) was chatting with a few of the city council members onstage as more people squeezed in.

I searched to see if Deckard was around the stage, but I couldn't find him.

"Every time you tried to ask him out before, there was always an excuse. The clouds were moving too fast. The wind was too windy," Rochelle said.

There was a chance I hadn't hidden my reluctance as well as I'd thought. I had wanted to ask Deckard out B.M. (Before Miles, not Bowel Movement). It wasn't that I was waiting to hear from Miles Asher. I never even thought of him after he'd left. The two men had nothing to do with each other. I wasn't even thinking of Miles now. Who brought him up? Not I!

"I know it sounds like those were lame excuses, but it never felt right," I said.

I was sure Deckard had been the guy for me. On paper, we

just made sense. But then Miles Asher blew through town and confused me.

"Are you sure you actually like Deckard?" she asked.

"He's a walking green flag. He's perfect."

"Nobody is perfect. Not even a little. That's the sort of thinking that leads to never making a move," she said.

"He's adored by the whole town. He's so cute and nice and comes from the best family." Here, Rochelle's eyes narrowed like she doubted the Sparks family was the best. I went on. "He's the only one who regularly checks to make sure the guinea pigs are okay in the worst weather. He volunteers at Golden Sunset. He writes poetry."

"He does?"

"In my mind, he does."

She crossed her arms with a huffed laugh. "You know, and I realize that this may not hold much weight having just professed my loss of edge because of said husband, but you don't actually need a man at all," she said, lazily flipping out a hand.

"Please. I know. It's not that I think that."

But I loved it here, and I wanted to build a life. And if Deckard chose me, then I could stay here. Rochelle wouldn't understand.

My eyes moved over the crowd again, finally spotting him talking to a group of curious tourists. He smiled affably, his little flop of light brown hair slowly falling forward, so he had to push it back.

My hands went cold in anxious anticipation. My stomach clenched in what must have been the signs of a crush.

An idea flashed like a bolt of lightning: Deckard and I, arm in arm, dressed to the nines, waving to the town cheering us on as we get into the limo and head to the Governor's Ball. Then the town would think me worthy. Then I could relax a little.

Rochelle was still using her lawyer tone when a shape

moved into the direct path of my staring. "I'm just making sure that you actually like Deckard and aren't projecting a vision of some life you feel you need to have to prove yourself to this town because—"

"I'm going to take him to the Governor's Ball!" The idea burst out of me before I could lower my voice. It was perfect. I'd be alone in the limo with him, and I could come clean. And then we would date, and all would be forgiven. The town would still love me. All would be fixed. "I'm going to ask him to the Governor's Ball."

"You got a ticket? How?" Her indifferent facade cracked as she almost shouted.

"Shh, keep your voice down," I warned her as several residents looked at us.

She lowered her voice to gossip levels. "I heard the mayor couldn't even get a ticket. Hence the reason for all this hullaballoo today." She gestured all around us, where the crowd strained to see the stage set up on the gazebo.

"No ticket yet. But I can feel it. I'm winning today." I let the warmth of the truth spread through me. A hopeful anticipation buoyed me. Once I was alone with Deckard, the truth would be revealed.

"Ah." Rochelle's dry tone threatened to dash it all.

"Don't 'ah' me. That's the real-world equivalent of texting me 'k.' I don't care for how much of your disappointment is revealed."

"Tell me how you know you're winning the drawing today. The drawing that the entire town entered. The drawing that you have a one-in-a-few-thousand chances of winning." She side-eyed me.

"I just know." I lifted my face toward the sun and let it warm me. The air was still chilly this high up in the mountains, but it held that hopeful flutter of warmer days coming soon.

"And what if they don't call your name for the big prize?" she asked.

"Then it wasn't meant to be." My insides warred. I had to win those tickets. I couldn't make any more excuses.

She held my gaze for several seconds too long. I had to look away, my focus going to the crowd instead. "You know what? I think this is a great plan."

"You do?" I dropped my arms and looked back to her, suspicious of her sudden support.

"Yep. You win those tickets today, and you can finally ask out Deckard and get everything you wanted."

"You think I need a man now?"

"Man, no man. I just want to see you happy. I want nothing to get in the way of that. If you think asking out Deckard will make you happy, then I support you."

"Okay." Why did her support only add to my growing anxiety?

"Plus, I have a good feeling about this lottery . . ."

Whatever Rochelle had been saying regarding her sudden change of heart faded away as alarm bells blared in my ears, blocking out all other sound. It was as if the whole world paused, except for the one man who entered my field of vision.

This wasn't happening. This *couldn't* be happening.

"Natalie?" Rochelle snapped her fingers in front of my face. "You there?"

The town faded away. My focus narrowed in. It was him. It was the man that I wasn't thinking about. The man that I *never* thought about.

My entire body went hot and cold at the same time. My heart began racing out of my chest, as if to run away.

I'd spent weeks looking for him in crowds, hoping to spot his half-annoyed, half-amused grin above the heads of the towns-folk, those bright blue eyes glancing around condescendingly.

And here he was, chin tucked, eyes riveted to the phone in his hand as he moved through the crowd without a care in the world. His broad shoulders twisted confidently, moving himself out of the way with dexterity that didn't vibe with his performed disinterest.

"Oh my God. Don't look now." I gripped Rochelle's arm and tried to tuck myself behind her to hide, which was immature while simultaneously being as successful as trying to house-train a wild guinea pig. I would assume. Not that I tried.

Not after that first time.

But it was most definitely him. Bane of my existence, enemy of all.

Miles freaking Asher.

Chapter 3

Natalie

My palms grew sweaty. My heart tried to escape my chest. My stomach flipped as though floating away.

From all the rage, no doubt.

"What?" Rochelle turned in a full circle, searching for the source of my freak-out, drawing all the attention to her ridiculously beautiful face. "Ah."

"'Ah' again?" My eyes widened, and I looked around frantically. "More of an, *ahhh*," I screamed quietly, not wanting to draw attention to us.

This wasn't happening. I had finally decided to ask Deckard Sparks out. I had a plan that made sense.

"Why is Miles back? I thought he was gone for good after last time." Even Rochelle seemed confused.

"I don't know. I had no idea he would be here. No. No. This cannot be happening."

"Well, this complicates things." She tapped her fingers along her lips. "He's cuter than I remember. I think your hatred of him repainted him in my mind as some sort of hunched gremlin creature, but he has Nerdy Hot Guy energy."

"Ugh. The better to hide his ugly insides."

"I'll-take-care-of-your-needs-first vibes."

"*Pfft*. He isn't aware of anybody else's needs."

My neck went hot at the thought of Miles *caring* for someone else first.

"He's coming right at us now," Rochelle said, lips hardly moving.

"Of course he is. You're a beacon of gorgeousness, calling the unprotected masses to come crashing to your shores," I grumbled.

She chuckled. "Yeah, I'm sure that *I'm* the reason that he's coming over here."

I peeked around her arm to see that, sure enough, he was locked on and moving in.

"I'm *so* onto him," I said, narrowing my eyes.

"I'm sure you'd like to be." She clicked her tongue. "You know, now that I think about it, your fixation with Deckard began shortly after Miles left."

"Objection!"

"Overruled." She shook her head. "No. It's true. Are you asking Deckard out to get revenge? To prove that you are over Miles?"

No, I was asking out Deckard because he was *here,* and he was loved by all. Unlike Miles Asher, who left the taste of batteries in my mouth. Not that I've licked a lot of batteries.

Not after the first time.

"No. I didn't even know Miles was back," I whispered. My heart continued to hammer. My hands smoothed back my hair. Was my outfit cute? What? Who cared? "Why is he even here?" My muttered rant continued. "He made it clear that he hated this town and couldn't wait to leave."

"What a jerk," she said.

"To dutifully quote *Mean Girls*, 'He doesn't even go here,'" I said.

"You sound like you are about to wax poetic about our little town."

"I would never." (I did all the time.) "I just think this is literally the most perfect place to live, and why he can't see that makes him a huge pretentious jerk."

"It's weird how protective you are about this town."

"It's a totally normal thing to be protective about."

"Yeah, but you aren't even from—"

"Do not finish that sentence."

"Okay. Okay, sorry. I forget how weird you are about that too."

"If you keep calling all of my charming personality traits 'weird,' then I don't think I want to hang out with you anymore."

"Aw. Please forgive me. Your love of this town is perfectly in proportion to your hatred of Miles."

"That didn't feel like an apology."

"Huh. I tried." She shook me off her arm and out of my hiding spot. "He's almost here." She kept her gaze locked forward, watching him in her periphery.

"I was so glad when he left," I said.

"Really? You seemed pretty upset. You talked about it a lot—"

"Are you close enough to flick him?" I asked.

"Unfortunately, no. But how do you feel about a spitball?"

"Feels a little vulgar. But keep it in your metaphorical back pocket."

Rochelle tucked a little wad of paper into the pocket of her jeans.

"I'm thinking a stinging barb with plenty of wit that makes him feel emasculated and also stupid for existing," I hissed.

"Your turn-ons are intense."

"Look at him." I glared. "Even the way he walks through the crowd. Like he doesn't want to be here. Everyone just parts for him. Probably because they don't want to get his stink on them. That's not fair. He actually does smell really nice. Which, while we are listing them, is also an annoying trait."

"Are we listing them?"

"You can see in his eyes, he's coming to use me again." I circled around Rochelle, still attempting to hide behind her tall, lithe frame. "That's all he does. Mines this bounteous brain for its best bits and then claims them as his own."

"That was a lot of alliteration," she said. "John is waving for me to come over. It seems there may have been a churro incident."

"Don't you dare leave now." I tried to hold on to her, but she slipped out of my grasp easily and spun away like the gorgeous gazelle she was.

"Trust me, I'd rather stay and watch you two flirt in your super weird—eh, normal—way, but alas, duty calls." With that, Rochelle sighed and walked off mumbling, "All I do is help people."

Miles sauntered up (because he was an actual grown human man that *sauntered* in real life). Heat spread up my neck, and I could not get my pulse under control. I focused on my breathing instead.

"Why'd your hot friend leave?" he asked, hardly looking up from whatever was so important on his phone.

Really? After how he left. After everything, *that* was the first thing he said to me. I couldn't believe this was happening. This was not how this day was supposed to go.

"She's married." My back teeth ground together.

"That doesn't make her less hot. Shame on you for boxing her in."

In through my nose, out through my mouth. I would not let him bring me down to his level. Any reaction from me would give him what he wanted. I refused to have any sort of feelings about him being back in town. I didn't even notice. Nope. Too busy living my best life.

"Why are you breathing like that?" he asked, rocking back on his heels to look at me as he tucked his phone away.

"Can you please be quiet?" I asked as politely as possible, even though my jaw seemed to be locked. "I'm trying to hear the mayor."

"Why? This is a dog and pony show," he said with an expression of boredom. "The winner of that ticket is going to be somebody in the mayor's office or on the city council."

"That's not true."

"I forgot you love the mayor. She can do no wrong. You even saved her precious son."

My nostrils flared, and a sick feeling passed over me. "Please, go away."

"Aren't you curious as to why I'm back?" he asked. He even had the *gall* to put a hint of hurt into his voice.

"I'm sure you need something from me."

"When you put it like that . . ." He chuckled nervously. "But you're right. I need your help."

Oh, that's rich.

"You are the last person on earth I would ever help again," I said, finally lifting my head to briefly cut him with my gaze. It took all my strength.

The sharpness of my words must have hit him, causing him to bring a hand to his chest in mock shock. "You're not as nice as you make yourself seem to everyone."

The truth of it was ice in my veins. He saw through the facade, and he could see my ugly insides.

"I am very nice. Stop. Talking."

"That's a shame. I meant it as a compliment. Nice is expected, unimaginative."

"Go. Away." I growled the words. My sweet mask was slipping. He did this to me. He brought out the worst version of myself that I tried so hard to keep hidden.

"Can't. Now I'm invested to see who wins the big prize. Isn't that why we are all here?" The mocking tone boiled my blood.

This whole town was a joke to him. It had been since day one. I highly doubted that he cared at all about who won the tickets. He wouldn't even be here by the time of the Governor's Ball. God, he better not still be here by then. He's already ruined some of winter and the start of spring. He can't have summer too.

"Why are you *here*?" I glared at the ground.

Sometimes—and I wouldn't admit this to anybody—I struggled to look directly at Miles. Even before I vowed to hate him forever. He was just so . . . hard to look at. He made me feel like my insides were going to vibrate out of my skin. Like I was this ball of intense energy with nowhere to go.

Now, I had to force myself to meet his gaze to show dominance, like a bear, or whatever animal you're supposed to do that with. I should probably look that up later, given my close proximity to a variety of wild animals. Slippery Slopes was nestled in the valley of a mountain and surrounded by dense protected forests.

The mayor stepped up to the microphone, and the crowd around us surged. All at once, I was pressed forward from behind, and I stumbled on one of the large decorative stones that lined the edge of the grass. I was about to crash face-first into the pavers when a strong grip caught me and yanked me back. The action caused Miles's front side to be pressed up against my entire back. His touch caused a rush of rage throughout me. It was this physical burning presence of him that made my stomach go all liquidy and my legs shake.

"Come on. Back up," Miles snapped to the people in our direct vicinity. "It's the Governor's Ball, not a new car."

The crowd barely acknowledged him as they kept their focus onstage, but they did give us a little breathing room.

I shrugged him off while I muttered a thank-you, which he acknowledged with a grunt. His hands were back in his pockets as he looked around the crowd, avoiding my gaze. I'm sure that small act of civility was the source of his visible discomfort.

I was lightheaded and tingly from the post-anger adrenaline rush.

"That's it? You're not even going to listen to what I have to say?" he asked after another moment.

"So you can get what you need and leave all the faster?"

"Yes. That's what I do—"

"That, I'm aware of." I scoffed.

The mayor announced herself, and I stood on tiptoes to try to hear her better and to block him out. Which didn't actually make sense, but neither did turning down the radio in the car when lost.

I strained to get a better view of Mayor Sparks, but apparently, everybody over five foot five was parked directly in front of me today.

"Here." Miles grabbed my hips and hefted me onto the same stone that almost tripped me. It lifted me a few inches over the heads in front of me. His hands dropped from my waist as quickly as they'd arrived. Along with that same flush of anger in me. He must really be desperate. All this faux chivalry suddenly.

How dare he . . .

I narrowed my eyes. At least I could see better from here. But it also meant that we were close to the same height now, and his proximity behind me was tangible. His exhales moved the loose hairs from my tight bun at my neck. I swallowed and focused on the stage.

Mayor Sparks spoke.

"Thank you all for coming on this beautiful spring day. What perfect weather to choose a winner for this year's Governor's Ball on the Fourth of July in our state capital of Santa Fe." The crowd whooped and clapped. Mayor Sparks nodded with a polite clap of her own. "I want to remind the people of this very civilized and well-mannered town, I did not have any control over the number of tickets that were donated to Slippery Slopes. I know so many of us want to go to the elusive and exclusive Governor's Ball, but allocation of tickets was based on population, and I was lucky enough to even get a second ticket for the winner to take a guest. Let it be clear that I myself do not even have a guaranteed ticket. I have been entered into the lottery like everybody else."

Around us, the crowd shifted on their feet in anticipation.

"This is feeling a little Katniss Everdeen," I mumbled, wishing Rochelle was still here to get my joke.

"I was thinking Shirley Jackson's *The Lottery*," Miles said, and my shock must have shown on my face that he knew either of those references.

I bit back the barb that sat so perfectly on my tongue about him being able to read. I was a civilized, well-mannered citizen of Slippery Slopes, as Mayor Sparks had just mentioned.

"No smarting cut about how I can't read?" he whispered low into my ear.

I shuddered in disgust at his proximity, smoothing down the hairs on my arms. It wasn't the first time he got in my head.

There had been a moment when he first arrived that I thought our connection was rare and genuine. But maybe I'd been desperate for a closeness that wasn't there. No more of that.

"Please stop talking," I repeated for what had to be the tenth time.

"Nobody knows this town better than you. Or at least has such a hard-on for it," he added entirely unnecessarily.

I curled my lip at his crude turn of phrase but didn't let him goad me. When people showed their true colors, I wasn't surprised when they acted poorly.

"And I will admit that maybe I have been shortsighted in my initial reaction to this town . . ."

He needed my help again because his project was failing. Got it. I loved helping people, but I hated being used. There was a crucial difference, despite Rochelle's thoughts on the matter.

"Now, the moment you've all been waiting for." Mayor Sparks spun the giant cage filled with little plastic balls. The crowd went silent, as if everyone had taken a collective breath in. "This is very exciting. And the winner is . . ." She stopped the cage to unhook the little metal door.

The whole square was silent, save only the happy babble of a nearby baby and the squeaks of a passing herd of guinea pigs.

I flicked a look to Deckard, but I'd lost him in the crowd. If I could just see him again and remember why I wanted this. How he was the right choice. Somewhere near my ear, Miles buzzed on, but I'd long since tuned him out. There was only Mayor Sparks and her mouth as it moved around two words. She read the ball before turning it for the crowd to see.

"Natalie Weatherby," she called out loud and clear, and the world took in the breath that had escaped me in a gasp. "How wonderful! Our local hero."

Mayor Sparks smiled genuinely, lightly clapping the palm where she still gripped the ball that had my name on it.

"Huh. I stand corrected." Miles's words cut through the ringing in my ears.

The world slowed down as everything around me faded to a blurry haze, like in a dream, where I could only see what was right in front of me.

There was a beat of silence as the announcement sank in before the clapping and cheering began, along with a fair amount of disappointed grumbling.

I felt a weight gather on my shoulders as gazes found, then settled on me, one by one. First, only a couple who knew who I was, then a few more, hearing the growing murmurs surrounding me.

The whole town would look at me. They would all see the truth written on my face. I was no hero. I would only disappoint them.

"Over here!" Miles called out enthusiastically, waving his arm over his head. "Natalie is right here." He bent his head and whispered in my ear, "Aren't you so happy? Real tickets to the big barn dance."

His deep, whispered voice was the only thing to penetrate the shock of my name being called. There was a glint in his eyes that made it impossible to look away from him once I noticed it. My mouth opened and closed as I tried to move my body.

The teasing smile on his face melted away as I stared at him. A furrow of concern creased his brow. "Natalie?"

"I-I . . ." I couldn't seem to move or speak a sentence. I had to come clean now. I had promised Rochelle; I had made a plan. The pressure of this realization pushed my skull in from all sides.

Without looking, I could imagine Rochelle's shocked expression as she watched me. This was what I wanted. This was my great, big plan.

So why did it feel like I couldn't breathe?

Because Miles showed up and ruined everything.

Chapter 4

Miles

For someone who just won what was *apparently* a hell of a prize in this oddball town, Natalie Weatherby looked like she was seconds from passing out. I stepped closer to her, feeling slightly remorseful about calling the whole town's attention to her—and about pretending to notice her friend, like I didn't care about Natalie. It just felt important in the moment to show her that I hadn't been thinking about her.

Because I was a huge asshole.

In my defense, she'd been so cold toward me. It threw me off. Callie would say I acted extra annoying when I felt any negative emotion. But what did a best friend know anyway?

Was it a bit of stage fright that had gotten to Natalie? The entire town did seem to be searching for her now.

Based on the greenish hue to her skin, maybe she didn't want the whole town looking at her? But she was the literal town representative. This was her time to shine.

I had expected her to have a positive reaction to my return. After my talk with the mayor this morning, Natalie was the first

—and only—person I wanted to see. Stupid of me, based on her frigid body language and cutting remarks. I wasn't expecting a parade or anything, but we had hit it off the first time I was here for work, and I had hoped she'd be happy to see me. What a joke.

Who was ever happy to see me?

Just add it to the pile of crap that was this day. This was why having friendships was overrated and helping people was the worst.

Natalie's friend came back over, glaring at me. "What did you do? Why is she frozen?"

I held up my hands. "Nothing." Aside from somehow branding myself as her mortal enemy from the moment I rolled back into town.

"Natalie Weatherby?" the mayor called over the speakers. "Want to come up and collect your prize, doll?"

Natalie's friend gently shook her, ducking to meet her gaze. "That's you, Nat."

Natalie blinked her wide eyes. She swallowed once.

"Natalie?" her friend repeated.

"Natalie, you're needed in the principal's office," I said in a crackling announcement voice, hoping to break through to her.

The other woman rolled her eyes at me. The crowd around us inched closer, growing more disturbed and homing in on her.

"Seriously, Natalie, the mayor wants you," her friend said.

I threaded my fingers through Natalie's icy ones and squeezed once, just to check for a pulse or any sort of reaction. She blinked and closed her mouth with a swallow. Her gaze moved to our entwined fingers before life returned to her eyes, fire flaring in them. She yanked her hand out of mine.

She turned toward her friend, giving me her shoulder. I had really pissed her off. The worst thing was I hadn't even been my usual shitty self with Natalie. I had tried . . .

"I didn't think I would actually win." Her voice was hardly a whisper.

"Clearly." I rubbed my hand where her fingers had just been.

"Yes, you did. You literally told me. And you were right! Wild." Her friend shook Natalie's shoulders excitedly. "Now your Prince Charming awaits. But first go get those damn tickets before this crowd picks you up and shoves you up there." She flicked her wrists to wave away a few crowding people. "Shoo. Get back. Let her breathe."

Natalie plastered on a smile as large and sincere as a plastic jack-o'-lantern's. "Yes. I know. Yes. This is great." Her voice wobbled as she spoke with forced enthusiasm. Couldn't everyone see she was terrified?

"I can't believe it. You were right. I will never doubt you again," the friend said.

"You doubted me?"

"No. No. Never."

A man, presumably the friend's husband, came up and slung an arm over her shoulder, his other hand tugging along a little girl gnawing on the end of a churro. "Why does Natalie look like she's going to puke?"

The other woman shrugged before gently prodding Natalie in the direction of the stage.

This conversation was leading to several more questions, but before I could ask who Prince Charming was, Natalie finally found her motion setting.

She weaved her way through the crowd toward the podium set up in the center of the gazebo. With shoulders back, she went to collect her supposed prize.

I watched her as she disappeared into the crowd, people patting her on the shoulder and congratulating her, others joking about being her date.

The first moment I ever saw her, I told myself, *Not so fast*. I wasn't going to be one of those tourists who dallies with the locals. I was many terrible things, but never a cliché.

She was stunning though. It wasn't even her figure that drew me in first. It was that smile of hers. Not the one currently cemented to her face. The real one she flashed me that first day we were introduced by the mayor. It was so warm and kind and seemed to shine out of her whole being. Her welcoming brown eyes revealed hidden depths the more we spoke. Her bright blond hair that was determined to escape from any style she put it in. I was desperate to see that hair down, loose and flowing. Had I ever seen a blonde with curls like that? It was like she'd stepped out of a rococo painting. It made me want to find out if those hairs were as soft as they seemed. She drew me in and threatened me as I watched her retreating form.

Also, those jeans did phenomenal things for her ass.

"You know what's great about Natalie?" the other woman asked loudly, drawing my attention back to her and her little family. I didn't like the look she was giving me—like she'd heard me cataloging her friend's finer assets. Then again, I had been staring.

"She's great with power tools?" I asked. "She can juggle a variety of citrus fruit?"

"Huh. The guessing *is* fun," she said to herself, and then to me she said, "but no. Everyone in this town loves Natalie."

"Sounds terrible," I said. I raised my eyebrows in question. I highly doubted everyone *loved* her, but her friend was clearly going somewhere with this.

"And Natalie loves everyone," she finished.

"So cute," I said dryly.

"Everyone but you," she added.

"There it is." I sighed, looking for an excuse to get away.

"I cannot figure out what you did to piss her off so much that she can't even look you in the eye."

I had noticed Natalie struggled with that. I thought maybe my strikingly good looks were too much for her to handle. "I genuinely wish I knew that too."

I thought Natalie and I had hit it off from the get-go. We'd spent a lot of time working together for this assignment, and she never acted entirely miserable. I even thought that maybe there was a—it didn't matter because now, apparently, I was on her no-eye-contact list.

And so what Natalie didn't like me? I ignored the sharp tug in my solar plexus and focused on why I was here. And it wasn't to make friends. I sure as hell wasn't about to be treated like a pariah by a town that had more Sasquatch museums than it did banks. I was here to help Callie and get on with my life.

"It's a shame because Natalie is the type of person who will do anything to help a friend or neighbor. But once she feels wronged, you are dead to her, for all intents and purposes. Don't let those cute cheeks fool you, she has a dark side."

And I'd hoped to get to know it.

The thought came unbidden and I shoved it back down.

"Let me worry about that. But thanks for the warning," I said.

"Oh, is this the guy—" The woman turned and shot a look at her husband before he could finish that sentence.

"Really wished I could have heard how that ended." I extended a hand to him. "Miles Asher."

"I've heard all about you," he said with a warm smile that didn't match the implication of his words. "I'm John. My wife, Rochelle, is the one giving you the dirty look. And this is our daughter, Olive. She'd introduce herself, but she's really into that treat right now."

The little girl bared cinnamon-sugar teeth at me before getting back to business.

"Any ideas on how I can get in Natalie's good graces?" I asked John, since he seemed far less threatening than the other two.

"You would love that, wouldn't you?" Rochelle butt in, crossing her arms.

"Yes. That's why I asked."

"Natalie loves this town," John offered.

"Don't you help him," Rochelle said to her husband, who quickly became my closest ally in this town.

"Look at him. He looks so pitiful," John said.

"Pitiful?" Never mind to all of that then. I didn't need an ally after all. And I definitely didn't want pity. I was here as a favor. The faster I got this job done, the faster I could get back to reality. Where people were in touch with reality.

John ignored me and spoke to his wife. "Look, I know he hasn't made the best impression in Slippery Slopes, and sure, he's a little pretentious—"

"I'm hardly—"

"And maybe he still thinks that we are some backwater stop on the way to a real city."

"It's not?"

"But Natalie and Miles want the same thing." He gave his wife a look that softened her whole demeanor without her moving a muscle. "She wants him gone, and he wants to be gone. By helping him, you're helping Natalie get closer to Deckard."

So that was who the Prince Charming in question was. I hadn't spent much time in Slippery Slopes, but even I knew the town's Perfect Son. The mayor's only male heir was beloved by all. That made sense, him and Natalie. How very quaint.

Rochelle's eyes narrowed, belied by a soft smile that curved her lips. She leaned into her husband. "Don't try to out-lawyer a lawyer." She pressed her lips to her husband's, and I moved my attention to the child that stared unblinkingly back at me. I smiled, but her gaze never wavered. Just one unending stare. I took a half step back.

"John's right," Rochelle said, and it was safe to look at the couple again. "Natalie is protective of this town and wants what's best for it. Tell her just that and she'll help you, I'm sure. My dear friend's biggest fatal flaw is that she can't help but help people. Even people who don't deserve it." She tacked on this last bit with a pinched smile.

"Great. Yes. Any ideas more specific than that?" I asked.

"Just don't dick her around. And figure it out." Rochelle had clearly reached her threshold of speaking to me because she dragged her family closer to the stage where Natalie now stood, with plenty of color back in her cheeks.

"Thanks, very helpful," I muttered.

I leaned back against a tree on the edge of the crowd, settling in to watch Natalie's acceptance speech. Was that what this was? Was all this necessary for a bunch of bad food in a hot and overpacked glorified conference room? I hadn't been to the Governor's Ball, but these things were all the same no matter where in the country you were.

Natalie did look pretty with the sun shining on her and her smile more genuine now. It was easy to see why the town loved her. She attracted eyes to her as she rambled. I couldn't understand what she talked about, but just like me, the rest of the town listened dutifully.

Dammit. I sighed audibly.

"Nope." I shook my head and pushed off the tree. "That wouldn't do."

I strode away from the crowd and back toward Main Street. My phone vibrated with a call, and I winced. Not that I wasn't happy to see my best friend's name pop up, but because I knew the inevitable questions that would ensue.

"Hello, gorgeous," I said.

Callie's unamused face blinked back at me. Her normally bright eyes were dull, and her face was noticeably puffier than the last time we spoke. "Don't try and flatter me. I know I look like shit."

"I think you look beautiful." I tucked into a side street that smelled faintly of oil and trash but was, at least, empty.

"I appreciate your attempts. But anything you and Mags say can't be trusted. I know this pregnancy is kicking my ass," she said. Her words were tight like she was winded just from speaking, even though she was clearly lying in her bed.

"Your hair is extra shiny." And it was true, her dark blond hair, thick and healthy, had grown down past where the screen's frame ended.

"It's because I'm being pumped full of vitamins and supplements."

"I'm sorry." This was the reason I was here. This awful worry that churned when I looked at Callie. When I thought of her wife and soon-to-be child. Callie couldn't be flying, let alone gallivanting all over Slippery Slopes, trying to finish this project.

"No, I'm sorry. I'm such a grouch. This pregnancy is making me feel like I'm failing as a mother already." She seemed so defeated. "It was supposed to be all glowing skin and affectionate belly rubs and now . . ." Her eyes rolled to the ceiling as they filled with tears. "Bed rest and crying all the time." She gestured to her face before her arm flopped heavily back down.

"Callie," I said as my chest seized with sympathy. "You aren't failing. You are doing exactly what the doctor said. What was the last update?"

I glanced to the town square, and though I couldn't hear

Natalie anymore, I could see her moving her arms happily as she spoke, gesturing like a mime entertaining an audience.

I looked away. I hadn't even meant to seek her out.

"Same," Callie said, and I refocused on her. "Continued bed rest. This baby isn't due for three more months. I'm never going to make it."

"You will because you have to. You've handled the worst in humanity to get what you need. But I'm sorry you're having such a hard time. I wish I could help more. I'd be pregnant in an instant."

She snorted. "That's what Mags keeps saying. But this was my choice. I wanted to carry for us. I just thought I was going to smash it out of the park."

"To be fair, you usually excel in all things."

"Right? This is my first dose of reality, I guess. My mother said that when I told her I was pregnant. She said, 'From here out you have no control.'"

"Ominous."

"But I'm starting to understand. Anyway. I don't want to talk about swollen body parts anymore. Tell me how the meeting today went."

"But you just said you didn't want to hear about swollen body—"

"Oh my God, Miles." But she laughed as she chastised me, and I felt better, like I'd helped in some way.

"No. It was fine. The mayor sent her hellos and wishes for good health. She liked what she saw so far with the video. She's excited."

"And she said why, right? They're going to showcase the film at the Governor's Ball if it's good enough. The mayor pulled a lot of strings to get this chance to show off Slippery Slopes. It'll be a huge boon for both of our careers."

"She did. And it will be."

"I was meant to be there. This company was our baby, Miles, and now . . ."

"You're having an actual baby." The words settled low into my consciousness. It was a reality I hadn't processed, this idea that things were changing. But all I could do at this moment was comfort Callie. I waited until she met my gaze. *See, Natalie, some people can look me in the eye.* "Look. I know you're frustrated that you can't be here to finish these shots, but this is, at the end of the day, still just a job. Your actual baby is number one."

She nodded and let me lie to her. But the truth was, we both had everything riding on this. And we were both painfully aware of the fact that I was shit at interviews. But the last thing Callie needed was to feel any more anxiety when her pregnancy was already so high risk.

"I know. God, I sound so awful. All I do is feel guilty all the time," she said.

"Then, from the little I know about parenting, you're right on track. If you didn't care, you wouldn't worry," I said.

Her bottom lip trembled as she met my gaze and nodded. "Thank you. This sucks. Okay. And tell me how it went with Natalie. I really do want to talk about work."

"Well, about that. A little snag."

"Oh, Miles, what?"

"The mayor thinks I should tap Natalie as our interview person in place of you."

Callie's thought processing was written all over her face, ending with a nodding frown of approval. "That's actually a great idea. She knows the town, people are comfortable with her," she said, warming more to the idea as she spoke. "And you and Natalie really hit it off. The first time you guys met, it was like being the awkward third wheel on a first date, so that should be—oh, no Miles, why are you making that face?"

"I'm not." I grimaced.

"What did you do?"

"Callie. I'm offended. And here I just made you feel better."

"I'm sorry, Miles, but you do know this is your MO. Roll into towns, annoy everybody we meet, or worse, don't even pay attention to them. You play the pretentious asshole because you never have to deal with the consequences and then you leave, never to be seen or heard from again."

I mean, yes, but ouch. I wanted to say that it had been different with Natalie. That I even sent her a message after, and I *never* talked to anybody once I left the town. I certainly wouldn't admit that my feelings were a little bit hurt from her ghosting me. But maybe after her reaction today, Callie's opinion of me wasn't totally off.

Before I could answer, she inhaled a gasp. "Do not tell me you slept with her."

"I did not sleep with her," I said. "And I really wanted to." I said it jokingly to take some of the truth out of it. "But I'm maturing. I didn't want to break her heart." I scratched my eyebrow with my thumb, hiding my gaze from Callie.

"Wow, you must have really liked her. I felt that chemistry, but damn."

"Please. You know I don't operate that way." I brushed away some fuzz on my shoulder.

Natalie had been so mad. She wouldn't even look at me. I wanted it to be like the first time I was here, when I made her laugh so easily. Her cheeks turning bright red and her curls bouncing, it had been so easy to make her blush . . .

"So you say. How did you screw the pooch then?"

I sighed. "I don't know."

"Well, figure it out. If Natalie came recommended by the mayor, then you need to get her help."

"Yeah, yeah."

"And don't do the thing where you act all pretentious and too good for things."

"Am I an asshole or a pretentious snob? Make up your mind, Callie."

"Both. You're definitely both." She took a deep breath in and out. "We need to get this movie played at the Governor's Ball, Miles. This is the chance we've been waiting for. Once this baby makes their debut, we are taking over the documentary world."

Again, the two missions seemed incongruous, but I wasn't going to push for more information.

"What is it with this dance? Are they handing out gold bars? It's a bullshit event designed for the state government to sit around and tell everybody how amazing they are."

"Yes, see. That was a perfect example of both asshole and pretentious snob."

"I don't get it. You should have seen today. They had a whole event just to pick the winner of the tickets. Natalie won, by the way . . ." I thought again of the shock on her face. The coldness she imbued toward me before that.

"Was she happy?"

"She wanted to win, from what I could tell."

"So then, this event is important to her, isn't that enough?"

"I don't care—"

"It's important to me then," she said impatiently. "Listen to what Natalie needs and make sure she gets it."

"She's really pissed. I'm not sure how to fix this," I admitted, poking at some bricks in the wall.

"From what I gathered, Natalie is one of those helper types. But they're usually the ones who need the most."

I frowned. "Natalie is beloved by all. Her best friend even said so when she was mildly threatening me."

"If Natalie is the one helping everyone, there's probably something she needs help with."

"Oh, good. Another person I get to help out of the kindness of my heart."

"Yeah, that's two whole people. Watch out, world, the next saint is coming through."

"I'm basically a nonprofit at this point."

"Ugh. I have to pee or cry. I'm going to go. You can fix this." Callie sighed and shifted.

"Yeah. Sure."

"Love you, babe."

"Love you. Sends Mags a kiss."

"Yep."

Call ended. I sat for too long, staring into space. I moved back toward the stage where Natalie was surrounded, having finished her impromptu acceptance speech.

"Take me, Natalie!" someone shouted, and a few others followed suit.

Natalie's color paled again. She was surrounded by her beloved townsfolk, but she wore that plastic version of her smile and hurried off stage. I made my way toward her, weaving through the dense crowd as they surged her, calling her name and making demands.

Was this ball really that important? Couldn't they see that the woman was overwhelmed?

I wanted to be sympathetic, I did. But there were things that I needed too, and this couldn't wait for her to defrost to me. Plus, I hadn't really done anything wrong.

I elbowed my way to Natalie and went to her side, becoming a self-imposed bodyguard as I huddled her away. With hands resting gently on her waist and lower back, I guided her on, all the while elbowing anybody who got too close.

"Let the woman be. I'm sure she'll announce who she's taking soon," I shouted.

Natalie stumbled as I moved her to the side street and back to the hotel I was staying at around the corner. Once we were in the lobby, she seemed to register who I was. I tried not to feel hurt as she quickly brushed off my arm.

"Thank you," she said, talking to the collar of my shirt.

"Who would have thought they'd lose their mind over a fancy dance in the capital." I shuffled on my feet, hands back in pockets. "This is feeling more and more like *Hunger Games*."

She guffawed a laugh. It popped out like she had no control of it, and some color returned to her cheeks. It was like that first week all over again. She met my eyes for a flash of a second. A sort of happiness spread through me.

"Yeah, I think it's about the free champagne for some and rubbing elbows with the governor for others. But it is a big deal to get to go." Her gaze went sort of hazy again.

"I'm sure it will be great," I said instead of making a quip about yokels and big cities. Progress.

"Okay, well, see you later." She moved to leave, and I stepped forward to stop her.

"Wait. I still need your help."

I couldn't let her go now. I needed this to happen. Callie and Mags and their little baby needed me to step up. I may be a fuckup to most of the world, but I could at least prove myself to them.

Her features hardened before she nodded. "Of course. You weren't helping me at all. You just wanted to get me here so I can help you."

"Can't it be both?"

"Not with you. There's always an angle."

"Always? Look, I'm sorry if I offended you, but like I said, I need your help."

"Wow. Some apology."

"I don't have time for this," I growled, running a hand through my hair. How was I supposed to get her help when she was set on being the world's most difficult person?

"And I already told you, I learn from my mistakes."

"Rochelle said you help people all the time," I said.

"People who live here. People who want to be here."

"Are you seriously that much of a snob against tourists that you won't hear me out?" I was panicked and lashing out, but she was out of line too.

"I'm the snob?" She shook her head, gaze still roving over the floor. "I'm not wasting any more time on you. I have a date to go get."

I smothered the involuntary wince at Natalie's mention of the word *date*. Callie would flick me if she saw that. This was going swimmingly.

Natalie might need help, that was true, but I had nothing to offer her.

Chapter 5

Natalie

"That arrogant . . . self-serving . . . and he thinks that I'm . . . Ugh!"

A full day after the Governor's Ball lottery, and my anger for Miles Asher's return to Slippery Slopes was just as fresh.

I stomped my way toward Grizabella's Cat Cafe.

No more waiting. No more hesitation. I was asking Deckard to be my plus-one today so that I could tell him the truth.

I'd spent the entire night tossing and turning. Every day I carried this lie, the harder it became to shake. I never meant for this to happen.

And for Miles to just show up and derail everything. And how he talked to me as if he hadn't completely used me and left. It didn't help that when I'd gone to collect my award, I'd completely lost the plot in front of the whole town. It was one thing when I was prepped and ready to talk with notes and points to hit, but when let loose in front of a group of people, I just spoke whatever came to mind. It was like there was this claw machine in my mind, digging through old chests of useless information and facts and tossing them out without any rhyme or reason.

It wasn't until Mr. Graves, resident mooch, shouted, asking where the free food was, that I was broken from my nervous verbal spillage and gently directed off the stage by Mayor Sparks. I couldn't believe I'd won the tickets. I really hadn't thought . . . I mean, sure, I'd hoped. It was good. Now I had to come clean to Deckard.

"Ugh." I stomped more vigorously.

No more excuses. I'd made the ultimate bet with myself when I said that if my name was drawn, then I was asking Deckard to the ball. I'd made a promise to myself, and I was not about to break that.

Miles wasn't the reason for this sudden decisiveness, either. He meant nothing. I would ignore him until he left. I had helped him and his partner the best I could the first time they were here. There was nothing he needed me for now.

I stopped in the middle of the road, fists balled at my sides as I took a deep breath to calm myself. I didn't want to stomp through this town and have everybody see me all worked up. I was the town representative for a reason.

"Good morning, Tess." I waved happily to the owner of Slippery Snips and all-around gossip.

"Good morning, Natalie." She looked like she was thinking up a way to talk to me, and I knew that if she pressured me to talk, I'd end up blabbing about everything and nothing and watch myself become a disappointment to her in real time. "Congratulations on the tickets," she called after me.

"Thank you!" I walked on, head down, on a mission.

See that, Miles? Suck it.

I was a ray of freaking sunshine. I stopped and looked around, worried the people of the town could read my dark thoughts, but I laughed off my concern immediately.

There had been a discombobulating bit of freedom in my interactions with Miles yesterday. I was so shocked to see him that I didn't have time to prepare. I said exactly what was on my mind. Or at least what was appropriate to say in the middle of town.

There had been no pressure to perform. I didn't care if he liked me. I didn't care if I hurt his feelings. Okay, I cared a little. Hurting people never felt good, even when they'd hurt me first. But I didn't have a filter with him. I didn't have to feel grateful or pretend to be happy and nice. I was just me. And he was right. I wasn't *nice* all the time. It was a scary truth that needed to stay hidden.

I might not even be *good*.

I had my whole life, thanks to this town, and I owed it to them to make sure I was the best Slippery Slopes representative—which sounded like a made-up job, but it was a real thing I'd been doing since I turned eighteen over a decade ago. Officially, I ran the shuttle tours all week, twice a day, through peak tourism season. But I also had more miscellaneous roles now, volunteering for different city departments and running most of the social media accounts. Although Gabe had started to take on more and more as my eager young pupil.

I was the unofficial welcome wagon for people important enough that they deserved special attention, but not important enough that the mayor herself couldn't handle it.

I knew more history and facts about Slippery Slopes than anybody else. Except for maybe Ned Fled, the oldest man in town. Now there was a trove of information. It was my knowledge that was the reason Miles was assigned to me when he and his partner, Callie, arrived the first time. I was meant to be their official Slippery Slopes tour guide. And it was great . . . at first. Callie was the one who was meant to return to finish the project now that the weather had warmed up. I wasn't ever supposed to see him again.

But I wasn't thinking about Miles. I was focused on Deckard and my plans.

I was determined. Deckard was the future. There was nobody more beloved. I could imagine us hand in hand, stopping to talk to our neighbors, smiling broadly. We would be the perfect couple, the Golden Couple. We would be as much a part of this community as the recently restored Jane Smith statue.

I shook my head clear and pulled my shoulders back. In the camera of my phone, I made sure my teeth were food-free and my hair wasn't too poofy in its braid before I rounded the corner.

I walked into the cat cafe full of determination. It was relatively busy, and I couldn't scan the tables quick enough to see if Deckard was in his usual spot working on his laptop. Various cat pedestals and cats filled the welcoming space, and the aromatic scent of coffee filled the air. To my relief, nobody queued at the counter. I could take my time, say things as I'd rehearsed them.

Bec Perkins waved to me with a warm smile from behind the register. "Hi, Natalie. How are you?"

"I'm here to see Deckard," I said on a rush. Then I realized I'd been rude. "I mean, hi, Bee. How are you?"

She didn't seem surprised or hurt; she gave an open smile. "I'm great. Deckard isn't here today."

I finally let myself look around the cafe. At Deckard's usual table sat Bee's boyfriend, Owen, a large, intimidating man who used to work for Benny Jr. but was now hunched over what looked to be an anatomy book. He sneezed loudly, startling a few cats that had been sleeping around him.

"Oh," I said. All at once, the wind left my sails.

But was I also relieved? Just a little bit. Maybe asking

Deckard out here in the middle of town with his best friend watching wasn't the best strategy? He might feel pressured to say yes. Maybe it would be better if I wrote him a letter? Maybe send a casual text. An aloof, *U Up?* Just kidding. But playing it cool would be better than him knowing I'd been thinking about him and planning all this. The last thing I wanted was to seem needy or creepy. I needed to play this just right.

I worried the inside of my bottom lip as I turned in a slow circle, scanning the room.

"Do you want a drink?" Bee asked when I turned my focus back to her.

A small group of older ladies came in behind me dressed in leggings and carrying rolled-up mats. Probably from the midmorning classes at Yoga and Yogurt. I scooted to the side to make room for them to reach the counter. Then, at the last second, I sidestepped back in front of them to keep my place at the start of the line.

"No, thank you. No. But actually, do you know where he is?" I tried to play it casual, but my voice did this weird hitch up at the end.

"I'll be right with you, ladies," Bee said to the group chatting happily behind me.

The bell above the door rang again, and a couple of tourists came in. The crowd shifted forward. My heartbeat quickened.

"He's usually in by now," Bee explained, returning her focus to me. "Maybe he went to work at the library instead today? Sometimes he prefers that. And it was pretty busy here yesterday and stuff with the lottery. And you know how the hot springs are this time of year with the tourists." She raised her eyebrows at the couple that just entered.

The bell rang again as though to prove her point. It was the reverend and her husband.

"Welcome in," Bee called over my shoulder. The volume in

the cafe had increased considerably since I first entered. I flinched as she continued, "I'll be with you all in a minute. Feel free to pet a cat while you wait. They're all available for adoption through Whisker Wonderland, the local no-kill shelter." There was a hiss followed quickly by a gasp. "Maybe avoid Eva. She's got a soft center, but she shows her love aggressively."

She leaned forward and lowered her voice for me. "That's Deckard's favorite cat."

"Oh—I—that's good to know." A sudden flush burned my cheeks. Bee looked at me knowingly, and I couldn't meet her gaze.

I turned to watch a serene, sleek all-black cat, perched on a raised cat bed, lick her paw, unimpressed as the man from the tourist couple held his hand out for his partner to examine.

A nervous dread prickled the back of my neck as I clocked how crowded the cafe had suddenly gotten.

"Okay. Thanks." I started to back away, trying not to bump into a table or a tourist or a cat.

"Do you want me to tell him you came by looking for him?"

"No!" I answered too fast. I unclenched my jaw and softened my voice. "Nah, it's fine. I'll see him when I see him." I went to coolly play with the waving cat statue next to the register, almost knocked it over, then fumbled to straighten it. Sweat prickled my pits as I felt several gazes turn my way.

Nobody could know why I was here but it was like being the center of attention yesterday all over again.

"Okay," Bee said, happy expression still in place. Her eyebrows lifted as a new thought came to her. "Congrats, by the way. About the tickets. Are you so excited? I would not want that pressure. Whoo-boy, no, thank you. I mean, I wouldn't *hate* the attention. But all those people wanting the extra ticket? Like, no matter what I did or who I chose, I would be disappointing someone." The cafe quieted around us as Bee went on.

A sinking feeling came over me, filling my toes and fingertips with ice. "I mean, the mayor herself wanted to go and couldn't get a ticket. And how could anybody let down the mayor? I mean, nobody is going to be happy—hey, are you okay? You look sort of pale."

"Yeah. I-I just gotta go." I couldn't feel my face. My heart raced.

The reality of the lottery had just punched me in the gut.

Bee was right. There was no way I wouldn't disappoint someone.

"Oh, you're the woman who won?" one of the yoga women asked, and her friends started to nod and speak at once. "How fun! Now, have you already decided who you're taking because—"

The reverend stepped forward. "Oh, Natalie, I'm glad you're here. I was actually going to see if you'd given away your ticket yet."

"Wait now, Reverend Smith." The yoga woman she'd inadvertently cut off spoke up. "I was just asking—"

A new person spoke up. "My grandson is coming to visit, and I was going to see if Natalie wanted to meet him and maybe hit it off."

It was Maybel. Maybel was one of the first people who gave me a place to sleep after the accident happened. She let me stay at her B and B for weeks. I couldn't possibly disappoint her.

But there was a similar story like that for at least a dozen people in this town. Everybody would want this extra ticket. I didn't want to offend anybody. There was Bob, the grocer, who gave me my first job in Slippery Slopes. He never even blinked an eye at my untraditional education. He set me up as a cashier once he saw I could count well enough. There was Conor Finkle, the head librarian, who let me take classes on the computers and stay late if I lost track of time, never even making a comment about it.

How could I disappoint any of them? Would they still be so eager to have that ticket if they knew the real me?

Liar! Cheat!

I tried to soothe my thoughts, but my heart raced so hard it shook my eyeballs.

I should give the tickets back. I should come clean about not deserving them. But everyone would hate me and make me leave town. I was alone; I had nowhere else to go. The crowd moved in. The air became stifling and full of bodies.

Liar, liar!

This was not how this whole morning was supposed to go. This was not the plan.

And just when it felt like I was about to burst from pressure, there he was. As my frantic eyes moved over the room, I spotted him, leaning (always leaning) near the back.

Again. Miles Asher.

Of course, he was here. I wanted to hide. He couldn't see me like this. He'd be even more smug. I hadn't even noticed him when I came in. Had he already caught my humiliating flailing?

When my gaze first snagged on him, I could have sworn he was glaring darkly at the crowd, but when I looked back at him, he was watching them all with a half-smile on his face, hands in his pockets, as if he delighted in my impending doom. Of course, he'd gain pleasure in my faltering after how we'd left things yesterday.

He stepped forward, about to add to my mortification. Or maybe he'd "help me" as he had yesterday, only to tell me later that I owed him. To think he called me a snob.

Me! The one who spent her entire life traveling the country in a modified van as a home with two hippie parents, living in one commune and then another.

It was too much. I was here, pushed into a literal corner, with no plan, no way to make sure everybody was happy. Most people were going to be mad at me, and I was going to be sick. What if they demanded I repay their kindness for my being so self-centered now?

"Natalie," Miles said, effortlessly pushing through the crowd to get to me. They made space for him without him even trying.

I didn't trust the ease with which he moved, the confidence that propelled him. As though anywhere he went, space would be made for him. When he was at my side, he swung his arm over my shoulder and smiled a huge grin down at me. "Tell them who you're taking to the big ball."

Oh, *God.* I couldn't speak. I couldn't lie. I couldn't even move.

"Cat's got her tongue," he joked, nodding to the cats around us. "I'll tell them. Because we are friends, and you are clearly overcome."

I had to say something before he did what I thought he was going to do. There was no more time to waste.

I had to say—

"Deckard Sparks," Miles said coolly.

All at once, the people around us tilted their heads and smiled.

Sharp faces relaxed into smiles and nods.

"Oh, that's perfect. She saved his life, and now they're meant to be."

"Such a handsome couple."

"Can't compete with that."

Bee was silent behind me, but I swore I could *feel* her gaze boring into the back of my head.

Still, I couldn't speak.

"I know. These two crazy kids are bananas for each other,"

Miles went on in a voice that I'd never heard him use before, corny and saccharine. "But we need your help." Like a magician playing his audience, he leaned forward conspiratorially, and they all mirrored his action. "She's going to surprise him. So don't go ruining it by spilling the beans." He mimicked zipping up his mouth. "Mum's the word."

Everyone agreed with joyful hand clasping and fake mouth zipping in solidarity.

What was *happening*?

What sort of magic spell had he just cast?

He'd said *Deckard's* name. For a moment, I had thought that maybe he'd say his own name. I'd been so sure. He'd commit himself to me. Blackmail me for help. That would be in line with his typical behavior. And I would be furious. Bound into a verbal contract witnessed by all. With no way to get out of it.

That would have been the worst. Of course.

Still too stunned to do anything but smile, I let myself be led out of the crowded cafe.

Once in the fresh air, I turned to look up at Miles and found a hair-raising smile.

Why had he done that? And why was he looking at me like he had me exactly where he wanted?

"Looks like there's something you need after all," he said, sending a chill of foreboding down my neck.

Chapter 6

Miles

"Why? Why would you do that?" Natalie moved out from under my arm immediately. Her eyes were wide, almost amber in the midday sun.

She was pissed at me, but at least she wasn't so pale anymore. Couldn't the locals see how the pulse at her neck rose? Couldn't they see the fear in her wide brown eyes? She was like a scared puppy being mauled by sticky-fingered toddlers, being backed further into the corner.

"I was helping." I shrugged.

And I had been. I'd found my in with Natalie. She looked like she was seconds away from offering up her firstborn to appease the needy masses. She needed help, and based on the conversation I'd overheard—not eavesdropping—moments before, she'd been in search of Deckard Sparks. It was easy enough to put two and two together.

Her Prince Charming, that Rochelle spoke of, was Deckard Sparks. Of course. Son of the mayor, the town's golden son who could do no harm. The life she saved and, therefore, was destined to be with.

It made perfect sense, the two of them. Now that I knew what she needed, it was clear what to do.

I swallowed down an unexpected taste in my mouth.

"Helping *who* exactly?" She glared at my collar, keeping her voice low.

We stood in front of the cat cafe, and a steady stream of people passed by us.

I opened my mouth to answer, but she didn't let me. She leaned in close, voice menacing. "Because 'help' usually *helps* the person you're meaning to . . ." She gestured wildly.

"Help?" I offered.

"I didn't want to use that word again," she grumbled.

"I got the crowd off your back, and I got you one step closer to getting in Deckard's pants."

Her lip curled. "Don't be crude."

"Wasn't that why you were at this unhygienic fur ball of a cafe? To ask out your Prince Charming? Was I wrong?"

"Yes. No. It's not really any of your business."

"But your extra ticket is meant for him?" I clarified. It would be absurd to think she'd ask me. I toyed with voicing the idea for a second, to see the mortification on her face, but even I had lines I wouldn't cross. See? More progress.

"Yes!" she shouted and looked around. Another group of people passed by, and she plastered on that jack-o'-lantern smile. She lowered her voice again. "We can't talk here."

She growled as she grabbed my hand and tugged me across the street. My fingers threaded through hers, and I wondered if she realized she was essentially holding my hand for all the town to see. It was fun to imagine a world where she'd willingly claim me as hers. But it wasn't possible. Not when Deckard existed.

She led me around the corner to an older two-story building full of tourist shops. In the alley behind it was a flight of worn wooden stairs that led to the back entrance of the stores. At the very end of a walkway was a small doorway that I would have missed until she ducked into it. The looming mountains behind us seemed close enough that I could almost reach out and touch them. It was a stark reminder that this strange town was plopped in the middle of a mountain valley. Natalie glanced around surreptitiously before she pulled a key from her bra. My eyebrows shot up.

To be a secret key nuzzled in the warmth of her—

"Don't ask," she said.

"I wasn't about to," I said and followed her as she pushed into a dusty-smelling room. "But am I allowed to ask where we are?"

She flicked on an overhead light, illuminating a small, cluttered space no bigger than a guest bathroom.

"I used to come here when I first—" Whatever she'd been about to say was cut off with a sharp shake of her head. "It's my Thinking Place."

"It's a dusty closet." Though there was actually a good smell in the air. Really good. I took a deep inhale and then realized it was the sweet, clean smell of her and hoped she hadn't noticed.

"Yeah, well, it's mine. But it's not exactly a known public space. So don't tell anybody."

"There goes the content for my next newsletter," I said.

But what I really thought was that Natalie had shared a part of herself with me that nobody else knew about. And I wasn't sure why that made me feel sort of sick and excited at the same time.

"So you're squatting," I said.

"I don't live here." She moved aside to reveal a massive

circular chair, or maybe a small couch, that took up most of the space.

"Is that a kinky sex chair?"

"Oh my God, no. It's a reading chair."

"It's the size of a small bed."

"It's comfy."

"How did you even get it in here?"

"It wasn't easy," she said with a frown. "But it was worth it."

"For when you sleep here?" I teased.

Besides the not-a-sex-chair that took up half the space and was covered in a blanket, there was a small side table with a stack of books. She caught me looking pointedly at the obvious napping spot. "Okay. Sometimes I nap between tours or whatever if I don't feel like going all the way home. But Pat, the city maintenance guy, knows I use it. He doesn't care. So long as I don't share that he sometimes spends the night with Mel, the owner of Grizabella's." She covered her mouth. "Crap. Don't tell anyone about that either."

"Another newsletter ruined." I shook my head remorsefully.

She chewed on her lip, clearly still irritated but struggling not to be charmed by me.

The small space left barely enough room for the both of us. The warmth of her body sent an unexpected frisson through me. Did she smell this good last time? I remember thinking about strawberries and lemon, but also a hint of mint and a shot of liquor. Like sipping an ice-cold cocktail on a summer day while watching the sun slip behind the crest of a mountain and holding a gorgeous woman's hand.

Where the hell had that thought come from?

"It's for when I need to get away, you know? So I can let it all hang out." Her hand gestured to where a sports bra was balled up on the floor.

We both looked at it and then looked away.

"I just tell people to leave me alone," I said, tucking my hands in my pockets and scooting back as best I could until I ran into a wall.

"Of course you do. Sometimes I need a space to breathe and relax my cheeks," she said, and I focused back on her. This time, my eyebrows shot all the way up. She scolded with an eye roll before using her fingers to rub her cheeks in circles. "These cheeks. I have to do a lot of smiling in my work."

"But probably you also need to rest your other cheeks." I flinched as she smacked my arm.

"Anyway. With Deckard. I did plan to ask him to the ball. I *do* plan to. But there is a certain way to go about these things. And now. Oh, no." Her head fell back as her arms went limp at her sides. If she were a cartoon character, water would spray from her eyes in arches. "He probably already knows. Bee heard everything. She probably texted him the moment you made that insane announcement."

"Even better. Problem solved," I offered.

"No, no. Not solved. Even worse." She shook her head, and a single overhead bulb created a halo of light around her. It cast shadows that elongated her lashes and made her lips more full. She was incredibly alluring when she freaked out. Did she know this about herself? "Are you even listening?" She clapped twice in front of my face. "Deckard probably thinks I'm some weirdo who's going around the town telling people that we're dating even though we've literally only talked like three times."

"Woah. Only three times? But you saved his life. I mean, that counts for something."

She spun away with a growl.

"How long have you lived here?" I asked when she turned back, collected. I'd assumed they were friends, at least. That they volunteered to pet stray dogs on the weekends together or shoveled paths in the snow for the elderly.

"That's not the point." She went back to glaring at the shelf behind my shoulder.

"It feels relevant. How do you even know you like him?" I asked. Again, not that I cared.

She crossed her arms and gave me a look very reminiscent of Callie "calling me out on my dipshit-ery," as she'd say. "So every woman that you've slept with, you've had deep, meaningful conversations with first?"

"You got me there." I scratched the back of my neck. "I just didn't think *you* were the type."

"Yeah, well, you don't know me at all," she said with bite, meeting my gaze for the first time.

"You're right about that." But I did know about her secret room where she went to let down her guard, which nobody else knew about. I didn't look away. I let her sit in the discomfort of this moment. Of whatever this animosity was between us.

She moaned again, and it reminded me of Callie, helpless on bed rest back in Oregon. I couldn't quit now, despite the screaming desire to leave this place and never look back. I broke away from our glare. I needed her help, not to push her buttons.

But it was so fun . . .

"Listen. It's not a big deal," I said. "I'll go back there and tell everyone I got my wires crossed. I'm a bumbling fool who knows not what he speaks of." Again, with the old-timey talk . . .

"No. No. Then I'm right back to where I was."

"I could tell them that you're taking me," I offered. I hadn't meant it seriously. I didn't even want to go to this glorified barn dance, but I had wanted to see her reaction.

A sort of confusion quickly passed over her features, then faded. She shook her head. "No. That's way worse. They'd never forgive me for taking an outsider."

I didn't even feel hurt a little bit by that. I scratched between my brows with my thumb. "And why do we care so much about what this place thinks?" I asked.

"*We* don't. I do. You wouldn't understand. You've never stayed anywhere longer than what? A year? Isn't that what you told me?"

Turned out she did remember our conversations. And also, she wasn't wrong. I couldn't care less what this town or anybody here thought of me.

But I did care what Callie needed, and what she needed was for me to get Natalie's help.

"Okay. Go find Deckard and talk to him. Tell him I messed up and you wanted to clear the air before the town gossip mill got to him," I said. She worried the inside of her lip. "And while you're talking to him, maybe add on 'Oh but hey, since we are already here and discussing it, we should go to the ball together since we are both oh so perfect for each other and everybody loves us.' Yada yada yada."

"What a solid plan." She turned her chin away.

"What's your hang-up with this guy?"

"I don't have a hang-up. I just want to ask him the right way."

I looked around the space for a solution and it occurred to me. The way she froze when she won the tickets, then in the cafe . . .

"Are you shy?" I asked. She scrunched up her face. "But you have no problem saying exactly what you want to me."

"You don't count."

"Clearly. Okay, but you give those great tours. You're a great public speaker."

Her mouth opened and closed. A hint of color stained her round cheeks. "I'm not shy. This feels different. Deckard is the mayor's son."

"What is it that you're afraid of exactly?"

Her mouth opened and closed. "Nothing."

As she spoke, my eyes took in the room. Not like she would notice because she was still too busy avoiding my eyes. Next to the not-a-kinky-sex-chair was a stack of what appeared to be romance books with blue aliens on the cover? Noted. Next to that was a stack of candy bars, and wait, was that a canister of those weed gummies? Was this her contraband stash? Did she keep any other secrets here?

It suddenly felt illicit to be here, but in a thrilling sort of way.

"Deckard, well, I think he's sensitive. And I get that. He's—"

"Practically perfect in every way? And then you saved his life? How very romantic."

Her face did a weird scrunch as she wrapped her arms tighter around her core.

"Not to be the feminist of the two of us, but he's still just a man," I finished.

"Deckard has more green flags than you would even know what to do with." I ground my jaw as she spoke. "He knits sweaters for the guinea pigs. He has five really cool older sisters who are extremely protective of him. That's a lot of pressure— don't roll your eyes. He's a good person."

"What does that even mean? Nobody is just good or just bad. We aren't six anymore." She swallowed, and a furrow formed between her brows. "Every person contains multitudes." Her jaw dropped, but her eyes flicked around the room, and she closed it again. "You're putting way too much pressure on this. Look. You're both young, hot, perfectly single people. The story writes itself."

As she studied the floor, that curious, nauseous feeling circled my gut again. What had I eaten for breakfast? I had to get out of here.

"I have an idea. And before you get all worked up, actually listen to what I'm offering," I said.

"Okay."

"I can help you get Deckard to be your date. Help you work up your way to clear the air with him and maybe even ask him out. It'll keep the town off your back"—her eyes narrowed skeptically—"while you help me finish this film and conduct the interviews I need. We both win." I held up a hand as her mouth opened. "And before you go accusing me of using you, think of this too. This is the mayor's project. This is for the good of the town. The town that you love *oh so much*. It's what she would want. It'll put you even more in her good graces."

"I'm already really busy."

"I'll work myself into your schedule. I promise this can be good for us both. I know you think I'm some manipulative mastermind, but I'm just trying to do my job."

I could see her defenses melting, see her turning over my words and actually processing them.

Her gaze moved to the wall. Her eyes flicked back and forth as though she was working through a complicated math equation in her mind.

"Also. The faster you help me, the faster I am out of here," I added.

"Deal," she said, finally meeting my gaze again.

I huffed. "Probably should have led with that."

"So I help you with interviewing locals, and you'll help me ask out Deckard?" she clarified.

I nodded. "If we do this right, the timing will be perfect. We have a little more than two months before the Governor's Ball on the Fourth of July. I will be out of here by the time you get to go to prom with the quarterback, then you can get married and live happily ever after with all your little golden-haired babies." She shot me a look. "What?"

"Nothing. I think this could actually work." She extended her hand. I raised my eyebrows with a laugh but shook it in return. A jolt passed down my spine at the feel of her long, delicate fingers. Then her lips curled, and she added, "And you can go back to your frozen ice castle to play with yourself."

"You *do* subscribe to my newsletters."

Chapter 7

Natalie

I glanced around my Thinking Place, making sure I had everything I needed as I slid into my neon green tour vest. It was like putting on the mask of the person I was best at being. I was ready to shine. Today would be another full day of sightseeing, with a group down from Denver who chose the "Town and Terrain" tour. That package included a trip around Slippery Slopes in the city's minibus before driving up to Cabezón Trailhead. They'd all completed the signed waivers that ensured they'd been hydrating and acclimating to the elevation for the 1.5-mile loop, and that they were in good health and not at risk of elevation sickness. Inevitably, despite this clear warning, there was usually about one person a month who still got altitude sickness.

I packed some high-fat and high-protein snacks and extra water alongside the usual first aid kit, but Denver was around the same elevation, so I wasn't too worried about this particular group.

I had a twist of guilt as I thought of Miles waiting around to hear from me. Well, now he knew how it felt.

No. That didn't feel good either. I knew he was trying to do his job, but nothing about his plan, even though it made sense, made me want to rush. Besides, we had loads of time. I wasn't avoiding Miles, but I wasn't adjusting my schedule for him either. I was genuinely busy.

He was here for at least two months, and the interviews he needed would only take a few days, tops. There was no hurry.

It had nothing to do with my resentment toward him. I was a professional and would do what the mayor and this town needed.

But the anxiety lingered in me over our interaction last week here in my Thinking Place. I hadn't spoken to him since. Ironically, I hadn't been thinking when I brought him here. I'd wanted to get him away from the prying eyes and ears of the locals. Tess from Slippery Snips and her group of gossips had been walking by right at that moment, of course.

It was an actual miracle that I hadn't heard from Deckard yet or been brought in by the sheriff and accused of stalking. The town had actually managed to keep Deckard out of the loop, buying me a little time to figure out how to talk to him.

Miles had asked what I was afraid of, and I had been so close to spilling my guts. Telling him that if I messed this up, then I'd never be accepted by this town. This town that had raised me from the worst moment of my life. How could I explain how important that was? I couldn't. Not with him, someone who so openly delighted in mocking this situation already.

The secrecy and lies made me twitchy and jumpy. My hidden candy stash was dwindling at an alarming rate, and I was hanging out here more than ever. I still caught whiffs of his pretentious cologne or aftershave—whatever that alluring, woodsy, earthy man smell was that he'd had on.

When I was all packed and ready to go, I realized I'd dilly-dallied too long and run out of time to get coffee. I liked to be at the meeting area, town hall, at least ten minutes early to make sure the van was ready to go.

Maybe I could pretend that a stop for coffee and pastries was part of the tour.

I hurried down to Main Street and made my way toward the other end, where the government buildings were.

I'd even been avoiding Rochelle because, without a doubt, she'd want to know where things stood with Deckard. And I couldn't tell her that I needed Miles as my quasi-confidence coach to get me to work up the nerve. How humiliating. But I actually did think Miles could help me with Deckard. I hoped whatever it was about Miles that made it easy to speak my mind with him could be transferred to my interactions with Deckard. But Rochelle wouldn't get it. She was the type of person who didn't back down until she got what she wanted. I needed to work up to that.

Why *had* I brought Miles to my Thinking Place? Because I didn't care about his opinion of me. I didn't care that he knew that I sometimes read alien romance and binged on sugar before crashing to nap.

I didn't care about Miles at all.

I lifted my chin and walked with pep down toward town hall.

To my surprise, there was already somebody waiting at the covered bench.

I skip-hopped to get there faster. I appreciated an eager beaver and those who respected carefully constructed timetables.

"Hi, thanks for being early. I'm Natalie—" I stopped as I rounded the bench and came face-to-face with a grinning Miles.

My defenses were instantly raised.

He'd left so suddenly last time. For weeks, I'd looked for him everywhere, spotting him in strangers. Moments like this, where I'd turn a corner, sure that I'd seen him, only to realize it was another tall man with light brown waves and blue eyes. My heart would choke my throat thinking he was back, only to be dashed again.

And now suddenly he really was everywhere. It was too much.

"Hi, Natalie. I'm Miles. The man you are systematically avoiding." He held up a cup from the cafe on the other side of Main Street. His bright blue eyes were stunning in the early-morning New Mexico light. "Coffee?"

I looked away as I took the cup with a "Thank you," and didn't comment about how Grizabella's was better.

"You are welcome. Two creams and a sugar, if I recall correctly." I nodded and hated that he remembered. He grinned at me over the rim of his own coffee as he sipped. Then he held up a grease-stained paper bag that smelled deliciously of fried dough and frosting. "I also brought doughnuts if you're hungry."

"What are you doing here?" I asked, even as my stomach growled traitorously.

"I'm here for the tour." He gestured to the van.

I thought the tour had been full, but there might have been a seat free. With shoulders to my ears, I pulled out my phone. "There's a waiver you must sign. You can't just—"

"Signed it," he interrupted with a chipper tone as I saw that, in fact, he had filled it out last night at 10:54 p.m.

"Great." A building tension clenched my jaw. At least there would be plenty of other people to distract me. No risk there of us being alone together again. My body and brain weren't always on the same page when it was just Miles.

"I figured, since you are clearly so busy, that I would meet you where you were at. This Cabezón Trail, listed on the itinerary, is on the list Callie provided. I should be able to get some good shots with this gorgeous weather. Maybe we could find some people to chat with."

No matter what other anger I held on to, it was ridiculously pleasing to hear that he'd read my itinerary for the day.

Hmm, maybe Rochelle was right, and I did have weird turn-ons.

"Where is Callie? Wasn't she supposed to be the one to come back?" I'd meant to ask him that the first two times I saw him, but I'd lost track of what I wanted to say.

"She couldn't make it. I'm here instead." There was a brusqueness to his tone that indicated that was all he would say on the matter.

"Right. Well, thanks for the breakfast." I took a sip and winced. "Just so you know, Grizabella's coffee is better." I couldn't help myself. This really was so much worse.

"There it is. She's waking up," he said. "I've missed the real you."

And the implication that he knew me warmed my chest more than the itinerary reading had. I turned on my heel and spun away. He didn't know me. Nobody knew me, not really. "I have to do some checks before the rest of the group arrives."

"Take your time, I'll wait here and read over the itinerary again. Very good, by the way."

A moany squeak escaped me as I went behind the van. Hopefully, he hadn't heard it. I did my usual checks of tire pressure and the likes. The city maintenance guy—and local snow-plow driver—Pat, filled the gas and did his own safety checks, but I liked to restock the snacks and add a few other personal touches. They went a long way with the tourists and were often mentioned in my five-star reviews.

When it was about five minutes *after* the allotted meeting time, I started to worry.

Miles stood and made his way over to where I sat in the driver's seat, double-checking dates and sign-ups.

"Nobody's here yet. Time for a quick snack," he said.

"Thanks," I said distractedly as he handed over one of the doughnuts wrapped in wax paper. It wasn't unheard of for one or two people to be late; things happened. I allotted a buffer for this in the schedule. But a whole group not being here? That made me suspicious.

I looked up at Miles. Miles chewed happily. Suspiciously happily.

He wouldn't sabotage my business just to get time with me, would he? That would be more outrageous than telling half the town I was dating Deckard Sparks when he didn't even know me.

But I didn't know Miles at all, it turned out. I wouldn't accuse him of anything, but maybe I'd fish around. My cell rang as I finished my freaking delicious breakfast.

Damn that, Miles Asher.

I carefully wiped my fingers on the wet wipes I brought before answering the call from Maybel, who ran the local B and B.

"Hey, Maybel," I said with my friendly tone. The one that had been absent since Miles arrived.

"Hey, Natalie. Bad news, kiddo. Looks like the Sanchez crew hit up the shrimp tacos at Tony's Tacos on the way down here . . ."

"Oh, no." Well, that answered that. There was no way Miles could have done that. That was the second time now I'd thought

Miles had been awful but he hadn't been. Rochelle was right, I did carry a chip on my shoulder about him.

"I know. I wish we could issue a warning about that place, but Benny Jr. owns it and I can't risk pissing him off."

"I hear ya." I tapped my fingers in a pattern on my lips as she continued on with the more graphic details of her last twelve hours. When I glanced up, Miles was watching the action closely as he listened to my half of the conversation. I tucked my fingers into my palms and forced myself to be still.

"It sounds like a rowdy church service with all these prayers to the porcelain gods." The greasy breakfast roiled in my stomach at her colorful euphemism.

"Thanks for letting me know, Maybel," I said.

"Yeah. No worries. Hey. Have you talked to Deckard yet?"

I twisted away from Miles to respond in a quieter tone. "Not yet. I will though. Soon."

"I told you about my grandson coming to visit, right?"

"You did. Listen, I gotta go."

"Yep, yep. See ya."

When I ended the call, I let out a long sigh and walked over to Miles, who'd been pretending not to listen.

"The Sanchez party isn't coming," I said with finality as the realization that I had an excuse to cancel today's tour buoyed my mood. "Also, this is as good a time as ever to remind you that eating seafood in an isolated mountain town in the middle of the desert from a guy named Tony is never a good idea."

"Noted." He pulled a face. "What else did Maybel have to say?" The way he asked told me he already knew the answer to that.

"Nothing."

"Oh really? She didn't ask about your extra ticket?"

I grumbled.

"You know, I can help with that too? Whenever you're ready."

"Okay. We will see about time." I looked to the horizon. The sun had finally lifted high enough that Slippery Slopes was no longer covered in the long shadow of the nearby peak. From up here at town hall, the whole city was spread out below, and the golden light moved through the valley, illuminating eastern windows, like lights being flicked on.

"It's so pretty," I said.

Miles came to my side. "Yep, very nice. But we should get going. Time's a wasting."

I frowned. "You can't be serious," I said. The relief of canceling today's event had been in sight.

"I paid for this tour."

"I'm not wasting the gas or my voice for one person." I scrambled for an excuse. "Plus, you don't even want to go. You're only here to . . ."

"To what?"

"I don't know. Prove some point?" I threw out a hand.

His jaw clenched and actual anger moved over his features.

Was I being a jerk? I didn't want to spend the whole day alone with Miles. He was too good at . . . I don't know, getting past my defenses. Making me feel things that I didn't want to feel. He brought out the parts I kept hidden. I didn't want to drive around this town with my worst qualities on full display.

"Natalie." I'd tentatively met his gaze at his serious tone. It'd become slightly easier with time, but the way he said my name had the unwanted side effect of making me aware of everything and nothing all at once. The world blurred when he locked his gaze onto mine, and yet I felt like I could see every detail in his blue eyes. "You really think—"

Whatever he'd been about to say was cut short by the frantic footsteps of somebody running to the shuttle. Gabe, local jackof-all-trades, with his light red hair and a sweaty face, stumbled up to the still-open bus door, panting. "Sorry, I'm late. It took a while to, uh, help with things—" Here, he made a face, sticking out his tongue as he indicated projectile vomiting.

"Hey, Gabe. What are you doing here?" I asked.

"Hi, Natalie. I thought I might crash the tour since there are —oh, hey, Miles. Nice to see you here. What a good time this will be." Gabe looked so hopeful, guilt twisted my chest.

"Tell me I didn't miss anything," he said, still short of breath as he moved to come aboard. He looked worriedly between us. "You weren't going to cancel, were you?"

"Well, actually, we were debating if maybe we should reschedule since—"

"Noooo!" He moaned out the word so long, I froze in my tracks.

"Oh . . ."

Miles stifled a laugh.

"But I guess, I understand. I'm sure I can find other work to do." He stared over my shoulder with a shell-shocked look. "Thank goodness, I don't trust anything from the ocean."

Miles tossed up his hands. "I'm on your side. I wanted to keep the tour."

"Please," Gabe begged.

"Come on, Natalie. Let's give Gabe the VIP tour."

"All my tours are equal in quality and content." I sniffed with derision.

Gabe looked so damn excited it tugged on my heart. At least he wanted to learn about the town and wasn't just here to antagonize me or whatever it was that Miles was doing. Plus, I was a sucker for nerds. Especially ones who geeked out over a topic I also happened to love.

"Okay. Let's go learn some history," I finished with a smile.

"Yes!" Gabe punched the air.

Miles went up into the bus, shaking his head. I heard him softly mutter, "Nerds." But for some reason, it had me smiling instead of feeling defensive.

As Gabe made his way up the steep steps of the shuttle, Miles grinned broadly. "Great to have company, bud." He patted Gabe on the shoulder in a chummy manner and grinned knowingly at me. "Should we get a move on?"

I could do this. We were doing this. No big deal, I gave tours all the time, and this was no different. I would make sure to avoid Miles at all costs, like the professional that I was.

Chapter 8

Miles

Some pro Natalie was.

We'd been on this tour for an hour already, and she hadn't even looked at me once.

Gabe had nearly all her focus that wasn't taken up by driving the minibus.

Not that I expected anything different. I had watched every subtle twitch of muscles in her face as it fell the moment she registered me this morning.

It hadn't stung. Whatever. I was here to get these shots and bounce.

To be fair, Gabe asked great questions too. You could tell the kid was all about this small-town stuff. He was as eager as Natalie was to talk about the boring history of this place.

Okay, so it wasn't entirely boring. Not the way Natalie talked about it. For such a random small town, the history was rich, and the interactions with the nearby indigenous communities was a refreshing change of pace. For all my resistance, Natalie was incredible at this. She was as charismatic and lively as though she had a bus full of people and not just us two. And her earnest excitement about the different shops and the people who ran them was infectious. I was about to suggest we stop at Trailside Treats to try Ellie's handcrafted red chile fudge. Except, between the shitty coffee and greasy sugar that started my day and the constant stops and goes (through no fault of Natalie's—she was an extremely competent driver, even as she spoke) I was starting to feel carsick.

I was content to watch Natalie and snag the occasional shots as I could. Once we got further up the trail, I would get some drone footage. All had been cleared with local regulations and rules. She looked damn cute in her little dorky visor and vest. What a nerd. A superhot nerd. Whose ass was seriously filling out those hiking pants. People of the town waved to her/us as we slowly drove around, and Natalie smiled eagerly in return.

So it was a good thing that Gabe ended up carrying most of the conversation load. Even if I did feel like it was a major blow to the bro code. I knew that his interests lay with a certain bartender, but he could have at least checked to see if I was interested. Not that I was. But a bro would have checked.

I pressed my thumb to the growing headache pulsing between my eyebrows. Was I seriously threatened by a college student whose current biggest flex was that he "didn't trust food that swam where it pooped"?

I needed professional help.

By the time we drove somehow even further up the mountain, I was more than ready to be on solid ground again, and with no desire to hike.

"Okay, you guys ready?" Natalie buckled the straps of her pack. She said, "you guys," but her gaze only loosely flicked over to me.

"Super ready." Gabe was stretching his arms above his head in a pre-hike warmup.

"You said this was a short hike, right?" I asked, not at all wanting to do any of this.

"One point five miles," Gabe answered.

Natalie beamed at her star pupil.

"What's with the pack?" I asked.

I wasn't stalling per se, but I wasn't liking the looks of these two. They seemed a little hardcore for what was supposed to be a family-friendly beginner walk.

"Safety first. I'm first aid trained, and this is part of my duties. Plus, you never know." She patted a canister on the side of her pack.

"I trust you with my life," Gabe said seriously. "Did you know—"

"Yes," I cut him off. "She saved Deckard's life. She's a real wonder."

Natalie stared into the woods, avoiding both of our gazes.

"The trail is extremely safe. The pack just comes with the job."

I nodded, noting not for the first time how cagey she was about the whole life-saving thing. I guess gracious humility was another stellar quality I'd never be able to live up to.

At first, the hike felt great. With my feet on the ground and the sun on my face, my energy returned some. Plus, it was beautiful up here. The air was unlike anything else; even though we weren't that far from town, it felt completely cleansed of all things man-made. Gabe and Natalie kept a brisk pace, chatting happily back and forth about his research and the places he'd visited for his thesis. I hung back, focused on my footing. These sneakers weren't terrible for walking, but the gravelly dirt and damp leaves meant lots of slipping. There were still patches of snow in some areas, and there was mud where the sun shone.

About twenty minutes in, things took a turn for me.

There was more of an incline on the trail than I'd expected, and all of my equipment meant I was carrying at least twenty pounds of additional weight. Which wasn't much by itself, but combined with my lack of real food, my hands were starting to shake. It got to the point where I couldn't even get the camera to focus. I should have swallowed my pride and asked to stop to eat a protein bar, but the other two were completely unaffected. I had the built-in excuse to stop and "take a photo" every so often, but that wasn't helping. My heart pulsed in my eyes and seemed to cloud the edges of my vision at times. I was fairly active by nature of my job. One time, Callie clocked us getting over twenty thousand steps in one intense working day. I did my part to stay fit.

But this beginner hike was killing me.

I suddenly felt so embarrassingly winded, so fully tired, I thought if I didn't stop to take a break, I might pass out. I would never hear the end of it.

"Hey, uh, you two. You go ahead. I need to take a longer shot, and it will take a few minutes," I said, trying not to sound as out of breath as I felt.

"Okay," Natalie called without looking back, and an emotion surged through me that had me biting my cheek.

I was scared. What I felt was not normal, and she was going to keep going, and I was going to sit down and never stand up again, because I was too fucking proud to say that I needed help.

I would never see Natalie or those angelic curls again.

I swayed so violently, I had to grip a large pine to keep from tipping over completely, the sharp bark cutting into my palm.

"Woah, bro. Are you okay?" Gabe called from where they were, already several yards ahead of me.

I blinked, and when I opened my eyes, he was already in front of me, leaning forward with a worried expression. "Dude, did you eat at Tony's last night too? You look seconds from—"

I held up my arm to cut him off. It took a large portion of my energy.

Natalie came jogging up a second later, and my humiliation grew. "What's going on? Oh my God. Are you okay, Miles?"

"I don't know," I admitted. "I don't think it's food poisoning, but I feel off. Like really sick but also dizzy. Weird." I tried to explain but it was costing more energy than I had.

"Did you warn him about altitude sickness?" Gabe asked Natalie.

"I did," she said.

"I did too." Gabe's brow furrowed.

"You signed the waiver," she accused me. "You read the part about altitude sickness."

"I skimmed it." I found a massive exposed gray rock and let myself fall onto it, carefully shrugging off the camera equipment. "I'm okay. I just want to hang out for a minute."

"Shit. Miles." Natalie shrugged off her pack and rummaged around in it.

"Oh, dude, that's serious stuff. You shouldn't mess around with that," Gabe said.

If I had any more energy, I would've rolled my eyes. But I worried the momentum of it would cause me to fall backward. This town was almost as obsessed with blood oxygen levels as it was that damn ball.

Natalie pulled out a water bottle. "We can hang out a minute. You need to sip some water," Natalie said, unscrewing the cap and thrusting the bottle toward me.

My stomach revolted. I turned my head to the side.

"I know, but you really need to. Just a few little sips." I did as she said.

It was weird. I was equal parts humiliated but also loving that Natalie had to look directly at me to make sure I was okay.

As she squatted in front of me, she rested a hand on my knee, maybe for balance, but maybe not.

"You're really pale," she said.

"It was a long winter," I said weakly.

"He jokes. That's good." She fished for my arm, which flopped limp at my side. My breaths were coming fast, and I could still feel my heartbeat in my eyeballs. She placed two warm fingers daintily on my wrist and squinted as her gaze flicked between my eyes. "Your pulse is racing." Her fingers moved to my neck, maybe thinking my pulse would be different there? She moaned. "Dammit, Miles." But she didn't have the ice-cold mad face; this was more of a worried mad face.

She pulled out her phone and messaged somebody before she placed her hand on my chest. "Okay. Your breaths are short too." Her phone pinged a response, and she quickly scanned the message before coming back to meet my gaze. Natalie was fully in work mode, and damn, it was hot. "I'm pretty sure that you have altitude sickness. The good news is, it's super common and most likely mild."

"The bad news?" I asked, jaw clenching as my mouth filled with saliva. I would not vomit in front of this woman, so help me God. I had to keep some dignity intact.

Instead, I focused on where both her hands now rested on my knees.

"Bad news is, that it's really unpleasant for a few hours." Natalie turned to look up at Gabe. "Hey, Gabe, can you stay with Miles while I run back to the shuttle to meet the doctor?"

"No." I said it so fast that both turned to me in surprise. I wanted her to stay. Yes, it was melodramatic, and probably I was going to be fine, but I had the sudden and overwhelming surety that if she left right now, I wouldn't be okay ever again. "I don't want us to get lost coming back."

"It's the only trail. If you stay on the marked path, you'll be fine," she said.

Gabe flicked a look between us, and maybe there was some such thing as a bro code after all, because he said, "Actually, do you mind if I go meet the doctor? I need to check in at work, and I left my phone on the shuttle."

"Are you sure?" Natalie asked, worrying her bottom lip.

"I'll be fine."

"Okay. Thank you so much, Gabe. Tell the doctor that we're coming back slowly, but if she can meet us on the trail, that would be great."

Gabe nodded.

"And be careful. The last thing we need now is a broken leg."

"Got it," he said and then jogged quickly but carefully out of sight.

"Good kid," I said as she watched his retreating form with a worried look. I was relieved he was gone. My pride was slightly less wounded with just Natalie. I groaned until she turned back to me.

Also, maybe I liked having her undivided attention.

"I know this sucks, and it's probably the last thing you want to do, but we need to get you to a lower altitude."

I groaned again.

"I know. But it will start to help right away. You need more oxygen." She pulled a brown square from the bag and started to unpeel its wrapper. "After you slowly eat a few bites of this protein bar, we are going to start heading down, okay?"

I curled a lip at the bar. "Do you have any other flavors?"

She huffed. "Glad to see you haven't lost all your charm."

I forced down a few bites of that god-awful bar and was slightly less nauseated by the time we got moving. But my head still felt like it was stuffed so full of cotton it was going to explode. I was ready to go to bed and call this day a wash. At least some of the shots I'd taken before the shaking took over were good.

As we walked slowly back toward the trailhead, Natalie kept her arm locked through mine, carrying a surprising amount of my weight. I had to be safe, so I let her help me.

"Were you able to get what you needed?" she asked after several tedious minutes.

"I think so. Good old Steady Hand Asher, as I'm known in the business."

"Is that right?"

"Well, soon enough I will be."

She laughed softly, like she used to. It was so nice being arm in arm with her, making her smile. Sucked that I had to almost die for it to happen. This could be the start of a friendship again. Maybe she wouldn't go back to icing me out now.

As the terrain flattened, I recognized the start of the trail. Gabe was walking at a brisk pace with a brunette woman in her early thirties behind him.

As the two approached, Natalie clicked her tongue. "Do not even think about it. She's incredibly off the market."

"I wasn't." And I hadn't. Weirdly, I didn't even notice the finer features of the good doctor. I'd been too distracted by making Natalie laugh.

Hmm. Troubling.

"I already have enough . . . enemies in this town," I added to keep things light between us. I felt her look at me, but I kept my eyes locked on the trail ahead. "I guess now that you mention it, she is easy on the eyes."

Natalie scoffed. "She doesn't date."

"Okay, okay. Stop trying to hook me up with her." Natalie frowned as I walked on my own toward the doctor.

After doing essentially what Natalie did but with better tools, I was deemed fit to live another day.

"He'll be okay. You were right, Natalie, it is acute mountain sickness. So long as he takes it easy and doesn't try and hike anymore, at least until he's acclimated, he'll be fine." The doctor looked back up to Natalie. "Another life saved," she said dryly, before packing up her bag.

Natalie looked like she might get sick and thanked the other woman again.

"Just take your time getting him back down to town," she said before walking away.

Natalie nodded. They really seemed to downplay what I thought for sure was going to be the end of me, not thirty minutes ago.

After a few minutes of logistics, Gabe and the doctor drove off back to town.

Once the tires on gravel were no longer in earshot, Natalie and I sat in silence. The mountain was full of sounds once my ears adjusted. Natalie was leaning against the shuttle with her head back as she watched a flock of passing birds fly way overhead.

She looked tired. I'd sort of ruined her plans for the day.

"Sorry about the tour," I offered softly.

She pushed off the van, seemingly surprised, and briefly met my gaze. "Oh. Uh, don't worry. These things do happen. Hence, the waiver," she said.

Risking all my pride, I stepped closer. "Yeah. I'm terrible about reading the fine print."

Her eyes widened as I moved even closer. I felt a little better and wanted to be friends again at least. I wanted to go back to the easy camaraderie we'd had the first time I was here.

"Thank you for taking care of me too. You were amazing all around today."

Color flooded her cheeks. All I wanted was for her to get back to the place where she easily met my eyes.

"Thank you." She backed up until she was flat against the van, staring at my collar. Closer, but not quite.

I moved until there were only inches between us.

"Maybe tomorrow we could look at somewhere else on Callie's list?"

I could see the moment her shields shot back up, preparing her excuses. "I'm really busy."

"Of course." And just like that, back to square one.

"You can't show up and expect me to drop everything for you."

"I wasn't asking that. I was asking to make our next plans," I said, frustration in my voice.

She slid to the side to get on the bus, but I couldn't go back to town. Mostly because I wanted to hash this out once and for all, and a little bit because the thought of moving again did terrible things to my insides.

"I'm busy. I have a full life here, despite what you think," she said.

"Natalie. Come on."

We would leave here and be right back where we started, but I was sick and tired—quite literally—of the brush-off.

"No. Natalie. Wait. Stop. I'm not doing this anymore." My tone was serious, as was I.

She froze and turned to me with a worried frown.

My stomach lurched.

"We have to talk about this elephant in the room. I can't take it anymore. But first—" I held up a finger before I sprinted to the porta potty and threw up the protein bar.

Dammit.

Chapter 9

EVEN THOUGH I WAS STILL FRUSTRATED, I COULDN'T HELP but pity Miles. When he came back around the corner, his color was gone, and his eyelids were heavy.

I handed him a fresh bottle of water and the unopened travel mouthwash I kept for this exact situation.

"I cannot get in that bus yet," he said in a rough voice, shame hanging his head.

"We can wait a few." I winced in understanding.

He went to where he'd been sick, and I heard the familiar sounds of gargling.

I wasn't ready to have whatever conversation he'd been wanting. I didn't know what either of us would say, but I knew I didn't do well with head-on confrontation. I cared infinitely until I didn't.

A few minutes later, he returned to find me doing work on my phone.

"If you think you can handle it, we should try and get you back down into town. I'll drive slow around the curves."

He closed his eyes and let out a long breath. "Only if you promise to talk to me. This whole thing where you pretend I don't exist is starting to suck." I must have hesitated too long because he added, "You'll be driving, so you won't even have to look at me. Which is your favorite thing to not do."

"That's . . ." But I trailed off because I had no defense.

My guilt for this whole day was too much. I'd been so determined to avoid his accusing gaze and all that it made me feel, I'd missed the early signs of his pitiful illness. I was better than this.

"Okay. We can talk," I said. "But tell me if you're going to get sick again."

"I think that's all she wrote. I regret the battery acid coffee. Let me tell you."

"Antacid?" I held out a package of chalky tablets.

"You're a saint, prepared for everything."

"Like I said, you aren't my first. If the drive up doesn't get them, the—" He went still. "You get the gist."

I hadn't even told him about the aerial tram tours I offered, where somebody almost always got sick or froze with fear. There had been an incident last New Year's Eve where the tram got stuck and Bee Perkins and Owen Campbell were stranded up there together. I'd have thought that would have slowed things down, but ever since it was remodeled, the tram was more popular than ever.

On the winding road back to town, Miles sat in the seat behind the driver's where Gabe had been on the way up. I was fully aware of where his hand rested on the back of my seat near my ear. Already that heady scent of his filled the air around me, and I fought from inhaling deeply.

"Remember the first time you were here with Callie?" I asked because, as it turned out, I couldn't stand the silence after a few minutes. Normally, I'd be happily spooling out facts, but I didn't think Miles cared about the lost gold rushers who founded our town.

"I do remember those two weeks of my life, yes." I ignored his sarcasm.

"Did you get sick like this last time?" I asked.

"No. Not like this." After a thoughtful beat, he added, "But we didn't hike up anywhere. And actually, now that I think about it, we were in Utah before we came here, filming a commercial for this small ski town, so maybe I was already acclimated. Who knows. Very embarrassing all around. Taken down by the actual air I breathe."

I laughed. "If it makes you feel any better, professional athletes come to places like here to train their lungs."

"Hmm. It helps a little."

"But then again, we get a lot of retired couples too, who manage fine. Maybe it is you. If only there had been an informative document you could have read."

"Or the several dozen warnings I got about it since I've been back. I don't remember people being so concerned about my blood oxygen levels last time, but maybe that's because I was distracted."

His stare was tangible on the back of my head. I flicked my gaze to the rearview mirror to find him studying me. Something about the intensity of how he watched me had me softening more. "Just another mile until we're back. Are you doing okay?" I asked and looked back to the road before he noticed me watching him.

"I'm fine. Only a mile? Wow. It felt so much longer driving up."

"That's because you're feeling better."

"I still want to talk about the elephant in the room, Natalie. Or the minibus, as it were." His voice got closer as he leaned toward me. "Even if you've managed to stall most of this drive."

"I don't know what you mean."

"Maybe you don't like me. I get it. I'm not for everyone. Those people are wrong, but they are entitled to that opinion." I scoffed, but he went on. "But don't forget, I remember what you're like when you're being professional. And this isn't professional."

He wasn't wrong. Shame burned through me, holding my tongue.

"We need to work together. This job is important to me. When you said you would help me, I thought that meant you would take it seriously too."

"I am taking it seriously," I said, the embarrassment making me defensive. "I have a life here that's really busy. But I know this is important."

"Do you? Because it seems like you're half-assing it and I didn't take you for the type."

I took a deep breath in. He was wrong though. I hadn't been professional last time either. I'd let myself get way too close to him. I was not sure how to proceed with him now. In a lot of ways, it felt easier to pretend to hate him, somehow, it didn't hurt as much.

He waited in heavy silence as I found my words. "I find it difficult to work with you. But I will try harder to make an effort in my schedule," I finally said.

"Can you tell me what I did? What changed? If we're going to work together, then you're going to need to be able to look me in the eyes. Can you tell me whatever it is that I fucked up so we can move on and I can get out of your curls faster?"

His fingers gently tugged one of my curls that had come loose behind my ear, and it sent a sharp jolt through me, even though there was no skin on skin. I was too aware of him.

"It's not—you didn't—"

"If we're going to work together, you're going to need to

be able to at least look me in the eyes." Without thinking, I found him in the rearview mirror again and quickly looked away.

"For more than that." He sighed and sat back. "If I knew what was so offensive about me, then I could try to tone it down. Except my natural good looks, I can't help those."

I bit back a smile.

Maybe it was the vulnerability of his words, or the guilt for maybe hiking a little harder than necessary to prove some sort of childish point, but I felt myself weakening, as always, under his direct attention.

"I guess I felt, *feel*, protective of this town."

"Oh," he said in surprised understanding.

I spoke carefully, chose my words intentionally. He'd hurt me and it cost so much to admit that. I wasn't ready to. There wasn't a point. "It seems to me that you rolled in, got what you needed, and then left. You left and didn't even look back. Like this town meant nothing to you."

He made another sound of understanding but dragged it out longer this time. I watched the roads, now more congested as we pulled into the edge of town.

"I really don't want to talk about this. It makes me feel like an absurd person," I admitted when I found him in the mirror again, frowning in thought.

"Well, we have to talk. Sometimes you have to talk about uncomfortable things," he said.

"Or we could go back to me making witty barbs and you taking them on the chin."

"I guess that's better than nothing." The gentle, sad way he said it . . .

Frick.

"It's just that . . ." I sat up, pretending to be very focused on the road. Completely out of his line of vision in the rearview.

"This town really liked you. You made a large impact here, and then you left. And it sucked. For the town."

That familiar crush of embarrassment grabbed me as I thought again of how I'd been so sure he'd call or text after he'd left. When he was here, we'd sent a lot of messages to each other. He'd ask some inane question that could have been easily looked up online, and I pretended to be annoyed by his inability to do a simple internet search. It was great. He made me laugh so much and it all felt so good. And then, like that teenage girl who could never properly read the room, I waited around for him to come back. Heat burned up my neck now thinking about it.

He sat for some time in silence as I worried I'd shared too much, given too much away.

"We're back," I said, quietly pulling the van into the lot.

With the bus parked and the engine off, the silence was deafening. I stood up and stretched.

He stood up too, grabbing the overhead bar but keeping a large space between us. My body felt this pull to lean forward.

I chewed the inside of my lip, desperate to leave and stop feeling so much, but I could tell he was building up to speak.

He cleared his throat and winced, putting a little more space between us. "God, I'm going to take a shower for an hour when I get back to the room."

I nodded, completely unsure where things stood. Had that been enough of the elephant? Was that his hint that he wanted to go?

He rubbed the space between his eyebrows with his thumb, as he so often did, and let out a long breath. It tugged at my heart because it reminded me so much of the guy who I met the first time, the guy who I never would have thought could be so callous.

Maybe I was a naive schoolgirl.

"Callie has mentioned to me that sometimes I can come on a little strong," he started. I stilled, greedy for any facts about his life away from here. "This is going to make me sound completely arrogant, but you already think the worst of me, so I'll just say it." I didn't think the *worst* of him. He was dead to me. Or at least he had been. I wasn't sure now. "The thing is, I'm kind of an asshole. I never stick around for very long, and I have found it's easier to speak frankly rather than mess with . . . fripperies . . ."

"Fripperies?" I asked, biting back a smile.

He shook his head and cleared his throat. "I'm nervous."

My shoulders relaxed, and a smile tugged on my mouth.

As he spoke, his shoulders sort of scrunched up to his ears, and he leaned to the side, as if telling this truth about himself made him become one of those plastic toys you blast with a hair dryer to shrink. "The downside to this is, I'm not so great at long term. I've been doing some version of this job since college. I've never needed to stick around. I do what I've got to do and I leave, on to the next assignment."

An unexpected crushing sensation weighed on my chest. I understood what he was saying on a rational level, that he was good at his job and he shouldn't be condemned for that, but on a much deeper level, it meant that I was like everybody else.

I hadn't made any sort of impact on him.

I was no different than every other small-town woman in every other town he'd been through. Thank God, I hadn't slept with him. My emo, needy little heart wouldn't have been able to take it. No matter how old-fashioned it made me. I didn't feel that attraction to very many people. I needed to work up to it. And I had really worked myself up with Miles.

But if I had slept with him, I would have felt even lower when he left, and that hardly seemed possible.

I clenched and relaxed my jaw as I counted by twos. If I

could make it to one hundred, then I wouldn't cry. I wouldn't make an absolute fool of myself in front of this man who was literally just doing his job.

"I want to be clear that I never do this maliciously or even on purpose." Here, he looked to the side, and his shoulders unfurled. "Callie actually thinks it's a natural defense mechanism because—" He shook his head. "The point is, *God*, I didn't mean to share all this. The point is, I am sorry, Natalie. Truly."

Shit. I didn't make it to one hundred. I ground my jaw as tears burned the backs of my eyes. This was absurd. I was absurd. We were basically strangers.

"Natalie, please look at me."

I swallowed and met his eyes on me. It felt like trying to lift up a bus, holding his gaze while simultaneously trying not to let tears form.

"I am sorry. I never wanted to hurt this *town*."

So much for my subtlety.

And it was so much worse to see his sincerity, to understand that this had all been a routine stop on his journey through life when it had taken such an emotional toll on me.

"Also," he said, and I managed to keep holding his gaze. "You should know, this town did have an impact on me. I didn't forget it as soon as I left. I haven't stopped thinking about this place."

What did that mean? Did it change anything? It made me feel better, maybe, but also worse?

I shook my head, looking at his dusty sneakers. "But you never reached out or—"

"Hey! I sent that email a week after I left. Didn't you get it?" His face seemed hopeful.

My mouth hung open, and my head shook as I went back through every message and email to see if I'd missed something.

Wait.

"Do you mean the email you sent to the mayor and cc'd me on? The one where you asked if anyone had seen your beanie that you left?"

"You did get it." His forehead creased. "Why didn't you respond?"

"Yeah, the *mayor* and I got it." I tossed a hand out with a shake of my head. When I'd seen his name pop up in my inbox, I'd been so ridiculously hopeful. And then it all crashed in the one-line email I still had pathetically memorized. "I wasn't even the main recipient."

"It was an excuse to talk to you," he admitted, and my mouth fell open.

"I thought it was you using me again. Or the town again. If you wanted to talk, you could have asked *me* how I was doing. Or asked about literally anything." My voice was high and my throat tight, so I made myself take a breath. "Th-that would have made all the difference," I admitted.

"I know. I think I knew that on some level." He scrubbed a hand through his thick hair. "But I was never meant to stay. I was always leaving."

"Just like with this trip."

"Just like with this trip," he repeated.

An understanding as clear as ever passed through me. Miles and I had shared a connection. I hadn't imagined it. But that didn't change the fact that he was ultimately leaving. That my life here would continue. Maybe he had been trying to protect me in his own cowardly way. I needed to go to my Thinking Place and process this.

"But I'd like to put the past behind us. Start over. As friends again?" he asked hopefully.

He had been trying to end *things* cold turkey without leading me on. He was a nonconfrontational little jerk, but to be fair, he'd been clear from the moment they arrived that he was always meant to leave. I was oversensitive about people leaving this place. I had hoped differently; I thought that maybe our connection was enough.

It didn't matter now. We had new plans, and he was right. The past was the past.

"You're not the only one with flaws," I admitted. "I have also been told by my overly honest best friend that I have a habit of keeping score and holding people to really high standards."

"And I was an asshole for . . . well, my whole personality. I'm sorry for it." He smiled, and I met his gaze with a smile of my own. His grin grew and I hated that it made me feel so good to be the cause of it.

"I'm sorry too. I will be nicer," I said. "We can work together and both get our needs met."

"Absolutely, and then I'll be out of your curls forever." He tugged on one again with a soft smile that made my heart do a flip.

"Perfect." Exactly what we, the *town*, wanted.

Chapter 10

A STRANGE THING HAPPENED NEXT.

Maybe it was the way I kept replaying my last conversation with Natalie, the way I kept seeing the genuine pain in her eyes every time I closed mine.

But I felt like shit. Not only from the altitude sickness—please, it's not always about the altitude.

The next few days, I laid low and told myself that I was giving Natalie space before I reached out to her for another assignment. But the truth was that an incredible shame weighed me down.

I wasn't a conversational mastermind, but it was clear her hurt hadn't just been on behalf of the town. Obviously.

No shit, I heard Callie say in my mind.

Mind-Callie was right. I left a trail of destruction, and I'd never had to face the consequences before. And this was why facing the consequences of my actions sucked.

I paced the small hotel room, unable to decide what to do next.

I wasn't an evil person; I didn't enjoy hurting people. I assumed they never thought of me again, or it wasn't that big of a deal. Even though I had wondered once or twice, in the loneliest hours of the night, what it might be like to stick around some place, I wasn't built for that.

I'd hoped my thoughts of Natalie would lessen with time and distance. I thought that I'd imagined how drawn to her I was, how easy it was to talk to her. Because the scary thing was, I didn't often meet a person who I felt like I understood inherently, and they understood me in return. Did anybody? It was so rare.

Human connection was terrifying.

Most likely, though, I really was attracted to Natalie, and these last couple days were meant to apply some distance from these pointless *feelings*. I already had a best friend and was really more of the lone-wolf type anyway. Only weirdos had loads of friends. Hadn't I read that on a bumper sticker once? Probably.

What I needed was a good conversation with my close friend to feel safe and loved and appreciated.

"Hey, dumbass. How's it going being a total loser?" Callie answered my call from the same spot in bed she'd been last time we spoke.

"Oh, God, I miss you." I placed a hand to my heart and let out a sharp breath.

She chuckled and her chest heaved. "I miss you too."

"Am I seeing things or are your boobs huge?" I leaned closer to the phone. Propped up by the pillows, her *pillows* were almost to her chin. "We talked last week."

"You're not crazy," Callie said with a shake of her head. "I'm maternal as fuck now."

"It's weird when you talk about my wife's boobs," a voice called from off-screen. Mags landed in a happy thump next to

Callie, kissing her cheek and shaking the whole screen. "I feel like this isn't the first time we've talked about this, Miles." Mags had short hair, shaved underneath, and the energy of a youth. I don't think she'd sat still in ten years. She rested her head on Callie's shoulder in a rare repose.

"Probably not." I shrugged. "I wasn't saying I wanted to motorboat them. I was pointing out a fact. Your mammaries are glam . . . mer . . . ies . . . or something. That worked better in my mind."

"Gross," the two women said, lips curling in unison.

Within the next two seconds, Mags was already bouncing back up. "I'm off to play pickleball," she said before kissing Callie's cheek again. Then she dropped her head below the camera and said in a soft, cooing voice, presumably to Callie's belly, "Bye, little baby bean. Keep kicking ass." (*Hopefully* to her belly.) Resuming her brisk tone, she said, "See ya, Miles. Try not to be such a total boner all the time."

"But then, how would I get a rise out of you?" I said, grinning and waiting for them to laugh at my hilarious joke.

They did not laugh.

Mags left with another disappointed sigh as Callie shifted herself higher. "Ugh, freaking giant boobs and belly and everything." I waited until she stopped shifting. She let out a long sigh. "Okay, work talk now, please."

"Did you see what I uploaded to the shared site?" I asked.

"I did. Some of those shots you got were great."

"That's Steady Hand Asher."

"Wow. You are still trying to make that non-nickname happen."

"Greatness takes time."

"I think the bigger issue is that the nickname sucks," she said.

"Could be."

"And while I appreciate the obvious dedication to the work, I couldn't help but notice there weren't as many frames as I'd been expecting," she said in shortened breaths. "We have a lot of footage to shoot and only a few more weeks. I know it feels like a lot now, but you know how fast these things go."

"I do know. It's been sort of a pain getting Natalie to work with me. Through very little fault of my own."

"Miles," she said with an edge of good-natured irritation. Hopefully, it was good-natured.

"*But*," I added, with the lift of my pointer finger. "Natalie and I had a really good talk, and I think things will be easier from here out."

"You had an actual grown-up conversation? Miles Asher, why I never thought I'd see the day," she said with a tacky, transatlantic accent.

"We have grown-up conversations all the time."

"You mean like earlier when you talked about motorboating me?"

"I said I *didn't* want to, and you know that we do."

"I'm kidding, yes. I am the very lucky exception to the never-get-close-to-anybody rule." She smiled genuinely at me as I frowned. "But if you cleared the air with Natalie, why are you in your hotel in pajamas at three o'clock on a Tuesday? This is precious daylight you're wasting."

"This is very expensive loungewear, thank you very much. And I got sick. But I'm okay," I added quickly when her face transformed in a flash with worry. "I've had to take it easy for a few days."

"Please be careful. Did you read the pamphlet Natalie made about altitude sickness?"

My head dropped back, and I let out a silent scream off camera.

"I can't have you going on bed rest too. Then we will never finish this video."

"Don't worry. I feel totally fine now. In fact, I'm meeting up with Natalie tomorrow." Just as soon as I respond to her last message. From yesterday. That I'd left unread. An image of Natalie checking her phone, her big brown eyes pinched in disappointment, filled my mind.

I rubbed at my throat where I'd had nonstop heartburn since the humiliating puking incident.

"Since we are still talking about Natalie, and not to be a jerk, but when you two are out tomorrow, do you think you could focus more on the shot list?"

"What do you mean?" I slid my laptop over and opened it. I set the tablet on the desk before I logged on to our shared site. "I got everything for Cabezón. Didn't I?"

"You did, but, and no offense to Natalie here, because she's undoubtedly lovely, but maybe get a little less of her in some of the shots."

"What?" I frowned as I started to click through the uploaded videos. I remembered thinking once or twice that the sun was illuminating her in a particularly appealing way. Or noticing that when she shared facts, her eyes lit with this sort of magnetic energy. And when she laughed, her whole being seemed to glow.

Surely it wasn't that much.

But it was. A lot.

"Huh," I said as I continued to scroll through everything. "I guess I didn't realize how often I accidentally got her in the shots."

I flicked a look at Callie. Yep, there was that "calling me out on my dipshit-ery" look.

"Anything I should be worried about here, Miles?" she asked seriously.

I shook my head. "No. I think that must have been when I started to get sick. I wasn't thinking clearly."

She held my gaze a beat too long. "Because you promised me you could do this."

"And I can." I shut the laptop, unable to think clearly with Natalie's face paused on my screen.

"I have all the faith in the world in you. And also, please don't fuck this up, Miles. I love you tremendously, but please, *please* don't ruin this because you're thinking with your zoom lens, so to speak."

"You mean my penis?"

"Gross." Callie grimaced. "I'm already so down about not having any control and not being out there doing this myself."

Another wave of guilt passed over me. I seriously hated emotions.

"I know. And it's all going to work out."

A guilty thread tugged in my mind. I had been thinking about Natalie way too much. It killed me that I'd hurt her. When I pictured her face during our last talk, I felt like punching myself in the zoom lens. But Callie was my person, and the only one who continued to put up with my shit since college, longer than anyone really. I wouldn't let her down. Time to get back to work and focus on why I was here.

"Callie." I held her gaze as I spoke. "You know that the work has always and will always come first."

"Yeah, I know." She rubbed her belly and let out a long breath. "I thought that too once, and now look at me." Her arms flopped out, but a smile tugged her mouth wide. "I don't even remember what my toes look like."

Chapter 11

Natalie

Rochelle and John had joint offices on the second floor of the business center located in the heart of Slippery Slopes. The business center is one of the oldest buildings in town, and remnants of the original wooden staircase are still visible today, tucked away behind the cement stairs added in the 1960s.

Jeez, even my thoughts were narrated like a tour guide. I needed a hobby.

A hobby that didn't involve obsessing over whether or not Miles had texted me back.

When he first returned, my anger and hurt were so strong that I thought I'd never feel anything else. But seeing his pain and shame over the inevitable fact that he'd had to leave almost undid me. Then, when he said, "I haven't stopped thinking about this place," had he actually meant Slippery Slopes? I doubted it, based on how he looked at all the rampant guinea pig gangs.

And yet I was right back to sitting around waiting to hear from him. This was why I hadn't told Rochelle everything. Because I knew exactly what her reaction would be. *Do not waste time on that sorry excuse for a douche canoe. I've said it before, when a guy is ready for commitment, there is no mistaking it. Look at John.* But John wasn't like most men. He was obsessed with his wife. Obsessed. And of course he was. She was incredibly sharp and knew New Mexico law better than anybody else. Also, yes, the whole model thing.

Speaking of John, I waved to him as I passed his office. He smiled and waved back, even though he had his phone cradled to his ear.

A second later, I was jerked roughly into Rochelle's office.

"Hey, hey," I said, holding up the delicious New Mexican food I'd brought from Tres Conejos. "Be careful with my Cojones!" Out of context, it sounded bad, but what did they expect, naming their restaurant "three rabbits"? Not a single Slippery Slopes resident referred to it by its actual name.

"Nothing better than greasy, hot cojones. But hurry, close the door behind you. And lock it," Rochelle said with agitation, as she paced, a stress ball barely clinging to life in her hand.

"What's wrong?" I asked, looking behind me as I obeyed her.

"I can't stand to look at him," she said. Her arm flailed in the direction of her husband's office across the hall.

A wave of anxiety passed over me. It wasn't just my own conflicts that I avoided at all costs. I hated seeing anybody fighting. I set down our lunch and fidgeted with my fingers.

"What's wrong? What happened? I don't tell many people this, but I know the best places to hide bodies," I joked.

Though I really did know that.

"As a lawyer, I'm pretending I didn't hear that. As your best friend, aw, thank you." Despite having told me to close the door, Rochelle went to peek through the short blinds. "But no. We aren't fighting. Just look at him."

I copied her, covertly looking through the shades and across the hall into John's office. He was leaned back in his chair, feet propped on his desk, laughing at the person on the phone. He lobbed a much happier-looking stress ball into the air before smoothly catching it. He seemed like normal, affable John to me.

I leaned back to look at her. "What am I missing?"

"Really? You don't see it?" she asked, disbelieving.

I shook my head.

"He's just so hot. He's obviously tormenting me." She groaned and let the blinds snap shut. "All because last night I may have purposefully worn those yoga pants he likes, but then accidentally fell asleep after Olive went down. He's clearly getting revenge. How am I supposed to work like this?"

I looked again, though I was fairly certain I would never see what she saw. No offense to John. This time, when he tossed the ball up, it came back down on a different trajectory, smacking him in the face. He jostled back in his chair before laughing and bending to pick up the ball.

"See?" Rochelle gestured emphatically. "God, he's been doing that all day." She fanned her face.

I couldn't think of anything to say, so I just went back to where I'd set our lunch down.

"Right. So, I brought us your usual. Number four, two carne asada tacos with guac."

"Did you get green chile?"

"Yeah, but on the side because Amanda said it was super spicy."

"*Pfft*. She always says that so the tourists don't try and get their money back. Gimmie, gimmie."

"I also got tortilla chips and queso."

"Hell yes." She was already dumping the green chile on her first taco. "Any margaritas tucked in there too?"

"I wish. But do you really want to waft the smell of booze to your next clients?"

"Can't be any worse than the last guy," she said, and I huffed a laugh. "But you're probably right. It would just make me sleepy."

We sat in companionable silence as we situated our food on the small coffee table. I picked off the cilantro from my own tacos.

Rochelle rolled her eyes.

"What? You know it tastes like soap," I said.

"That's not why I'm rolling my eyes. Just say you don't want cilantro when you order."

I waved her away before flicking off the disgusting green bit still stuck to my finger. "It's too late. I've been ordering this for like five years. If I say anything to Amanda now, it'll be the talk of the town."

"Headline news on the *Slippery Slope Sheets*, I'm sure." She shook her head. "You care way too much about what this town thinks of you."

I shrugged because, yeah, *duh*.

I already felt like I was hanging on by a thread. If I lost my best friend, I would never survive. There had been so many times I'd tried to tell Rochelle the truth about Deckard. And every time I chickened out. I couldn't handle her looking at me like an outsider.

After we had inhaled our first few bites, I said, "Okay, I've waited long enough. What's the juicy gossip you had to share?"

She swallowed her bite and wiggled her shoulders. "Remember how Miles is back in town?"

"Mm-hmm." I took a huge bite, focusing on my taco and not her eagle-eyed, scary lawyer gaze.

I hadn't told her everything about Miles. She didn't like him for reasons all her own, reasons that were central to me and the pain he inflicted when he left. I knew if I told her about his desire to help me with Deckard, I'd second-guess myself even more.

"Of course you do, I forgot he was annoying you at the ticket thing. Oh, how's it going with Deckard?"

"Wait, first this." It was always best to keep her on track.

She nodded and then took a split second to reorient her thoughts. "The mayor told her daughter—"

"Which one?" I asked.

"Dottie? Or is it Daphne? Who's the one that had the part-time clown business?"

"Dottie."

"Okay, so the other one. Who sometimes works for the crystal shop?"

I nodded, taking another bite. "Yeah, Daphne," I said around my mouthful of taco.

"Well, she told me that her mom told her that the reason that Miles's hot chick partner, Callie, didn't come back is because she has a high-risk pregnancy." She paused for a reaction. My eyes widened appropriately. The food in my stomach suddenly weighed ten pounds. Miles hadn't told me that. He'd been mildly evasive when it came to Callie. Rochelle went on. "The only reason Miles came back was as a favor for her because she couldn't."

My last bite scraped down my throat as I swallowed it in surprise. "Oh. That makes sense, I guess."

After Miles and I spoke, I held on to the nugget that he'd had feelings or whatever the first time he was here. A little part of me thought maybe the reason he'd come back was because he'd been secretly missing me too. But like he said, he was just here for work.

Always for work.

This was why Deckard was the right and obvious choice. And yes, I didn't need a man, yada yada yada, but Deckard was *here*. He loved this place as much as I did. Deckard, who would look handsome on my arm in his tuxedo, who the whole town loved. It only made sense.

No more pathetic pining over a short-lived, doomed-to-fail connection with a man who would be leaving.

"I know, can you believe it?" Rochelle asked. "I should feel like an asshole for being so mean to him when he's literally here against his will to help his bestie." She took another bite. "I mean, I *don't* feel bad, but, like, maybe I should a little."

"Totally." *Against his will.* "Callie was great." I reached for a different topic. "I hope she's going to be okay."

"Me too. But who would have thought that Miles had any inkling of not being a total selfish prick."

"Yeah."

"He's still a total pretentious douche canoe though, and so we hates him," she said in her Gollum voice.

"Totally."

"And you aren't going to pay any attention to him because if he was interested in you, he would make an effort. That simple."

Called that.

"Totally," I said.

Rochelle threw down her paper napkin. "You have got to stop saying totally. What is your major malfunction? Do you need a hard reboot?"

"Nothing. No, I'm fine." I smiled.

Her eyes narrowed, and she pointed at my face. "Fake smile."

She was going to find out anyway. I sighed and sat back. "It's just that, I might have sort of agreed to help Miles again while he's here."

"Natalie. My love." She crumpled up another napkin and tossed it at me before crossing her arms and leaning back.

I ducked out of the way. "Don't give me the mean lawyer stare. You know it scares me." I gave her a sad face.

"Only if you don't give me that sad face." She uncrossed her arms and leaned forward again. A large burp came out. "Oof. Sorry. This green chile was killer. Heartburn." She rubbed at her esophagus.

"Tums?" I reached for my bag.

"See? This is why you are too good for him."

"Because I always have antacids?"

"Because you care. Because you are a nice, decent person, and he's always going to take advantage of that to make his own life easier. Why are you helping him?"

If only she knew the truth about me, she would think we were a perfect match.

"He apologized. He needs my help." I sighed. "I'm terrible at saying no . . ."

He had looked at me with that sheepish smile and those blue eyes, and any hope for me went right out the window.

"Just promise me you smothered those feelings you had for him. Promise that you're onto his ways by now. I mean. Do what you got to do." Her eyebrows raised suggestively as mine lowered in suspicion. "But don't let him play you. Guys like that are the worst."

I knew she meant well, but I couldn't help but feel a little coddled, a little talked down to. We were the same age. Just because she was married with a kid didn't mean I wasn't aware of the ways of men too. I had been hit on once or twice—not as much as her, but I wasn't that naive.

Or maybe I was.

I didn't know.

"It's going to be fine. We put everything on the table and

were very clear about what we wanted. The faster he gets out of here, the faster we all win."

"Amen to that."

"Plus, knowing he's helping Callie actually makes more sense."

She nodded, her mouth twisted in concern.

"He seems to think he can help me get Deckard," I added.

She sat forward with a gasp. "Oh my God, that reminds me. There's more gossip I wanted to tell you. The stuff with Miles and Callie"—she waved her hand through the air—"that's whatever. But guess what else Daisy said?"

"Daphne."

"Whatever. She said that Deckard was talking about you."

"What?" I sat up. Unconsciously, my hand went to my hair, as if just the mention of him meant he'd appear.

"Yep. She said that he said that you looked—" She tilted her head in thought. "What was the word? Right, 'shell-shocked' when you won the tickets."

"Oh." I deflated. "That hardly feels complementary."

"No, no. Listen." She smacked my knee. "Then he said that any guy would be lucky to go with you to the ball and that you are a 'sparkling representative' of this town and that he owed you for everything you did for him."

"Really?" My stomach pitched. I needed to talk to Deckard now more than ever. "Sparkling," I repeated softly.

"And, oh! You're really gonna love this part. The mayor was there, right? Because it was one of the grandbabies' birthdays. And Mayor Sparks said something along the lines of how amazing you were and that the town was really lucky to have you."

It was like a firework went off in my chest. I felt like I might lift off the ground with pride. Even if those words were based on a lie, I couldn't believe how much hearing them lifted my spirits. "Really?"

"Yep. She said you were like the daughter she always wanted."

"Shut up, she did not."

"She did." Rochelle nodded with the satisfied grin that only the best gossip could provide. "I remember because that's when Darbie—"

"Daphne."

"That's what I said. That's when Daphne got pissed because the mayor literally already has five daughters. Sort of a sick burn if you think about it. But maybe the mayor meant it in terms of your love of the town."

I sat back, sucking my lips in and trying not to smile with my whole being. "The mayor really said that?"

Rochelle nodded with a knowing grin. "See, you're halfway there already. Take advantage of whatever Miles the Dingus offers, but don't let it be a one-sided relationship. Because you aren't going to repeat what happened last time. Don't let him take advantage of you. And if during your time together, he sees what could have been his if his head wasn't so far up his ass, then it's a win-win."

This had nothing to do with Miles. I wasn't even thinking of Miles that much. Sure, he popped into my head from time to time, but this was about Deckard and the mayor and the town and finally being worthy of their love. Miles and I could work together and accomplish both our goals.

I was pumped full of food and motivation.

It was time to make everything right.

"You're right. I can do it. I will use him to help me get Deckard."

"Hell yes!"

We both stood with our newfound motivation.

"No more waiting for the perfect moment. I can do it."

"Heck yes." We went to the door together. "I'll follow you out. I have to talk to John about, um, some important law stuff."

We said our goodbyes, and as I walked down the hall, I heard her say, "I'm onto you, you dirty flirt. Now take off those pants," before she closed the door to John's office.

Chapter 12

Miles

Despite my constant crap-talking, one great thing about small towns was that if you were looking for a specific person, it took only about three people until they were located. Especially if that somebody was as universally loved as Natalie Weatherby.

I stood at the tour bus stop and asked the worker tinkering under the minivan, "Excuse me, do you know when Natalie is coming back?"

He rolled out. I was taken aback by the man. He was well-built and fairly good-looking. I wasn't sure why that surprised me. How often did he work with Natalie?

Was that jealousy I was experiencing again? *Really, Miles. How juvenile.* My internal scolder sounded more like Callie every day.

"Who's asking?" he said in a gruff voice as he squinted his eyes to look me up and down. "Oh. It's you."

"Miles. Hi. Not loving that tone."

I frowned, but before I could explain myself, he added, "Natalie doesn't have an afternoon tour." He wiped the sweat from his brow with a rag at his waist, and it was straight out of a Diet Pepsi ad. Ridiculous. It wasn't even hot out. "Heard her saying she was going to have lunch with Rochelle."

"Thank you."

"Yep." He watched me in a moment of brief hesitation, like he'd been planning to say something else. Maybe he wanted to fight it out? That would be a shame. I was a lover, not a fighter. Also, I was wearing my nicer shirt. Instead, he shot me one last glare before rolling back under the minivan.

I spun around in the direction of the law offices of Rochelle and John—no idea what their last names were—and spotted the woman in question on the sidewalk, stomping determinedly in my direction. I walked to meet her in the middle. Natalie was as lovely as ever in a pair of jeans and a blue top that hugged her figure nicely but was hidden under that oversized neon vest of hers. Her hair was still pulled back and covered with the matching visor, but the braid seemed softer than the tight twist it was normally in, and a few more curls hung down to frame her face. Her makeup looked more deliberate too, more eyeliner. Had she dressed up to see me?

"Your timing is terrible," I said, coming to a stop in front of her. "One minute earlier and you would have saved me from that barrel of laughs."

"Terrance? Oh, he's great. Don't let the gruff demeanor fool you," she said, with a wave of her hand.

"Oh yeah? You two good friends?"

"I think so. Fairly good." She tilted her head from side to side in thought. "We work together often because he's a mechanic for the city, and he hosts a pottery night that I sometimes take tourists to."

An artist too. Of course.

"Why not ask him out to the ball then," I said, playing it cool as a cucumber, not at all jealous. But honestly, the man's muscles had muscles.

She narrowed her eyes at me, a slow smile spreading over her features. "I think Michael might be offended."

Another man in her life? "Who's that?" I asked, a hair too quickly.

"His partner."

"Ah." I rocked back on my heels. I might have felt silly for jumping to conclusions, but he had looked like he wanted to punch me in the face.

"You look terrible in green," she said, cocking her hip to rest a hand there.

"You have to admit the man is shockingly built."

She nodded and patted my cheek. "Don't worry, you're still the prettiest princess of them all."

I batted away her hand but then taunted her by not releasing it. I couldn't help but notice that this time she didn't instantly shove me away. In fact, every time I touched her, she allowed it a fraction longer. I would have to test this theory. I might be able to hold her hand for five whole seconds before I leave in a few weeks.

I quelled the turbulent feeling of delight and dread that thought gave me.

"He did not seem to care for me." I started to follow Natalie as she walked on. "I don't remember, did I meet him last time? I usually leave a good taste in people's mouths. Or at least a taste. You know what, never mind."

Her pace quickened slightly. "There's a chance I had some unkind things to say about you before. I should probably let him know everything is square between us now."

On the one hand, she had talked about me. On the other

hand, that might explain some of the dirty looks I'd received since returning.

"Anyway, I was looking for you." I avoided her gaze as I pretended to study the busy town around us. "Sorry, I haven't responded to your text yet. I was, you know, getting my blood all acclimated."

"I hadn't even noticed," she said flippantly. *Ouch.* "I was looking for you, too, actually," she added, and it softened some of the sting.

"How'd you know I was here?" I asked.

"I put a tracker on your phone." She said it so matter-of-factly, I almost believed her. But then her smile cracked, and she said, "Also, Maybel told me you were going all over town asking for me."

"Stalker."

"Takes one to know one."

She was meeting my eyes, and with her firecracker wit, it was like there had never been any weirdness at all. This was better, this *friends* business. It was better than being invisible, at least.

"Are you ready to head up to the hot springs?" I asked. "I'll need to swing by the hotel to get my equipment."

"Not yet. First, you're helping me with Deckard." She rolled her shoulders and bounced on her feet like she was gearing up for a boxing match.

My eyebrows shot up. "Go help you beat him up?" I looked pointedly at where she was jabbing the air.

She dropped her arms with a scoff. "No. I'm going to go ask him to the ball. Today's the day." She couldn't have sounded convincing even to her own ears, but I wasn't about to question it.

"Wow. Okay, good for you," I said and waited for her to lead the way. "Go for it. Ask away." I gestured in the general direction of Main Street.

She blinked at me expectantly.

My blink in return was just as full of expectations.

"You're going to have to talk to *Deckard*, Natalie. I'm Miles. Have you hit your head?"

She rolled her eyes with a groan. "You're the one helping me. So help. That was your end of the bargain, and I'm cashing in." She nodded with determination.

I fought back a laugh. She'd honestly rehearsed this before she found me. She must have. This also meant that she had dressed up for Deckard and not because of me. It was ridiculous that I'd assumed anything else. It made no difference. I rubbed at my chest.

"Okay. Okay, don't sic your lawyer friend on me. Actually, she was sort of hot when she threatened me. Maybe do—ouch, no hitting." She was back to bouncing and jabbing the air and snuck one in there for me. Her curls bounced, and her attempt to be fierce fell painfully short. She was adorable. "I'm kidding. I'm here at your disposal. What do you need?"

Her arms dropped to her sides, and she shrugged. "I don't know. You're supposed to know. You're the tutor, and I'm the tutee."

"Heh. Tootie. I think it's mentor/mentee."

She ignored me. "Give me the pro tips. What do I need to do?"

"Go up to Deckard and say, 'Please date me, oh, perfect one' and bat those eyelashes at him and do your cute little pleading face you do."

"Rochelle hates that face." She hid a grin as she turned her head away.

"It's very powerful."

She let out a huff. "I can't do that. The whole 'going up to him' thing. We've already established that."

We were walking along cozy Main Street when I stopped and looked her up and down. She faltered to see the hold-up.

"He's got two eyes and you're hot, so what's the issue?" I asked.

"I-I," she sputtered, and a flush burned up her cheeks. It was obvious that she was hot. Did she not know that? There was no hiding it. "I'm not good at that."

"At what?"

Her face flushed even darker, and she looked around and stepped closer, like we were exchanging secret military codes. "Being seductive."

I swallowed. "Are you trying to seduce him or ask him to the ball?"

"Yes. Both. I don't know. You're supposed to be helping me, and you're getting me all in my head about it again."

I looked her up and down once more. She was sexy in a perky collegiate sort of way, but those tour guide clothes hid many of her finer features—like her bright eyes and smile.

"Look, I'm going to say something, and it's probably going to get me punched in the junk, but you asked for my help."

She made a grumbly sound of assent.

"Maybe skank it up a little?" I suggested.

Sure enough, her fists balled.

I turned slightly to protect my goods. "Obviously, you're perfect as you are and all that, but you look too . . . wholesome. Maybe he doesn't know about this edgier side of you?" *The side you only shared with me,* I thought protectively. "I saw your naughty little book stash."

Instead of flushing again, she bit the inside of her mouth and shrugged. "What do you suggest, then?"

I stepped closer and tapped my lip in thought.

"Lose the Tour Guide Barbie accessories . . ."

She scoffed.

"And maybe . . ." I gestured for the vest, which she complied with easily enough, taking it off and thrusting it at me. With my free hand, I unsnapped the top couple buttons of her shirt in a quick flick that she hardly had time to react to because I was pulling off her visor at the same time. More curls had come loose to frame her face, accentuating her wide eyes that blinked in surprise.

We both looked down to examine her full breasts, pushed up and still mostly hidden but with enough cleavage revealed that it was clear she was packing.

I tore my gaze away reluctantly and gestured to her hair. "Take out the braid and zhuzh your hair a little."

"You cannot be—"

"Zhuzh!" I demanded.

"I don't even—"

"Fine. I'll do it."

I stepped nearer, and her eyes widened infinitesimally. My movements were slow lest she bite, but she didn't stop me as I came right up to her, as though I might embrace her in my arms. Instead, I reached behind her shoulder to grab her thick braid that hung down her back and carefully eased off the elastic band before thumbing free the twists of the braid. The angle had me so close that her sweet aroma and heat infused me.

"Just so you know, it's going to be all frizzy now," she said softly.

I looked down to find her gaze inches from mine, eyes flicking back and forth.

I hummed an acknowledgment but went back to work. A full body frizz would only add to her natural allure. Her mouth was slightly parted, eyes wide as I loosened the tight hair at her scalp, releasing more of that heady, addictive scent. Her lids grew heavy, eventually closing as I rubbed my fingertips along her scalp, tugging gently at the strands, teasing the roots. Her head fell back into my hands as she relaxed, like I had found her reset button. Every second that passed without her realizing just how close we were felt like a small gift.

When her eyes snapped open, I stepped back, putting a professional amount of space between us. "That's probably good," I said, voice thick.

"Yep. I'm just gonna shake it out." She flipped her head over, and I took the moment to collect myself after whatever the hell that had been.

When she snapped back up, I had to hold in a moan because her look had the exact impact I'd been hoping for. It was like she'd been tossed around a mattress in an athletic round of hide the salami. Her hair didn't look fluffy, it looked wild and free as it was meant to be. Even her lips looked more full and glistening.

"Yep. Good." I stuck my hands deep in my pockets, careful not to drop her tour guide stuff, and studied the surrounding mountains.

"You have to see how archaic this is," she said. "It's offensive to assume that a quick makeover à la nineties rom-coms can attract a man."

"Physical attraction is always the first step for a man. Don't be naive."

"Not all men."

"Not your very sophisticated Deckard?" I grew more irritated. It was getting harder to not look at her, and if I heard any more about how perfect Deckard was, I might flip a table.

When I finally looked, she glared daggers, and anger made her more alluring. "I am not naive, I just don't think that zhuzhing my hair and undoing a few buttons can make me—" She'd spun to look at herself in the reflective storefront of the yoga studio. "Aw crap, I look like a sex kitten." She turned to examine her reflection more. When she saw her ass, she lifted her eyebrows appreciatively. "Okay, fine."

"Listen, you and I both know that sexuality is a complex spectrum, and everybody revs their engine their own way. You don't need to woman-splain everything I do to help you, or we're going to get nowhere fast."

She put a hand to her heart, affronted. "You cannot take that word. Womenkind has been mansplained to for centuries."

I dropped my head back and groaned. "I'm just saying it might give you the confidence you need to talk to Deckard if you're in character, more alluring than you might normally act."

She pursed her lips. "I guess I do feel more powerful."

"Good. Own your sexuality."

We came to a stop in front of the cat cafe. Did the guy live here?

"Who'd have thought you'd be my feminine sexuality guru?" she said.

"It's right there on my business card."

She threw her head back to laugh. The action exposed her neck, and I was seized with the overwhelming urge to pull her into my arms and inhale up the side. I cleared my throat and swallowed down the churning acid.

"Okay." She peeked a look through the window and wiped her palms on her jeans. "I'm pretty sure I see him in there. I just need to say—" She moaned and wrapped her arms around her middle. "What do I say, exactly?"

I pulled her arms back down. "Just go with the flow, let it happen naturally," I offered, still warm from her laughter.

"No. Terrible plan. I need a script."

I chuckled. "We could Cyrano this up. Get a tiny earpiece like a spy, where I tell you what to say?"

"Where would we even find a spy kit? Actually, I bet a few

shops would have some." She shook her head. "No, I can't handle additional listening in this plan. I'm going to be flustered as it is, trying to talk."

What was the deal with this guy that she was so nervous about him?

"Fine. Um." I looked around. "Practice on me then." My words hovered in the air between us, the reality of what I'd said. They sounded much better in my mind. Had I thought about them at all before they came tumbling out.

"Wh-what do you mean?" She huffed a nervous laugh.

"If you can't go in there yet, pretend with me first." I stepped closer and tried to smolder. "Hi, I'm your lover boy. Everything I touch turns to gold, and I have a massive—"

"Miles!"

"—baseball card collection. Why, Natalie? What did you think I was going to say?"

She groaned. "If he ever said that . . ." She shoved me away, and I grabbed her wrists. My thumbs swept across her pulse points without meaning too.

"Okay. I'll be serious." I cleared my throat and neutralized my features. I met her gaze and pretended that I was a man who was allowed to be as openly attracted to her as he felt. "Hello, Natalie."

All at once, her demeanor completely shifted, and she became that person I'd seen on the lottery day. Her hands pulled out of mine, and she froze.

It was the weirdest thing, this mental block of hers. How could I get her around it? Did I really want to help her? I didn't have a choice.

I was still close enough that I lifted my hand to her chin easily. I put my thumb below her bottom lip. It was full and warm and pillowy soft, and I was overwhelmed with the urge to suck it into my mouth to taste it. The heat of her nearly touching me had every muscle in my body flexed with tension. Her mouth parted in soft surprise.

I used my thumb to gently tug her bottom lip as I spoke in a high-pitched voice, "Hi, Deckard. Would you like to be my plus-one to the Governor's Ball that everyone around here is weirdly obsessed with?" As I puppeteered her mouth, her grin grew to the point where I couldn't control it anymore with my thumb. We both tried not to laugh at the funny bubble-popping sounds her mouth made.

Finally, her laughter broke through, and a surge of joy passed over me.

"Why, yes, Natalie, I'd love to go with you. I thought you would never ask!" I gathered her in my arms and dipped her back. She fell easily with the flow, one leg kicking up into the air, her hair cascading around her as she laughed with her whole being.

It was an incredible sight.

She was breathtaking. I'd been over the top and myself, and she'd laughed. I'd made her laugh her way out of that catatonic state.

She was still leaning back in my arms when my heart began to pound dangerously in my chest. Worse than the altitude sickness. I wanted to kiss her so desperately, I couldn't even think clearly. I gazed down at her, and all I could think was how amazing this woman was. My arms held her tighter, her hands were on my chest, and we moved closer together by fractions of an inch.

Her smile slowly melted from her face, her gaze flicking down to my mouth and back up. Was I imagining this invisible tether bringing us closer together? Was she imagining closing this space between us to see what would happen?

Or was this still a part of the act—pretending I was the man of her daydreams?

The door behind us opened with the soft *ting* of a bell, breaking whatever trance we'd been in.

"Hey, Natalie," a man's voice said.

Deckard Sparks, in all his goodly glory, stood there, eyes dancing with a friendly light as they bounced between Natalie and me.

"Deckard. Hi." She swung up so quickly that she almost toppled both of us. She pushed out of my arms and stepped back. No person in history has moved faster than Natalie did to put distance between us.

That felt great. Really, really great.

Deckard was the picture of easy affability, with a to-go coffee cup in one hand and a laptop bag over his shoulder. I extended an arm to shake his hand. Not punch him. I wasn't Terrance the mechanic after all. "I don't think we've met. Miles Asher."

"Hey. Deckard Sparks." He shook my hand and it was perfectly pleasant. "Nice to meet you. Oh, right, you're here filming that thing."

"That's me," I said flatly.

That thing.

"My mom has really high hopes for it. Sorry, the mayor. That sounded like a flex, but trust me, it wasn't. I meant, it sounds like it's going to be great. And I didn't know if you knew that I meant the mayor. 'Mom' slipped out." He chuckled, but the tips of his ears went red.

"Thanks, man."

I looked between Natalie and Deckard. Really? This dweeb had caused her to go fully catatonic again?

"Well, I won't keep you two. I wanted to congratulate you on that ticket," he said, turning to Natalie, the statue. "It was nice seeing you again." He hesitated.

"Thank you," she said with her wax-lips smile.

Deckard gave her one more long look before glancing back at me and saluting another friendly wave, then strode happily across the street.

Natalie spun and began walking in the other direction. I followed her to the Thinking Place, without saying anything.

Well, this debrief should be fun. At least I hadn't fucked up anything this time.

I didn't think I had at least.

Chapter 13

Natalie

THIS WAS ALL MILES' FAULT.

What the crappity crap was that?

What was *any* of that?

My brain was a confused wash of regret and humiliation as I walked at full speed toward the Thinking Place, fully aware Miles was hot on my heels.

It hadn't been Miles' fault actually. Not entirely. I was a mess before he got all up in my faculties, jumbling them.

I was grateful he wasn't speaking. I was back to not being able to look at him again, but not from anger. From that other emotion that still lingered right under my skin, making me buzz.

What had Miles been thinking? The way he spoke to me, flirted with me, held me. I ignored the thrill that shimmied through me.

He'd held me in his arms. He'd looked at me like . . . like I don't know exactly. Unmasked? Raw? It made my heart flutter and made me feel like I was going to puke all at once. Sure, I'd had feelings for him the first time he was here, but I had shut it all down. Put that regret behind me. I had taken Rochelle's advice, and I wasn't letting myself slip back.

But then I slipped without meaning to, and now here I was, falling.

No. Nope. *No.*

I finally stopped to look at him once we were back in the safety of my space and the door was locked behind us.

"Not a word." I held up a finger.

He held up his hands in a gesture of innocence, his mouth in a flat line.

But with his mouth closed and his body a few inches from mine in this safe space, his thoughts were impossible to know. And he looked at me with that neutral yet penetrating face. *Don't think the word* penetrating *at a time like this,* I reprimanded myself. I was so mad at him again, I wanted to take him by the collar and shake him. I trembled with the force of it. My entire body was tense with the need to take him in my arms and squeeze that stupid, patient look off his face.

He'd done it again, he'd discombobulated me. He'd *held me in his arms* like I was precious, like we were on the cover of one of my alien books. People didn't do that in the real world. He couldn't just—

He swallowed audibly in the quiet space, causing me to focus back on his lips. Time slowed down. The air was heavy. My heart thrummed.

He would leave.

This all had to stop.

"Fine. A few words. Speak. Your silence is somehow worse," I said with a rasping voice.

Worry or confusion passed over his features before that smooth mask he wore was back in place.

"Wow, that was intense," he said.

"Get it all out."

"My eyes are burning. The chemistry was so explosive between you two," he teased, hands back in his pockets.

How could he even joke about chemistry at a time like this? When my anger for him made me feel like there were chemical reactions boiling throughout my body. When I wanted to push him into that chair and straddle him so that I could more easily stop him from talking.

"Clever," I mumbled.

"That went so much worse than I thought it would."

I bit my tongue to keep from shouting that it was his fault. If I hadn't been all *swooned* up, then I would have been better. But that wasn't true at all. I would have probably acted exactly the same.

"This is what I'm saying. I need help," I said.

"He literally gave you the opening. Lobbed it right at you, slow and steady down the middle. All you had to do was swing." He spoke emphatically now, really getting into the role, gesturing the actions.

"Please, stop. This isn't helping. I'm already embarrassed." My head went back and thumped against the wall.

"More embarrassed than throwing up in front of your hot tour guide?" he asked softly, and when I lowered my head, he had a sheepish look of apology.

For those keeping track at home, that was the second time today he'd called me hot.

My mouth lifted a little, and tension melted from me. "Maybe about the same."

"It's okay. I'm here to help, remember?" he said. "Okay, so the direct approach is out."

I nodded.

"There goes my concerns that he might be gay, and you were barking up the wrong tree."

"That was never in question," I said.

"Maybe not for you."

"No. Well, he's at least bi," I said to be fair. "He's dated many women in town. But also, Slippery Slopes has a large queer community. Third highest in the state. Also, his sister is openly gay, and so I don't think he'd feel like he'd have to hide that side of himself."

"Okay, gotcha. I could not care less who he gets his rocks off to."

"Also, he's a huge ally. Every June, he marches in the parade with his mom and sisters holding a big—"

"Okay, I get it." Miles held up his hands in a plea to stop me. "He's perfectly progressive. A life worth saving. I needed to see for myself. I'm checking boxes, that's all. But the good news is he definitely sees you in a non-platonic way. I'm going to take a quick second to say I was right about that." We both looked to my breasts, which absolutely stole the show.

"He did?" I asked, meeting his eyes again. "I didn't see him notice."

"Yes." Miles gave me a flat look. "As men, we learn many a way to subtly check out women, and he pulled them all off."

"Ha." I couldn't help my guffaw of a laugh. "You guys think you're subtle but you are so not," I teased.

"Some chauvinist men might lack finesse, but not I. Nor your boy Deckard, it would seem. I've looked at your boobs five times since we've been in here. Your ass twice."

"What? How?" I turned in a circle, wondering if there was a mirror behind me.

"Three times." I stopped and crossed my arms, though yet another smile tugged on my lips as he continued, "The point is, I caught him looking at you. It's good news."

"I guess he might be shy?" I said in an attempt to stay on task.

"Could be. Could be." Miles nodded thoughtfully. He

leaned back against the wall, and for the first time, I wished for some furniture in here that wasn't the one not-a-sex-chair. But there wasn't a need for more furniture when I never had company.

"Or oblivious, maybe, but no. Again, it really did seem like he was giving you an in by mentioning the ticket like that. Maybe he's waiting for you to make the first move. Is he sort of a nerd?"

I clicked my tongue. "Please. What does that even mean? I mean, he and Bee Perkins kept to themselves mostly in high school."

"Who is Bee Perkins?" he asked.

"The girl who works at the cat cafe?"

"Doesn't ring a bell."

"You've seen her several times at least. Pretty brunette, bright tights, and a patterned dress?"

He waved the segue away. "Doesn't matter. So Deckard and Bee?"

"Looking back, I vaguely remember them being super into *Terraformative*."

"The books or the show?"

"Does it make a difference?"

"I guess not."

"Both, I think." I leaned back against my side of the wall, our body language mirrored. "They would dress up for those midnight releases at the bookstores."

"Ah." His steepled fingers tapped at his lips. "So, yes. A huge nerd. This lines up with some running theories."

"We're all nerds about something," I said, defending Deckard.

"I'm not," Miles said, dropping his hands in a casual shrug.

"Okay. Fair. What running theories have you got? Oh, but

first, before I forget. Could you tell me more about the best drone to use for filming the mountains? A friend was asking."

"Have you got an hour? It's not so simple." He chuckled with arrogance. "I mean, it really depends on what your end goal is. Because there are so many options. If you're looking for more of a—" He stopped when I crossed my arms and lifted my eyebrows. "Ah. I see now that this was a trap and I've walked right into it." I nodded. "Fine. Point made. I am a closet nerd too."

"Let's assume, for now, that Deckard is not going to be forward with me. Nerd or not," I said.

"Then you need to meet him somewhere where there are fewer people and chat with him about what he's into. You both need to feel safe to relax," he said.

I nodded, liking his line of reasoning.

"I was surprised to see you so tense." He shrugged with his hands in his pockets, giving him that stupidly sexy appearance of ease. "You're very charming and funny when you're with me. I mean, like on the tours and stuff. Like you were with Gabe. What's the difference?"

He was handing out compliments like tissues these days. Had he been like this last time?

"I don't know," I said, staying focused. "It just feels different when I'm in work mode. Like I'm Tour Guide Barbie," I said, to quote him from earlier.

"That gives me an idea. Has Deckard ever been on one of your tours?"

"I don't think so actually," I said.

"Have him come on a tour so he can see that side of you. Maybe offer a private tour. Say he won some raffle, since you all love those so much." He rubbed at his esophagus.

A private tour. I could showcase the best side of myself, and then maybe once we were comfortably away from the prying eyes of the town, then maybe I'd be bold and explain the misunderstanding.

"That's actually a really good idea. Thank you, Miles." This was a good plan. I would be in control. I'd know what to say. I could give tours in my sleep.

"Of course. I told you I would help you, and I was sincere." He grinned, but his fingers rubbed at his chest.

"Do you need another antacid?" I asked.

"Maybe. I thought I was feeling better but I guess not." His thumb pressed between his eyebrows. "I think that I need to maybe go lie down back at my room. Let's wait on the hot springs?"

"Are you sure?" I asked, now concerned.

I stepped forward to press my fingertips to his forehead. His eyes fluttered closed with a surprised intake of breath.

Without opening his eyes, he said, "Yeah. We've got loads of time. I want to lie down."

He opened his eyes and stepped back to put some space between us. As much as this closet of a room would allow.

"Okay. Yeah. Let's check in with each other in a couple days?" I asked.

"Yep. Yes." He was backing up to the door. "In the meantime, you dazzle Deckard."

He smiled but looked like he was fighting back being sick. Maybe he wasn't ready to be out and about. His stomach had turned as quickly as his flirtatious mood.

"Feel better," I said.

He left, and for the first time, I felt hopeful about my approach with Deckard. I did know how to be a competent, well-spoken person. So long as I had my comfort space and was in control.

This was good. I had a plan.

I was closer to getting what I wanted. Miles and I both were. Nothing to worry about.

Chapter 14

Miles

I was so sick of these four walls of my hotel room, I thought I would scream. On the other hand, if I left the room, then she'd be out there.

Natalie.

Walking around all beautiful and charming and burrowing her way under my skin.

And I was a big chickadee-chicken.

The worst thing about agreeing to help other people was that it really highlighted what a piece of shit I was most of the time. Caring about other people's wants and needs was hard work. I was a single man who traveled the world for a living, only ever worried about my own immediate wants and needs.

And now, suddenly, two different women required help. I bumbled both exploits.

"So dumb," I groaned, stepping out of the shower and wrapping a towel around me.

I didn't bother rubbing the steam from the mirror. No sense in seeing the pathetic schmuck who'd be staring back at me. The used up packet of antacids I bought from the mini-mart down-stairs was on the counter. My reprieve from hiding these last few days was over. I couldn't lock myself away anymore.

Callie called and chewed me out yesterday because, for days, there had been no new uploads.

"Get your head out of your ass and get some shots or I'm sending Mags down there and she really won't like leaving my side."

The threat was enough to spur me into making plans with Natalie for today.

How could I handle seeing her? Being near her? Last time I tried to play it cool, I had my hand running through her hair before bending her back in my arms, seconds from kissing her. And I could. Not. Stop. Replaying it.

A sturdy and sudden knock at my hotel room door made me yelp in shock. "Hey, Miles?"

Had Callie sent Mags to drag me around town by the ear until I got the rest of the shots? I stared, frozen in the direction of the intruder. The only entrance to the room was right next to the bathroom, which meant mere inches separated us.

Maybe if I stayed very still . . .

"I know you're in there. I heard you scream like a little girl," Natalie (thankfully, not Mags) called through the door. "What are you doing?"

"First of all, it was a very masculine shout of surprise." I made my way over. "And I'm getting ready. What are you doing, stalker?" I unlocked the dead bolt.

"Can you let me in? Mr. Graves was wandering downstairs, and I don't want people to see me—" I opened the door to Natalie. "Thanks."

Still beautiful. Still with that hair and smile and soft-looking skin . . . And those breasts (though more covered than when I last left them, sadly).

Fuck.

I stepped aside to let her in but she froze in her tracks, staring at me and blushing red. Her gaze lingered where my hand gripped the towel around my waist, flicked up and around my chest, shoulders, and arms, and then back to the towel. It must have been only a fraction of a second before she blinked away to stare pointedly into the room behind me, but I wished for an eternity. No judgment here. I hadn't stopped thinking about the feel of her in my arms for the last four days.

"Control yourself, Weatherby," I said, turning away and going to the closet. Inside me, an absolute hurricane of pride ripped through any remaining modesty. I'd strip naked and prance around this room if she looked at me like that again.

Dignity was for men whose self-worth wasn't eclipsed by lascivious fantasies.

After a long pause, Natalie cleared her throat and stepped cautiously into the room with a mumbled, "You wish."

"Vividly. About ten minutes ago," I mumbled in return. "What are you doing here?" I asked, debating letting the towel fall so I would have access to both hands. After all, she was the one who chose to come up here. But it would be a little too much, even for me. Her presence rendered moot any tension released in the shower, and I was too close to becoming an actual creep if I got an erection.

"We're going to the hot springs today." Her voice was less strained and more annoyed now. "Please tell me you didn't forget."

"I didn't forget. I *meant*, why are you up here, in my room?" I debated between two shirts in the closet: a green and a blue.

"You said you were going to meet me downstairs. Like twenty minutes ago. I wanted to make sure you hadn't OD'd on that cologne you wear." She circled the small space, examining every detail. Thankfully, a lifetime of hotel stays kept me neat and tidy. "Green one," she added, without a noticeable look my way.

I grabbed the blue shirt.

"Wait, what time is it?" I asked.

"Twenty after noon." She gestured to the hotel alarm clock.

"Shit. I must have lost track of time in the shower." Our eyes met, and it was my turn to spin around before I gave my indiscretions away.

I mentioned the breast thing, right? The release of tension? That was half the shower right there. The other half was spent torturing myself on whether I should ask her how her date with Deckard went and then feeling nauseated. This place did not agree with me. Could I be allergic to a whole town?

"Apparently," she said. "And we have to go today or you'll be delayed even longer. We're expecting a few inches tomorrow."

"Who's 'we'?" I awkwardly pulled my shirt on with one hand. "And a few inches of what, exactly?" I asked when my head poked through. I hadn't meant to say it like that, but it would appear that I lived in the gutter now.

She had moved to sit primly in the desk chair. She stared pointedly *not* at me. "The town is getting snow," she said. "Big storm blowing in overnight."

"But it's so nice out." I went to the window and looked out, still gripping my towel around my lower half.

"Yeah, but it's spring. We usually get at least one more big storm before it really starts to warm up."

That meant more days being trapped in this room and not making progress. Just great. I regretted not getting out more when I'd had the chance, in the same way I regretted not chewing freely before biting the inside of my cheek.

Natalie leaned forward to rub her hand over the sheets. "Huh, these are nice. I wonder what the thread count is."

The angle made it apparent that she hadn't buttoned up all the way after all, and *sonova*, I was thinking about her breasts again. Not that I'd really stopped. Natalie caressing the bed I'd spent so many hours thinking about her in made me realize my time in the shower had not been nearly enough. My breaths quickened, and my nostrils flared. And I was so very thankful I had not dropped the towel.

We were in a hotel room with a perfectly good bed. Only one thin towel and a flimsy excuse separated us.

She looked up at me, and as our gazes crashed, she seemed to realize the same thing.

"You know what, I'll just meet you downstairs." She scrambled to the door as fast as she could, and I held my towel with white knuckles.

"Good idea." I focused on the sheets.

"I have my SUV today."

"Okay."

"It's forest green. You'll see me."

"Sounds good. Be right down."

"Yep. Yep. Bye."

She couldn't leave the room fast enough. I would need to remember to ask if we could stop at the shop for more Tums.

And maybe another bottle of lotion.

It was really dry out here.

The trip up to the hot springs helped me get my head on straight. Driving through the town, seeing other people, it helped remind me of my reasons for being here.

Natalie, for her part, chatted happily about local life I didn't care about. Still, I enjoyed listening to her talk.

And admittedly, the history of the springs was sort of interesting.

By the time we got to the trail leading to the hot springs, I had assured her repeatedly that I was better and could handle the hike out. And aside from more persistent heartburn, I did feel fine, even carrying all my heavy equipment.

"People claimed healing powers. Spiritual revelations. Very mystical. We're lucky to have any access to it at all. Most of the pools are part of the surrounding Rez, but they leased several pools to the city—so long as their strict guidelines are adhered to, and we don't abuse our privileges."

"Huh." I grunted as we hiked up.

It was a nice, warm day. The only thing hinting at the coming storm was a heavy wind that occasionally swept up under the trees. It was hard to believe that it would snow tomorrow, but I'd been around long enough to know that nature was wild and unpredictable. After rounding a switchback, there was a break in the trees that showcased all of Slippery Slopes below.

"Hold up." I shifted my camera around and got the sight in focus. The small town had the air of a hidden hamlet, nestled as it was between several mountains. Though large enough to have a relatively good-sized infrastructure, seeing it from up here, from my bird's-eye view, gave the town the feel of a hidden treasure. The snow on the peaks, the verdant valley speckled with homes and buildings below—it was incredibly picturesque.

God, Natalie had infiltrated my self-narration.

"Isn't it wonderful? Sometimes I can't believe I live somewhere so perfect." She was at my side, hands akimbo as she took a deep breath in and out.

"You've seen one town, you've seen them all," I said, because I was a contrary asshole and somehow admitting that this place got under my skin felt like giving something up. I wasn't ready to think about it.

"Nah," she said, unbothered. "That's not true."

The way she'd said it implied she actually had been around to see what else was out there. I knew she'd had a life pre-Slippery Slopes, but she never talked about it, always shifted the conversation away. The last time I was here, I'd been too focused on charming her to notice how little she'd given away.

She was a little enigma, that one.

When I looked up to see what I could find hidden in her features, I had to clench my jaw to keep from making a sound. She was beautiful. A streak of golden sunlight found her through the break in the trees, highlighting her like a glowing beacon. She had her foot up on a rock while looking wistfully on the valley below, a soft smile on her face. Her golden curls, which had been piled into a slicked-back ponytail, were now breaking free in little wisps around her face. A sheen of sweat and a glow of exertion gave her an ethereal radiance. She was so wondrously breathtaking; it made no sense that there wasn't a line of people following behind her at all times.

I faced the camera to her, focusing on the soft Cupid's bow of her mouth and the slight slope of her nose, the almost invisible spattering of freckles high on her cheeks that was only visible in this exact light, like a gift from the sun. The sound of the shutter—and maybe my lack of commentary—had her turning toward me.

"No, no." She held up a hand to block me. "Just focus on the town and nature."

I looked up and over the camera to hold her gaze. "Please," I said, and it came out sounding rougher than I intended. She must have heard sincerity in my tone because her smile fell away with her hand. "I just need . . ."

I couldn't finish the thought. Not even in my own mind. Because it felt like if I didn't capture her exactly as she was at this moment, I would die. At least, a part of me would die. This exact version of Natalie needed to live on with me forever.

"Okay," she whispered. "I don't know what to do." She chuckled nervously.

"Look at your home. Focus on whatever you were just thinking about."

She nodded and briefly closed her eyes. When she opened them again, the self-consciousness had melted away.

I took a few more shots. "What are you thinking about?" I asked, unable to help myself.

"How lucky I am to be here." She took another deep breath in and out. I thought she might be dreaming of a life far away or wishing for more. But she was grateful. Her outlook on life clawed at my throat, made me feel even more like the bitter man that I had become. She was a wonder. "The mountain air makes me sentimental," she said with a shrug as she shot me a look.

One last photo, that contented, peaceful smile made for me.

I swallowed and lowered my camera with a trembling hand.

"We can keep going now," I said, voice gruff.

She nodded, and we started off again.

"Guess what?" she asked after a few minutes.

I was still lost in thoughts of that moment and the strange grip it'd had on my chest. I was ready to go back to our playful banter. "You found a way to keep the rampant guinea pig population under control?"

"Ha. Not likely. But nice answer. Some people don't even try to guess," she said with mock annoyance. "I gave Deckard a private tour, like you suggested."

I stumbled on some loose gravel.

"Yeah?" I asked as she put a hand on my shoulder.

I shifted the weight of my pack.

"You okay?"

"Loose stone. Tell me about your private show," I said.

"Ew. Don't say it like that." She released my arm. "It went well. I guess." Her nose scrunched up, and her head tilted from side to side. "I think I mostly just spit facts at him. There wasn't a ton of back-and-forth, in hindsight."

I clenched my fists to keep from asking for more information. Had he seemed into her? Was he desperate to touch her at every opportunity? Was she just as eager to be near him? I swallowed all my questions down as she went on.

"You were right to suggest that. I was a lot more relaxed. Maybe in time it'll feel more . . ." She searched for the words, glancing up at me and then quickly away. I patted my pocket for my stash of Tums. "Well, I think in time we have the potential to grow more comfortable with each other. It was a great start. It felt really good to talk with him. Well, at him mostly."

"I hope you used protection with all that information sharing," I grumbled.

"What?"

"That's really great."

She was quiet for several steps. "Yeah. So, thanks."

"One step closer to what you want," I said.

"Yep."

We went silent for a little bit. I focused very hard on my walking, keeping any and all asshole thoughts to myself.

"It's strange," she said. "I think you were right about him being a little shy or needing less people around to be comfortable. I'd assumed that he was better with social stuff because of his giant family and his mom. He's always out in public and he seems so good at it."

What I wanted to say was, if I heard any more facts about how wonderful Deckard was, I was going to throw myself off the side of this mountain. But I settled on, "People might think the same about you."

She nodded, blowing air through her lips. "Just goes to show that you never know what really makes someone tick."

"What makes you tick?" I asked. I needed to change the subject. The abyss was becoming far too appealing.

"Oh, me? Nothing. I mean, nothing special. I'm pretty average."

Well, that was a load of shit.

"You seem to hold the town in high regard. You haven't always lived here, right?" We hadn't talked about too much personal stuff last time I'd been here, and with the days going by so fast, I found that I was becoming desperate to know anything about her.

"Not always." Her pace picked up so that I couldn't see her face. "I came here when I was eighteen."

I waited patiently, the silence stretching until she sighed. "I was raised in an RV, a glorified van really, by my two loving, but flighty, hippy parents, traveling all over the country, never settling in any place for more than a year or so. Usually a few weeks at a time." *Pretty average, my ass.* "When we stopped here ten years ago, they died in a car accident, and I've been here ever since."

I stopped. It was like someone reached into my chest and squeezed my heart. My physical pain at learning her tragedy was jarring and unexpected. "Wait, what?"

She also stopped and spun to me, shoulders back and chin high. "I know. I didn't want to tell you and turn into the sad orphan girl. Don't quit being your charmingly acerbic self now."

"I wouldn't know how." I said it jokingly, but I wanted to hold her. I wanted to find her at eighteen and protect her from what had to have been immeasurable pain. But she started walking again.

I kept my tone light and followed after her. "Hippies, huh? But you seem so—"

"Tightly strung?"

"I was going to say . . . Yeah, no, I guess that's the best way to say it."

Pieces were coming together to form this person in front of me, but there was still so much I didn't know or understand. So much I get to learn.

"I get it. Everyone expects me to be this flower child, this carefree spirit, when they hear about my parents. Sometimes we roll the opposite way though, don't we."

I couldn't help but laugh at the irony. "Yeah. We do."

"And, well, traveling so much as a kid meant I was never really in a stable, typical environment. I was mostly home-schooled. The few times we tried public schools, it was a disaster." She huffed a laugh. "Never knowing if what I said was extremely weird made me a shy kid. One or two times making small talk and being looked at like I was a total freak, well, it was enough to keep me from talking altogether. It would seem that showering at truck stops while your mom stood by with a Taser wasn't a universal childhood experience. Over time, I got over my shyness some. Having loads of information at my disposal helped. I learned everything I could, read everything I could, so that I wouldn't misspeak. I learned I do better when scripted. Controlled."

Thankfully, I was bogged down with equipment, because I wanted so desperately to scoop her up and hold her. But she'd said she didn't want to be seen or treated differently. She didn't want to be pitied, and I understood that.

"Ah. Makes sense," I said. "How did you—what did you do after they died?"

"I was completely lost. I think things would have gone really bad if this town hadn't stepped in. If I had been anywhere else." She shook her head. "But I was saved. I literally had nothing and nobody. I'd spent my whole life being with my parents, and that one time I decided to not be with them, because I was having some dumb late-teenage fit about who knows what, that's when the semi lost control. That was it. Over in an instant."

We'd stopped walking, and her gaze had gone off into the distance. When she spoke again, her voice had regained some control.

"Slippery Slopes didn't even blink. Even though I was technically an adult and they had no reason to help me." Her gaze went far away as she spoke, a crease forming between her brows. "The mayor and town rallied, like I was a lifelong citizen, and they took me in without even a second thought. I never wanted for anything. They helped me get into online classes to get my GED and then a bachelor's in communications. Everybody made sure I always had clothes and food. I mean, I was used to going with very little. That was my parents' whole thing; they wanted me to learn to live simply. But my whole life was in that RV. I can't really think about it."

I nodded.

"I haven't left since." She shrugged and started walking again, as though to say that was the whole story. But it wasn't, there were many more untold depths to her. I couldn't . . . She was . . .

"Incredible," I said honestly. I hurried to catch back up with her. "I can see why you love this town."

"I do. I owe them everything." The determination in her tone had me narrowing my eyes.

What had she meant? What did she owe them? She had been paying it forward in all the ways I could see.

"Do you ever miss traveling, if that was your whole childhood?" I asked, feeling like this question was more important than I wanted it to be.

"Sometimes. I miss seeing all the different towns and noting how similar we all are, but also how we make ourselves stand apart." I understood now why she'd made the comment about Slippery Slopes not being like other places. For her, there would never be a town that could compare. "But mostly traveling reminds me of uncertainty, of never settling. My parents were great in a lot of ways. I was more educated than a lot of my peers and saw so much of the world, which helped me keep an open mind and have acceptance of all types of people."

I nodded, but I could tell her thought wasn't finished. "And also?" I offered.

"And also, it always made me long for a solid, real place to call my home."

Her gratitude for Slippery Slopes made more sense now, but she seemed to wear it as a chain around her neck. She lived as though she owed her existence to this place.

"Where do you go for trips these days?" I asked, trying to keep things light even as my thoughts darkened on her behalf.

"I don't really. I love it here. Why would I go anywhere else?" She turned her head away, pretending to follow some unknown distraction. Hiding a truth from me that she didn't want to share.

"I guess we can't all be rolling stones," I teased, rubbing at my esophagus.

There was a tension in the air now. Her shoulders were stiff. She didn't want me to see her as a "sad orphan," but that wasn't even close to anything I'd been thinking. Still, she needed me for the kind of help that she couldn't get from this town because she loved it so dearly. I could push her in ways nobody else could, because she was safe to be what she considered her worst self with me. And that was a new and terrifying feeling. It was a sense of purpose that I wouldn't fuck up.

I would keep things on track. For her.

"Okay. So. Next phase with Deckard. Now that he has seen your professional, competent speaking side, time to let him know you're interested in him sexually."

She stumbled, and I caught her before she face-planted.

"Loose stone," she said.

Chapter 15

MILES'S LOOK WAS OF PURE TEASING. AT LEAST IT WASN'T pity. Try as I might to keep myself walled off from him, he had a way of bashing through every barrier I set up.

Okay, maybe I hadn't been trying that hard. Maybe it had been nice to share with someone who wasn't so close to it all, the way I could share my Thinking Place with him. He had no connection here, nothing tying him to any of the shared histories.

But there was no doubt he delighted in catching me off guard.

I sputtered some incoherent words back at Miles's last comment.

At least he wanted to stay on track with the relationship coaching, or whatever this deal we had going was. I could do that. I could be malleable to his advice. Even though it had me wondering if I was sexually interested in Deckard. Was he what I wanted? I wanted him to like me. I wanted to make sure I didn't upset the town. But was I attracted to Deckard?

I must have thought so at some point, because I had told Rochelle he was a "cutie with a booty" or some nonsense. But at the moment, I had difficulty remembering my reasoning. After spending time with Deckard on the tour, I'd hoped more physical feelings would develop, but everything I wanted from him primarily centered around how I would be perceived being with him. It wasn't a path of introspection I enjoyed going down.

"Have I gone too far?" Miles stepped up next to me, and heat emanated off him.

And his smell. Goodness.

When I'd stepped into his hotel room earlier, it was like being embraced in his (slightly damp) hug. His intoxicating scent, still heavy with his shower steam, floated around me. His hair was loose and glittering with water, untouched, unperfected. He was just there in his towel, the image so compelling in its simplicity. I saw a side of him I never had. It was like seeing him as a boy. Like, how you see someone sleeping, their vulnerability and innocence exposed.

It shook me more than I wanted to admit. No matter how I tried to trick myself, I was very attracted to Miles. That didn't take me any time to decide. Before him, I thought this level of draw to a person existed only in fiction. I had found people good-looking but that was very different than this intense pull, this all-encompassing desire to bite him or shake him or bury my fingers deep into those curls and suck on his lips and inhale him until one of us passed out.

"You've gone quiet. I knew it. I went too far," he said, his brows twisted with mischief.

"No. I just—I was thinking about stuff." He frowned at me, and there was a hint of worry there. Maybe he, too, wished I hadn't shared so much about my past? Maybe he wanted to keep things in the here and now, on our plans.

"Stuff, huh? Very philosophical."

"I was thinking about sexual attraction," I said honestly. "Sex."

He cleared his throat and focused on his steps. "Sex isn't bad. It doesn't make you bad, and it certainly doesn't have anything to do with the town."

I stopped and blinked at him for the sheer audacity of it all. "Obviously. I know this. Miles, you're going to get my feminist card revoked if you keep talking like that to me."

"Well, you've gone all Frozen Natalie. I'm trying to shake you out of that."

It was weird how well he knew me already. Unsettling.

"I wasn't—listen, what does me wanting to boink Deckard have to do with the town?"

"Boink?" He curled a lip in distaste.

"I regretted that word choice as soon as it came out." This was why scripted speaking was a million times easier. Even though I hadn't ever filtered myself around him before. "I'm not saying that I want to, I just . . ." I took a steadying breath. Again. *Discombobulated.* I'd never even thought that word before, and now it was part of my regular vocabulary. "I'm not afraid of that side of myself . . ." I trailed off because maybe he was actually right? I was the poor orphan girl to this town, not the sexpot trying to seduce everybody's golden son. "It's just that there are a lot of women going after him, and I don't want to be like all the rest. And that *area* isn't my strong suit to begin with."

"Maybe because you said *boink.*"

I laughed despite myself. "Miles."

"It's not a strong suit because you feel like you have to hide it, I suspect. It's not *not* there." He looked up at me with that damn boyish charm of his. It made me want to take his face in my hands and just squeeze.

"Maybe not everybody is like that," I countered, because it was a reflex with him.

"Probably not. A spectrum and all that. But you can be, can't you?" He was about to refer to my alien books again, I could feel it. "I mean, look. I'm not saying you have to go full-tits-out, so to speak, though, again if you'd like a direct approach—"

"Miles." I raised my hands to possibly strangle him.

He flinched back. "But I'm suggesting that you can show more than one side of yourself. You contain multitudes. Let him see that."

He wasn't wrong. There was so much of me I kept hidden. I mean, didn't we all do that? Didn't we all feel like we were inherently different or wrong, and so we showed only the best sides of ourselves? Isn't that really the whole point of social media? Even so, I was very guilty of presenting a very specific image. Not like Miles, who seemed so free to be whoever he wanted to be all the time. Must be nice.

Or maybe this was a test? Maybe he thought I would rebuff him, blush away. What had he called me? *Wholesome.* I'd show him wholesome—a whole lot of *some.*

We had just made it to the hot springs, and a few of the pools already had people. My favorite pool, the one tucked off to the side, known mostly to the locals and left out of the travel guides, was unoccupied. (I did have some gumption to protect the pool's sanctity to the locals.)

"Trust me, I can be seductive," I said, a plan forming as I turned and made my way over.

"It's extra convincing when you can't meet my eyes when you say it."

"Whatever, just get your shots."

"I intend to," he said.

He followed me around the edge of the cliffside, where the water poured up over the edge, like those fancy infinity pools. I set my stuff away from the water, and he did the same. When he lowered to rummage through his equipment bag, I took a deep breath in and took off my boots and pants, followed by my shirt.

"I'm thinking I'll start over there first, then maybe we can get some interviews and . . . woahhhmygod. You are naked." Miles stared, wide-eyed, not even trying to look away in the name of modesty.

"Control yourself, Asher," I mocked him as he had me earlier. "It's just a bathing suit." I tossed my hands out and looked down at my basic black one-piece. I wore it when I swam laps at the community pool. It wasn't exactly scandalous. After all, I tended to swim during the senior water aerobics class, and Ned Fled had a heart issue.

"I can see that. But why are you wearing it? You never said we were getting in the hot springs." He gulped, eyes moving frantically over me, and then looked around, trying to stay locked on my face.

I shrugged. "It was assumed. You come for the footage, you stay for the magic waters."

"No. I didn't assume. No."

"Bummer." I bent over into my bag to get my towel. Yes, I did it in a sexy way. I'm human, sue me.

My actions were justified when I heard a low moan from his direction.

"Natalie. I almost fell off the side of the mountain. You have to warn me before you do stuff like that."

"Get your shots. I'll be in here." I tested the water with a pointed toe, hiding another satisfied grin.

He grumbled and went off to work. A few people signed waivers for image use, and I took my time sinking into the water. It really was incredible up here. I realized I should visit more often. I should go anywhere more often. Miles's question about travel had me thinking about my predictable and safe life. I didn't think the occasional day trips to Santa Fe or Taos counted, not like how he'd meant it when he'd asked me. Why didn't I travel? It could be argued that I did enough of that in my childhood. That's what I should have said and left it there.

I let the buoyant water lift my legs as I spun slowly, pushing off with my arms, reveling in the weightlessness. I floated on my back in the water, my hair fanned out around me. Half of me was submerged while the other half was exposed to the licking breeze of the open sky, sending goose bumps over my arms, pebbling my nipples.

Or maybe, I should have said it was none of his business. I didn't have to explain things to him. Not everybody traveled. Sure, I missed seeing new parts of the world, but I hadn't been lying. I always did want to come back here when it was all done. I couldn't imagine an untethered life again; it made me feel awful just thinking about it. Slippery Slopes was my home.

It didn't matter. I had no time for traveling anyway. Why was I even thinking about this?

I let the natural bubbles relax the tension called Miles from my shoulders and back. I fully relaxed.

"Enjoying yourself?" His deep voice pulled me from my serenity.

"I had been, yes." I blinked open my eyes to find Miles with the sun behind him. "I guess that's over now. Did you get what you needed?"

He nodded, hands deep in his pockets. How long had he been standing there watching my introspection?

Maybe it was the relief of sharing my parents' deaths with somebody new, or maybe I felt I wasn't making enough progress with the Deckard situation. Whatever it was, I was compelled to prove that I could follow Miles's advice and be the person bold enough to ask out Deckard. I wouldn't lose track of the goals.

Plus, it was nice to turn the tables on him for once. He thought I should skank it up? Well, guess what? I was skankier than the skankiest—okay, yeah, no, that was beginning to feel offensive and super out of character.

But I could be seductive. It wasn't hard with Miles. In fact, it was weirdly easy to slip into this side of myself.

"Are you sure you don't want to come in?" I stood up and climbed onto a higher step, taking a break from the intense heat of the pool. Even though it was a mild spring day, the cool air caused steam to curl off my skin. I cupped my hands in the hot spring and brought them up to my chest, letting the hot water run in rivulets down my chest and arms. The water was drastically warmer than the air, and my nipples were hard against the thin nylon material of my bathing suit.

Miles shifted, and when I looked up, he had his camera out.

"No more pictures of me," I groaned.

"I won't if you don't want me to, but it's actually really incredible with the steam coming off you and light slanting through the trees like that," he said in a businesslike tone.

I turned to give him my back at least as I poured more water down my back and shoulders. It was silent as I focused on the distance, trying not to feel self-conscious.

"Amazing," he said. After another minute or so, I shivered. "Okay. I'm done," he said.

I sank back into the water to my shoulders. I stared up at him, not fully using my face, but close to it. I didn't know why. What point was I trying to prove? Or maybe I just wanted him to join me. There was nobody around, and I felt safe to be with just him.

"You'll regret not coming in," I said. "I brought an extra towel for you to use."

"I didn't bring swim trunks. I didn't know."

The water was just below my chin as I stepped to the deepest point in the pool. I didn't let my gaze drop. "You don't have to wear clothes."

He didn't move. Just blinked with the slightest, almost imperceptible flare of his nostrils. If I said it matter-of-factly, maybe it wouldn't sound desperate.

I groaned. "It feels amazing. I already feel more alive."

"Weird. I'm sure I've died," he growled.

"You're overthinking it."

Our gazes clashed, and I saw the challenge there. I wasn't backing down from whatever this taunt was. All at once, he shucked his shirt and boots. He hesitated for only a beat before he pushed his pants down and off. His clothes joined mine in a pile. He wore a pair of boxer briefs. I blatantly stared, as he had at me, but before I could see more of the gorgeous body I'd only glimpsed earlier, he was already lowering himself into the water. I moved to settle at his side.

"Woah." He was quickly neck-deep and floating next to me, color high on his cheeks as he noticed how close I was.

We sat in silence. Now that I had him here, I suddenly didn't know what to say. Maybe I was a big chicken.

I leaned on my hands again and let my legs float. Our calves and our thighs slid against each other, smooth and hot. Neither of us spoke, but neither of us pulled away. My pounding heart, the heat of the springs, and his nearness all flustered me. The only sound was the soft popping of bubbles and the wind in the trees. Occasionally, a laugh from one of the other groups would float over, but other than that, it was peaceful and quiet.

"What's my next assignment, oh wise one?" I asked eventually. If we focused on Deckard and the goals, then maybe this tension wouldn't feel so all-encompassing.

"So. This seductive side," Miles said. "It needs exploring." His gaze was fixed forward, a grim determination set on his face.

"I don't know how . . ."

"Practice on me then." His Adam's apple bobbed up and down.

That again. It was pretend, we both knew it. So why did it feel as loaded as the last time he said it?

Our legs still rubbed against each other in the hot water, the natural bubbles seeming to push them closer. Nature's hookup plan.

"If I were to seduce him, it would be simple. Deckard, I mean," I added, growing bolder.

Miles's eyes blacked out when they flicked to me, inching closer. No jokes to be found. He was as still as I'd ever seen him, save his rapidly rising and falling chest.

"I'd probably touch him a lot." I slowly lifted my arm toward him, giving him plenty of time to stop me. But all he did was watch me with a clenched jaw. Slowly, I dropped my hand to his shoulder, the one further away from me. I ran my fingers slowly from one side to the other. Water droplets fell from the path I left, running down his defined chest. Goose bumps broke out over his skin. "I might 'accidentally' brush him with my breasts." I leaned toward him. My nipples were still hard as I pressed into his side.

"Yep." His voice came out tight. He cleared his throat and tried again. "Good. Men. Boobs. Classic combo." He was stiff and had his hands clenched under the water. His head was turned to me, eyes moving over my face, as if on high alert to what would happen next.

Prey caught in the predator's snare.

For once, I was in a position of power. I felt heady with this side of myself.

This was so out of character for me, and yet it felt so natural, so predetermined. What was I even doing? Who was I kidding with this? But I couldn't stop. It was more than wanting to prove myself to him. It was that I wanted to prove my sensuality to myself too. I was more than my perfectly controlled image. I was complicated, and I was a woman with wiles that were to be wielded.

I could be many things with Miles.

"And then, I'd just go for it, probably," I said with a shrug.

"It?" He laughed, but instead of explaining, I showed him.

I smoothly pushed to float over and above him, and then lifted my knees to straddle him.

"It," I repeated.

I rested my knees on the stone, and his hands, tentatively at first, came to rest politely on my waist. My wet hands snagged in his hair as I ran my fingers through it. He was watching me so closely, with such tender anticipation, I wanted to weep.

"Uh, Natalie, you should know." Color rose high on his cheeks.

"It's okay." The shifting water had me brushing against the length of him. He was as hard as the stone beneath us, and it made me feel powerful. "It's just practice."

"Practice," he repeated with a shaky inhale.

I took a few deep breaths in and out, our gazes locked on each other. Both of us were breathing so hard that when our breaths synched up just right, my breasts brushed against his chest. The muscles of his jaw clenched, his nostrils flaring. He watched me closely as the thumbs resting at my hips began to move, almost imperceptibly at first. It was electricity shooting through me. It was burning heat and icy trepidation all at once. Then his thumbs moved with more intent, swirling on my hips, his other fingers gripping with a ferocity that caused me to fall further onto him. There was no chance I might float away now. His erection, even more distracting now somehow, sat between us.

The tension shifted. He had to have noticed it too, because I was just a woman straddling his lap, and he was rock-hard, and I just wanted to grind against him until I came, and this . . . this couldn't be normal. This couldn't be helping toward my goals, right? But it was like being intoxicated and high and turned on, and I couldn't imagine anything other than this moment, and I wanted him so bad.

"Then what?" he asked, breathy and deep.

My gaze fell to his mouth. He licked his lips unconsciously. I swallowed. "I might ask if I could kiss him?"

Miles's whole body went rigid. His nostrils flared as I lowered my head, tilting it slowly, intentions clear.

"If he was amenable to it," I added.

His eyes moved back and forth between mine. They flicked to my mouth and seemed to trace the edges of my face. "Of course, he would be amenable to it. He's probably been desperate to kiss you since he first saw you."

"Hmm."

My arms slid to wrap around his neck, and I leaned forward, my breasts pressing into him. He swallowed audibly as I moved closer in tiny increments.

I rode a roller coaster that couldn't be stopped. I didn't want off this ride. Adrenaline coursed through me, making me feel more alive than I had in years. Decades maybe.

"Natalie," he said with a low, gravelly voice.

His hands on my hips tightened. I tilted my head and he did the same. When our lips met, it was a shock to my system. I'd been wanting to feel any part of him for so long that I never thought it was really going to happen, and now that we had touched, I couldn't hold back. I gave in to him fully.

I opened my mouth to deepen the kiss, and he matched me with the same eagerness. His pressing tongue, his soft lips made firm by thinly held back desire. I shifted on my knees, distantly aware that the hard stone might be rubbing them raw. But I didn't care as I ground myself against him in a wanton way, feeling completely out of character but also so fully free in my body.

I *wanted* this. It didn't feel like acting. I wasn't a good person. This wasn't practice, or if it was, it didn't matter because I just wanted to kiss him like this forever. The heat spread over my neck and up my cheeks. His hands tentatively moved up my hips and over my waist, his thumbs rubbing circles, his touch tentative. I grabbed his head and pulled him harder against me.

No subtlety in my demand for more. I felt him smile against my mouth. He lifted me up effortlessly, thanks to the buoyancy, bringing me more firmly against him, and the noticeable shape of him rubbed right where I needed it most. Desire loosened and made me feel heavier than ever. I was restless and desperate. I was quickly losing control. I wanted to grind against him; the thin fabric of our clothes wouldn't stop me from getting what my body so desperately desired.

I had meant this as some way to prove myself to him, but I was out of control. I think he was too. We were both lost to the heat of the moment, the feel of skin on skin, the desperation making the steaming air around us thicker.

I wanted more. I needed more.

"Miles, I want—"

A laugh from down the path filled the air. I quickly flailed back off his lap before a group of teenagers came around the corner. A shadow passed over Miles's features as I scrambled out of the water. God, what if I knew one of them? What if they told people in town that I'd been straddling the outsider set to leave when I was meant to be taking Deckard out?

We were pretending. This wasn't real.

I wasn't thinking clearly. I'd gotten caught up.

"So, yeah. Something like that," I said, lamely grasping on to the pretense as I hurried to get dried off and dressed.

It had been nice to just let go for a minute and act in a way that didn't feel like I was putting on a performance. But it was over now.

"I'm sure Deckard would—any man would—" He scrubbed a dripping hand over his face. "Yeah," he finished lamely, water still clinging to his lashes.

I tossed a towel to Miles, and he got out of the pool, wrapping himself up. I didn't even look at him. I couldn't. I was back to that.

Once we were dried off enough that we could put our clothes on, we headed back down the trail. The winds picked up as we made our way much quicker and more silently to the car. By the time we were in my SUV, the wind was fierce.

"There it is. Spring in all her glory," I said, watching the dark clouds on the horizon.

"Maybe we should go warn those kids?"

I'd been thinking the same thing when they came barreling down the trail, arms full of quickly grabbed towels and backpacks. They laughed and piled into their car before driving away.

We drove to town, and I couldn't believe how many different excuses my brain made up for why we needed to spend more time together.

"I will go upload these. Callie's on my case," Miles said as we pulled up to his hotel, making it clear he wanted to go back to his room. Alone.

"Sure. Of course."

I'd gone too far. I'd confused things and messed up. I'd been so close to making more plans with Miles, but I'd chickened out. There was no point. The distance and my cooling loins—that was a terrible way to think about it—meant that my brain was back in control. And probably for the best, even if somewhere deep in the depths of said loins I heard a sad trombone. *Womp womp.*

"I'll see you next week?" he asked.

I nodded. "Make sure to stock up on some food in case the storm hits harder than expected. Otherwise, the town is used to it, so it shouldn't disrupt too much."

Across the street, Mayor Sparks was chatting with a new deputy whose name I couldn't remember.

I lowered in my seat.

Miles followed my gaze and then looked back to me. "Good luck with Deckard."

He got out of my car quickly, slamming the door loudly enough that the mayor shot a look our way. I felt my cheeks flame. Miles gave me one last long look before turning away and going into the hotel.

Chapter 16

Miles

I LAY ON MY BACK, STARING AT THE CEILING OF MY HOTEL room for hours. I wasn't sure if I'd actually gotten any real sleep. I just know that after I uploaded the videos for Callie (making sure there were no traces of Natalie), I tried to shut off my brain. It was as effective as using my thumb to stop the spray of water from a hose. The howling winds outside whistled through the windows, and occasionally the building would creak from the intensity of the spring storm.

My mind wouldn't stop replaying every moment of the previous day. From Natalie first showing up to my room—her heated gaze roaming over my body—then to the confession about her past and learning how much pain she carried in her, and lastly to the torturous tease in the hot spring from which I was sure I would never recover.

I groaned as I rolled over, desperately ignoring the hard-on that would not stop. Maybe if I suffocated it. My hips thrust into the bed, and I groaned again, remembering how Natalie had gasped when my thumbs had begun to test her gentle skin. God, if she'd reacted so intensely to such a delicate tease, how was she going to be when I took my time touching every inch of her?

"No," I growled out loud in the silent room.

It wasn't going to happen. It was all just make-believe until she could have the real thing, the better man. But dammit, I wished my body would get the memo.

I wasn't an idiot. Not completely, aside from putting myself in that situation to begin with—why, oh why, had I joined her in that hot spring? I knew why: because I was a man and she'd looked up at me in a way that no mere mortal could say no to.

But Natalie had been just as into it, and that's what my brain kept circling back to. She couldn't fake the way she kept toying with her lips, biting and tonguing them. She couldn't blame only the hot springs for the flush that spread up her chest and neck and cheeks. That soft, raspy moan that escaped her when her core brushed over my hard cock couldn't be faked. Or her quick breaths as our kiss became more intense. That kiss. I would never feel another kiss like that.

"Ugh," I groaned again. My hand was back around my cock as I rocked into my palm.

I had to stop this. This wasn't why I was here. This wasn't going to make my eventual leaving any easier. My heart had a sharp moment of panic.

On *her*. It wouldn't make things easier on her when I left. I was used to it.

I thought of her face when she'd explained how hurt she'd been the last time.

It crushed me. I had been directly responsible for her pain.

There. That was an instant boner killer.

I flopped onto my back and groaned.

Eventually, I must have fallen asleep when my body physically wouldn't let me be awake anymore. I tossed and turned in between stress dreams about missing flights and forgetting to put my pants on. By the time I woke up and couldn't stand being in bed anymore, a white light glowed around the blackout curtains that spoke of daytime. I rolled into a sitting position and scrubbed at my face.

"I'm ignoring you," I said to my morning wood tenting my shorts before blowing out a long breath.

I went pee (awkwardly), brushed my teeth, and threw on some clothes. By the time I was coherent enough to process information, the clock said it was almost eleven. Damn. And I hardly felt rested.

There was a knock on the door, and I thanked my former self for having had the forethought to push back my breakfast date the night before.

I opened the door to find Gabe and his goofy smile. "Thank you," I said, grabbing the tray. I turned around, and he followed me into the room. We weren't friends, I didn't do that, but Gabe did like to fill me in on what was happening with The Bartender.

"I brought a few more bottles of water too," he said. "Can't have you getting sick again."

"I will never live that down."

"Not likely, no." He sat in the chair. "I only have about five minutes. The manager wants me to go shovel the path."

"What is your job here, exactly?" I asked.

"Oh, I don't work here."

My eyebrows shot up as fear made me look to the door.

Gabe started to cackle. "You should have seen your face." He gestured down to his outfit. "I'm in the uniform, you've seen me talk to Benny Jr., the owner."

I grimaced. "That guy seems like an asshole."

"He is, but he owns half the town, so what can you do?"

I sipped my coffee with a sound of assent.

"But yeah, there's only a few of us on staff because he's also a cheap ass," Gabe explained. "So I just do whatever is needed in the moment, I guess." He started laughing again. "I can't believe you thought I was serious. Did you think I was some sort of stalker? Man, you need more friends."

I huffed a breath out of my nose. He wasn't wrong. Well, he was. But I didn't need or want more friends. One was plenty. One had me hanging out with a busboy in my hotel room in a small town running rampant with giant vermin.

I gestured toward him. "Okay, so bartender."

"Last night we hung out, but I felt like he wasn't into me. Or he's just not interested in being more than friends, and maybe I read the situation all wrong?"

"I won't presume to know how every guy operates, but the fact that he wants to spend time with you speaks for itself. If he didn't, he just wouldn't, right?"

Gabe nodded, eyes locked on me like every word I shared was gold.

"Did he seem to listen to what you were saying? Did he hold your eye contact for a long time? Ask you questions?"

Gabe nodded. "Yeah, all that. But he didn't, I don't know. There was no flirting."

"When you want to be around somebody, you will find any excuse, no matter how weak, to do so." As the words hung in the air around my head, I pointedly ignored the indication. "Maybe he's worried about the same thing you are, maybe you need to be bold and push things further."

"Oh, man." He looked like the day on the tour when we'd described all the shrimp taco sickness.

I leaned forward and put a hand on his shoulder. "Better to know either way than live with this doubt, right?"

"But it could be the end of a friendship."

"Then it wasn't a solid friendship. Look, a long time ago, I made a pass at a woman who was not interested in me in that way, at all. But we've been best friends for over ten years now. Trust Bartender to be made of stronger stuff than that if you're meant to be in each other's lives."

Gabe nodded, his fists balled like he was pumping himself up.

"How are you? Things going okay with Natalie?" he asked.

Why had he brought her up? Were thoughts of her written all over my face? Did he know something?

"Why?" I asked too quickly.

"She's still helping with the movie thing?"

"Oh yeah. It's fine." I rubbed my chin.

"Did she ask Deckard out yet?"

I shot a look at him. "How did you know about that?"

"I thought everybody knew. Except Deckard."

"Don't mention that to her." I rubbed where my heartburn returned. "You know Natalie pretty well, right?"

"I think so. As well as anybody can. She's sort of closed off, isn't she?"

I blinked in surprise. "Natalie? I thought everyone loved her."

"Nobody knows where she disappears to on her days off. She's not at her apartment."

"Really?" I asked.

"She's a mystery. But yeah. She's great. We do love her. That's well established, but she's also very private." His eyes narrowed. "It's understandable. Going through what she went through. Must be hard to get close to people without the fear of losing them."

Was Gabe an armchair psychologist in addition to his numerous other jobs and his PhD in small towns? He shook his head and smiled.

"Sure wish she'd let somebody in," he added. "We all want that for her."

My mouth opened and closed. Thoughts swirling. Natalie was an open book; her hopes and dreams so clearly written all over her face, easy for anyone to read. How was that not obvious to everyone?

"Anywho. What do you want to know about our girl Natalie?" he asked.

I cleared my mind and focused. "I was hoping to . . ."

What had I been hoping for? To know what her favorite flowers were? What ice cream she always chose?

To what end?

"You know what, never mind."

"I knew it. You're into her."

"I'm leaving here in less than a month," I said.

"Are you looking for love advice?" Gabe's chest stuck out like a proud bird.

"I honestly don't even know." I chuckled at myself.

"Looks like the tutor has become the tutee."

"Mentor/mentee. This town needs more dictionaries. But yeah, sure."

"I wish I could help. But Natalie is a closed book. So many people have tried to get to know her, but she has this wall. Don't get me wrong, she's amazing and kind, but you can just tell she doesn't open up to anyone easily. I wouldn't take it personally. Especially since you're an outsider and soon to be leaving. She'd never let herself get close to you."

"She is interested in Deckard," I said robotically.

"I will say, any guy that she does finally open up to is a lucky bastard."

I scratched the back of my head. The pit of whatever lurked inside me threatened to swallow me up at those words.

"Yeah. Definitely."

"Welp, that snow won't shovel itself. See ya later, Scorsese."

"I'm more of a videographer—you know what, it doesn't matter. Thanks for the coffee."

Gabe said goodbye, and I rubbed my chest in a circle. It was like I'd been seared with a hot poker. Maybe I'd see a doctor when I got home.

I didn't actually have a primary care doctor. You had to have a primary residence for that sort of thing. Natalie was a closed book to everyone else? Seemed impossible.

Coffee in hand, I went to the window and blinked when I opened the blackout curtains.

"Woah."

It was a snow-covered wonderland. Even the little pink flowers on the trees that had just begun to blossom were covered in snow. Easily half a foot. The town square was packed with people, and there were several bald patches where giant snow-balls had been rolled. Snow people of all shapes and sizes decorated the square. One ambitious tot struggled with a snowball (though that felt like an understatement) twice his size, determined to push it like his older sister was doing.

That woman from the cat cafe- I could not remember her name—was out there too, handing out cups of hot beverages to people. Hard to believe that a couple days ago, people were sunning themselves in this square. But everyone seemed to enjoy it, rolling with the punches. What had Natalie said, snow was good for everyone? It meant a wet spring. I supposed that snow had a lot of charm in its own way. I couldn't imagine living in a place so cut off like this; the nearest Apple store was three hours away. And sure, the stars at night shone brighter than I'd ever seen. And the sense of camaraderie and neighborliness was so damn wholesome.

I chuckled to myself, thinking again, always, of Natalie.

What would it be like to be down there with her, holding hands, drinking hot chocolate handed to us by . . . *Beverly?*

But no. I wasn't the guy of Natalie's dreams. It would be her and Deckard down there. Shiny, gorgeous couple that they were, surrounded by the town that loved them.

It wasn't just that I wanted her. I did. Incredibly. *Unfortunately*. It was a physical attraction worse than any I'd ever had before. Thoughts of the things I wanted to do to Natalie consumed me like nothing else ever had. Worse than any pain. Worse than the time my and Callie's car broke down and we had to walk what was easily seven miles with all our gear across the Arizona desert, without water as the sun baked us.

This was still worse.

Every cell yearned for her, not just to hold her, touch her, soothe her, but to be near her, to talk to her.

I wanted to hear her smart mouth and soft laughs. To learn everything about what made her who she was. I was truly a man possessed. I'd never thought it would be like that. I found myself wanting to know and memorize all her preferences for what she liked. To hear about her childhood as a tiny little carefree flower child running through fields, long tangled hair flying behind her as she laughed. I *ached* to know every single part of her.

What the fuck was happening?

I thumped my head against the thick glass of the window, cold enough to chill my fevered thoughts. But there wasn't a place for someone like me in a town that was so perfect. So untainted. I didn't fit here.

My phone rang, and when I saw who it was, I groaned.

Could she hear me thinking about her?

"Good morning, Natalie," I said.

"Oh, sorry. Is this Miles?"

"You called me." I laughed.

"No, I know. You just sound different."

"Different how?

"I don't know . . . just uh, different. Not bad. Not bad at all.

Deeper? Gravelly? No, it's good. Just wasn't expecting that," she rambled.

Was I imagining it, or was she flustered by my morning voice? Well, midday voice. I laughed a low rumble. I swear I could feel her shiver through the phone. Was this all it took? Hearing my voice and I could have this effect on her?

I felt incredibly powerful. Something had changed at the hot springs—maybe those waters were magic.

"Natalie, it's me. What can I do for you this morning?" Did I need to phrase it like that? Did I need to use her name?

No.

But she didn't need to straddle me at the hot springs yesterday either.

A choked, squeaking sound came through the line.

We were playing a dangerous game of chicken, with my cock on the line—that was a chicken joke.

"Have you looked outside?" she asked, back on track.

"No, why?" I lied totally unnecessarily, lest she knew about the unfettered daydreams.

"Really? Because I see you."

I straightened, terrified. I almost jumped back to hide before I realized I needed to get a grip. It wasn't like she saw my thoughts.

I searched the crowd down below again and spotted her immediately. How had I missed her the first time? She wore black snow pants and boots, a large parka, and a purple beanie with her wild curls flying all around her. Her cheeks and nose were pink with the cold, but she had a huge grin on her face as she waved happily.

I smiled and waved in return, my reflection in the glass showing a lovesick fool with a goofy grin.

"Can Miles come out and play?" she asked.

She was so fucking beautiful it was going to kill me. I should say no and put the distance between us. I was leaving, and even if I wasn't, she was far too good for me.

But then Gabe's words entered my mind. Any guy who she shared herself with was lucky. I was the lucky bastard. For some reason, Natalie had put faith in me, and I owed it to her to help her with whatever she needed.

Even if it killed me.

"Is that not right?" she asked uncertainly. "I thought that's what kids say. I was trying to be funny, but maybe it wasn't right."

"I will be right down," I said with a laugh.

"Bring your camera to get some shots and interviews. It's amazing down here."

"Good idea."

Work. Right. The whole reason I was here and the reason I wouldn't be able to stay.

I may not have forever with Natalie, but I have right now.

Chapter 17

Natalie

IT WAS ONE OF THOSE RARE SPRING DAYS WHEN EVERYBODY came out to delight in the final snowfall of the year before summer. That was the only reason I came to get Miles. With everybody jolly and playful, the conditions were right for him to get more interviews and video of Slippery Slopes. I didn't need to overthink it or worry about it. I was allowed to enjoy somebody's company without it being any more than that. People were attracted to people all the time without feeling the need to make a pass or cross a line they couldn't uncross.

Because when I woke up this morning and saw the beautiful blanket of snow covering the town, it was Miles who I thought of first. It was Miles who I wanted to be with. Deckard was long term, so it would likely take more time to get there with him. And yet, it was getting more difficult to remember why Deckard was the right person for me. It felt too easy with Miles, suspiciously so. Could things that feel good and easy ever be the right choice? Doesn't true love and a life together require a certain amount of work and effort?

I'd need to feel out Rochelle for her thoughts.

Miles came out the front entrance of the hotel, and my physical jolt in response was so strong, it was like I was being pushed toward him. The lies I told myself "wouldn't hold up in court," as Rochelle would tell me. His hair was mussed from him clearly having just woken up. He wore an easy, sleepy smile and a winter hat and heavy coat. His voice on the phone this morning did very strange things to me. I didn't know that sexy phone voice was a thing for me but *ka-ching!* New kink discovered.

His smile was warm and genuine as he stepped up to me.

I handed him a cup of coffee.

He took a sip and winced. "What is this?"

I faltered, reaching for the cup. "Did I get the order wrong?"

He smiled so fully it made my insides squirm. "Just messing. It's perfect. You remembered my order?"

"I guess." I shrugged.

"Stalker," he mumbled before looking at me over the edge of his cup and taking another sip.

"Whatever." I bit my lip as I turned away to hide my smile.

"Is this Beth's coffee you spoke so highly of?"

"Bee," I corrected with a laugh. "Why can't you remember her name?"

He ignored me and spun in a circle, taking in the people. "So, this is a snow day?"

"It is. Perfect snowman conditions."

"We must partake."

"It'll be good to get some interviews too, with the town all happy and rosy."

"I will let you do your thing. Let me get the camera set up," he said.

We walked around the square as I chatted with the locals. Miles was there with the camera on his shoulder. Sometimes I'd look up to find him staring at me, camera angled away from his face, a smile on his lips as I spoke. I fought from blushing or grinning too much.

Then he'd have people fill out a waiver as I moved on. He was doing that when I found Rochelle and her family.

After exchanging hellos, John and Olive went back to making snowballs.

Rochelle leaned in and asked, "How goes it with all that?" gesturing to Miles and his camera.

"Fine. Easy. It's fine."

"Okay, glad we cleared that up." Her penetrating gaze lingered on me, but whatever she'd been about to say was cut short.

"Hey, dingus," Rochelle said to Miles as he approached us.

"Hello, scary lawyer lady," Miles replied.

"Hey!" John called over. "That's Mrs. Scary Lawyer Lady."

"Thanks, hon," Rochelle said to her husband. To Miles and me, she said, "Actually, can I get in on this interview thing? I can casually mention the law office."

"Sure," I said happily. "Where do you want to stand?"

"No, no, Natalie. Miles can handle it solo," she said.

Miles, who'd been getting his camera ready, froze, eyebrows raised, flicking me a look of trepidation.

"I don't mind—"

"No. I insist," Rochelle said. "And look, there's Deckard Sparks talking to Bee and Owen. Why don't you go say hi, Natalie."

Miles and I shared another look. I wanted him to insist that he needed me, but he turned back to his camera to mess with the lens.

"That's a good idea," Miles said. "I can handle things here."

I felt thoroughly dismissed and sick to my stomach. My feet were filled with lead as I made my way over to Deckard. He and Bee spoke animatedly about the newest *Terraformative* book.

"One of the best ones yet."

"Agreed," Deckard said.

"Hey, Natalie. How are you liking the snow day?" Bee asked. "Back for more hot chocolate?"

"Hi, Bee. Deckard. Owen." I waved to them each in turn, and they all smiled back. Actually, Owen sort of didn't frown as deep as usual, and that was about the same as a grin.

I looked up to find Miles holding the camera and Rochelle talking. All seemed normal enough. They must have felt me watching them because Rochelle turned at that exact moment to give me a friendly smile and a thumbs-up. Miles didn't look in my direction.

A nervous pang tightened my insides, and my palms grew damp in my gloves as I turned back to Deckard.

"No. I'm good. I wanted to, um . . ." The three of them looked at me expectantly.

It was like being eight years old again, going up to a group of girls in matching clothes, as I wore worn, out-of-fashion jeans from a donation bin, and somehow saying all the wrong things.

I didn't fit in here. I would screw this up. My neck burned. I couldn't think of what I was meant to say, and matters took a turn for the worse when Mayor Sparks approached.

"Hi, all. Are we having fun?" the mayor asked.

We all smiled, and suddenly, it was like being a kid as the principal approached.

Deckard's smile tightened, and he nodded.

The mayor turned to me, dressed in chic winter clothes. I was painfully aware of my wild hair that I hadn't bothered to tame falling from my hat. "Natalie. How are things with Mr. Asher? I've got high hopes for this video."

Had she asked that because word got back to her that I'd been found straddling the cameraman in the hot springs? Did she think that I was wasting the town's resources? Did she think her son was a better match for me, like the rest of the town must have?

"All is right on track," I lied. "I was about to go help him now. Nice seeing you all."

I turned and left before I could fumble anything else, my smile plastered on my face.

When I found Miles again in the middle of the park, he was frowning. Rochelle had stayed behind with her family, but she wore a smile as she waved goodbye.

"You okay?" I asked Miles.

"Yep. Are you okay?" he asked me.

"Great."

"Great," he said.

We walked without speaking until we were on the edge of the grassy area, almost to the statue of Jane Smith. Somebody had knocked the snow off her and the baby the statue held in her arms. Probably Deckard. Because that was the sort of thing he would do.

"Did you do it?" he asked.

"What?" I asked, confused and lost in my own thoughts.

"I saw you with Deckard. Did you ask him out?" His tone was brisk, businesslike. Like the answer mattered little to him either way.

"No. The mayor came up. His friends were there. I got all weird. Like I always do."

The muscles in his jaw relaxed as his gaze moved around my face and hair.

"It's like you're so wound up. You just need to breathe or have an amazing orgasm or something." He let a frustrated breath out. "I don't know."

The suggestion came so completely out of nowhere that had I been in a car, the airbag would have gone off.

"What are you talking about?" I asked, appalled.

"You need to get on with it. With Deckard." He pressed his thumb between his eyebrows.

My anger grew with his cool indifference. I dragged him behind the statue, hidden from prying eyes and gossips. "You are such a man. Oh, I just need to get off, that will cure all the world's problems."

"It might help." He tossed out an arm. "How often do you get yourself off?"

"Stop. We are not having this conversation. This is absurd."

"You're overthinking this," he said.

"What else is new?"

He sighed and rubbed the back of his neck. "Look. I'm not here much longer."

The stark reminder was another airbag in the face. "I am fully aware that you can't wait to leave."

"Our time is limited. And I'm the person helping you with this stuff, okay? I'm not trying to embarrass you or whatever you think my ulterior motives might be." His eyes were hard as he spoke, and a determined edge in his tone matched.

"I don't think you're going to live stream my most embarrassing moments," I said. "But it's personal and I don't want to talk about it with you."

"Who will you talk about it with around here when I'm gone?" My mouth dropped open but closed when I realized he was right. "Isn't this the stuff you wanted my help with?" he added more softly, finally meeting my eyes.

I bit my bottom lip. "You really think an orgasm will help?"

"It might, honestly. If you're more relaxed. Don't think of it as this super emotional thing. It's a release of tension, right? It's not that serious. It's getting off. It's like sneezing or coughing."

"I mean, no, but sure. Maybe for you," I said, painfully aware of how red my face must be.

"You really have to make things so difficult." He groaned, and his head fell back. He'd been so flirty, so kind when he first came downstairs, and now he was this crabapple. Maybe being around the townsfolk and talking to them really was that hard for him. Maybe this had been the exact reminder of why he needed to get out of here as fast as possible. And to think that I'd invited him out to have a nice time and get to know the town more.

"I'm just asking how often you relax. In a sexual manner," he said.

I glared and glanced around to make sure nobody was near enough to hear. "You know that I'm not seeing anybody."

"Okay. That literally has nothing to do with what I asked."

"I can't believe we are having this conversation," I mumbled. "I don't . . . really. I don't really think about it, okay?"

"Sex?"

"Or getting off. It's not on the forefront of my mind."

"Ever?"

"No. I'm not wired that way. If I'm with someone, it's different. But it's sort of like, out of sight, out of mind, I guess." I shifted in my boots.

He rubbed his thumb over his bottom lip. My focus was pulled to the action. Was it no longer out of sight? Was I having a reaction just talking about it with him?

"Okay. Okay. I'm not judging. Desire is also a spectrum, as we've mentioned, like most things. That's fine. But do you get sexually aroused?"

I would not tell him that he had managed to sexually arouse me on more than one occasion, and it was a shock to every cell in my body. There was no faking what happened at that hot spring.

"I do," I said, clenching my jaw.

"Okay. Good, that's a starting place."

I tried very hard to be as methodical about this as he was being. I could come at this scientifically. Maybe he was right. He had been right about the tours and boob display. And even though I hadn't asked Deckard out today, I had gone up to him with minimal panic. That was some sort of progress.

I was the one who wanted Miles for his help. Clearly, the things I did were not working. If I needed to change myself in this area, too, I could work on it.

He went on. "But it's not like you do it when you wake to start the day. Or to help you relax, to go to sleep. Or sometimes in the middle of the day, just because—"

"Okay, got it. Nope. Not really. It's difficult for me to get to that level of reaction. I'm go, go, go all day, and then I pass out." I cleared my throat. "But when it does happen, I'm into it."

"Hmm." I could tell he wanted to say more—probably about how great sex was better than anything. He would know, wouldn't he?

"Hmm, what?" I asked.

"I'm thinking. Because it could be like exercise or eating, right? Or I don't know, mantras and positive self-talk. You don't really *need* it, but you might notice a visible improvement."

"I will try it," I conceded, ready to move on.

"When?"

"Oh my God, I'm not discussing that with you," I said through my teeth.

"Try it tonight. Light some candles. Go to your Thinking Place, where there is no pressure." I hated that he knew I had already planned on that. "Read the horny literature."

I couldn't help but snort. "Okay. Please change the subject. How did it go with Rochelle?"

"Fine. It was fine." But his gaze was focused behind me

when he spoke, and he started walking. "Actually, I want to go back and upload what I got today and get out of this cold."

"Okay." That was weird and abrupt, but his mood had turned. I walked him back to the hotel entrance. The sun had fully come out, and the snow on the roads was melting, water dripping all around us, flowing into the street sewers. The snow day was over. Summer would be here soon.

Deckard was here. Deckard was the future, and even though my attraction to Miles felt borderline unbearable, my future in this town was more important. I wouldn't end up alone and lost in the world again.

"Before you go in, I wanted to let you know next week is the anniversary of my parents' deaths," I said softly, the words tumbling out. I couldn't stop them. I felt like he needed to know. The town remembered, but whenever it was brought up, it was awkward for everyone, so it was easier to smile and pretend it wasn't on the forefront of my mind.

"Natalie. I'm so sorry."

"No, it's—" I shook my head. "I want you to be prepared that I might go a little MIA. But it's normal and I don't want you to be worried."

"When can I see you again?" he asked, and it made my heart thump loudly against my chest.

"I guess when I have news? Or when you need me?"

He sucked in his lips and I thought that he might add more. Instead, he reached out to tug lightly on a loose curl tickling my cheek. He swallowed with a small crease between his brows as he watched himself perform the action, like he wasn't the one touching me. Then, without saying anything else, he turned and went inside.

Chapter 18

Miles

THE FOLLOWING FEW DAYS WERE A BLUR OF GETTING SHOTS and spending time with Natalie under the flimsy excuse of working toward our shared goals. We spoke most days, more than once. More often than not, we started with a work question or with some other reference to an earlier topic, which led to a meandering conversation throughout the day. There wasn't a day I made it until noon without thinking of a reason to reach out to her. At this point, it was ridiculous to pretend like I wasn't eager to talk to her.

And what that meant, I wasn't sure, and I had no desire to examine it too closely. Time was passing, and we both felt my imminent departure like a silent third party in every room.

But all the while, her friend's threats lingered in my head. And threats they were. When Natalie walked away, Rochelle made it clear that she wouldn't put up with me using Natalie for any sort of exploits, boinking or otherwise.

I believe her exact turn of phrase was, and I quote, "I've got a friend that knows the best places to hide a body." Then she drew a line across her throat before Natalie shot us a glance, and Rochelle smiled sweetly. It was enough of a reminder that I needed her to stay on track with Deckard. No matter how much it made me sick to see her talking to him on the snow day and know that my time was coming to an end.

So when Natalie had been unusually quiet this Sunday evening, it was her well-being I was worried about that drove me to call her. I'd been working on my laptop and decided to do a quick voice call through the computer rather than get up to grab my phone. That way, I could, in theory, still do work if she needed information. It was important to keep the appearance of professionalism.

"Hello?" she answered almost immediately.

I cleared my throat to keep from smiling.

"What are you doing?" I asked by way of greeting.

"Just working." Her voice was high and tight.

"Aren't you supposed to be taking the day off?"

My heart hammered in hopeful anticipation of a few minutes of easy back-and-forth with Natalie. It was just a phone call, I reminded the needy voice in my head.

"Miles?" she asked with hesitation.

"Yes, it's me. That's why my name popped up when I called you." I chuckled. "Natalie, I'm very concerned you don't understand how technology works."

"I just can't get over how different you sound on the phone." She laughed nervously.

"I can't tell if it's a good or bad thing."

"It's good. You sound . . . I mean, not to stroke your already impressive ego, but you could easily monetize your phone voice." An electric charge had me sitting up straighter. I was thrilled just like last time, knowing I had some sort of superpower in that regard.

"Hang on." I tapped the button to change the call to a video call instead of just audio.

"What's that? Oh." After a moment, Natalie's face, shrouded in darkness, took up most of the screen. "Hi," she said.

"See. It's really me," I said with a wave.

I couldn't see her well, only the blue-white glow of her screen illuminated her.

She waved back with a bashful smile.

"I can hardly see you. Where are you?" I asked, tilting my head to see her over the edge of my glasses.

"You're wearing glasses," she said.

I realized too late that I'd forgotten to take them off. My vanity took a blow.

"Ah. Yes. I'm over thirty now, and working this late on this small screen can strain them." I reached a hand up to take them off.

"No, don't," she said quickly. "I mean, if it's straining your eyes. Don't take them off on my account."

Honestly, a man could get an *impressive ego* going on like this. "I'll keep them on if you tell me you like them."

She scoffed, but then she lifted her chin. "I like them. As much as I like your phone voice."

She was in rare form tonight, and I was here for every second of it. But wasn't this playing with fire? Hadn't I just been telling myself to stay away and listen to the scary lawyer lady?

But I was weak, and knowing that Natalie liked me, at least on some level, made me fucking feral.

"They stay on." I pushed them in place before running a hand over my jaw. "So why are you up working?"

My mind raced with too many options that were not conducive to a professional relationship, especially after hearing her say "stroke."

"I wasn't working. I lied." She cleared her throat. "I was trying to relax," she said, heavy with innuendo.

Heat burned up my spine. I was determined to not be a pervert. Maybe she really was just relaxing. "That's good. You work very hard."

She made a choked sound and bit her lip.

My heart beat a little harder.

"I went out with Rochelle for a girls' night and had a glass of wine."

"Good girl." Now I was being a flirt. I couldn't help it.

"I was thinking about what you said about my sensual side, and a glass of wine helps with . . . *that*."

I squeezed the comforter next to me. "Where are you?" I asked.

"My Thinking Place."

Where she went when she needed to be her most real self. I noted the flicker of a candle behind her . . . Had she taken my instructions seriously?

"What are you doing, *exactly*?" I asked.

"You said you wanted an update on that."

"On what? Remind me." I said, shifting back against the headboard.

"Enjoying some alone time with myself," she said flatly.

"Yes. That." My voice cracked, and I swallowed. "For the sake of progress."

"It's not going great. I can't seem to—if you're working, I can go."

"Don't you dare hang up this call, Natalie." I sat forward and tried to make out more details around her. I clicked on the light next to me and hoped it would illuminate her on the other side.

She blinked in the brighter light, the color high in her

cheeks. She was in the not-a-sex-chair, lying so that her hair sprawled all around her.

She was fucking gorgeous.

"Tell me exactly what you were doing before this call," I said, half hard already. If I was wrong about this and she wasn't in the midst of touching herself, I would feel like a complete asshole and pervert.

But if I was right and Natalie had accepted my call in the middle of getting herself off, then I just may be the luckiest man on the planet.

"I was trying to relax," she repeated but this time with a notable implied meaning.

"Natalie. Darling. Yes or no, were you trying to get off?" I asked directly, because there would be no beating around the bush . . . at least not the way . . . never mind.

Instead of shying away or being embarrassed, she held my gaze as she nodded. "Yes."

"Fuck." I looked up to the ceiling, fully hard now and a little bit closer to death. "And is there any way I might be able to help you?"

Please let me help you.

She nodded. Her bottom lip had to be swollen with how hard she bit it.

I couldn't tell if this was an incredible gift or some sort of twisted karma.

"Whatever you need," I said.

I had to tread carefully here. Surely, she didn't want me to physically help her. If that was what she wanted, I would be there faster than if I could teleport.

"Maybe you could give me some ideas. I'm overthinking things," she said.

"Overthinking what part?"

"The fantasy. I can't imagine the person or the scenario. It's like I'm trying to write out a whole play and I'm getting lost in the weeds of the details."

"You want me to give you ideas to make it easier? Scenarios?"

"Yes."

"And you are going to touch yourself?" I asked.

"Yes. Or I could go. This is—I can't believe I'm saying this. I just thought you might have a setup that wouldn't be so complicated."

She couldn't remove herself from the pressures of being here and the people she knew. She needed a stranger in a new place, at least for the fantasy.

"I can absolutely do that," I said.

"I could listen while you talk, and if I like them . . . I could tell you if I like your ideas," she said cautiously.

Part of me wanted to get off this bed and do twenty push-ups from pure adrenaline. Not that I would even be able to lower to the ground with this fucking hard-on right now. Yes, that was a not-so-humble brag.

Another, less confident side of me wondered if she only liked the sound of my voice because it didn't sound like me? According to her.

There was also this worry that this was some sort of test from the universe. Natalie was special and lovely. She did so much while maintaining good humor and humility. She worked too hard, in my opinion, so I could do this. I could give her whatever she needed.

"Are you sure this is what you want?" I asked. She'd already closed her eyes. "Look at me, Natalie."

Her eyes fluttered open, and her mouth parted. "Yes. This is what I want."

I swallowed. "Okay, you can close your eyes again," I said.

She leaned her head back.

"Are you lying back in your chair?"

"Yes."

"Set your phone on the table next to you. Keep the camera on you. I want to watch you as you listen."

She squeaked but did as I said. The camera shook before she set it down. Only her upper half was visible; her hands were just below where the camera stopped. She wore a loose T-shirt that had been cut around the collar, so her shoulder was exposed. She was not wearing a bra. I wanted her to move the phone so I would be able to see if she grew tempted to touch herself. Would I be able to handle that if she did? Or did she really just want me to provide fodder for after we disconnected?

"If you don't like anything I say, just tell me to stop, okay?" I said, voice low.

"Okay."

"This is to help you learn what you like, so you can't be afraid to speak up."

"I won't." Her chin lifted as she swallowed and got situated.

"Are you comfortable?"

"Yes," she said.

"Remember, these are fantasies. You don't have to worry about the moral weight they carry, not here, not ever. They are safely yours and nobody else's business unless you want them to be. Fantasies are so varied and intimate, so don't feel any shame if one thing works or doesn't."

She opened her eyes to look at me with a coy smile, eyebrows lifted.

"Am I mansplaining your sexuality again?" I asked.

"Yes, but it's cute. I feel safe with you, don't worry."

She closed her eyes and leaned back again. And thank God,

because if she saw the impact of that statement on me, it would give my feelings for her away.

"Just relax," I said.

"I told you that's not my forte."

"I want you to pretend that you are lying there, in your chair, in your safe space."

"I don't have to pretend, I am—"

"And he comes in."

"Who?" she asked, breaking the tension and giving me a confused look.

I clenched my jaw and rubbed it. "Whoever you want it to be." Her frown deepened. "Or it's a faceless man, an amalgamation of men from your past you've been attracted to." I could say Deckard, but I didn't want to say his name right now. I didn't want him to be in this room. Even if he was who she thought of, I didn't want to know. "He is whatever man you want him to be."

Her eyes roamed over my face, seeming to linger on my glasses, then my mouth. "Okay." She leaned back and let out a breath.

I released the bedspread from my grip. The covers were wrinkled where I'd been squeezing.

I couldn't believe this was happening, and at the same time, I would die to keep it going forever. What a gift this was. And I was the man for the job.

Limiting it to one fantasy would be the only struggle when I'd had so many involving her just in the last fortnight. But I had to think about what Natalie might want and need. She needed to feel safe to explore her wants.

"You're lying back in your chair," I started again. "You are reading your book when you start to fall asleep." I leaned into the gravelly sound of my voice. It was easy because I felt like I was growling, barely holding on.

Eyes closed, she lay perfectly still, except her chest, which rose and fell quickly. Her arms were locked at her sides.

"A man comes into the room. You barely hear him as you're halfway to sleep, but you know him. You feel safe. And you know why he's there. You know what he wants, and you aren't scared. You want him. You've been waiting for him. You've seen him watching you all day. You know how desperate he is to taste you. You've never felt so needed by someone before."

I waited a beat to see if she was still okay. Her shoulders tensed and relaxed as she let out a long breath.

"You pretend to be asleep to see what he'll do next. You feel the blanket covering you slowly being drawn down your body. You're not wearing any clothes. You can almost feel his eyes moving over the shapes of your breasts, the curve of your waist, your smooth calves and thighs. You can feel how badly he wants to explore your body. You're having trouble sitting still because you want him to touch you already."

She arched her back, biting her lip. I wished I could see her hands, but her arms were still. If she was affected, she wasn't letting herself go any further.

"Is this still okay? Should we try something else?" I asked.

"No. This is good," she said after a beat when she realized I had asked her a real question.

"Do you want to go? Be alone?" I asked.

"No. I need to know what happens next."

I chuckled. "Without the blanket on, the cold air makes your nipples hard. You wish he would touch them. You wish he would hover over you and take a breast into his mouth and suck on your nipple until you are soaking wet." At this, she gasped, and I felt powerful. "His hands grasp your ankles, and he pulls your legs apart to see if you're—"

"Wait." She shook her head and looked at me. "Sorry. Stop."

Shit. *Shit.* I freaked her out. I was lost in the heat of the moment. My heart pounded so hard it moved my whole upper body.

"I'm sorry, was that too far?" I asked. I felt coiled and tense and terrified my deviousness would put distance between us.

"No. It's good. It's really great. I just . . . I think I need—"

"Tell me." I brushed the heel of my palm hard against my cock. I hadn't meant to, I just needed to push it down.

"Tell me what you would do if you were here," she said on a rushed breath.

"What?" That couldn't be what I thought I heard.

"If I were someone you wanted, a stranger you picked up at a bar, maybe. Someone *you* wanted desperately. We didn't know each other, but we went back to yours and . . . I want to know what you would do. Just pretend and tell me what you'd do to me, this stranger you want so badly."

My cock rioted. It was painful against my jeans. If I shifted, I would feel a wet spot like I was a fucking out-of-control teen.

A stranger? No. I wanted *Natalie* desperately. I wouldn't need to pretend she was anybody else.

"I will tell you what I would do, Natalie, but could you do me a favor?" I asked.

"What?"

I moved the laptop off me, adjusting to give my cock some breathing room. I rested it on a pillow next to me so that it captured me from the chest up, mirroring Natalie on her side. I propped my head on my hand, elbow bent, ignoring the erection trying to get her attention just off camera. It was almost like we were next to each other. Never more than now did I both wish that were true and feel grateful it wasn't. I wouldn't be able to control myself. I wanted to touch her so bad. I wanted to be what made her call out in pleasure.

I couldn't be in the room with her, but I could do this.

I could do this for her. I could be what she needed to unlock another part of herself that she deserved. I couldn't think too much about who would eventually reap the benefits without the now familiar pain ripping up my esophagus, but I could give her this. I took a risk. I asked what I really wanted.

"Can you touch yourself for me?"

She blinked up at me, her full lips swollen from biting them and her eyes dark with desire.

Chapter 19

Natalie

My eyes shot open to see if I'd really heard what I thought I had.

Miles was a disheveled, sexy mess. His darkened gaze burned into me. He had one hand holding up his head, and the other wasn't visible. What I wouldn't give to see it.

I couldn't believe what he'd said. I wanted to. I wanted to so bad.

I was already so close that I would probably get myself off in no time.

All night at the local bar with Rochelle, I'd been thinking of the assignment he gave me, anxious to get home and get to work, and wondering if there was some truth to his logic.

Mostly wondering if I even cared anymore about asking Deckard out.

I couldn't confess the truth of it all. Not even to myself. I tried to bring it up to Rochelle to work through it, but I didn't think she'd understand. Plus, there wasn't anything tangible to share about Deckard, and the first thing she'd ask would be when Miles was leaving.

But I didn't want to think about any of that.

Right here, right now, I didn't want a fantasy about some stranger. I wanted Miles to tell me what he would do to me. Even if the woman he imagined wasn't me, I could put myself in her shoes. That was what I needed. Miles with that voice and those fucking glasses and that naughty mouth of his.

I was already so close. I was so needy, I couldn't stop squirming. He had to see what he did to me.

"What do you think, Natalie? Can you get yourself off?" His voice was low and teasing, but tense. I hoped this was impacting him as much as it was me.

"Only if you do it too," I said, acting braver than I felt. I was terrified he'd say he was only doing this for me, that I was making a fool of myself. That I'd once again misread a situation.

But then his nostrils flared, and he swallowed thickly. "Are you sure?"

And why should I doubt Miles when he'd been the one here and helping time and time again? I wouldn't be this brave with anybody else but him. It had to be Miles.

"Yes. It will help me feel more comfortable if we are both getting off," I said, and it was mostly true.

But also, I wanted to watch him as he went over the edge. I wanted to hear his dirtiest thoughts and see what he looked like when he was lost to his desire.

"Okay," he said. He held my eye contact as his bed shifted and the camera shook. I realized that he couldn't have had me on his phone when I answered, and now I was sure this was his laptop. I couldn't see anything lower than his chest, but after some soft shuffling, he hissed a groan of pleasure.

"Are you touching yourself?" he asked me when he opened his eyes again.

I imagined him lying on that hotel bed, that bed I'd run my fingers across, as he touched himself. It was enough to drive me over the edge right then. There was such a delicate intimacy to this, so scary and tenuous, but also the most exciting thing I'd ever done. I felt dangerous and wild and out of control, and I loved this side of myself.

"Are you?" I asked.

He nodded, his shoulders rising and falling as a flush spread up his neck. I wished he'd take off his shirt but that felt like getting far too close to ogling him.

"Tell me, Natalie."

I shook my head. "Not yet. I need you to tell me what to do."

"Fuck." His arm moved roughly for a quick moment before stilling. He closed his eyes for a brief reprieve, biting his lip before finding me on the camera again. The tiny version of myself that I saw in the corner of the screen was unrecognizable. She was flushed and wild, hair everywhere, eyes dark, mouth parted. No control. Far from perfect.

"Remember, I'm just a stranger you picked up. I can be whoever you want me to be." I couldn't believe I was saying this. I couldn't believe how bold I was.

His head went back, and I got to explore the long angle of his neck, his Adam's apple moving on a growl.

"I would start by kissing you," he began. "As soon as we were alone, I wouldn't be able to wait a second more. I'd push you up against the door and kiss you like I've been wanting to all night." My fingertips went to my lips without thinking; they tingled, and it shot heat down my back. His glasses, his voice, the straining of the muscles in his neck, his clear desire, and heat being in this moment with me. I moaned and closed my eyes, letting his voice wash over me.

"You taste incredible. I wouldn't ever want to stop feeling

your tongue slide against mine. I'd slowly wrap my fingers in your curls. All night I'd been watching them bounce, and I wanted to know what they felt like. I tug them slightly to bring your mouth closer to mine, and I'd kiss you more deeply until I felt your neediness for more match my own. Until you arched against me, begging with your moans, for more."

I let out a slow, shaking breath. I wouldn't overanalyze the fact that this pretend woman had curls too.

"Then I would need to taste you all over. I'd start with your neck, slowly kissing up the long column there, inhaling you." There was a moment of quiet before he added, "Touch your neck now."

I followed his instructions.

"Good," he said. "Then I'd move to your collar. I'd probably lift off your shirt and push down the straps of your bra to run my lips over the shape of your shoulder."

My fingertips followed the path of his words. I didn't take off my shirt, because apparently, we weren't doing that, but I lifted up my hem and went under so I could follow his instructions.

"Then, eventually, slowly and carefully, after I'd touched you everywhere else, and you were practically begging for relief, I'd find your breasts. I'd feel the heaviness of them. I'd cup you, run my thumbs over your nipples. Play with your nipples, Natalie."

I gasped out as I did. Back arching off the chair. It was true. By the time I got to touching my breasts, my skin was already on fire with need, my nipples were hard, my breasts heavy and needing to be played with.

I was throbbing, and we hadn't even gotten to my underwear yet. This was going to kill me. I clenched at emptiness. It wouldn't be enough. I needed more to fill me, but at the same time, I couldn't stop now.

"Fuck, I'm so hard," he said breaking character, and it was hotter than anything else he could have said.

"Miles," I moaned, feverish, reckless. Shifting and unsettled.

I was desperate for more. Flushed and aching. I wanted to dip my fingers lower, see how wet he'd made me. I was so sensitive all over, yearning. Needy.

"Touch lower now," he demanded.

I traced my fingertips down my rib cage, stomach, lower. I find that I'm soaked and swollen. I dip a finger in and find I'm drenched. I touch myself like I'm alone, like I need to get off.

"I can hear how wet you are," he growled.

I whimpered. I opened my eyes. His face was damp with a sheen of sweat. His arm was moving so quickly that the camera shook.

I might have felt embarrassed at how right he was, but there was no shame here, not like I'd felt with men in the past. It was filthy, but I felt free and sexual, and it gave me a new sense of power that I didn't know I had.

"God, Natalie. You are so gorgeous."

I rode my hand, squirming and pressing as much as I could to get what I needed. It was incredible and not enough. It was pure delight and frustratingly painful. I wanted him in me. I wanted to feel full of him as I rode him. I wanted to be the woman he was fucking into the mattress.

I opened my eyes at the last second, hot and turned on by the jerking movements of his arm. I was the one he was looking at. He was jerking off for me as if he were lying here next to me.

"Ahh," I called out, pushed suddenly over the edge. I came and came, wave upon wave, no breaths in or out, just a silent scream as I pulsed.

"God, you're incredible. That was . . ."

I blushed but smiled as I looked at him. His eyes were totally blacked out and flicked all over the screen, and I wondered how much of that he could even see. Or was it the idea of it, just like with me, that felt so exciting?

I couldn't believe that I'd done that.

I didn't even recognize myself, but then again, I did feel more powerful and confident. I was still pulsating as I slowly pulled my hand away.

"Show me your fingers." He gasped.

Only slightly shamefully, I held them glistening up to the camera.

I thought about licking them, but he didn't ask. It didn't matter, a moment later his head was thrown back, the tendons of his neck powerful as he lost himself.

"Fu—" he called out, half word, half groan.

He shifted, reaching off-screen. "Sorry, just need to clean this up. Man, that got everywhere. Sorry, you don't need to know that. But honestly, I'm a little proud. I haven't come that hard in a long time."

I chuckled. I couldn't help but feel a surge of pride and hope. "That made me feel like I could conquer the world," I admitted.

"Good. That was the goal."

Imagine how I would feel if we had sex.

The thought took me so suddenly, I wished I could shove it back down. This was supposed to be a release of tension. This was meant to relax me, but I felt needier than ever. If out of sight, out of mind was true, then touching myself with Miles had put my sexual desire to the forefront of my mind. It would be all I could think about.

Not that we would. Not that he'd want to. That had all been his fantasy, and yet at the end there, he hadn't been saying anything about another person. He watched *me* closely.

"Are you okay?" he asked.

"Of course. Just tired. You weren't kidding, it's a great way to help get to sleep."

"Yeah. Well, glad we could help each other."

My heart pounded in a new way. I felt an icy chill of nerves.

Now what happened? How did people recover after getting themselves off in front of each other? There was no tourism pamphlet for that.

He lay back a moment later.

After using a tissue to wipe my fingers, I stretched back with a yawn.

"Thank you. I hope—" I started.

"Thank *you*. That was incredible." His tone grew serious. "I know you said you'd had a glass of wine, I don't want you to regret this," he said earnestly.

I fell back, hiding my face as a wave of nerves crashed over me. "No. Not at all. It was one glass hours ago, and honestly, I think I needed this. More than I knew. You were right. Once again."

He chuckled. "Okay. Because I'd hate for this to change things. I'd hate for you to be uncomfortable around me."

"Never," I said easily. "I think I proved I might be a little too comfortable around you."

I knew that I wouldn't be able to share this moment without wanting more. I wasn't built like that. I would love to be able to have emotionless sex, but turned out, in that regard, I just couldn't.

Darkness moved in as the ebbs of residual pleasure flowed away.

"I'm glad," he said.

I yawned again.

"Good night, beautiful," he said softly. "We'll talk tomorrow."

I nodded as my blinks took longer. I loved how he said *beautiful*, even as I started to fade away.

We ended the call, and when the screen went black, it reflected my face.

Shame washed over me. Not about what we'd done but about the person I thought I should be. I was getting mixed up.

I thought I would feel better. I had. But only for a moment, because now I saw how reckless I'd been. I was finding excuses to share parts of myself with Miles when he wasn't the one I was supposed to want, for so many reasons. I was acting out because feeling anything thrilling was better than feeling the darkness that crept in along the edges when I was still for too long, if I thought too much. I stayed moving to escape the pain, but it was time.

I was back here. Alone, so painfully alone, and falling for a guy who would be gone in a few weeks. Who had no interest in building a life with anyone, let alone me. I wished I could let these moments be enough.

My dark thoughts grew like roots in my brain throughout the night. The wine was long worn off and all that remained was the crash of sadness.

It wasn't helped by the time of the year. The new flowers blooming, the smell of the cottonwoods. It caused a familiar pang of despair, deep and aching.

It didn't make any sense. A few moments ago, I'd felt like I could fly. Now I was so painfully sad it was like I couldn't breathe.

I knew the anniversary always made this week hard. But it hadn't hurt like this in a while. The raw freshness of pain ripped through me.

But what else could it be but the anniversary of my parents' deaths?

Chapter 20

Miles

I WAS FULLY ENTRENCHED IN THE RELIGION THAT WAS Natalie. She consumed my every thought.

I tried to focus on my work. I did everything I was supposed to be doing, but I couldn't get the sounds of her coming out of my head. Or her face when she laughed freely at a joke I made in poor taste. Did she know how much I had given away when I shared my fantasy of her? Was it so painfully obvious that she consumed my thoughts?

And worse than that, I knew at any moment she would no longer be anything close to mine. Not that she was close to that now. But she would ask Deckard out. And she would ask him soon. She was running out of time, less than a week? I could only hope that he already had plans.

"No," I said out loud to myself.

No matter how much it made me physically sick to think of them together, how could I be so selfish as to hope for it to stop? This was what we'd agreed to. I was being a better man for the sake of her happiness.

And it sucked.

How could this be happening? How could I be in this deep? I needed to get out of here. I needed to leave. This was all happening too fast.

But I also needed to know: Had she already asked him? Was she done with me now that I'd gotten her off?

Fuck, I wished I could stop thinking about it.

But she'd been so quiet these last couple days.

"Shit," I said, remembering too late it was the anniversary of her parents' deaths, distracted as I'd been by the last time we talked.

I was dressed and downstairs before I could even question it. I would make sure somebody had an eye out for her, that she wasn't alone, that she was safe. Then I would leave her be.

I went first to Gabe, who said that she'd left a message earlier, and she sounded fine. After finding her Thinking Place empty, I went around town subtly asking a few others about her whereabouts, including the grumpy mechanic who gave me a look like it wasn't my business. And maybe it wasn't. But I found I couldn't stand the thought of her being alone.

I was truly resorting to the worst when I called her best friend. Rochelle had exchanged contact information with me after she threatened my life on the snow day.

"What's up, dingus?" she answered.

"Hey," I said.

"See, now I feel bad calling you names if you aren't going to taunt back."

"Sorry. Uh . . . You're a tall gazelle of terror." I stood outside the hotel, not ready to go back in and give up.

"Better. Not your best work. Something must be amiss for you to call me for a reason other than cajoling repartee."

"Is Natalie with you? I've been trying to get a hold of her."

"No." Her tone changed, cooled. "But she's fine."

"So is she with you?"

"Today is a day that she likes to be alone," she said.

"Alone? Really?"

Silence met me.

"Look." I pressed my thumb between my eyebrows. "I know it's the anniversary of her parents' deaths. That's why I wanted to check in on her."

"She told you about them?"

"Yeah. And I know she wants to be alone, and I won't bother her, I promise. I just want to make sure she's okay." I debated telling her how Natalie had been radio silent the last two days, except for sending a few short texts that were overly friendly with too many exclamation points. Even for her.

The sounds of Rochelle's family in the background quieted with the click of a door.

"Should I be worried?" she asked.

"I don't think so. I don't know. I want to check on her."

"Shit. I can't get away right now," she said.

"No. It's okay, I don't expect you to. Do you know where she might be? If she's at a bar drinking her feelings or out in a cabin in the middle of nowhere? I figured she wouldn't be drinking at either of the two places in town because she wouldn't want anybody to see her, but I checked her Thinking Place too and—"

"She told you about her Thinking Place? She only told me about that, like, two years ago, and she still won't tell me where exactly it is. I've narrowed it down to Main Street, but I cannot figure out—"

"Rochelle."

"Sorry. Okay, well, yeah. You're right. She's probably taken a rideshare service to that biker bar en route to the next town over. It's not the nicest place, but when your only goal is to get wasted, it gets the job done."

"You let her go alone? Every year she does this?"

"Look. Don't guilt me. You can't roll into town and think you know all about her. Usually, we have someone there to keep an eye on her, but she doesn't know that. Or I'm with her, but I'm up to my ears in work right now, and Olive has strep, again, and John—I don't have to explain myself. But Natalie is a grown woman, and this is how she mourns. She's okay."

But she wasn't okay. I couldn't shake the feeling that I needed to be with her. "Sorry. That wasn't about you. I'm just worried about Natalie. She's been quieter lately."

"Shit." Rochelle sighed. "You're right. I've been so distracted. And it's not an excuse, but she's the type that would gnaw off her own arm before letting anybody know she wasn't okay."

"Extreme example, but yeah."

"Will you text me if you find her and let me know she's okay?"

"Yeah, will do."

I was already back in my rental car before I ended the call.

After a forty-minute drive through winding and sketchy back mountain roads, I found the even sketchier bar. The squat adobe building with a single neon sign that said Beer was as charming as Rochelle had described it. I never thought I'd miss the comfort of the Slippery Slopes bar scene. There were a few tables and a sticky floor, and that, in a nutshell, was the entire ambiance. But it did make it easier to find Natalie.

She was easy to spot in any room. She sat hunched at the bar, trailing her finger in condensation as she rested her cheek in her other hand. I watched her for a moment, still debating if I should bother her or if I should keep my promise to leave her be. When a man and his friend across the bar talked back and forth and were shooting her looks, my feet moved toward her.

I stood next to her, and the bartender was on me in a minute. He had large arms covered in tattoos and a lip piercing that rang a bell. Had he been her former fling? Could I take him? I was taller than him, but he was girthy. I hated that I used that word to describe him.

"She's got a date, back off," he warned, and my mouth dropped open.

"Terrible customer service," I said.

"Ah!" Natalie said with a squeal. "It's okay, Oz, I know him from work."

His entire demeanor changed.

"Sorry, bud, I've been keeping pervs off her all night."

"Just glad to see she wasn't out here unprotected."

"Oscar." He extended a hand. "Most people call me Oz."

"Miles. Most people call me M.I. for short." I shook my head as I returned the gesture. "That was a terrible mileage joke. Nobody calls me that."

He huffed a laugh, his voice noticeably more friendly now. "Can I get you anything?"

"Water for now," I said. He lifted his chin and went off.

I turned to Natalie, and she looked at me. Her jaw dropped open. "Glasses," she whispered. "Ka-ching!"

My hand went to my face, where my glasses still sat on my nose. I had meant to leave them in the car. "I need them to drive at night."

She wiggled her eyebrows up and down and then closed her eyes when the action seemed to make her dizzy.

"How did you find me?" Natalie asked.

"It wasn't very hard."

After a few quick fruitless laps around town, several phone calls, and one awkward run-in with a group of chittering guinea pigs, and voilà.

"I'm sad," she said.

"I know. I'm sorry." I sat on the barstool next to her, and she immediately turned so her knees brushed mine.

"And worse, now I'm a cliché too."

"How's that?"

"A sad drunk girl at the bar. I'm basically a flashing red sign for predatory men."

"I'll take care of you. No men will even look in your direction. I'm extremely threatening."

She snorted.

"Offended."

She turned to me fully, reached up, and ran her hand through my hair. "Yeah, those disheveled curls and that charming smile really scream 'I'll punch you.'"

I smiled. Maybe I shouldn't love drunk, touchy Natalie, but she was quickly rising to the top of my favorites. Right under watching-me-come Natalie.

"So many curls. We could never have children." She'd mumbled it so quietly I wasn't sure that she knew she spoke it out loud. "They'd be cursed to silk pillowcases and a fifteen-step post-wash treatment."

I ignored the tightness in my throat. "Oz and me, then. To protect you," I clarified. "Probably more Oz than me, to be fair." I swallowed the lump in my throat at the instant image of curly-haired mini Natalies toddling around town, being absolute menaces and charming the locals out of all their treats.

"I didn't want anybody to see me like this," she said. "I'm such a mess."

"You're far from a mess. You're beautiful." She gave me a watery smile. "We've all been here," I said.

She leaned forward and whispered, "I actually don't even like drinking. I had to hold my nose to take my first shot."

If she didn't drink much, she was going to be miserable in the morning.

I leaned forward, too, and whispered back, "Then why am I finding you three sheets to the wind?"

"Three sheets to the wind. Who says that?" She snorted before my question sank in. Her chin quivered. "Because I don't like being sad more than I don't like drinking."

Pain like being punched in the solar plexus.

"No," she said, stretching out the word. "Don't look at me like that. I can't stand being looked at like that. I'm supposed to be pathetic alone."

"Natalie, do you really want to be alone?" I asked.

"It's complicated." She frowned. "Everybody in Slippery Slopes has either totally forgotten about their deaths, which is fine, I wouldn't expect them to remember a tragedy ten years ago. It's that, or they're treating me like I might have a meltdown if they even mention their names. I've never done anything to make them think that. I've never been anything but appreciative. I try so hard to be appreciative of all that I've been given."

Her hand balled into a white-knuckled fist on the bar top. She held on to everything so tightly all the time. I put my hand on hers and rubbed it until she relaxed it again.

"I know you have." I wanted to tell her that she didn't have to be an indentured servant to the town's kindness, but the timing didn't feel right.

She mumbled something about being alone again, but I couldn't quite make it out. Maybe she really didn't want to have company, and I was overstepping.

"If you want, I could leave?" I asked. I wouldn't actually leave, I'd sit in the booth and keep an eye on her until she was ready to go.

She grabbed my arm. "Don't go."

"I won't." I put my hands on hers.

We both looked at where both my hands clasped hers before

she narrowed her eyes at me. "Promise not to look at me like I'm sad. Or ridiculous. Or pitiful."

I didn't think she was any of those things. I thought she was incredible and strong and resilient and beautiful. I wanted to embrace her just so my arms could give her strength until she could stand on her own again. I yearned to take care of her. None of these were feelings I understood or was used to. My tongue was stuck to the roof of my mouth.

"Definitely don't look at me like that," she mumbled, a flush growing up her neck.

We held each other's gaze, and I wondered if thoughts of our last conversation still haunted her like they haunted me.

"What were their names?" I asked, threading our fingers together. My heart hammered with fear that she would call out the action, but she looked at me, confused. "Your parents?" I clarified.

A soft smile spread over her face. "Paul and Mary," she said.

"Ah, they're just missing their Peter," I said.

"People always made that joke." She laughed, her eyes soft as they looked into some distant memory. "Not as much anymore. Most kids today don't know who they are."

"Aren't you a kid today?"

"I'm almost thirty."

"Ancient. Soon you'll be wearing glasses and listing your ailments."

"I like your glasses," she said softly, holding my gaze.

I had to bite my tongue to keep from saying *I like you.* But she must know that already, no point in saying it out loud.

Instead, I shifted the topic back. I couldn't have her looking at me like that when she'd been drinking this much.

She took a sip of the water Oz set down in front of her. I gave him a nod in thanks. I suddenly realized where I knew him from.

"Don't you work at the Slippery Slopes Hotel?" I asked.

He leaned forward on crossed arms and nodded. "Yeah. I pick up shifts here too. You're Gabe's friend, right?"

I almost scoffed because no. I wasn't Gabe's friend. I had a friend already.

"Aw, Gabe. He's the best. Isn't he the best?" Natalie looked between us, her eyebrows contorted like she'd seen a puppy.

"He's great," the bartender and I both agreed.

"He gets it. Unlike some people." She nudged me with her shoulder and almost fell off the side of the stool. I put an arm around her to keep her upright.

"He gets what exactly?" I asked, feeling only mildly threatened.

"How amazing Slippery Slopes is. I know *you* hate it."

Oz raised his eyebrows as if to say, *You've done it now.*

"I don't hate Slippery Slopes," I said, holding up my arms, the picture of innocence. "It's actually really grown on me."

"I told you, you would learn to love it." She leaned forward, all smug like.

"Let's not get crazy," I said equally as smug, leaning closer. "I said I was learning to appreciate it."

"I wish you would love it," Natalie said with a sigh.

My gaze fell as that sharp pain returned. She was referring to the town and nothing else. "It has some redeeming qualities that I typically find lacking in other places," I admitted.

Better than saying, I was falling so fucking hard for *this town* that I couldn't remember what being on solid ground felt like. That might give a little too much away. Especially when even telling her I liked her was too hard.

She shook her head, looking at me. "You're so nice for how much of a pretentious tool bag you sound like."

"Callie's said something along those lines before," I said.

"Do you need anything else?" the bartender asked. Quite honestly, I'd completely forgotten he was there.

"Keep the waters coming and maybe some fries or chips if you've got anything to soak up the booze?" I asked.

He nodded but seemed to be hesitating. He looked between us and back at me like he wanted to ask me more. Instead, he stood up straight again. "I'll let you two get back to it. Glad Natalie's got a friend here tonight."

Again with the *friend* word. Throwing it around like confetti.

Natalie and I weren't friends. We were more than friends. There wasn't really a word to describe us though, was there? And that's why we didn't need to talk about it.

Once he was gone, I turned to Natalie. "What were your parents like?" I asked.

"Paul and Mary?" she asked. "Yes, I did call them by their names. They were hippies, like I've mentioned." She smiled again, and I wished I had my camera to capture this new think-ing-of-her-parents smile. She went on to talk about them, and I listened intently.

"My dad was convinced that he could replicate any bird call. He would try it all the time. In the middle of a crowded national monument, he'd make the most ridiculous squawking sound you ever heard, drawing all the attention around him." She stopped to laugh, even as her eyes glittered with moisture. "I am sure I was embarrassed at some point, but I can't remember it with anything less than fondness now."

"He sounds great," I said, letting her go on.

"My mom was quieter, gentler. She had this incredible intu-ition for when somebody needed to talk. She would just listen. And really mean it, you know? If we were at a truck stop, she'd wander to the bathroom, and when she hadn't come back, we'd look up to find her hugging a sobbing waitress."

The fries came, and I was happy to watch Natalie demolish most of the basket as she drank her water.

"They sound incredible," I said.

"They are." She shook her head. Frowned deeply. "*Were.* It's been ten years." She spread her fingers flat on the bar and leaned back with a shake of her head. "I can't really wrap my mind around it. It feels like it just happened, and then it feels like a lifetime ago. I was a person who I don't even remember. It's like I look back and I see a little girl, terrified and hanging on to whatever she could."

I took her hand again, wishing I could wrap her in my arms. "I've heard that there isn't really a linear timeline on grief. However you feel for however long is exactly how it's meant to be."

"You're right," she said. "I still feel that way most days though."

"Like what?"

"Like this sad, sheltered girl who's playing dress-up as an adult, and any minute somebody is going to figure out that I shouldn't be here and I'm not who I say I am."

"I don't think anybody ever really feels like an adult. One day, we notice our body hurting more, but it's confusing because we still know exactly how it feels to be a kid. It's weird."

"You're trying to make me feel better."

"I'm really not," I confessed. "I'm only a couple years older than you, but I certainly don't have any clue what I'm doing. My best friend is having a baby. She is making a whole human with her family, and I don't even have a place to live."

"You don't?"

I quickly shook my head. I hadn't meant to make this about me. I didn't want to talk about me. "Nobody feels like an adult. Literally everybody is faking it."

"That's a relief." Her shoulders lowered on a heavy sigh. "I know I shouldn't feel so . . . I shouldn't complain."

"I think in this case, you're good."

"I have a good life."

"And you can be sad. Both things can be true," I said, giving in to putting my arms around her.

She looked at me. Her blinks had slowed down considerably, as though the truth of what I said had settled in.

"Yes. Both things can be true. It doesn't have to be either-or." I shook my head in agreement as she processed. "I don't usually talk about this stuff," she admitted, her mouth a few inches from mine.

"Okay." I lifted a shoulder. "Practice on me then," I said softly, so only she could hear.

She sucked in a soft, sharp breath. Her gaze flicked between my eyes, roamed to my mouth, and back up.

"It doesn't feel like practice when I talk to you," she said. "It feels necessary."

I squeezed my eyes and took a bracing breath. When I opened them again, I had leaned infinitesimally closer.

"Miles—" Her eyelids fluttered closed, and I couldn't tell if she was leaning in to kiss me or to fall asleep.

Either way, she was in no state to be here anymore.

"Let's get you home," I said. She nodded after a beat and dropped her head to my chest.

I kept my arm around her, whispering to Oz as I closed out the tab, telling him I'd be driving her home.

"Thanks for looking out for her," I said. "You're a good guy. I can see why Gabe likes you," I added coolly, not making eye contact with Oz as I signed the bill and started getting Natalie ready to leave. When I looked up, Oz was collecting our glasses, and there was a soft smile on his face.

Natalie made it two minutes into the drive before she fell asleep deep enough that she snored softly. I had to wake her when we arrived on the edge of Slippery Slopes to figure out where she lived.

"Just turn up here."

It was a side street I didn't recognize, mostly dark this time of night, save a few glowing porch lights on the small houses that lined the quiet road. I drove slowly, wondering which house was hers.

"Here," she said.

I rolled to a stop in front of a small single-family home with no lights on. "This will be my home one day."

I huffed a small laugh. "Is that right?"

She nodded her chin up and down. "Mm-hmm. And I'm going to have a yard full of wildflowers for the local bees and butterflies."

"Is anybody living here now?"

"The couple that owns it lives in Florida most of the time. They're trying to sell it."

"You should buy it," I said. It was such a random detour. This house had to mean more to her than she let on.

She made a soft sound of acknowledgment. "Maybe. Not until . . . not yet." Then she lifted her hand forward. "My apartment is just around the corner," she said with a jaw-cracking yawn.

I glanced back at the cute home one more time, wondering if she noticed that she hadn't mentioned Deckard in her plans for the future.

Not that she'd mentioned anybody . . .

I pushed the thoughts away, my mind already filled with too much tumult from tonight's intimacy.

Thankfully, I was able to get her into her apartment, take off her shoes, and tuck her into bed. I was sure there were crucial bedtime routines that I missed, but she hadn't been sick, and she was home safe now. She fell asleep in her bed almost immediately.

I sent a picture to Rochelle. Partially to let her know that she was okay and partially to ensure that she gave Natalie shit about her sleeping position—sprawled like a starfish, mouth open.

Thanks for the update. She sure is beautiful, isn't she? Her text reply read.

She is, I said simply.

I got some water and medicine for her inevitable hangover and set it next to the bed with a protein bar I found in her pantry.

I ignored the desire to snoop, instead sitting in the chair next to her bed. It was almost three a.m. at that point, and I wanted to make sure she'd be okay.

I'd leave in just a minute.

"Miles?" she asked, her eyes still closed.

"Yeah? Do you need anything?"

I came over to her, trying to hear her murmured ramblings.

Grabbing her headboard, I leaned down to brush away a few curls from her face. In her half-asleep state, she grabbed my palm and nuzzled into it. I swallowed down a wave of unexpected emotion at the gentle touch.

"Don't go," she whispered.

"I'm right here," I said roughly, feeling my heartbeat through my whole body.

She slurred something else about lies and monsters. I frowned and hovered closer.

"What's that?"

"I didn't save him," she said. "It's all a sham. I'm a dirty liar, and when this town finds out, they are going to hate me forever."

Her hand dropped mine, and her breathing leveled out to that of a gentle sleep almost immediately.

I stumbled back to the chair and fell into it clumsily. I ran a hand over my mouth. She was not going to be happy about sharing that with me, but it was another clue to understanding this enigmatic wonder.

Chapter 21

Natalie

I STRETCHED IN BED, KICKING MY LEGS OUT AND PUSHING my arms up above my head as I tried to remember how I got home.

I felt great. Aside from the strong taste of regret in my mouth, I felt lighter, comfortable. I hadn't been expecting that this morning. I'd been expecting the usual douse of post-drinking heaviness. The lonely ache that hit me upon waking each morning alone.

Today, I was hungry though. I barely ate some fries last night when—

A slow smile spread over my lips before I fully opened my eyes.

Miles.

He'd come to check on me. I knew I would've been safe with Oz and then taking a cab home, but Miles came for me. My heart fluttered with the memories of us laughing and talking. It seemed hard to believe that the man who once caused me so much eye-twitchy rage could now be the source of my lightness.

When I finally blinked my eyes open, my phone said it was still earlier than nine a.m., but I didn't want to sleep anymore. I found Miles a moment later, asleep in the chair across from me. His arms were folded tight around him, chin down, legs long and crossed at the ankles. It couldn't have been comfortable for him to sit like that all night. But knowing that he'd stayed to watch over me had me feeling unaccountably warm and happy.

I had been so sad the last few days—of course I had, that part was normal—but this morning I felt the lightness that came with a good cry or a good conversation. And I'd had both.

I didn't feel quite so lonely.

I did need to pee like crazy, though, and brush these teeth.

With sneaky stealth, I grabbed some clothes to change into and went to wash away the smells of stale beer and grease that lingered on my skin and in my hair.

A quick shower and I was back to my old self. I left my hair loose and long, not wanting to do the full curl routine. I'd regret it later, but today I would pretend to rock the frizzy beach wave look. The weather had warmed back up, and today should be a sunny day in the sixties, so I pulled on jeans and a tee to keep things simple. By the time I tiptoed back into the room, Miles was leaning forward, head down, rubbing the back of his neck.

"Good morning," I said. I tried not to sound too perky. Rochelle told me it could be a lot first thing in the morning. "I didn't wake you, did I?"

"No, falling asleep like I was jammed into an airplane seat did." His eyes moved up and down me. His nostrils flared, and he looked angry as he glanced away. When I looked down at myself, I saw that my soaking curls had dampened my shirt and left my nipples hard. "What time is it?" he grumbled.

"Perfect time for brunch," I said, hoping that he wouldn't want to bolt away yet.

"Oh, God. You feel great, don't you?" He slowly stood up to stretch. With his hands on his lower back, he arched his chin up to the ceiling. His disheveled button-up rode up enough to reveal that little slit of yummy man tummy. I'd been so close to seeing it all, watching as he got himself off. I still couldn't believe that had happened, and here we were talking like it was nothing.

But then I met his eyes, and I'd been caught staring, and there was a liquid heat there, so maybe he'd not totally forgotten either.

"Yeah, starving but good," I said and spun to make the bed, an act I never normally did, but I had no idea what else to do with my hands.

"Give it five years," he said. "You won't be waking up so bright-eyed and bushy-tailed. I didn't even drink, but the lack of sleep has me feeling like I did."

"You're just jealous that I can hold my liquor."

"Yeah, well, we shall see next time . . ."

He trailed off, not looking at me. Because there wouldn't be a next time. Next year, I would be alone again.

"Hopefully, I'll have a better coping mechanism by then. Though I vaguely remember thinking that last year too." I turned back to him.

"Sorry. I didn't mean to stay here, I just . . ." He scratched at the back of his head.

"No, it's fine. Thank you for showing up last night," I said sincerely.

"You didn't have to be alone. I would have gone with you," he said.

How could I tell him that that would've been worse? That I was already feeling too reliant on him. I couldn't let myself fall for someone who wanted to leave forever. I had to be what this town needed.

"Thank you."

"Hopefully, next year, Deckard will be there to help you."

"Yeah, hopefully." We both stood awkwardly.

"Want to go to breakfast?" I asked.

At the same time, he said, "Well, I will get out of your hair."

"Oh," I said.

"That sounds good, unless . . ."

Good thing there was nothing awkward about any of this. I fought to keep my hands from twisting in my shirt, like a nervous teenager. I didn't want him to go yet. I wasn't ready to stop talking.

Choice made, I said, definitively, "No. I want twigs in a blanket."

He made a face. "Do I want to know?"

"It's normal pigs in a blanket but with a name more sensitive for the local animal life."

He laughed for the first time today.

Deb's Diner was decently crowded this morning, but Miles and I were tucked in a side booth near the back. If he had any comments about the Sasquatch-inspired decor, he stoically kept them to himself.

Food almost entirely devoured, I slowed down to a normal human rate of consumption.

I'd already caught several amused eyebrow raises from Miles.

"No thanks, I don't want any," he said.

I shoved the remaining fragment of a pancake at him. "Help yourself."

"I'm good." He chuckled.

He'd eaten a Slippery Slopes omelet, which was really just a Denver omelet with New Mexico green chile.

"I will miss the chile," he said as he dabbed his forehead with a paper napkin.

"So, what's next for you?" I asked after the sausage sweats started to kick in. I sat back with a sigh and focused on my coffee.

"I was thinking a slice of pie," he said, pretending to look at the dessert menu next to the napkin holder.

I wasn't sure why I pressed. He'd expertly avoided any sort of probing questions since he'd arrived. "I meant after Slippery Slopes and this job for the mayor. Do you have the next assignment lined up?"

"Callie usually decides what's next. I go where she tells me," he said, suddenly very interested in eating again.

That hardly sounded like a solid plan. The way he talked about getting out of here, I thought he had a new job lined up.

"Okay. Right, so, then what're you going to do?" I asked.

"Go where Callie says . . ." He looked confused by my question.

"I guess I figured since her baby is due soon that she might be staying put for a little while. But if Callie already knows your next assignment?"

His eyes flicked frantically from side to side. "Yeah, sure, she'll have the baby, but that's like what, a couple weeks? And then I'm sure she'll be ready to get back to it. She gets restless too."

Restless. Was that what he called his fear of ever being still?

"You guys haven't talked about it?" I asked.

"Not really. Immediate bed rest wasn't really her plan," he said with a growing frown.

"No, right. Of course not." Better to shift to safer ground as he all but eyed up the door to run out of there. "You guys met in college, right?"

"Yeah, she lived off campus and let me crash with her when —for a while," he said, shifting in the booth, flicking a look out the window.

"Where was this?"

"California. Then, when she graduated, we started making films together. This tourism commercial niche was only ever meant to be temporary until we could make real films."

"Real?" The waitress came by to top off our coffees, and I thanked her.

"More than travel tourism videos and commercials. Callie has always wanted to make documentaries that move people."

"And what do you want?"

"To be where Callie is."

"Are you in love with her?" I asked bluntly. My heart needed to know. Not that it mattered or that it would change anything, but it might help explain why he'd always kept himself so guarded, always on the move. It would make sense. This reluctance to be away from her.

He looked up at me, his entire body totally frozen. Then he laughed like I'd told the funniest joke. "No. No. Men and women can be friends without it being sexual."

"I didn't say it was sexual."

"You really do need to renew that feminism card."

"Here we go." I rolled my eyes. "Don't deflect. Callie."

"I'm not in love with her. I do *love* her. She is the most important person in the world to me. She helped me through a rough time. We are each other's person." He rolled up the corner of his paper mat between his fingers. "Why do you keep making that concerned face?"

"No, I'm not. It's nice to hear things about your life," I said, and it was true. I was desperate for any scrap of his backstory.

"Oh. I guess I don't talk about it a lot because people always think I'm in love with her. Because I'm a man and she's a woman." He said this last part in a mocking tone.

"Okay, I get it." I frowned again. "I feel like I overshared like crazy last night. I meant that it was nice to hear you talk about yourself. That's all."

"You were great last night. Drunk Natalie is somehow even more adorable." I bit my lip to keep from smiling too widely at the comment. "You talked about your memories with your folks and what they were like. I liked hearing about it."

I smiled. "I liked being able to talk about them. Thank you," I said, but realized my voice lowered.

I looked around.

"Nobody can hear you," he said, and it filled me with shame. "Is there something else on your mind? Something you want to get off your chest?"

I bit my bottom lip. I had thought I dreamt my confession, but had I really spilled the beans?

"You told me about Deckard," he said.

I winced, hoping that I had imagined that slip. I shouldn't be surprised. I tried so hard when I was sober not to give too much of myself away to him. With lowered inhibitions, I was surprised I didn't confess far more incriminating information. But this was my biggest burden yet. It was so easy to share about myself with him, but this confession cost me so much. What he must think of me. What I must seem like to him.

And yet even in my anxiety-riddled worry, I still felt a slight sense of relief from sharing with someone. Even if it wasn't Deckard, like I'd planned. I lowered my voice again, looking around.

"I can't believe I told you that. That's honestly my biggest shame. Bigger than the Thinking Place. I feel like at any moment somebody is going to come forward and call me out for being the horrible liar that I am."

"I'm not judging you. It's nice to know that you aren't completely perfect."

I snorted. "If you only knew, I'm so far from it."

I clenched my fists; the buzz of sharing was addicting. Once I started with Miles, it didn't seem like I could stop.

"I know it just makes sense to be with him. Deckard. Especially now, because the whole town thinks that I saved him. But I didn't. It was just such a misunderstanding. I *had* been looking for him that day. I was upset about . . ." My eyes fluttered to him and then quickly away. "Something. I was going to ask him out."

Miles frowned but didn't speak. I wondered if he'd put together that it was when he had left the first time. I'd been determined to forget about Miles and finally ask out Deckard.

"When I came around the corner, somebody was already there. I had no idea who it was. I was lost in my own thoughts. I thought that they were hugging Deckard? Looking back, I realize they were giving him the Heimlich." I couldn't admit that I had been thinking about Miles. Hiding from the town because I was tired of being on and wanting to just move on. I thought that Deckard would help me with that. That our mutual respect might lead to more. "I couldn't get a good look at who it was, and they certainly didn't want me to see them. I called out a hello when I realized what was happening, and for some reason, the other person ran." I shook my head, trying to remember more details, but it had been late and dark, and I was only fairly certain it was a woman, but that was all I knew. "Deckard has no memory of what happened, but I'm just waiting for that to come out too. I feel like I'm living a lie, and I can't escape it. Deckard thought I'd been the one helping him. I told him that there was someone else, but he insisted it was me. And then Mayor Sparks and all five of Miles's sisters came around the corner. They had heard what happened, and they were so excited they wouldn't let me talk. I don't know if you have ever been around six very grateful and excited women, but it's hard to get a word in edgewise."

"Once or twice in Vegas, but we don't need to talk about it," he said with a cheeky smile.

I snorted at his stupid joke, obviously said to help break the tension. "I did try to tell them, but they didn't listen. They thought I was being modest. The rumors grew like wildfire. This town has us slotted to be some sort of perfect couple, and I can't tell you how scared I am all the time. It's been like that for weeks. I hide all the time I'm not working. I can't stand disappointing anyone. Just one wrong moment and I feel like I'll be living with the consequences forever."

"And you are too afraid to come clean now?"

"I keep meaning to. Especially with Deckard. That was the whole point of all this." His eyes flicked around, brows crinkling as my words settled into him. "I know you think I'm ridiculous for feeling so indebted to this town, but if I think about them hating me . . . I just can't stand it."

"Nobody would hate you, Natalie. This town loves you. They loved you last time I was here and you hadn't even 'saved' him yet," he said, eyes roaming over my face. "I just don't think you should be living your life for other people. I don't think they would want that either."

"I just can't stand the thought of disappointing them. After my parents died, I remember being in the hospital staring at the snack machine and thinking, how would I get money to get food? Where did they even keep money? I guess that sounds pretty horrible when I say it out loud."

"Death is—our brains do weird things in the face of trauma," he said. If he thought the segue was strange, he didn't comment. "I don't think there is a right way when it comes to any of that."

He leaned back now and sipped his coffee, too, gaze far away and thoughtful.

"Yeah. I don't remember a lot of details, but the first thing I really remember is having this moment, like this full, shocking realization, that nobody was coming. I had been sleeping at Maybel's for a few nights, already expending what had to be good income for her. Not just her, but everybody who was helping take care of me. I was sure that her charity wouldn't last forever. And rightly so, people had businesses to run. And it hit me. Like a truck. I sat there staring at the wall and thought, 'Nobody is coming for me.' Nobody was coming to figure it out for me or make it better. I was completely on my own. I was a kid, and while I had some street smarts, this was different. That heart-wrenching pain, that fear, that wasn't going away. Nobody could help. Nobody could make the next choice for me. I was alone. Completely and utterly alone. It was this constant waking nightmare that I couldn't figure a way out of."

I must have been crying without realizing it. Miles scooted to my side of the booth and held me tight. "Oh, Natalie. I'm so sorry. I wish . . ." I looked up when he didn't continue his thought, leaving me to forever wonder what he wished. His thumb brushed a tear from my cheek. "I'm sorry."

I shook my head with a laugh. "I don't know how this keeps happening. I don't normally talk about myself like this. But the town, they were all there. I was never alone." I held his gaze. "I can't disappoint them."

He had to understand why it had to be Deckard. Why this was all so important.

"I understand." A seriousness crinkled his brow as he met my gaze. "I feel honored that you'd share that with me. That you share any parts of yourself with me. And I'm not going to tell anybody, don't worry." He lowered his head and kissed my forehead.

"Gosh." I wiped my nose with a rough paper napkin. "And I don't know anything about you. I don't even know where you live. Wait, am I crazy, or did you say you don't have a place to live last night?"

"I usually crash at Callie's between assignments. Though last time I was there, there was a crib in my room. So I don't know how much longer that arrangement is going to work." He scrubbed a hand through his hair on a laugh, but it sounded hollow. "I actually hadn't really thought about that." I must have had my concern written clearly on my face because he quickly added, "You're doing that thing with your face again. I'll figure it out. Maybe one of those extended-stay hotels."

I was about to offer him my hidden office or even the couch in my apartment. The words were right there, but I knew, I just *knew*, instinctually, that if I offered him a place here, he'd be running out that door and back to his hotel room faster than I could say twigs in a blanket.

"Where are you from? Do you have any family you can stay with?" I asked instead.

He shook his head. "I'm from a tiny town in Ohio. I don't talk to my family anymore. I, uh, sort of had the opposite upbringing of yours. Very strict religious parents, they essentially kicked me out when I was a teenager."

"What?" I asked, shocked. He'd shared his tragedy like it was completely normal behavior for parents to reject their children.

"Yeah. It's not that interesting. I met a girl online. I wasn't supposed to be online at all, so that was another big strike against me. I was never an easy kid to raise to begin with. Asked too many questions. Struggled with rules. And when I told them I loved her and was going to be with her, they told me that if I left, I wouldn't be able to come back. And I never did." He shrugged as though he spoke about an event as casual as deciding not to have pie after all.

"Miles, that's terrible. I'm so sorry." I grabbed his hand under the booth and squeezed. I had so many more questions, I didn't know where to start. "It's terribly romantic. The woman you met online," I clarified. "Don't tell me it was a catfish thing?"

"No." He huffed a laugh. "Thankfully. It easily could have been though. I did go to California. Alina was real and a sophomore in college. I crashed with her for a few months. It was great for me. I went wild, like a sort of Rumspringa, I guess. And way more permanent. But more than that, I felt like I was finally learning who I was. Getting to see all the things that I'd missed out on. But then Alina's school found out. Someone in her dorm ratted us out. To be fair, it was super illegal living with her. I wanted to get a place off campus and start our life together, but she told me that she was too young and wanted to focus on school."

"Oh, no." My heart ached for young Miles, finally learning about the world and already experiencing the pain of it.

"She was right though," he said with a clearing of his throat. "We were babies. And I had lived such a sheltered existence— she had to teach me how to use public transportation, among a hundred other things. It wasn't fair to put all that on her when she was just starting her own life too. It was too much to ask of anybody, let alone at that age. But yeah. I found a listing for a place. That was Callie. The rest is history. I traveled and saw almost all of America and other countries. Had my mind blown wide open. So, I guess to answer your original question, even if my parents wanted to talk to me again, I couldn't go back. I've seen too much. I wouldn't want to."

"Thank you for telling me all that." We were shoulder to

shoulder. Close as could be, physically but so much more. I wasn't sure how we'd gotten here.

"I guess I had a similar moment, as you did," he said. "When I was looking for a place to live and had nowhere to go. I knew I couldn't go home. I knew I was meant to travel and learn, once I'd had a taste of it. But I was so scared. And so alone. And again, I thought like you did, this like *oh shit* moment, nobody is coming for me. I am the adult now." He laughed. "I don't think I've stopped feeling that way."

Every bit of me yearned to take his pain away.

"Miles, I'm so sorry."

"It's okay. We both did okay, right?" he asked. His Adam's apple bobbed. "We will continue to be okay," he said.

"You're right." I smiled up at him.

"Orphan buddies?" he asked.

I coughed a surprised laugh.

"Too soon?"

"You're ridiculous." I leaned into him, resting my head on his shoulder.

His comfort was a balm to all my biggest fears. I'd never felt so secure as I did when Miles told me it would be okay. I wished I could give him that feeling of safety in return. But he wouldn't have that here or anywhere.

Not until he was ready.

I wanted him to lean down and kiss me. The desire to feel his lips again was stronger than ever. He, on the other hand, looked seconds from panicking. Had it really been so hard for him to share that? Did he think that I would judge him?

I put my hand on his cheek, noticing how he trembled before relaxing against me. If we weren't meant to have this connection, why did it feel so easy to be together? Why was sharing every piece of myself as natural as breathing with him?

I didn't know what I wanted as clearly now. Things that felt so important before were becoming hazy. But this. Touching him, talking to him, I didn't want it to end.

"Natalie." He said it almost like it pained him.

"Yes?" I whispered.

Our faces were hovering inches away from each other. He lowered his head. I wanted to kiss him. I didn't even care that we were here in the middle of the diner. Who was I?

"I want . . ." His eyes bounced back and forth between mine, reading me, waiting for me to stop him, but I didn't want to stop him. I wanted this.

"Yes . . ." I said.

I closed my eyes and pushed ever so slightly forward to make my choice clear. I wanted to kiss Miles here, in the center of town, in a busy diner, and consequences be damned.

A soft exhalation met my lips as my pounding heart shook my whole body.

But then. A beat of silence. Nothing. A whisper of cooler air.

"Natalie." He said my name again, but this time all the tenderness was gone. He was brisk and professional.

I opened my eyes to find him moving quickly out of the booth to stand.

"What—"

"Deckard's here. He sees us." Miles wouldn't meet my eyes. He quickly pulled some cash out and placed it on the table.

The whole thing flipped so quickly that there was no time to process.

I glanced to the door. Deckard was smiling and waving, but he hesitated, like he wasn't sure if he should come over.

I didn't want him to come over. I wanted to understand why Miles was looking like the building had caught on fire, and he needed to get away. But of course he was. This was all so confusing.

The decision was made when Miles waved Deckard over to our booth. My heart crashed to my toes. "Hey, man. How are you?" Miles asked, his aloof persona back in place.

"How are you guys doing?" Deckard asked, looking between us, shooting me a little wave because I was apparently still too dumbstruck to speak.

Why had Miles invited him over? Why had he popped our perfect bubble? My mouth was still parted in surprise. At least Deckard was used to my awkward silence.

"I have to head out, but we were actually just talking about you," Miles said.

"We were?" I asked, going unacknowledged.

All the thrilling anticipation that bubbled through me just moments ago dissolved, leaving only emptiness. Surely, he wasn't about to do what I thought he was going to do. That had always been the plan. Things were meant to be a certain way, but then he came and found me, and we shared, and that meant more than whatever was causing him to run.

"Oh, yeah?" Decked asked affably.

"Yeah, Natalie was wondering if you have plans on the Fourth of July?"

"Miles," I said without thinking, a harsh smile in place as I tried to get him to look at me. This wasn't how this was meant to go. This wasn't what we'd discussed. This wasn't even what either of us wanted anymore, was it?

If Miles heard me, he didn't react.

"I'm not sure. I don't think so. I'd have to check. Why?" Deckard asked me, smiling warmly.

"That's the Governor's Ball. Natalie wants to take you." Miles tapped the table where he'd set down the money. I was frozen in shock. If I called him out, he'd only leave faster. As it was, he was already glancing at the door, desperate to escape.

"Are you sure?" Deckard asked me, looking hesitant.

Miles refused to meet my gaze. He mumbled a goodbye and walked away without looking back, leaving out the front door of the diner.

Deckard started to speak again. "I'd heard actually that you might want to ask me, but then it's been weeks, so . . ."

"I, yes, I had been about to. I just—"

Through the window, I watched Miles retreat down the street.

"Well. I'd like to go with you. Shoot me the deets." Deckard shook his head. "I don't know why I said it like that."

"Sorry. I will, if you—I need to go. Sorry!"

I didn't look back at Deckard as I hurried out the door. I couldn't imagine how confusing that whole scenario had been for him, but I found I couldn't care about that right now.

I'd gotten what I'd wanted all along, but I'd never felt worse.

Chapter 22

Miles

WHAT THE ACTUAL FUCK WAS THAT? WHY DID I DO THAT?

I was such an idiot.

Anger burned like wildfire, ripping through my body. I rubbed at my chest as I walked quickly back to my hotel, where I could hide from the dipshit-ery that had been the last few minutes.

She'd just been sharing again and so upset, and it killed me that I couldn't take her pain away. And so I started talking. Talking about shit that I never talked about. I wasn't that guy. I didn't want her knowing about my pathetic past and my even more pathetic reliance on a married lesbian who was slowly cutting me out of her life.

"Miles!" Natalie shouted from several yards behind me.

"Shit," I muttered, not slowing my steps. I couldn't have her see me like this. Couldn't let her know just how out of control I felt right now.

My heart raced as I rounded another corner, walking

without thinking. Thoughts pounded through my skull so hard I barely knew where I was going.

She'd been looking at me like she wanted to kiss me. And I wanted to kiss her more than anything in the entire world, and I thought that if I could do that, then maybe being here wasn't the most insane thing. Maybe kissing her was a truly good thing I could do in my life. What could I have done to deserve her looking at me like that, like I was . . . worthy of her lips?

But then he'd walked in. Deckard. The good man. The right man for her, and I knew it was a sign from the universe. No more practicing on me. No more being the fill-in for the real thing. This was over. Her assignment was accomplished and so was mine.

There was no need to be near each other anymore.

I felt so sick I wanted to die.

If she reached me now, I had no idea if I would push her into his arms or pull her into mine.

She was going to be pissed. She had her plans and her scripts and her certain ways of doing things, and I just threw them all out the window.

"Miles! Seriously? Wait!"

Well, I was pissed off too. What was she doing looking at me like she wanted to kiss me? Was that going to be practice too? I was just a stand-in. And what was the point of her asking me all those questions? What had she meant with all that?

I kept letting myself get closer to her. We were toying with each other, to no good end. This didn't feel like friendship, this felt like torture. I wasn't going to be here. I wasn't staying. The plan was to get her with Deckard. So why did I feel like I was the one who drank last night, seconds from losing my breakfast?

I stopped and spun back to her as she came to a stop before me. Her hair flew wildly all around her, still smelling as it had when she'd just gotten out of the shower. Knowing that she had been naked and soaking a few feet from where I woke up this morning was worse than the pain in my back from falling asleep in the chair like that. She would have tasted like heaven. I wanted to drop to my knees and worship her.

It was at war with myself. My mind and body wanted the same thing, but some fucked-up sense of chivalry kept me from giving in. Wherever that part of me lived, I wanted to cut it out of me.

"You had no right to do that," she said, low and with venom.

"Isn't that what you wanted? Wasn't that the plan?" I asked, trying to keep my voice level even as it shook.

"You know that wasn't—and I—" Her arms wrapped tight around her. "You took the choice away from me, and that wasn't okay."

"The choice of what?" I asked.

Maybe if she admitted it to me here and now, that I wasn't alone in this, that I wasn't losing my mind all on my own, then we could . . . I didn't know.

Her mouth opened and closed, her gaze moving all over my face, looking for something. Her chest rose and fell quickly, and she swallowed whatever had been on her lips.

"Of how I asked him. When I asked. You shouldn't have done that."

"There was never a choice," I said and held her gaze. Anger melted into something worse. Something like hurt. "I was helping you. You were never going to do it."

She looked like I'd slapped her, but she didn't argue with me. A group of parents and kids with backpacks walked past us.

"Can we not do this right here?" she asked.

"God forbid anybody see that you're a human being with feelings and not just Tour Guide Barbie," I spat.

It wasn't fair, not after what she'd just shared with me. But I panicked and lashed out like a trapped animal.

Her brows furrowed. "You aren't going to be here. I have to live here." She jabbed a finger at her chest. "You've made that abundantly clear, so yeah, excuse me if I don't want to share my dirty laundry with the town."

"Me being the dirty laundry? Right?" I was the thing she was ashamed of. "Only I get to see the ugly truths."

It was a low blow. I saw the moment I crossed the line, her hand went to her chest, and her brows crumpled in on themselves.

"I'm sorry. Fuck!" I turned and kicked the air. "Can I just go? I don't want to be around you right now."

A mother from the group that had just passed turned around and came back. "Natalie, are you okay?" she asked, putting herself between us.

God, I felt lower than low. I was mud on the paws of a guinea pig. A passing woman thought that I was the exact man that I had been trying to protect her from just last night.

I tugged on my hair, unable to explain why I felt so out of control. I didn't want to be like this; this wasn't who I was. I didn't care. I sure as hell didn't feel.

"I'm fine. It's fine. Thank you, Janet," she said.

"I was glad to hear that you asked out Deckard. We all hoped you would. You deserve a good man." She squeezed Natalie's shoulder before she walked away. The woman, Janet, turned and shot me one final warning glare over her shoulder.

"Word travels fast," I said sulkily when it was just us.

Natalie's eyes welled suddenly. She blinked rapidly at the ground. "I don't understand what has happened. Please, can we talk?"

I didn't understand it either, but seeing the hurt written all over her features crushed any other emotion that had been motivating me. My brain screamed to leave her there, to let her follow the correct path back to Deckard and their white-picket-fence life, but something much louder, much scarier rooted me to the earth. This desire to help her, soothe her, hold her, just be near her overwrote every rational thought I had.

I spun on my heels and started walking.

When I could tell that she wasn't coming, I called over my shoulder, "I'm heading to the Thinking Place. Are you coming?"

* * *

As soon as we were inside, she laid into me. "That was an extremely asshole thing to do."

"Brand consistency." I smiled without emotion.

I crossed my arms and nodded. I'd take the lashing and then go lick my wounds in private.

"No." She shook her head. "I don't think so. I think you were trying to make me angry," she said.

She stepped forward.

I shouldn't have come here; this was a mistake. Being in this close space again, knowing that she'd made herself come to my words a few feet from where I stood, it was too much. I should have left her there at the diner with Deckard. Well, I tried to. She had followed me. She insisted on talking. Always with the talking.

I should leave. I should go back to my hotel room and get out of this town.

Like I did last time. Like I always do.

"I was just giving you what you want," I said, hands balled into fists at my side. "You know, I've never understood what it is about him that is just so irresistible. Aside from the manners, and the charm, and the charitable efforts, and the overall attractiveness." I grunted. I guess when I said it out loud like that, it was all so extremely obvious.

"He's here. He respects this town."

"You care way too much about what this place thinks."

"You wouldn't understand because you've never stuck around long enough for anything to matter to you."

"You aren't wrong." I swallowed down the hurt. "But at least I'm not lying about who I am or what I want just to fit into a place."

"That's true. You've always been extremely up-front about being a huge asshole," she spat.

Her words hung in the air. The truth was what she needed to be reminded of, and now she could leave me be.

She swallowed and lifted her chin, not backing down. Somewhere along the walk back here, her anger had returned in full force.

Well, good. So had mine. Anger was easier than longing for a life that could never be mine.

"You know what? No. That's not true. You're not an asshole."

"Yes, I am," I argued, realizing with every word just how juvenile I sounded.

"No. You're not. You compliment me, you take care of me. You worry about me. If you were truly the horrible person you want me to believe you are, then you wouldn't do any of that. I know a thing or two about hiding who you really are. Except you hide the man who cares for me. I think this is all what *you* want," she said.

"Oh, yeah? Please tell me how asking the town's Perfect Son out for you is what I want."

"Because you are a chickenshit."

My mouth fell open. Partially because what the fuck? But partially because hearing her talk to me like this, being her most true self in her safe place, was disconcertingly sexy.

"I'm not the one who can't be honest about a stupid misunderstanding, but I'm chicken?"

"Yep." She tilted her head. "You wanted me to get mad rather than ask you any more questions."

Her words agitated me. They vibrated their way under my skin, like an itch I couldn't reach. It made me overstimulated and unable to hold back.

"You think I want this? I hate this," I said, shaking out my hands. She didn't flinch at the sudden rage that burst out. There was a serenity to her features that only made me feel more out of control. She wanted to talk, then we would talk. "I didn't ask for any of this. I don't want to be thinking about you all the time. I wish you didn't occupy my every free thought. You go against everything I want. I am fighting with myself all the time. And part of me fucking loves it. I can't stop wanting you." I grabbed at my hair and tugged. "And I don't know what part of me longs for you when sometimes my anger toward you feels just as visceral as my desire. Where my mind is the one counting up arguments against you, and at the same time also remembering the exact sound of your laugh and the shape of your lips. I'm being split in two. I made a promise to help you get another man and it makes me fucking sick. So no, I'm not getting what I want."

Her chest was heaving as I finished my outburst. Her eyes were dark, but her features were a mask.

"I know that I'm a placeholder and I absolutely hate it," I said.

"You want me?" she asked.

"What?" I asked, voice hoarse from the outburst. Of all the things to have responded to, that's what she wanted to have clarity on?

"Yes. Of course. All the fucking time. Have I not made that abundantly clear?"

"No, Miles. You haven't." Her gaze fixated on a place on the wall for so long that I wondered if she was over this conversation. "Then we should do something to release the tension between us," she said. "Because if it wasn't abundantly clear, I want you too, Miles. Badly." She stepped forward, swallowing. "I think about you all the time too."

I frowned, shook my head, and stepped back. "I'm not staying here, Natalie. I'm not. We've both been clear about this from the beginning. You didn't do anything wrong. I just—when you're so close and we're talking—"

"I know. I feel it too. It's confusing." She matched my steps, not letting me retreat or avoid this tension between us.

She was taking the head-on approach.

I was terrified.

The anger that burned through me moments ago raged in a new way. My heart thundered through my whole body. I couldn't tell if it was the anger I had for myself, or the rage I'd directed at Deckard and Natalie, or the fact that I wanted to take Natalie and fuck her against the wall so that I was all she could see. So that I dominated all of her senses, so there wasn't a fragment of room for anybody else.

I nodded, backing up toward the door. If I didn't leave now, neither of us was getting out of here untouched.

"It'll be less confusing if we release some of the tension," she said, like she was solving a math problem.

"Natalie, I don't think—"

"Then stop thinking."

She stepped forward, closing any remaining distance between us. She wrapped her arms around my shoulders and pulled herself higher, her breasts pushing into me. Her warm, soft body was everything my tense, cold, distant one was not. Her sweet smell filled my nose as the warmth of her melted the last bits of my willpower. She hesitated, hovering right below my lips.

"I'd really like to kiss you," she said. "I understand that

you're leaving. I don't think it will change anything, but if you don't think—"

I met her mouth with mine.

There was no easing into it. It was the unleashing of weeks, more like months, of pent-up desire. Our mouths clashed and our bodies crashed. My head tilted so I could taste more of her. I grabbed her back and pulled her tight to me. I reached for her ass and squeezed her closer. I devoured her. I wanted this to last more than two frantic minutes, and kissing like that was trouble.

I released some of the tension held tight in my body and softened my kiss. She sighed in between licks, letting go of whatever final barrier was in place. Our tongues became more languid as they explored each other, and she matched my shift in tempo. I cupped the back of her head and brought her closer, thumbing the edge of her jaw. She moaned with me as she found out how hard I was. The fantasy I had described to her was coming to fruition. I wanted to make that and so much more happen.

We kissed and kissed, and my hands roamed her. She held my shoulders, my back, anywhere she could get purchase to keep me tight. She trembled, and it shattered any residual control I had over this moment. There was only making her feel good. There was only tasting her pleasure.

Our lips parted when she stepped back to lift her shirt up and off. I was on her neck in an instant. Kissing where her shoulder met her throat, then lower, her collarbones, the middle of her chest between her breasts, inhaling her everywhere I went.

"Can I?" I looked up at her, hand hovering over her breast. It felt moot to ask permission at this point, as I had been lavishing the area inches above only moments ago.

"Yes. Please touch me everywhere."

I unhooked her bra and threw it to the side. I cupped her

breasts, tugging on her nipples to see how hard she liked it. She liked it when I pulled them enough to lift her whole breast up, and the erotic joy that brought me shot straight to my hard cock.

After lavishing her chest, we walked back until she hit the definitely-a-sex-chair. She fell back, and her curls were wild around her. It was a million times better than the call, and I felt like a king. I was overwhelmed by this fantasy come to life. I had no idea where to start. She helped narrow down my choices as she bit her lip, hands going to her waist to shimmy out of her jeans. Her cheeks were flushed, eyes dark as she watched to see what I would do next.

"Beautiful," I said.

She was truly a goddess, naked and on display before me. My eyes roamed every inch of her, unable to stay on one place for too long.

I dropped to my knees and stared at her long legs, the smooth beauty of her body like a buffet before me. I felt shaken by my yearning for her. I needed this to be wonderful for her. I needed her to know how badly she deserved to feel good in her body.

Starting at her ankles, I slowly slid my hands up her legs, caressing and teasing more sensitive areas as she responded to them. She gasped when my thumb brushed the back of her knee, and I stopped to press kisses there. She muttered my name, growing more restless with every second.

"Dreams do come true," I said as I put her feet on my shoulders.

She was smiling when I looked up at her from where I hovered above her core. My mouth watered, longing to taste her finally, but I tortured us both a little longer. I ran my thumb along the crease where thigh met leg. I brushed my lips, too softly, over her pussy, causing her to groan and arch closer. Her blond curls grew tighter around her hairline, where sweat was forming.

I tested her gently with an index finger that came away soaking.

"Good. You're so wet. So good," I encouraged her between kisses.

"Miles," she cried. Finally, after neither of us could take any more, I devoured her. My fingers, first one and then the other, found their way into her. Her muscles pulled them deeper as I licked and sucked on her clit. My body was hot and tight, attuned to her pleasure. My hand and mouth were soaked with her sweet desire. Sweat dampened my body as I tensed, her body coiled around me as she rode my fingers and face higher and higher. I listened to every sound, felt every muscle for clues of her needs. She squirmed and groaned until she roared out my name on a final gasp for air and then went silent.

My name, screamed from her lips, was a sound I would not soon forget. It was incredible. My ego had never been bigger than when I did that for her. The aftershocks of her peak helped my fingers slide out. I kissed her thighs and stomach, breasts and chest, making my way above her. My cock was hard against my jeans, pressing into her belly, and she reached for it. I groaned as she worked me over my clothes, and a wildness took over.

"Take off these pants," she demanded. "I can't get enough." She groaned with frustration.

I stood too quickly to divest myself of my jeans and boxers. I wobbled a bit when the blood rushed from my head, and she giggled. When I looked up, her heavy gaze watched me, chest heaving as she playfully drew her fingers across her breasts. She was so beautiful lying there, once again, sated and breathtaking.

I was out of control. Desperate and needy. She was too beautiful. Too soft and smelled too good. The taste of her would be in my mind forever. I would never be free of her now.

I climbed back over her body, positioning myself above her again. We kissed for a long time, until she was arching and rubbing against me. Her hot, naked skin slid against mine, and our bodies were needy for friction. I wouldn't last long.

I balanced in this awfully awkward position, one arm holding me up as I hovered above her. Her hand went back to stroke me. Her thumb moved over the tip, finding precum to rub all around. I groaned and shivered in pleasure. She brought her thumb to her mouth, her pink tongue peeking out to sample my taste.

"Natalie. Fuck."

The sight almost undid me. I closed my eyes and clenched my jaw. I'd never been so out of control and needy.

My whole body shook, from the strain of holding myself like this, but also from the incredible need to take her fully, bury myself deep within her. Every part of me burned.

"Miles, if you want—" she started as she slowly brought one leg up to hook behind me.

"I don't have condoms." I swore. I should always have a condom on me, wasn't that Guy Smarts 101? No, that wasn't why we were here. That wasn't my plan. Wouldn't that make things far more confusing for both of us?

She shook her head, biting her lips, cheeks flushed. "Just come on me." Her hands went back, her fingertips gently spread across her chest. I whimpered without meaning to.

"Fuck, Natalie." I stroked once down my cock and squeezed.

She ran a hand over her chest, and I almost came right then. "Here," she said.

"Fuck. Are you sure?"

She nodded and blinked slowly, full of wanton sensuality.

I pushed against her wet and swollen lips, coating myself,

using her to help me get off. I thrust against her, rubbing against her clit. I rutted her, as out of control as I'd ever been.

"God, that feels good. If you keep doing that, I'm going to come again," she groaned. I held her hands as I frotted against her, lost in every sensation. She was too good. This was all too good.

"Oh my God, Miles," she called out as she came again. She laughed in delirious nirvana, seemingly surprised as my entire body shook above her. She was beautiful. I wanted her so much. I couldn't find one place on her to keep my focus. My Natalie, so, so good. Those tits and that mouth of hers, and her face and waist and hips. It was too much. The final thread holding me back snapped.

"Fuuuu—"

I painted myself over her chest and breasts, coming harder than even the last time when she helped me. A deep, primal voice told me that I was marking her as mine.

"You're right. This reading chair is amazing," I said, panting.

She threw her head back and laughed.

Chapter 23

Miles

BEING IN LOVE WITH THE WOMAN I SET UP WITH ANOTHER man meant I was in a perpetual state of agony.

For once, I was acting in Natalie's best interest and wants. God, it was so stupid, and I hated it.

Everything was easier when all I did was care about myself.

Natalie was so hard on herself about a white lie that could easily be explained away. But even if that misunderstanding hadn't happened with Deckard, she'd still want to be with him, because she thought it was what the town wanted. She acted out of fear. Not that I was much better. The thought of losing Callie and the life I knew was behind every asshole remark I made.

Why was it that when things went to shit, they really went to shit?

By the time I got back to my hotel room after that glorious afternoon with Natalie, my phone had been dead for hours. As soon as it had enough battery to come back to life, I was inundated with very unhappy texts from Callie, wondering where I was.

Every time I let myself have a piece of Natalie, I was slapped in the face with the reminder that what we had could never be.

Callie informed me that she never got my last batch of files. This final group that meant I could finally leave. The good news kept coming when I discovered the images I'd uploaded to the shared site got corrupted before Callie downloaded them.

"You always check to make sure that they worked," she said.

"Yeah, I know, Callie. Thank you."

She winced, all humor gone from our previous conversations.

"Dammit." She winced again and rubbed her stomach.

"Are you okay?" I asked, even though I was still pissed at her for treating me like a distracted child that couldn't do his job.

Though, to be fair, I had been distracted, and I hadn't done my job. The one thing I was meant to be doing out here.

No, that wasn't true. I'd also been meant to get Natalie a date and at least I had succeeded in that because I was a stupid fucking dipshit.

"I ate food, and my body is rejecting it. I don't eat food, and the little leech rejects it. There is no pleasing this unborn creature," she said.

"Well, I can't imagine getting all worked up and yelling at me is helping the little leech?"

"You can't call the baby that. Only I can call the baby that."

"Fine."

"Find those files, Miles. This isn't the time to be messing shit up."

"Jesus, Callie. I know that. You're not *my* mother."

Not being able to have Natalie already made me short, fighting with Callie sucked the remaining wind from my sails. I hated when we got testy with each other like this. It was a sure sign we were both over a project we'd been working on and were anxious to move on to something else. We had ended the call abruptly, and I felt like a huge ass for being so short with her. But I'd let myself get lost in Natalie and in this town. I wasn't ever meant to be here. I wasn't meant for this life and it was fucking everything up.

For the next forty-eight hours, I was consumed in files, phone calls, and searching for things. Every file on my computer was searched and scrubbed. The pressure of everything slipping out of control compounded on me, making me anxious and tense.

It was a lost cause. I had to run around town and try to get footage that corrupted. The mayor was not pleased. For whatever reason, she had it in her head that I was trying to stay longer in this town on their dime.

Like I had any desire to be here any more than I absolutely had to be.

Maybe I had been distracted. Maybe this was exactly what I was meant to be avoiding from the beginning.

Natalie and I spoke in short, awkward bursts. I wasn't pushing her away after we'd been so intimate, but this was exactly what I'd been avoiding. I knew I'd mess things up. And instead of finding any sort of relief in our time together, it only made me want more of her. It was a small sip of water, only to find I'd been more dehydrated than I ever thought. I would never be sated.

Callie called on video.

"Just checking in—wow, you look like shit."

"Have you slept?" Mags added at Callie's side.

"I've been working for the last forty-eight hours."

"Miles. I'm sorry I was so impatient with you—"

"I just want to be back at your house and put this whole fucking town behind me."

Every moment that ticked by, a growing panic gripped my chest at the end of this trip.

"You must be ready to get back on the road," I said, hoping for any spot of good news.

Mags and Callie exchanged a look.

"I'm going to take a walk," Mags said, waving goodbye.

That wasn't ominous at all.

Mags left, and I focused on Callie. "I know you usually plan these things, but you know, on account of making a human, I thought I could try and look into some options."

She opened her mouth like she was preparing to argue.

"Okay, sure, you probably have a job lined up, no doubt," I added.

"Miles. You know that once the baby comes, we'll have to change things up a bit, right?"

"Yeah. I mean, we can figure out milking stations or whatever you need." I stood up and paced the floor of the hotel room as I gripped the phone. "Actually, having a baby around might make it easier to get people to open up and talk to us. After all, who can say no to a baby? Nobody. It'll be good for the little kid, seeing the world, traveling the country."

But even as I said it, I thought of Natalie and her experiences growing up and how hard and "other" it made her feel. Would it even be safe for Callie and Mag to travel all over the country with a baby? I would be there though. I could make this work.

As if Callie could see my mind working on overdrive, she held up a hand.

"Miles, I can't travel for a while. And even when I physically can, I don't know that I want to. It's going to be hard for the three of us for a while. We need to figure out a whole new way of existing."

Three of us echoed loudly in my head. I hadn't been part of their plans. I wasn't technically even related.

"Your life doesn't stop because you have a baby," I said.

Why was I the one having to tell all these women things they should have learned long ago?

Callie pushed herself up in bed with a wince, and a stab of guilt hit me. "Of course not. But it changes things irrevocably, and I have to acknowledge that too. I want it to. I'm ready to be still for a little while."

My throat was suddenly so tight I felt like it was the only thing stopping the acid from churning up from my chest.

"You're just going to stop traveling? Stop doing what you love?"

"Of course not. But it will look different now. You didn't think we would carry on as we were, did you?"

I ground my back teeth, looking away.

"You did. It's hard living on the road all the time. It's not for everyone. That's not even a life I'm able to do as well in my thirties. It's beginning to take its toll. Let alone adding a kid to the mix. We chose this neighborhood because of the schools, because we planned for the long term here."

"So that's it? Our entire business is over? Without telling me?"

"Nothing's over. We will still have plenty of work. And hey, after this thing for Slippery Slopes, you'll probably have offers for jobs way better than I could get you."

I sat back down in the chair; I felt like I would tip over if I didn't. I dropped my head into my hands. Without fail, when things changed, it was the same for me in the end. Alone. Always alone.

"Miles?" she asked. "Are you okay? I am sorry if this is

coming as a shock to you. But you are always welcome to stay with us when things settle down."

"I thought I lived there."

Her eyebrows shot up. "This is news to me. I must have missed the part where you paid for things or got your mail here?"

I scoffed. "I make up for it with unceasing charm and gutter cleaning."

"You are weirdly good at that." She smiled again. "Miles. You stay here sometimes before jobs, but this isn't your home."

"I mean, sure, technically, I didn't live there. But it's the closest thing I have to a home."

The confession broke my voice and caused her features to crumble.

She shook her head. She looked bone-tired and weary and I knew this was a terrible time for this conversation, but what the fuck was I supposed to do now?

"What the fuck am I supposed to do now?" I asked.

"Miles, I love you. You will always have a place with us. I will always love you. Mags will always tolerate you. But you are thirty-two years old. You need to have a place of your own to live. Or at least a roommate who knows they're your roommate."

I glared at the floor. "This is ridiculous."

"I won't stop being your best friend just because things are different. But life changes and shifts."

"Yeah," I said.

But I didn't believe it. First, it was this, and then I would go weeks without talking to her, and then I would be down to a hastily written email giving me updates on her life at four a.m. That's how this worked.

I knew that. That was why I was always the first to go. To leave. Because being left behind fucking sucked.

"I know. I'm sorry. I was being an asshole. Of course, you

stay there with your family, and I'll be the one to travel." I shook my head to clear my self-pity.

"Are you sure you're okay?"

"Of course."

"Look. I'm in so much pain and quite frankly, I don't even think I have the wherewithal to say this any other way, so I'm going to say something and you might feel an instant defensiveness, but I have to get it out, okay?"

"I'm already having so much fun, why not," I said dryly.

"One person cannot be expected to be everything to somebody else. Even if they love that person with their entire being."

"I don't know why you feel the need to tell me this . . . I know that."

"Do you? Look at me."

I saw now why Natalie had a hard time meeting people's gaze. It wasn't easy when they were stomping your heart out.

"I love you, Miles. I will always love you."

"It's not you, it's me, huh?"

Throat tight, feeling sick. Feeling like the world was zooming out around me. It was my parents kicking me out again without even a tear of remorse. It was losing my whole identity and family within weeks. It was Alina in the quad, telling me that I should find my own place to live.

"This isn't a breakup. Not even close. You and I are destined to be in each other's lives forever, but I've probably let us lean on each other too much over the years. I'm saying not one person can be everything to someone else. It's not fair to either party. It ultimately makes for disappointment. Look at Mags and me. We love each other to the moon and back, and this baby like nothing else. But I can't fill the hole where her weird sports ball games are. And she will never understand our love of the film world. It's not fair or reasonable to expect that. And even this little baby will need me, be reliant on me, and one day he will have to go out into the world and find his own people because even Mags and I can't be everything to him."

I swallowed.

"It's like . . . we are all so complicated and yet filled with these missing puzzle pieces. It's why we need communities and friends and families. It can't all be left to one person or that person will be suffocated under that pressure. We are each too heavy for someone else to carry the weight of us alone. We need to share the load. Like making a movie."

"Okay, I get it. I feel like this isn't just about you and me."

"It isn't. Things are changing here, but you've changed too. I see you. I hear you. And I saw those videos. You have feelings for Natalie, Miles. I've never seen you like that. But I think you think that you have to be this perfect, infallible person to be worthy of her, but she obviously trusts you. She's letting you see something in her that nobody else sees. She's sharing her load with you, but she isn't expecting you to take the whole thing."

"I want to be everything. I want to be perfect and be the perfect man because that's what she deserves," I said, knowing I could never be enough.

"What she deserves, what we all deserve, is to find people who love us exactly as we are. People we feel safe with, even when we are scared."

I shakily voiced the thoughts that were stuck in my head. "I've never been still. I've never stayed. I leave everybody in the dust rather than feel anything at all. What if I fuck it all up and I'm stuck in a town that hates me and lets wild animals run the streets?"

"Oh yeah, that guinea pig thing is really weird. I forgot about that," Callie said.

"Right? And nobody talks about it." I dropped my head back. "See, you get me."

"I do. And I always will. Even as the external stuff changes."

"Look, I don't want to talk about this right now. I have to go send these remaining files."

"Miles." Callie looked ill.

"I'm fine. I gotta go."

We ended the call, and I felt even more like shit. Callie's accusations sat heavy on me.

"I couldn't ever be enough for Natalie," I mumbled to myself. I pulled at my hair, and my eyes burned. The hotel room was completely dark, and the bright light of my laptop screen was blinding me. My head was pounding, and my eyes were strained. I should take a break to eat something, but every minute that passed, I felt like punishing myself more.

I couldn't stay another moment in this godforsaken town.

There was a knock at the door.

"Jesus, what now?" I grumbled to myself. "What?" I yelled to the door.

"Hey, uh, Miles? I was wondering if you had a second to talk?"

"I really don't, Gabe."

There was a beat of silence. His voice lowered but also somehow lifted in a whispered yell. "It's just that Oz and I went out last night and we were at this club down in—well, that doesn't matter, but I sort of and then he—actually is there any way I could—"

I pulled open the door so the whole floor wouldn't have to worry about his sex-ploits.

"Listen. Gabe. I really do not have time for this."

Gabe's face fell. "I just thought, since you've been so helpful with—"

My phone started buzzing in my hand. It was Callie again. Giving me more life advice probably. "Fuck me."

"And I really am not sure what to do—"

"Jesus, kid, don't you have a friend you can talk about this with? I'm kind of busy."

Gabe stepped back, color rushing to his cheeks. "A friend?"

"Yeah, somebody who you're not hired to assist that you can talk to about this shit."

"I thought that's what you were." He backed up, fumbling as he tripped over his feet. "Sorry. I—you're right. I overstepped, sir. I apologize."

My phone started ringing again in my hand. "Shit," I swore, looking down at the number. I didn't have time to feel like such a jerk. I didn't have time for any of this. The pressure of all these entanglements felt like the barbed tendrils of a vine shooting up from the earth and tying me to the ground.

I went to call after Gabe as he walked away and tell him to come back later, but he was already gone around the corner.

"Hey, Callie. Look. I know I fucked up. I'm trying to find the files now—"

"Miles, it's Mags. My phone died, but I wanted to let you know we had to go to the hospital."

"What is it?"

"Just get here as soon as you can."

Chapter 24

Natalie

I CONTEMPLATED THE DRESS HANGING IN THE CLEAR BAG IN my closet. The ball was next week. The work was all but done. Miles needed a few more shots, but the flimsy excuse that he needed my help had run thin. He might even be done. Our time together was at an end, and it made me feel sick and shaky. I'd protected myself as best as I could.

It was a beautiful gown. The rich purple shade complemented my skin and hair, and it made me feel beautiful. Looking at it should make me happy. Deckard and I had chatted briefly about the color to determine what he should wear. The conversation was stunted and awkward. Great sign. Totally made the right decision. I didn't even lie to myself about telling him the truth. Whoever it was that had really helped him either must have moved on and left town or didn't want to come forward. My secret would be safe.

That should make me happy too.

It was very thoughtful that Deckard had even considered

my dress as he picked out his suit for the Governor's Ball. But of course he had. He was a thoughtful guy.

It was the reason I still had plans to go with him. It hadn't helped that Miles had fully retreated again. If telling me about his past sent him over the edge, then what we did together pushed him past a point of no return. It had been days since he last messaged me. But I hadn't reached out either. Too afraid to be left unread, like last time. Too afraid of how much our time together meant to me. Our mutual release in The Thinking Place was supposed to get him out of my system, but all it did was cause me to imagine a thousand other ways we could get each other off.

I touched my lips, thinking of him. Thinking of how amazingly he took care of me.

My feelings were addictive and out of control. I wasn't even mad that he'd put distance between us again. We both seemed to sense that it was necessary. When we were together, no matter how much logic we preached, our bodies had other ideas.

Nothing had changed. Not really. Aside from our physical relief.

Actually, that hadn't been helped at all either. Having him over me, coming on me, it only made me want him inside me desperately. Those weren't the only thoughts I kept having on repeat. I replayed how much he made me laugh, even when I didn't want to admit it. How comfortable in my skin I felt when I was around him, even when I was fully annoyed by him.

This distance was good. My aching heart was terrible.

Outside, lightning illuminated the sky, followed immediately by a crash of thunder. These all-out spring storms weren't uncommon this time of year, but they were still unsettling. Anytime nature reminded me of her immense power, it made me feel small and lonely. I thought about calling Rochelle just so I wouldn't have to be alone with my thoughts.

I needed to tell her how I'd crossed just about every line with Miles and how I'd been fooling myself to think that we could just be friends.

I wasn't going to take Miles to the ball. Miles was scared and leaving. Deckard was here and just what I needed. At least for the dance.

I held the dress up in the mirror over my body, standing on tiptoes. I'd been so sure about it when I tried it on in the store, but when I pictured Deckard on my arm, it felt all wrong.

A knock at the door made me jump higher than the booming storm had. Another crash of thunder, and my hands were shaking by the time I got to the door and peeked through the curtain to see who was there.

"Miles." I threw open the door to find him, shoulders hunched and a far-off look on his face. Rain soaked through his jacket and dripped in rivulets off his head. "What are you doing?"

His red-rimmed eyes peered up at me, tormented and tortured.

Miles in a towel had nothing on the vulnerability of the scene in front of me. He seemed so young and shaken as he stood there, rain battering his hunched shoulders.

"I-I wasn't sure where to go. I didn't have anybody else—"

"It's okay. Come in," I said and tugged at his soaking, ice-cold hand.

Something was very wrong. His reactions were delayed, and his thoughts seemed a million miles away.

"Stay right here." I ran to the bathroom closet and grabbed a few towels. "Are you okay?" I asked, tugging off his jacket and hanging it up. I couldn't care about the water in my entryway when Miles looked so forlorn. "Did something happen?" I used the towels to dry him as best as possible. His lips were blue, and he started to shiver.

"Callie is at the hospital," he said flatly.

I gasped and wrapped the towel around his shoulders.

"What happened?"

"Her baby is coming. Something is wrong with her placenta or blood pressure or something, and they need to give her an emergency C-section now."

"Is she okay?" I asked hesitantly.

"I-I don't know." His voice cracked—the first sign of emotion outside his catatonic state. "Mags couldn't talk long. They were prepping her for surgery. She said she'd text when she could. Callie's mom was coming too." His eyes went wide and wild, looking past my shoulder.

"She's going to be okay, Miles." I rubbed his shoulders through the towel, trying my best to warm him up. "I know it's so scary not knowing what's going on, but the doctors are professionals who are trained for this. She's got the best care, I have no doubt, and she's going to be okay," I said.

He finally met my eyes and nodded. "You think so?"

"I do." I held his gaze for a moment until he seemed to take in my words fully. "But I'm sure you're anxious to get to her. Let me just get my coat and my keys." I spun in a full circle, trying to decide what to do next as my mind raced. I couldn't stand seeing him like this. I had to make it better. I had to try to soothe his worry. "I'll drive you to the airport. You shouldn't drive in this weather. Not like this."

"I couldn't get a flight out until the morning. There was nothing else tonight," he explained.

I stopped my frantic search for my keys, which were apparently already in my hands.

"Oh. Okay. So no ride?" I asked. He came here for something then, and I was having a hard time understanding what he needed. My brain went into problem-solving mode. "Did you try both airports?" There was a small airport in Santa Fe, but the other closest one was all the way down in Albuquerque. "I can call—"

His head shook once. "There's nothing else even leaving tonight. Not anything I could get on anyway."

"Okay. I'm so sorry. You just come in, and I will take you to the airport first thing in the morning. We can leave as early as you want." Was that what he needed? A ride? "Did you pack anything? We can go back to the hotel and pack."

Again, his head shook once, his throat bobbing. "My bag is in the car."

"Okay. Did you drive your rental over here?"

"My car is in your parking lot."

"Good. Okay." I blinked at him. "Let's just get you warmed up for now. You can try to sleep a couple hours, and you'll feel better in the morning."

"I can't sleep." His arms hung limply at his sides.

"What do you need?" I asked, plainly at a loss for what to do next. Aside from trying to track down a pilot and rent a plane

. . .

"You." Miles stepped closer. "I just want to be near you. Please." His blue eyes were darker than I'd ever seen them. The lashes made little spikes from the rain. He'd stopped shivering, but he still needed to get out of those soaked clothes.

"I'm here," I said.

His throat bobbed as he nodded again.

"Come here," I said, and opened my arms.

It was the fastest he'd moved since he arrived. His arms wrapped around my waist, holding me to his cold and wet body. A shiver ran through me, but I didn't care as I gripped his broad shoulders in return.

"I'm sorry. I'm soaked," he said, but he released a sigh for the ages as I rubbed my hands through his hair. His head lowered again, his shoulders hunched until his forehead met my chest as his nose ran along my collar. His head rocked back and forth across my breastbone as his hands scooped me closer by my backend.

"It's okay, don't worry. I've got you," I said.

He shuddered out another sigh, and his hands began to move.

He pulled me tighter, almost too tight, but not hurting. His head went to my neck. "Oh, Natalie," he whispered, and it sent chills down my spine. I felt ashamed of how quickly I went molten under his touch. He was hurting, he sought comfort, and here I was getting turned on.

He dropped to his knees before me, head now at chest level, as I hunched to hold him to me, to take on his pain so that he could feel some relief.

"I'm sorry. I just need—" he said, his voice heavy with a tension I was getting to know well.

"It's okay." I gasped. My nipples grew hard under my sleep shirt as his ice-cold hand found the hem and slid underneath.

"I just need to touch you," he said.

I moaned some sort of sound as his head continued to snuggle deeper against me, his face fully between my breasts now as he rocked his nose back and forth.

"You're so good. So soft and warm, and you smell so good."

I couldn't speak. Delirious sensations overwhelmed me even as I struggled to know what he needed.

I started to get a better idea. But I was never one to presume.

He pushed up my shirt, and I gasped as his entire palm pressed against my abdomen, the tip of his thumb barely brushing the bottom of my breast. Heat flooded me, and I moaned despite the difference in temperature.

"Is this too cold?" he asked, but he didn't stop his exploration.

"No. It's—it feels good," I confessed.

He hummed a moan of contentment and continued to touch my warm skin everywhere he could. I pulled my sleep shirt up and off.

"Yes." He sighed against my chest. "Can I?"

His hand hovered centimeters from me. I grabbed it and placed it to my exposed breast. He massaged it, cupping and squeezing with one hand as his mouth found the other. He sucked at me, making sounds of pleasure that caused my toes to grip the carpet. I was heavy with desire for him, heat gathering at my core, burning the back of my neck.

I knew now what he needed and what I could do to help him. I'd give him love and support in the only way I could offer.

"Let's get these soaking clothes off of you," I said, my whisper soft but full of implication.

He leaned back, hand balanced on my waist as he tilted his head to meet my gaze. My hand cupped his face, and he turned to nuzzle into my palm and place a soft kiss there.

We didn't speak anymore as we both moved into action. We had a new plan. We always had been such a good team. We knew what the other needed, even if it took a minute to figure out.

"I didn't come here for this. We don't—I don't want to make you feel like that's why I came here," he said as I began to peel his soaking layers from his body.

"I know. I want to, Miles. I've wanted to since the first time you came to town."

He whimpered and it melted me. "You have no idea how long I've wanted this, Natalie. You have no idea. But I don't want you to—"

"I know, Miles. I know, and it's okay. I know in the morning you have to go, and I know that you are worried about Callie. Let me help you. Let me make you feel good, like you have made me feel good so many times."

"I don't deserve you. I'm not—"

"Shh." I tilted up his chin. "That's enough talking, I think, for a while."

The thing with having rules and setting boundaries to stay away was that it meant there was a desire to be together in the first place. And I had been setting and breaking boundaries with Miles since I first met him. It was ridiculous to think that everything wasn't always leading to this moment.

All pretenses of the last few weeks melted away. We both wanted this so badly and had wanted it for so long. We couldn't get close enough, fast enough. Our hands were greedy for each other.

He slid down my pants and stayed on his knees as he kissed me and licked me. "Let's go to the bed," I said, even as I held on to his head, not wanting this attention to end. He teased me up to great heights. I was already so swollen and wet for him. My whole body was tense and on edge with desire.

His eyes burned as he took a break to look up at me. His eyes were blacked out, and his mouth was shining.

He nodded and lifted me as he stood. I balanced on his bare shoulders, his arms banded around my backside. In any other circumstance, with any other person, I might have felt shame having my ass out on full display, but as always with Miles, I felt like I was exactly where I needed to be, exactly who I was meant to be.

Chapter 25

Miles

I HAD BEEN OUTSIDE OF MY BODY. MY MIND FLOATED UNTIL it brought me here, and all at once, I was brought back to life, to sanity. I was so lost, and she found me, scooped me up, and saved me. Natalie anchored me to the earth when I felt like I might float away.

Everything felt so perfect; there was no choice but to be in this moment with her. This wasn't why I had come to her, but now it all felt right. My body had brought me to her on autopilot, seeking the comfort of her simple nearness. But the second I touched her, I needed more. The moment I felt her desire in return, there was no going back.

I set her down in her bedroom before we tugged our remaining clothes off each other. Greedy hands and mouths were a flurry of activity, desperate to get the job done. We couldn't work fast enough, touch more of the other person. Bumping and jostling awkwardly, but laughing and happy. High on the euphoria of finally giving in.

Once naked, it was like a switch was flipped. We both

settled, calmed. We eased into the hours ahead of us, wanting to luxuriate. Now came the part where we got to enjoy each other.

She stood still for me as I looked over every inch of her, from the smooth curve of her neck to her shoulders, her rounded breasts, the bright glint in her dark eyes. I studied her and the perfection of this moment. My jaw clenched at the sight of her beautiful body. I'd never wanted anybody so badly.

"Miles?"

Hearing my name pulled me from my reverie.

"Sorry. I just needed to look at you."

She blushed and smiled. "You can touch, too, if you want."

"Hmm." I stepped closer so there was nothing between us except my obvious desire for her. "I think I might."

My hand cupped the back of her neck as I pulled her sharply to me, before sinking my fingers into her wild curls. How I loved these curls. I gently combed through her hair, like I had that day in front of the cafe, except with more need now, like I wished I'd had before.

She groaned, letting her head fall back into my hands, exposing her neck to me. I grazed my nose along the smooth column of skin, pressing soft kisses everywhere I went. I traced down her shoulders to lace our fingers together as I brought her in for a deep kiss. Goose bumps followed everywhere I touched, like I had a hitherto unknown superpower.

Her arms wrapped around my neck, pressing her chest firmly to me so that her soft, hot breasts were pressed firmly against my still-cold skin. We both trembled at the mismatched sensation of our whole bodies flush together.

"You're so cold," she whispered.

"I feel anything but," I said as she tugged me toward the bed.

We tumbled onto the sheets, never disconnecting, as though any separation might end this tremulous moment. I pulled the blanket over us, letting her warmth heat every inch of me, further cocooning us from what waited in the outside world.

Under the blanket, I explored her further. I let myself indulge in every inch of her perfect body. I was obsessed with her, consumed by need. I sucked her breasts until she moaned. I would never forget every breathy sound that escaped her. I ground against her as my hands messaged her ass, eliciting more moans. I licked her lips and in her mouth. I couldn't find an area of her that I loved the most, so I made a circuit of my favorite places, lavishing them with all my focus until she was flushed, panting, and crying my name. Demanding more from me.

It wasn't just me who was lost in this madness. She was right here with me. Her tongue chased mine, her hands just as curious as mine as our bodies arched and rocked in a rhythm. It felt too good to be true, but her shouts of need told me, her soaking core told me, her frantic heartbeat matching my own all told me. We were in this together. We both wanted this. No more rules or boundaries or other people. Just us, determined to wring the most amount of pleasure from the other.

I sank deeper under the blankets to make her come with my mouth again. Sweat beaded all over my body as she called my name, pulled at my head, and used my mouth completely uninhibited and wild. Like she absolutely deserved to. I was riding high with confidence as she came apart on my tongue in only a few minutes.

I shook with the need to take her as I came up from below the blankets. I was sure that I was a sweaty, disheveled mess as I licked my lips and looked down on her. But she just bit her bottom lip and writhed in place, dark eyes glinting with mischief. Without breaking my gaze, she reached into the bedside table to grab a condom.

"I love that you are always prepared," I said, grinning.

She shrugged coyly, and she was so fucking adorable I

almost lost control in that exact moment. But we weren't done yet. We weren't even close. I had six hours and I intended to not waste a single moment.

She sheathed me in a condom, and I watched in wonder as she held me, leading me to her soaking entrance. Then, I slipped slowly into her, inch by inch, as she dug her nails into my shoulders.

When I was finally seated deep inside her, it was like fully breathing for the first time. I didn't understand how I had ever lived this long without her tight heat gripping me. Everywhere I touched, or licked, or smelled brought me closer to some intrinsic understanding of life.

I'd never felt so human and vulnerable while at the same time so powerful and fulfilled.

I pushed up on my arms so that I could watch as I moved in and out of her. I thumbed over her clit and delighted as her back arched up off the bed, seating me more fully into her. She was so good and responsive. Told me exactly what she needed.

Just me.

Nobody else.

There was a possessiveness that engulfed me when I looked down at where we met. Nobody else could make her feel this good because I knew her best. I saw all sides of her, good and bad, messy and clean. The tragedy and hopeful joys of the future. I wanted them all.

If I could make this last a lifetime, I would. But we only had tonight.

I lowered to hold her hands as I rocked slowly into her, holding her gaze. My heart hammered in my chest with uncontrolled emotion spilling all around us.

She was perfect and beautiful, and she took me perfectly. Our bodies knew just what they needed. There was little talking. Just gasps, groans, and moans of encouragement.

This could never be enough.

This had to be enough.

I wouldn't think anymore. I sank into the sensations of her.

I came back to myself here and there in glimpses. Hours blurred together. I rocked into her, hands clasped. She rode me, taking the lead on what she needed. We held each other, spooning as I took her from behind. Never enough, never resting too long.

I only paused to take a moment to memorize what her breast looked like in my hand. Or how her stomach flexed as she rode on top of me. I studied how gorgeous her curls spread around us as she lowered her head to kiss me.

This was all there was.

The soft gasp as her back arched.

The responsiveness of her nipple as I sucked on it and then blew air to see it harden for me.

Her hand lowered to where our bodies met, and she broke apart again. Her sheen of sweat made her curls framing her face into tight coils. The heat, the wet, her release, it was too much. When I finally came, it was with the guttural roar of a man who'd spent months dreaming of this moment. I shook. I blacked out.

I kissed her forehead and cheeks and neck and thanked her profusely as her body shook with patient laughter.

"We really are a good team." She sighed as our sweaty bodies collapsed together.

I went a little delirious after that. Temporarily reprieved from my unrelenting need but not sated.

Later, after a short doze, we found each other in the darkness again.

I pulled her back to my front.

I kissed her neck. I was obsessed with her neck and shoulders. I was obsessed with every inch of her.

I never wanted this to end. I couldn't let it end.

I ran my hand over the curve of her hips, up to palm her breasts, waited until she mewed and arched back against me. Then I dipped my fingers lower, rubbed her, and tested her wetness. I complimented her and praised her for being so good. So, so good.

Then I was moving inside her again.

She was crying my name as I pressed on her clit, taking her, feeling her ass as I thrust.

There was no thinking. There was only feeling.

So good.

So right.

So perfect.

Chapter 26

Natalie

I picked a terrible time to realize I was in love with Miles.

But being able to help him would have to be enough.

We never really fully fell asleep. I think both of us were too wound up, even after the release of so much tension. We stared at each other across the pillows. There wasn't a lot of light in the pre-dusk morning, but there was enough that I could make out the outlines of his face.

He was so beautiful. I loved him so much. My heart ached with it, every muscle in my body did. It felt like the beginnings of the flu, which was an awful way to describe being in love. Nonetheless, I was filled with that same anticipatory dread for what came next.

"What time is it?" he asked. His voice was soft, but there was an edge to it now. A far cry from the whispered praise and encouragement from only hours ago.

"We should probably get going," I answered, even as my fever for him grew.

He nodded. The moment reality came back to him was evident in the sudden clenching of his jaw and his brusque movements as he got dressed. His gaze turned far away, his mouth turned down in focus.

I didn't regret sleeping with him. I never would. I didn't even regret falling in love with him, even though I knew what came next. He would leave here and not return.

I had to be realistic about these things.

We loaded my car with his bag and camera. Possibly, he didn't want to leave his extremely expensive equipment in a hotel room with no security team. Or maybe another sign he wouldn't be coming back. We decided it would be best if we took my car to the airport, but made plans to return his rental so he wouldn't be charged any more fees.

We didn't discuss his return. We both knew the truth. His work was finished, and now nothing but flimsy excuses could extend the visit longer.

The drive was silent from the start. All signs of the very vocal Miles were long gone. I knew that he was weighed down with worry, and the temporary distractions that I'd provided last night were just that.

There was probably a proverb along the lines of, "It is better to love and lose yourself to the pain of making them feel better while slowly drowning in your anguished misery, knowing you'll never see them again, than to have never loved at all."

Or something eloquent like that.

The town was still asleep as we pulled out of my parking lot and drove down Main Street. Miles had his head turned to look out the window, and I wondered if he spoke a silent goodbye. Would he even miss it here? I liked to think that he would at least miss me on some level. Even if he wasn't able to return the same depth of feelings. Or maybe he was ready to be gone and leave this place in the dust. I had hoped that our time together, my tours, and his time spent interviewing the locals and filming the best places would have changed his mind.

We'd had an incredible night, and now I had to live here without him.

The silence stretched on, down the long highway to the city. The airport was less than two hours away, but it was still not a close drive. The night played on repeat as the first bright light of early summer rose to the left of us. The stretch of the road ahead reminded me of countless drives from my childhood. It felt so different now. I missed this. I missed the road and traveling. But maybe because Miles was here, the idea of it wasn't so scary. Being with him always felt safe. After so many years of feeling like I was working off a debt, being around Miles felt like taking a deep breath in. Like taking a break from all the heartache. It had from the very beginning.

Our first time together last night had been like a train running off the tracks, out of control. Hot and quick and dirty and amazing. Maybe if we'd stopped there, maybe I could have still convinced myself that it was a physical attraction only.

But then the second time.

I gripped the wheel tighter as my insides fluttered and my heart raced, recalling how he'd seemed to find me in his sleep. How my body was already awake and ready for him before I was fully conscious. How he rolled on top of me and moved slowly, our hands clasped as he held my gaze. It was at that moment that I realized all hope was lost. It wasn't just physical need; my deep affection for him was so overwhelming that I shook from it. The aftershocks of my care still shaking me.

I was absolutely a fool in love.

We were more than halfway there when he finally spoke. It took me by such surprise that all I could do was listen.

"I googled maternal mortality rate in childbirth," he said.

"Why would you do that?" I glanced at him, looking for his phone.

He huffed a laugh, not smiling. "I did it when Callie first got pregnant."

"Is that what you're thinking about right now?" I asked.

"The maternal mortality rate in the US is one of the worst in the world."

"I know. I did something similar when Rochelle was pregnant. It's not helpful to think about it."

"It's worse for women over the age of thirty, and I'm terrified for them."

"It's going to be okay. I know that can't mean much to you right now, but she is going to be okay."

I glanced his way again to see his jaw clench.

"It doesn't make any sense," he said, shaking his head, not absorbing my words. "Why would humans be designed that way? That should be the one thing that doesn't kill us."

"I know. One of the many injustices women have faced throughout history. There are certain things that it just doesn't help to dwell on, and this is one of them. You are doing what you can do. You are going to be there for her, and you are going to support them."

Maybe it wasn't the right thing to say. Maybe I shouldn't promise things that I had no way of knowing, but there was no right thing to say in the face of scary stuff. None of us is well-equipped to handle these things. There was just being there for the ones we loved when they were going through the worst moments of their life.

Like this town had been for me.

"I'm so sorry you are going through this. I'm so sorry for Callie and Mags too." I extended my arm to grab his hand and held it. He squeezed my hand back, and the action caused a tightness in my chest.

"Callie is my only friend in the whole world," he said, the words seeming to tumble out of him. "I'm such a horrible asshole that I literally have no other friends."

I had to clench my jaw to keep from interrupting him. It simply wasn't true, but sometimes people needed to say their worst thoughts out loud, just to hear how wrong they sounded. The thoughts living in our heads held a truth to them that couldn't be sustained when spoken out loud to someone who cares about us.

"I have no family that cares if I live or die. It's just Callie. If I lose her—I can't—" His voice broke off, and he hid his face in our clasped hands, shoulders shaking.

"Miles." My heart broke for him. I'd never heard him so scared, so raw. So unbelievably out of touch with the truth. He wasn't alone. I stayed looking at the road as much as possible. I wanted to pull over and tell him the truth of my feelings, but would that be too much for him right now? All his thoughts were for his best friend. "Callie is going to be okay. You are going to be okay. You need to just focus on one thing at a time right now. You're going to fly to be with her. That's all you need to worry about."

"Callie is going to be okay," he repeated.

"Yes."

He drifted back into silence.

The more we drove, the more frantic I felt to tell him something, anything, about my feelings for him. We couldn't end like this. He couldn't go another moment thinking that Callie was the only person in the world who loved him. Even if he wouldn't ever love me the same way. Even if he went back to Oregon and I never saw him again, I had to tell him. It was my only chance. If he left again without talking to me, I wouldn't be able to handle it.

How could I not tell him? My love for him was exploding

out of my chest. It was desperate to wrap around him and make itself known. It wanted to comfort and ease and take all his suffering away.

Being in love was scary and awful, and yet it was as unstoppable as an avalanche in motion. But love was also the gift of humanity, and it should be spread, not locked down in fear.

When we exited the highway and drove into the airport, I had to make a choice.

"I'll park and walk you in," I said.

"No," he said, so quickly it was like he'd been preparing for it. "No, I—there isn't enough time. Just drop me."

There was time, but I knew an excuse to get away when I saw one.

"Okay," I said.

"Sorry. I just want to get there, and it's making me short and anxious."

I shook my head once, focusing on reading the signs for the departures lane. "No. It's fine, I get it. You just get to Callie."

I came to a stop in front of his airline and got out to help him unload his stuff. He set his bags on the curb. And I pulled him into a hug goodbye.

His whole body was tense, but for a brief moment, he melted into me. "It's going to be okay," I said for the hundredth time, feeling like it sounded so hollow. "We're going to be okay," I repeated his words to me from that day at Deb's Diner.

He made a grunt of acknowledgment, but his body shook as he squeezed me tighter one last time.

We pulled apart, and he collected his things, turning away. The panic gripped me by the throat. If he left now, without knowing the truth, I would never see him again. I knew it as sure as I knew anything.

I love you, Miles.

"Wait, Miles?" My voice shook.

He stopped. He glared at the ground, struggling to meet my gaze. He had to know. He had to feel it too. We were both so scared. But I could be brave for him, couldn't I? Finally, he met my pleading eyes.

My heart was in my throat. A few passersby pretended not to watch as they shot curious glances at the scene unfolding.

He stood braced and waiting.

"Callie isn't the only person who cares about you." I stepped closer, noticing a hovering security guard eager for me to move my car from the drop-off zone. The words were right there.

Just tell him what he means to you.

"The town, Slippery Slopes, cares about you, Miles. A lot."

Liar. Cheater.

His eyes shut briefly, and when they opened again, they were contorted in pain. His throat bobbed. "It would be so much easier if they didn't."

He turned and went into the building. I stared after him in a numb shock. It had hurt far more than I thought it would, even if I knew it was coming. I should have just said the whole truth. But if I'd shown myself anything these last few months, it's what a liar I really was.

Chapter 27

Miles

Callie was okay.

The baby, Otis, was okay, and so was Mags.

It had been by far the worst twelve hours of my life, but as soon as I got to the hospital, Mags found me to give me the news that my uncharged cell phone couldn't receive.

Natalie had been right, saying that everybody would be okay. But the pure terror I'd been living in left my body feeling depleted and vibrating with exhaustive energy. That sort of post-adrenaline crash that left me completely drained but unable to sleep. I was shaken and nauseous and tight with fear that didn't seem to dissipate.

It wasn't until I was allowed into the room and saw Callie propped up, a wrinkly little bundle in her arms, that my breath whooshed out of me in a painful guttural gasp of relief.

"Hi, Uncle Miles," she whispered.

I wanted to make fun of her for such an erroneous sentimentality, but my throat was so tight, my jaw clenched so hard that I couldn't speak.

"Oh, Miles. Are you crying?" she asked as I came to the bed and hugged her.

"Yes," I choked out.

"You sweet thing. We are totally fine. Admittedly, it was a little scary there. But it all worked out and look at Otis. Totally worth it to see this little guy's grand dramatic entrance."

"He gets that from me," I said, looking down at the new arrival.

"He's sort of strange looking," she said. "Don't tell Mags I said that," she added, glancing at the door.

"Like he's gearing up to return soup to the deli counter," I agreed, looking at the baby who was both too old and too brand-new.

"He looks like he wants to give directions to the store, but using only outdated landmarks and vaguely racist comments about the good old days."

I stared down at my "nephew" and decided there and then that he was perfect. "Nah," I said. "He's absolutely perfect as he is."

"Yeah, he is, isn't he?"

We stared silently at him for a few beats.

"Easily the second most handsome man in the room," I said.

"Easily." She smiled up at me.

"Where's Mags?"

"Went to get me some sushi and a turkey sandwich."

"Don't forget some unpasteurized cheeses."

I'd been fully aware of the sacrifices Callie made these last months.

We chatted for a while about various body-related changes that I really didn't want to know about, but we do these things for our friends. Maybe one day, when I was old and gray, I could share about my own bowel movements.

"I'm so sorry I wasn't here sooner. I'm sorry that I was such an asshole on the phone the last time we talked. I'm sorry that I'm such an asshole period. God, I don't know why I'm like this." I dropped my head in my hands.

"Miles, Miles." She grabbed my hand weakly. "I'm okay."

"Fuck. Sorry. I don't mean to be like this. Not when you just went through something so scary and so far off your birth plan."

"Yeah. It was scary. But I'm okay. And it's okay that you are emotional. We were too."

"I just thought—and then the last thing that I said to you. I couldn't—"

"It's okay. It's okay."

"I'm fucking everything up, Callie. It's all I seem to do."

"You're not. You're here and that counts." I let out a shaky breath and pulled the chair to be closer to them. She watched me closely. "What's going on? You have time to distract me before Mags gets back with the food. From there out, my mouth will be occupied."

"Gross. Is that advisable after such—"

She started laughing and held up a hand. "You have to stop." She closed her eyes and took a deep breath. "No jokes right now. Don't even be a little cheeky."

"You're a little cheeky. Literally hanging out in that hospital gown."

"Miles." She closed her eyes to take a patient breath, fighting a grin. "Stop trying to change the subject."

I sighed. "This isn't really the time to talk about me, Callie. Loath as I am to admit it. You just had a pretty traumatic experience."

"So then, just sit here with me. And when you're ready, you can talk."

And then we sat in silence for a while. I watched as the woman who I once saw knock out a full-grown man in a bar brawl hold a tiny little baby in her arms, and she looked so good.

"Are you scared?" I asked her after a little while.

"Yeah. I honestly don't know how anybody does this." She smiled and then looked at the baby. "But here we are as a species. Thriving."

"Brain chemicals, man."

"Are *you* scared?" she asked me.

My throat bobbed. "I am so scared. Just all the time. I am so scared, and I like Natalie so much, and I think I just about messed it all up to epic proportions."

"I didn't know things had gotten that serious with her. I thought you were just distracted on the job, but that isn't fair to you. I was really just terrified about being out of the loop and fearful that this video wasn't going to get done in time. I shouldn't have snapped at you or made you feel like you didn't know what you were doing."

"I'm sorry. I'm sorry I'm such a fuckup. I'm sorry that I couldn't be trusted to finish this one job."

"It wasn't you. It was me. I shouldn't have freaked out about a small mistake. It doesn't matter now. I don't even think I care about it. I mean, I do, but talk about a healthy dose of perspective."

I understood. I rubbed at my chest. The fear of losing her still so fresh.

"She told me the town cared about me," I said about Natalie.

"Well, that's nice."

I dropped my head back. "But that was a code, I think. I think she was trying to tell me that she cared about me."

"Why wouldn't she just say that?"

I sighed. "Probably because all I ever did was talk about how I couldn't wait to leave."

"Oh, Miles."

"I'm sorry, we don't need to talk about this right now. I know this is a horrible time." My throat bobbed as I said it.

"I want to talk about what's going on with you too. Tell me everything. Start from the beginning. Leave out the explicit bits."

"So you don't want to know about coming on her—"

"Miles," she warned.

I told her everything.

"I'm just not built like those people. I'm not really a lover," I said after I finished telling her again about what Natalie said at the airport. "I'm a rolling stone never growing moss."

Callie stared at me. "Is that really how you see yourself?"

"I mean—is that not what you said about me?"

"If I ever gave you that impression, then I am sorry, Miles. The issue is not that you don't care; you don't even have an issue at all. You are a deeply loving, deeply committed person."

"Oh, yeah, all those people around me all the time, I guess I didn't notice." I snorted.

"Yeah. You pushed all those people away though. That's your self-defense we talked about. You love so full throttle that it terrifies you. You probably sensed that you could fall hard for Natalie the moment you saw her."

I remembered how the world seemed to turn upside down the first time I really spoke with Natalie. How it felt like the ground shifted under my feet, and how I spent that first night in the hotel room staring at the ceiling with my heart racing, and I couldn't understand why. I'd told myself that it was just a physical attraction. I'd told myself that I was leaving. I'd gotten so good at telling myself all the lies that I needed to hear to numb out the fact that I had fallen for her almost immediately.

She was incredible. She was funny and thoughtful, caring and giving. She was a little wild and unpredictable and messy.

And she was honest. At least with me. She kept me on my toes, always unsure what to expect next, but somehow knowing exactly what she needed at any given moment.

"I don't think I've ever loved someone like I love her." I rubbed at my chest. "I've been terrified from the very beginning. So scared every moment and not sure why. Scared of loving her? Seems so silly now."

"It's not silly at all. You have been deeply hurt by people who were supposed to love you unconditionally. Your parents, the worst. And then Alina in college. But remember, you gave up everything to be with her. That's not on you. That wasn't because you don't know how to love. It's because you love with your whole being. No wonder you're scared shitless all the time. Love is vulnerability. You're a walking open wound."

"That should really be on a greeting card." I sat back and rubbed my forehead. "I feel like . . . like when I'm with Natalie, I'm wearing my guts on the outside, and with one look or one smile, she would decimate me. Like she could kill me. It really feels like that."

Callie huffed a laugh. "Yeah. Shit. That's love. It's vulnerability, but it's also the strongest thing you can do. Fear, running, anger, hatred—those are all weak and easy. Real strength is in the courage to love with your whole heart like you do."

"How *have* we made it this far as a species?"

She shrugged, her gaze flicking to the bassinet where she'd set the baby down. Apparently, "plastic baby cage" was not the right terminology. "Are you scared?" I asked again, my throat closing.

"All the time. Worse than I've ever been." Her nostrils flared with a watery smile. "But that's how I know it's worth it."

Everything seemed so clear now. Everything so painfully simple. I wanted to be with Natalie. Why would I do anything else? It was the most obvious choice I'd ever made, and at the same time, the scariest thing I would ever do.

If I was already scared shitless, I might as well be so kissing the woman I love.

Chapter 28

Miles

I was used to being a disliked asshole. I wasn't used to staying around long enough to apologize for it.

But if ever there was a time for change, it was now. And I had some serious apologizing to do.

I cleared my throat, palms sweaty as I approached him.

"Hello," I said.

Gabe looked up from the check-in counter at the Slippery Slopes Inn with his usual welcoming smile on his face. As he registered me, a coolness fell over his features.

"Hello, Mr. Asher. We weren't expecting your return. Unfortunately, your preferred room is no longer available." He clicked on the keyboard, avoiding my gaze.

"Hi, Gabe. Don't worry about it." I cleared my throat again. I put my hand on the counter between us, tapping my fingers anxiously. "I owe you an apology. I was such an asshole to you."

"I guess we have another room next to it that might suffice." He blinked up at me, looking guilty.

"Don't worry about the room, Gabe." I quirked a half-smile at him.

He swallowed and shifted uncomfortably.

It had taken me a week to get my shit in order, but I was back in Slippery Slopes, ready to make some amends. "I'm not here for a room. I wanted to talk to you. I'm here to help you. Talk to me, tell me what's going on with Oz."

Gabe looked over my shoulder toward the bar area.

"There's nothing to say," he said with a sniff. "I'm sorry I ever wasted your time."

"Man, I'm so sorry." I clasped my hands, elbows on the counter between us, in a position of apologetic supplication. "When I said that horrible stuff, I was in a shitty place but that wasn't your fault." I swallowed my pride and said the thing that needed to be said. "You are my friend, and I want to help you."

I hadn't ever said that out loud to someone, thinking it would cost me too much, but saying it now felt natural and right. Gabe was my friend.

He finally met my gaze, brows furrowed in cautious hope. "Really? You don't think I'm a pain in the ass. I know a lot of people think that about me."

"People think I'm an asshole." I shrugged.

"Well . . ." He smiled.

"Fair, but I'm working on that. And for what it's worth, I don't think you're annoying. And I think a lot of people appreciate you."

"Thanks, Miles."

"Now, tell me what Oz said last time you talked."

"He's not interested in me."

"Is that what he said? That he's not interested in you like that?" I asked.

"After you left, I ran out of courage, and I've been avoiding him. Which let me tell you, is really hard when we both live in the same small town and work at the only hotel." Gabe shifted on his feet.

When I looked over to Oz, he was looking at us. He quickly went back to wiping off the counter.

"I bet. That was my worst fear, not being able to run away from my problems."

"But you're back."

"I'm back." I smiled at him. "But you don't know for sure, do you, about Oz?"

He shook his head, his hands fidgeting without something to do.

"So then you have to go and tell him. Just put it out there. You shouldn't worry about anything but giving it your all, all the time. Nothing is promised to us. Time isn't guaranteed. Make your feelings known. It will be okay."

"Like you did with Natalie?" he asked coolly.

"I deserve that." I straightened my shoulders. "But I'm here to make amends. I'm here to tell her everything and apologize for being such a chickenshit."

"Good. Because she's worth it."

"I know. And I'm not worthy of her, but for some fucked up reason, she seems to like me. I hope. I'm going to take advantage of that while I can. Until she doesn't want to see me anymore."

Gabe nodded. He glanced at something on his screen. "It's time."

"What is?" I looked around. "What are you talking about?"

"They're leaving. Isn't that why you're here?" Gabe stepped around the counter, and I dropped my bags, distracted. We moved to the front door, and I already heard the rumble of the people outside. I had noticed a crowd gathering as I came up, but I'd assumed that it was just another random Slippery Slopes event, like maybe the Fourteenth Annual Thimble-Balancing

Contest or the Thirtieth Anniversary of the Time a C-List Celebrity Stayed in the Hotel.

Okay, so I was still a condescending prick sometimes.

My heart sank as we opened the doors to the crowd gathering in the park.

"I thought the ball was tomorrow."

"No, tonight. Tomorrow is the free night at the resort."

The sick feeling curled further in my gut.

"Shit." The crowd parted, and there she was.

Natalie was a beacon of light, as always. Tonight, she was more breathtaking than ever. She was always so beautiful, smiling on a tour bus, chatting with locals, gasping my name . . . How could I ever think that I didn't love her when images of her were all I saw when I closed my eyes? But this version of Natalie was on another level. On this warm summer night, she wore a shining satin gown in a rich purple that flowed down her whole body, except for the long slit going almost all the way up her left thigh. She glowed with ethereal beauty; her curls had been replaced by loose waves that flowed down her back. As she fixed her dress, I saw delicately strapped heels wrapped up her ankles.

I swallowed at the sight of her, heart hammering and mouth dry.

The whole town surrounded her as she smiled broadly, but people kept passing between us, and I couldn't see if it was real happiness or a jack-o'-lantern smile.

"Do it, Miles. Before they leave," Gabe said, putting a hand on my shoulder.

"I don't know." If I could only see her better. If I could only know with absolute certainty that this was what she wanted. I'd been so sure of everything when I left Oregon, so sure that she needed to know my feelings. But I didn't want it to be like this. In front of everyone.

If I could just see her. Maybe if she saw me.

But the crowd moved in closer.

She was swallowed up.

I pushed my way in, Gabe at my side, apparently okay, leaving the hotel unattended.

I was almost to her, hidden by a tree, when Deckard came to her side. They spoke quietly.

He was handsome as ever in his suit, perfectly matching her gown. It stopped me in my tracks. He turned to her and she toward him. She grabbed his hands and spoke as her smile grew wide. She had emotion in her eyes. She was happy. It was a genuine smile.

And all at once, that was enough.

The thing about being in love was that there was a frantic sort of impatience to it. I was desperate to start our life together right away. The need to race back here to be with her felt like the most important thing. But now that I was here and saw how incredibly beautiful and happy she was, that felt like enough.

I wouldn't ruin this night for her. This is what she deserved. An evening on the arm of the most perfect man in town for the most perfect woman in the world.

"What's wrong? Why did you stop?" Gabe asked as he came up next to me.

"I'm not going up there," I said softly.

"But—why?" He looked like he was trying to decide if he should intervene, glancing between where the happy couple was and back at me. "What happened to saying what needs to be said?"

I swallowed and looked back at him. "I don't want to ruin this night for her. She looks so incredible. She's wanted this for so long."

Gabe opened his mouth to say something and closed it.

"I love her, but I want her to be happy more than anything."

He nodded.

"If this is what she wants, I'm not going to stop her."

"But she doesn't know how you feel," he said. "Go up there and tell her."

"She wouldn't want me to do that to Deckard in front of his mom and the town. Even if she still has any feelings for me, that wouldn't be the right thing to do. I want to do the right thing for her, for once. I want to act like a man worthy of her love." I let out a sigh, arms dropping to my side. "Besides, my feelings aren't going anywhere. They certainly won't be gone by the time she comes back from the ball."

I swallowed, knowing the truth. My feelings wouldn't change but hers might. She might have the perfect weekend with the man that she's always wanted, and realize that I was never deserving of her love to begin with. I had been so awful for so long, I hoped it wasn't too late to show I was capable of change.

But that was a risk I had to take. If what we had was real, it would keep over the weekend. "Can you do me one last favor?" I asked Gabe. "I know I don't deserve it for how much of an asshole I've been, but it would mean a lot to me."

Gabe smiled. "What do you need?"

"Just make sure she sees this." I handed him a USB, which he took with a confused look.

"It's not a dick pic, is it?" he asked.

I threw my head back and laughed, a much welcome release of tension for the ball of nerves sitting heavy on my chest. "No. No. It's safe for public viewing, but I made it for her. I just want her to see it whenever she can. Later."

He held my gaze for a beat before pulling me into a hug. It took me a few seconds, but I eventually responded in kind and hugged him back. The knot in my chest unfurled a little more.

Friends, turned out, mattered more than the pseudo-safety of solitude.

She was happy, and that's all that mattered right now. I wouldn't ruin the perfect night that she'd been wanting for so long.

I went back to the hotel lobby to grab my abandoned bags and head home.

Chapter 29

Natalie

I was not happy. This wasn't right.

The voice in my head screamed so loudly I almost couldn't think. I had been so excited to wear this gown and get into this waiting limo. I'd felt beautiful, I was sure I had. But now it was all that same shiny facade that I always wore for this town. None of it was real.

So much of the town had come out to support me. I imagined Miles rolling his eyes at the ridiculous scene. Miles. I worried about him. Thought of him constantly. But aside from the few messages I sent about Callie, and to let him know he was on my mind, I gave him space.

I missed our nonstop texting conversations that lasted from the moment we got up until we fell asleep. I missed how easily I existed in my body around him. I missed how I longed for him and desired his touch as much as his laugh and intense focus.

But he'd left.

Here was the future. There were maybe fifty people clapping happily, smiling widely. There were John, Rochelle, and

Olive, all of them smiling for me. Because this was what I'd said I wanted. This is what we had all been working toward. Maybel and Fred, Tess and Conor Finkle. Terrance and Michael. Bee and Owen had shown up, likely in support of Deckard. This was the exact scene that I'd played on loop in my mind. The whole town beamed up at me.

Wasn't it supposed to feel right when you got what you wanted? Weren't all the pieces supposed to fall in place? Look at this town here to support me. Look at this handsome man waiting to take me away. I should be so happy.

But all that kept playing through my mind was, this wasn't right, this wasn't what I wanted. This wasn't true or real because I was living a lie.

Miles had been blunt, but he was always honest about how I let my fears control me when it came to this place.

I felt sick. My palms were damp, but I couldn't wipe them on this satin dress and ruin it. Why would I want to ruin something that I'd wanted for so long?

The mayor spoke to me, but I couldn't process her words. Everyone was here to see me off. I couldn't turn away now. And what would even be the point? Where would I even go? Miles had made it clear that I wasn't worth sticking around for. That his feelings didn't match my own.

I looked to John and Rochelle. Hoping to get Rochelle to catch my eye and tell me what the hell to do. I couldn't go on like this. John was pushing up his glasses and smiling at her, and she was laughing with her whole chest, her hand resting on him. They looked as in love as they did on their wedding day. And for the first time, I understood something about their relationship. It seemed like it couldn't be real, that ridiculous attraction, even after so many years, that desperation to be near each other and tell each other everything. The stupid inside jokes that absolutely nobody else found funny but would make them laugh until they couldn't breathe. Neither of them was perfect. But they were perfect for each other. They fought and changed, and also, they did it as a team.

I understood that now. That was what I wanted with Miles. I'd thought that Deckard represented a perfect pinnacle I could reach. I thought he could make me worthy of this town.

Rochelle broke away from the crowd and came up to me.

"Doing okay, Nat? You've gone all pale," she asked.

"Yes," I said robotically.

"Are you sure?"

I nodded enthusiastically. A smile plastered to my face. "No. I'm not okay. I'm not okay. None of this is real."

"What do you mean? Sure, it was rigged, but that doesn't mean you don't deserve to go." She put a hand on my shoulder.

"What?" I asked as my ears began to ring.

"What?" she asked, her eyes widening. "I didn't say anything."

"What was rigged?"

Rochelle winced. "The drawing. You were always going to win. The town wanted to thank you for everything."

The weight of my guilt almost pulverized me. My knees were seconds from giving out as I pictured myself being flattened like a cartoon meeting its demise by anvil. This couldn't go on. This wasn't right. Miles was right. I lived a lie.

"Excuse me. I need to talk to Deckard."

"Wait. Shit. Don't say that I told you. I kept the secret this whole time," she called as I started to step away. "Did I screw up?" I overheard her ask John, now at her side.

"I'm sure it's fine," he reassured her.

"Deckard?" I said, my voice lowered as I spoke to get his attention. He stood on the outskirts of the crowd, not really talking to anyone. He was a good guy. I hadn't been wrong about that, but he wasn't *my* guy. I knew it all along. I was forcing pieces that didn't even belong in the same puzzle to fit.

"Any excuse to have an event," he mumbled with a shake of his head, and a smile was plastered in place. "What? Did you say something?" he asked.

I pulled him away from the crowd to the quiet under the tree.

He was going to hate me. My knees trembled. My whole body shook with nerves.

"I-I can't go. I'm sorry." I spoke before I realized what I was doing. "Deckard Sparks. You are really like no other."

"So are you, Natalie."

"But—"

His shoulders dropped, and he braced himself.

"I can't go to the ball with you," I said, holding his hands.

"Let me guess. You're in love with someone else?"

"Yes. I love him so much." It was such a relief to say it out loud. "But also, I didn't save your life that day in town. I tried to explain that it was all a misunderstanding, but things got out of control so quickly and . . . well, I don't have an excuse other than to say that I'm sorry."

"Oh. Wow." He looked around. His hand reached to scrub his hair but stopped mid-action. "You know, it was all such a blur. You did try to tell my mom and sisters something when they showed up, didn't you?"

I nodded.

"They can be a powerful force when they're all together," he said, almost defeated.

"I'm sorry I didn't clear the air sooner. I guess it felt nice to be seen as a good person. Even though I was scared most of the time that I'd be caught."

"Who was it then that saved me?" he asked.

"I don't know. I keep wondering that too. I kept expecting them to out me at any moment."

"Huh." His gaze went far away as he put a hand to his throat as though recalling that life-threatening moment.

"You should still go to the ball and take someone you like."

He huffed. "I'm starting to think I'm cursed in that department. I don't think you can fake chemistry. And we don't have that. Wow, truly, the more I talk, the worse I make this."

I laughed and felt lighter than I had in many years. "No. It's true. I think I liked the idea of a guy as great as you."

"I'm not so great. So, can I ask? Is it Miles Asher?"

Thinking of him, I smiled with my whole face and nodded.

"I'll be honest, that day I ran into you guys outside the cat cafe, I had thought you were going to ask me. Truth be told, several people had already told me you'd been planning to, but then I saw you with Miles and thought, I don't even stand a chance. You glowed with him. But more than that, you seemed comfortable in your skin, in a way I'd never seen you before. In a way, I'm extremely envious of, in fact."

He confirmed what I already knew, but it tightened my chest, nonetheless. "Yes. I see now that he was always meant for me. I'm sorry it took me so long to understand."

"It's okay." He awkwardly patted my shoulder.

"I'd better go let everyone know. I have some things to clear up."

"You don't have to tell anybody. I don't think whoever saved my life is going to come forward," he said.

"I appreciate it. But this is something I need to do." We exchanged a tense hug, and I went back to his mother.

Mayor Sparks was speaking to a councilperson, but I tapped her on the shoulder, and she turned, surprised. "Hi, Natalie. Are you all set?"

"Not quite. Can I just say something really quick?" I asked.

"Of course. This night is for you," she said with an amused, albeit confused grin.

I cleared my throat. A tightening panic burned the back of my neck. The terror of having everybody look at me, knowing I was about to disappoint them, made me feel sick.

But I thought of the lie I'd let go on for too long. I thought of Miles and his belief that I was enough. That I shouldn't be living this one life for other people. I didn't need note cards or a script.

I just needed to be honest and be myself.

"Hi, everyone." The group went quiet to listen. My voice wobbled. I stopped. Took a breath and started again, speaking louder. "I can't believe so many of you came out for this. You don't know what it means to me. Ever since you took me in ten years ago, all I have ever wanted was to be worthy of your love." My whole body shook as I prepared myself for what I needed to say next. "But I don't deserve these tickets. I don't deserve to go tonight."

There was a gasp from the crowd as some people tried to argue.

I went on before they could; their protestations would make me feel worse. "The truth is, I didn't save Deckard Sparks. I don't know who did. When I found him, he'd already been helped and was coming back to consciousness. I tried to come clean, but the truth was . . . I didn't try hard enough."

I let the shock settle through the crowd. Murmurs and whispers spread all around.

"I loved the acceptance. I didn't want to disappoint you. I'm so sorry I lied. I know it doesn't excuse it, but I've been so scared of you all hating me." Here I looked at the mayor and her daughters. "I wanted to be enough for you."

"For me?" Ned Fled yelled in the heavy silence that followed.

I laughed with tears in my eyes. "Yes, Ned. And also for the mayor and her family. For Maybel, for Conor. For Bob the grocer. For you and you and you." I gestured to different people in the crowd. "You all saved my life." My voice broke. "I just wanted to be enough, to do enough in return. I just wanted you to love me as much as I love you."

I found Rochelle in the crowd. Her face was contorted in a confused frown.

"I hide parts of myself away because I worry you'll think me unworthy. And the last thing I would ever want to do is disappoint any of you. I can't ever express how much you all mean to me. You saved my life," I said, my voice breaking off as my throat bobbed. "And I think that I've spent so many years trying to prove that I was worthy of your saving."

A few faces in the crowd fell. Rochelle looked sad but not surprised.

"But I can't go tonight. I thought it was what I wanted. I thought it was another way, going with Deckard, to show I was a worthy daughter of the town. I wanted to be perfect. But I'm not perfect. I'm sort of messy, actually, and shy, and I have a lot of pieces of myself that I keep tucked away because I'm ashamed."

"Nobody's perfect," Maybel yelled.

"I know," I said with a head shake. "I don't think I realized how much of myself I hid away, thinking I was wrong or weird. But I'm just me. And some people like that about me. I have a secret room, and I have secret reading habits, and a sugar addiction. Amanda, I don't like cilantro on my tacos."

She looked side to side. "Okay." She shrugged.

"I'm afraid that any minute you are all going to figure out just how weird I am."

The whole town began to exchange looks as my confessions poured out of me. I lost the power to filter myself the longer I spoke. But I felt free. It was like I had been carrying a lifetime of guilt on my shoulders, and all at once, it was lifted.

"Also, I hate being alone on the anniversary of my parents' deaths. I want to be around people and talk about them and their wild life, and I hate that everybody pretends like it didn't happen."

"We thought that was what you wanted," somebody shouted.

"But we will be there next year," another added.

"Can we talk about the secret room?" Rochelle yelled.

"I'm sorry. I'm not ready to share its exact location." Rochelle pouted, and even disappointing her was a new experience for me. But I knew she wasn't really mad. My gaze moved over to Pat, where he stood next to Mel, their hands hovering close to each other. "I just never felt like I fit in here. You're all so warm and welcoming, and I just wanted to be worthy and not the weird little orphan."

"I like to rub softened butter all over my body and go down slides," Ned Fled yelled in support. "Makes me feel young again."

Several people looked at him. A mother pulled her child closer and whispered something in their ear. I imagined it was something about no more trips to the park.

"Okay. Great. Thank you for sharing that, Ned." I turned to the mayor. "I'm sorry you wasted the tickets on me."

"We're all weird." The mayor came to stand next to me again. She spoke to me, but loud enough for the microphone to pick up. "Slippery Slopes: Weirdly Wonderful. That's literally our motto," she said. "That's sort of the whole point. It's why we all get along so well."

"That's what Miles said too."

"The beauty of a place like Slippery Slopes is that it's a refuge for the ones in society who may not feel like they fit the mold, but in those differences, that's where we find our common ground. Our compassion and empathy for one another. We are a community in the truest sense of the word. And one little white lie gone wild won't get you banished like this is some old-timey Western," she finished.

I sniffled, realizing just how badly I needed to hear that, even if the truth set me free. It was still nice to feel accepted.

"Natalie, you never needed to be anything else. We love you as you are," someone else yelled.

After a moment, there was a laugh and then another.

"Those tickets were yours well before you *didn't* save Deckard. We got them for you," the mayor explained.

"I tried to tell her," Rochelle called.

"We never meant for it to be a point of stress for you. We got you this trip so you could enjoy some time alone, away from the town. You never take a break. We thought you could use a little trip. It's not much but it mixes things up a little. You work so hard."

"Oh," I said, shocked. "I appreciate it so much. But I think Deckard should go. Take someone else. Not me. I have something I need to go do."

I'd been such an idiot, so afraid for so long. And for what? Had I really thought they'd chase me out of town with pitchforks? No. But the anxiety had me thinking that their disappointment was just as bad.

And the truth was, I would have been okay either way.

I started to leave the stage when there was another shout.

"Wait, you can't go yet!" Gabe came running up.

"Why? What's wrong?" I asked.

"You don't have to go to Santa Fe, but you need to watch this," he said, panting.

"What are you talking about? I'm sure it's great, but I have to go," I said, glancing around.

My concern went unnoticed as a projection screen was lowered to my left.

I stood, uncomfortable in the high heels I chose to wear, as the footage that Miles had already shown me began to play. The version I'd seen wasn't totally done yet, but it was close enough, and it started just like this, with an incredible aerial shot of Slippery Slopes tucked in its cozy valley with the snowcapped mountains surrounding it, like a dragon curled protectively around its treasure.

"I've already seen this—wait, this is different." The next image was of me walking the Cabezón Trail. I didn't remember that being part of the video.

As the movie played on, an alternate version of the one I had seen unfolded. Except instead of the people of the town speaking about Slippery Slopes . . .

They all spoke of me.

"She's the treasure of Slippery Slopes," Mayor Sparks said on the screen.

I looked to her now, and she smiled at me with a nod. *Told you*, she mouthed.

There were pictures from before I even came here. There were images of my parents and me. Of me as a little girl with curls fuzzing around my head in a golden halo. The crowd oohed and ahhed.

"What is this?" My throat was so tight because this was clear proof that I was loved by not only this town but also the person who made this video.

And I knew who it had to be.

There were so many shots of me, making me look beautiful. The town loved me. I was worthy. I'd been so set on proving that I was lovable that I pushed away the man who might actually love me. Is that what this video meant?

Miles loved me too.

"It's a tribute to you, apparently. Looks like you aren't the only one in love," Deckard said.

"Gabe, where did you get this from?" I asked, frantic, heart racing.

"Miles gave it to me. He wanted to make sure you saw," Gabe said.

"When did he give it to you? Before he left last week?" I had already begun to hike up the train of my dress.

"No, he gave it to me just now. He said he had to go."

"He's here? I have to go!" I yelled, already heading to the hotel. The crowd cheered me on as I ran across the square in heels, forgetting all about the town, the ball, and the man I thought I needed.

Now I had to find the man I knew I wanted.

Chapter 30

Natalie

I had just made it to the front steps of the hotel when I almost ran smack into Miles. He had a bag over his shoulder, and he stopped suddenly.

"Hi," he said, sounding confused and glancing behind me in the direction of the festivities. His eyes moved over me, drinking every inch of me in. I would have flushed if I weren't already red from exertion. "You look incredible."

"Thank you," I said, panting. I stood staring at him in return. His glasses were on, and his messy brown hair was unruly. His broad shoulders and tall frame filled out a simple tee, stretching around the muscles of his arms. I longed to throw myself at him, but there was a rigidness in his stance, a tension in the air between us. My body wobbled forward, seeking him out without my control. "You can't go." I winced, stepping side to side. "And I should not have run in these heels."

"I can't stay here," he said. "What are you doing here, Natalie? Aren't you supposed to be in a limo right now?"

He was hesitant but strangely calm. He wasn't trying to

goad me into a verbal repartee, which was scary, but he didn't seem upset either. He seemed placid but happy to see me. I had to hold on to that.

"I saw your video," I said, holding up the hem of my dress as I came closer.

He rolled his eyes and pressed a thumb between his brows. "Gabe wasn't supposed to show you that yet."

"It was . . . incredible. I can't tell you how much it meant to me. Really," I said, pouring my soul into the words as I held his gaze.

"That's all I wanted." He ran a hand along the back of his neck. "That, and I wanted you to go and have fun tonight."

"I don't care about the ball." My brows furrowed as I thought. "I don't think I ever really did. I just cared so much about what this town thought of me. You were right."

Miles's frown deepened. "It's okay to care about things. I was wrong to make you feel shame about that. Caring about things and all, it's sort of the whole point, isn't it?"

I smiled, sadness gripping my throat and filling my eyes so I could only nod, holding back tears.

We stood staring, neither pushing the other too far. But if he wanted to leave forever, I needed to know.

"Why did you make that video for me, Miles?" I asked. Another step closer. He mirrored the action. My heartbeat shuddered. He was back here again, and he'd wanted me to see that video, and that must have meant that he had feelings for me.

"I wanted you to see how much you meant to the town. You were always so worried that you weren't enough for them, but they have been here loving you this whole time, and you never needed to change," he said. "It was important to me that you understood that. You have always been enough."

I swallowed. "The whole town?" He looked confused, so I clarified. "The whole town loves me?"

"Every single person who lives here loves you," he said, holding my gaze.

Everybody who lived here. That was frustratingly vague and probably a little hyperbolic. Despite her nonchalance, Amanda had seemed bugged about the cilantro thing.

My throat tightened. I looked into his eyes and waited. Had I really misread all of this? Was that video not a love letter? Was he really leaving after everything? We were never going to get anywhere if I was still too scared to admit my feelings. There was no going back. If he truly intended to leave, then he deserved to know he was loved regardless. Just as he had made that video for me.

He pulled his bag over his shoulder. The white knuckles where he gripped the strap were the only sign that maybe he wasn't as cool and collected as I thought.

"I feel like you're being way too calm about everything. I've missed you and you can't leave," I said. My head shook, and I reached for the strap of his bag. "You just can't leave yet, Miles."

He grabbed my hand. "You could come with me," he said softly, his words tight in his throat.

He laced our fingers together, watching the action closely. I wanted to go with him a million more times than I wanted to get in that limo and drive away with Deckard.

I opened and closed my mouth. I pulled my hand from his and held my hands close to my heart.

"I don't know . . ."

I couldn't just drop everything and go with him. That would be irresponsible, out of character. Wouldn't it? Or maybe it would be okay. Maybe I could leave this place and things would be okay? They wouldn't shut the made-up gates. I would still have a home to come back to.

He swallowed, watching me carefully as my mind raced in overdrive. His features still serene, but his hands were tucked deep in his pockets. "I'm not going to make you leave the place you love," he said simply.

My face crumbled. How was he being so calm?

"I was serious when I said that I wanted you to go and have a good time tonight. I want you to be happy, Natalie. More than anything. More than what *I* want. After a lifetime of only making selfish choices, I have come to realize that your happiness is probably the most important thing to me and—"

"Let's go." It wasn't a love confession, but I was done living in fear. I was ready to see where this incredible connection with Miles went. My feelings for him were like a plant that persevered even in the dark, even when I tried to starve and ignore them—imagine how they might flourish if I gave them the water and light that they needed. "I should pack. No. Screw it. Let's go. I have been wanting to take a trip."

"Are you sure?" His head was tilted, bracing but hopeful.

He was so handsome. I loved him so much. All I wanted was to be near him. I knew it sure as anything now.

"Yes. I want to go with you. I mean. I have to come back. I want to live here. This place makes me happy, *and* I want to be with you too. Both things can be true," I said, mirroring his words to me. A genuine grin began to crack his cool facade. "I would like to make that work somehow. We can try one step at a time. If you think you'd like that." My heart was hammering harder than it had when I stood in front of the whole town. "I love you, Miles," I confessed. "I should have told you that day when I dropped you off at the airport, but I was so scared. But I do. I love you and I want to go with you. But I do also love this town, and so if you leave—" My voice grew too tight to go on.

"You love me?" he asked, his sheepish smile growing.

"Yes."

"Okay. Great." The light in his face beamed through a full-wattage smile, and I let out a long breath. He reached for my hand and threaded his fingers through mine again. "Well, then let's go. I'll make sure you are back in time before your tour on Monday."

I was lighter than ever, almost out of my body with all the adrenaline coursing through me. He hadn't said I love you in return, but this was enough for now. If he needed time, I wasn't going anywhere.

"Okay," I said.

I couldn't stop smiling. Anticipation hammered in my heart as we walked back through the crowd to cross the town square. All at once, everyone noticed my return, saw his hand in mine, and the massive smile on my face.

I felt him shoot several questioning glances at me as we walked, as though he was sure that any minute, I would release his hand and realize my mistake. That wasn't about to happen. I squeezed his fingers harder and smiled up at him. I was proud to have his hand in mine. A few people in the crowd catcalled or whistled. Actually, I was fairly certain that Rochelle was behind most of the lewd comments.

We walked for several more minutes before my feet really started to hurt. These were not walking shoes. "How far did you park?" I asked hesitantly. "Not to ruin the big romantic moment or anything."

"We're here actually."

He stopped in front of a car I didn't recognize, parked next to the curb of a side street. "Since when do you drive a VW Bug? Is this your rental?" Flower decals decorated the exterior of the eccentric car, and crystals dangled from the mirror.

He laughed. "No. This is." He turned and gestured to the small house behind us.

My eyes took in the home we'd stopped in front of, too distracted as I was to notice where he'd taken me.

I laughed, waiting for the catch, knowing he wasn't cruel enough to taunt me like this.

"Very funny," I said.

It was my dream house. The one I never committed to looking into past finding out who the owners were, because I never felt worthy of staking a claim. I was always waiting to be asked to leave, like a partygoer overstaying their welcome.

"Not joking. It's my Resting Place. For the next two months at least," he said. "Or maybe My Staying Still Place. I haven't decided what I like better."

"Wait, what? Are you serious?" I asked.

"Just signed the rental agreement this morning. That's why I almost missed your exit. I got my dates all mixed up with this and the ball."

"Miles—"

"The owners are eager to sell it. If you know anybody. I'd love to stay here once the lease is up, but if somebody else were to buy it, maybe I could find a way to stay." He looked pointedly at me, dipping his head as the reality of all this set in.

I pressed a hand to my chest. It was too much. He was staying. He'd rented my dream home.

All this for me?

"But why didn't you tell me?" I asked, dumbfounded and confused, happy and scared to hope too much.

"I had planned on it, but then I saw you with Deckard, and I wanted you to have the ball, and God, you look so beautiful—I didn't want to take that away from you." His nerves began to show through now, and he pressed a thumb between his brows as the words tumbled out of him. "Plus, there's no rush. You look, seriously, so incredible. Did I already say that? Because I'm not going anywhere. I'm going to stick it out for a while here. I figured I would just tell you how in love I was with you after you danced the night away."

I mentally stumbled through his words as he spoke them, that last line filtering through.

"You love me?"

"Incredibly. Forever. It's incurable, I'm afraid," he said, holding my gaze.

"How are you so calm right now?" I let out a huffed laugh. I put my hand on my chest. My racing heart beat hard back.

"I'm not. I'm terrified. But also, I've lived in fear for so long that when I finally just decided to lean into loving you, it was the easiest thing I ever did. I want to start a life with you, Natalie. I want to come home to you in the evenings and wake up to you in the mornings. I want to be buzzing around you so much that I drive you crazy. Until the only way to shut me up is to kiss me. I want to love you and build a life here, and I am willing to wait. Even if you want to take your time, I will still be here."

"I can't believe this. What changed? You really want to stay?" I had so many questions. So many more things I wanted to hear and discuss.

"I just realized what really mattered to me. That I had been making every single choice out of fear instead of out of love. I want to be braver like you. You've made me a better man since the moment I met you, Natalie Weatherby, and it feels like an absolute miracle that our paths crossed. How could I not at least try? How could I be that afraid that I would let go of the most wonderful thing that ever came into my life? Actually, I am more scared than I've ever been, but also more sure. And so I think that confirms I'm making the right choice," he said with a small shake of his head. "It's confusing. Ask Callie to explain."

He dropped his bag on the front step before turning to grab my hands. "I know that I love you and that I want to be with you. And yes, fine. This weird little town has grown on me too. I have all these friends now, and it's a lot."

I huffed a laugh even as my eyes welled, and I felt shaken with relief. "You poor thing."

He shook his head with a frown, looking at the ground. "No. Actually, I might be the luckiest man alive. I feel like I've been given a second chance at life. I want to stay and be scared and feel all the things rather than run away and feel nothing. I'm sorry it took me so long to understand that. And I'm so sorry I was such an asshole."

"You weren't—"

"Don't try to deny it."

"I wasn't going to." I squeezed his hands and placed a kiss on his nose. "I was just going to say you weren't any worse than I was. We were both so scared. You missed it." I thumbed back to the direction of the town square. "But I gave a hell of a speech. Came clean to the whole town and then some."

"Did you now? Good for you. So your secrets are out."

"Yep. And you were right. They still love me. And even if they didn't all love me, I think I'm learning to love me. All my many facets. You make it easier to see that I'm worthy of that self-love because I was my absolute worst self around you, and that never seemed to put you off."

"You know, I thought it was hot," he said in a low growl. "I loved getting to see all the parts you kept hidden. It made me feel like I might actually be worthy of something." I pressed up on my toes to kiss him, a soft brushing of our lips, but it promised so much more. "So you told them where the Thinking Place is?" he asked.

"Let's not get too out of control." I stepped forward and grabbed his shirt to yank him closer. "I still need a place to meet you to . . . relieve some stress."

His hands slid down the cool, smooth fabric along my back, sending shivers through me. "That's fantastic news."

"I'm sorry I held on to the illusion of Deckard so long. I knew before the drawing that I didn't want to go with him. But I was still so hung up on you from the first time you were here."

"I know. God, I wasted so much time. I'm so sorry." His forehead dropped to mine. "I knew that first time I came to Slippery Slopes that I was falling for you. From that first meeting. I was kidding myself. So scared to put myself out there only to be rejected again. See. All adults are faking it. We are just a bunch of scared little children coping the best we can."

"I was so sure that nobody would love me as I really was. I was determined to hide my real self from the world. But you always saw me. You brought out the worst in me, in the best sort of way."

He laughed. "I have a habit of that. And you made me feel safe to love again. To try and stick around. I'm so lucky to have found you."

"Me too. And I don't intend to let you go anytime soon."

Chapter 31

Miles

Natalie giggled when I scooped her up and carried her over the threshold of our new home together. Not to presume, but God, how I hoped.

"I love this place so much, it's even better than I imagined," she said as she kicked off her shoes and looked around the front room. "It's even more adorable inside." Her eyes searched the area greedily as I held her in my arms.

"The stuff in here is mostly the owners'. But it's nice since I don't really have anything," I said. "It's like a practice run for real home ownership."

Natalie grabbed my face and turned it toward her. "Nothing about this is practice. This is all very real."

I kissed her and poured all my love into the kiss.

"You're sure you don't care about missing the ball?" I asked, still worried that I might be taking from her when all I wanted to do was give. All I wanted to do was make her smile this glorious, genuine smile.

"A silly little country dance? Please. Nah, let Deckard go

with whoever he wants. It was never about the dance," she added softly. Then her gaze moved from my mouth, around my face, and back to my eyes. "We should break in the house."

I swallowed, already feeling my body tense for her. She was incredible in that gown, but I couldn't wait to peel it off her. "I think that is a brilliant idea. But first, let me give you a little tour."

I set her carefully back on her feet, sliding my hands over her neck and shoulders as she shivered, biting her lip.

It wasn't a big house, but it would be plenty for us. She smiled and nodded as I made up a tour on the fly. I'd rented it with only a virtual tour, surprisingly, with the help of Rochelle. She was a big fan of my grovel plan.

"Here is the kitchen, originally built in 1975 and refurbished last year."

"Really?" she asked.

I shrugged. "No idea. But I sound like I know what I'm saying, don't I?"

She nodded seriously. "You should give professional tours."

"Yes, I'm known for being a real people person."

She threw her head back and laughed. We toured the rest of the cozy space: a living room, a kitchen, and two bedrooms, but I saved the guest room for last.

I held her hand as I flicked on the light. She gasped and held her hands to her mouth before laughing. "Is that my not-a-sex-chair?"

"No," I said seriously. "It's *my* definitely-a-sex-chair. I bought one for here. Because it's such a versatile piece of furniture, I needed one too. But this room is yours. I thought you might like a place of your own. A Thinking Place 2.0."

"Oh." Her mouth fell open as she saw the rest of the space. The small guest room was a larger, brighter version of her Thinking Place. Built-in bookshelves lined the walls.

"I built these shelves," I lied. "Okay, fine, they were here, but I knew you'd love them. You have your own bathroom. I don't want you to feel pressured to give up your own space. But I wanted you to feel safe and welcome here."

"I love it," she said and grasped my hands. "But I don't think I'll need it. I needed the Thinking Place to hide. It was where I went when I couldn't breathe under all the masks I was wearing. But I don't need to wear those masks now, not all the time. Or at least not so many. And certainly not around you."

"I'm glad. You are wonderful as you are. There is no reason to be anybody else."

"Thank you. I'm starting to understand that."

"I guess I'll need to start reading then," I said. "Since you don't want this room. I could put the camera equipment here—"

"No," she said, quickly covering my mouth with her hands. "I'll still need a reading room, don't get me wrong."

I smiled. "I don't want you to feel pressured to stay here. But I would love it if you did. Tonight, and every night."

"Miles. I want to be here. I want to be with you. You make me feel like I'm coming home. More than this town ever has. I feel safe with you. And I want you to feel safe with me. I love you just as you are, and I'm not going anywhere. Wherever that takes us." I couldn't help the tightness in my throat as she spoke. I had been so afraid to let myself love, so afraid of being rejected again, but the unmitigated joy her confession brought me was more than anything I could have ever dreamed of. "I knew from the moment I first met you. When you left the first time. I was . . . bereft." She rubbed a circle above her heart. "I felt like a piece of my heart left with you, and then I felt so embarrassed that I'd grown so attached to you in just a few weeks. But I think a part of my soul just knew you were meant to be in my life."

I brought her close and dropped my forehead to hers. "Me too. God, Natalie, I'm so sorry. I knew it too. The first minute I spoke to you. And it terrified me. I wanted to run away faster than I ever had. But I also couldn't wait to be close to you again. I always felt at war with myself when it came to you."

"Let's try and find some peace then, shall we?"

"I think so. I didn't know real love would feel like this. It snuck up on me. I'd been doing such a good job of living in safety, but it turned out I wasn't even living at all. I'm ready to be scared for a while. In the best sort of way. You have my entire heart. Please be gentle with it."

"Oh, Miles." Her voice cracked. "I don't know any other way to be. Let's be here now."

"Good idea. Plus, I have friends here." I sighed and rolled my eyes. "Honestly, it's so exhausting being so needed."

"You and Rochelle are really going to hit it off." She laughed.

"I probably have some apologizing to do to her, and the town too."

"I think anybody who saw that video you made me has more than forgiven you." Her brows furrowed. "Did you get the project done for the mayor?"

"Yep. She even has another job lined up for me. She knows the mayor of a town in Illinois looking for something similar."

"Oh, good." Her smile wobbled only a little.

"But I told her I'm on a sabbatical for a few months. Until I can convince you to buy this house and let me stay here."

"Good. We are going to need all the time." Natalie smiled, and we kissed. When she pulled back, she said, "I'm going to cut back on my job a little bit too. I want to relax and know what it feels like to settle into a home without always being afraid too."

After that, we didn't talk for a while. We made great use of the new reading/sex chair. Then we made it back to the bedroom to carry on and make up for lost time. We worked through several more fantasies she had tucked away without the rush or fear of when it ended. We luxuriated in each other, in the ways our bodies felt together.

We slept until halfway through the next day.

By sunset the following evening, we were ready to hydrate and take a break. We sat on the small porch, hand in hand as we sipped canned margaritas.

"This is perfect. I cannot tell you how often I imagined this exact moment," she said.

Her contented sigh brought me more joy than any choice I'd ever made. I had brought her some happiness.

I always thought loving somebody would feel like a burden, but instead it felt effortless, necessary. Meeting her needs was easier than meeting my own. And much more fun.

"I think I always wanted this too. I just never imagined it was possible," I said.

"I can't wait to start building a life here with you, Miles."

"I love you, Natalie. There are so many things I can't wait to do with you."

"Like christen all the rooms?"

"I'm glad to see you're finally reading my newsletters."

Epilogue

The Following Summer
Natalie

ONE THING THAT I NEVER EXPERIENCED AS A CHILD, always on the move, was the unmitigated joy of coming *home* after a trip. Traveling again refilled my cup in ways I didn't know I'd needed, nourishing a crucial piece of my soul that had been ignored. And now that I got to take trips with Miles for his work, it was as though I was fully leaning into all parts of myself. I was a complicated jigsaw with all its pieces finally put together. So many memories of my parents poured back in as we drove up through the gargantuan trees of the Pacific Northwest, or through the long, flat plains of the Midwest. My parents' memory was all over this country, and it was such a gift to find that part of myself again that I hadn't even known I was neglecting.

But there was nothing quite like rounding that mountain pass, coming around that bend, and seeing the sun setting on the valley of Slippery Slopes, glowing pink and welcoming me home.

I sighed loudly as the comforting realization set in.

"I still can't believe I own a home. I get to go home," I said.

"It's pretty wonderful."

"To our home."

"Eh, I just live there." He shot me a tense smile.

"You know that home is as much yours as it is mine, Miles. I couldn't have made that garden bloom the way you did."

"I did help break in all the rooms thoroughly. On that note, don't tell that to Mags and Callie when they bring Otis to visit next month."

"It would only be fair after the things I learned when we went to visit them."

He laughed, but the closer to town we got, the more the tension grew in the car. A year ago, I might have still feared that he was itching to leave, but now I trusted our relationship and commitment to each other.

"But really, Miles, it's important to me, to this town, that you know this is just as much my home as it is yours. Slippery Slopes loves you. I love you," I said, trying to ease his tension.

He grabbed my hand without taking his eyes off the road and kissed my knuckles. "I know that. I feel that every day. Sometimes I still get so scared. With great love comes great terror, it turns out. But then, I find you and just look at you or hold your hand, and I tell myself, I'm okay. We are going to be okay."

I squeezed his hand back. "And whatever happens, we will figure it out and grow together."

"That's right." His brows furrowed, and he let out a long, slow breath quietly, likely hoping I wouldn't notice.

Despite my assurances about our relationship, I found myself growing nervous.

As we drove further down Main Street and the town square came into view, I saw a crowd was gathering.

"Huh, I wonder what's going on tonight."

Miles made a sound but didn't answer.

When he didn't turn onto our street, my confusion grew. We had been flying all morning, but I had still hoped we could grab dinner at Deb's or maybe pick up some tacos (not from Tony's).

"Maybe there is a group aura cleansing from Chrysta? Her crystal shop has been doing well," I said.

"Maybe."

"Or senior yoga in the park?"

Miles was leaning forward, looking for a place to park with a crease in his brow.

"You're not guessing. Guessing the wrong answers is half the fun."

His laugh was forced. "Sorry. Yeah, maybe it's that."

I narrowed my eyes. "Is something wrong? You're acting weird."

"I'm always weird. Maybe life outside this town for a week made you normal."

"I shudder to think." I shimmied dramatically. "Nah. I'm a Slippery Slopes resident through and through."

Miles finally found a spot to park.

"Where are we going?"

"Just a quick stop. I told Rochelle I'd help her with something," he said.

"I love that you two hit it off, but I hate that you text without me." I pretended to pout as he helped me out of my seat.

I gasped as we walked into the town square. The little gazebo was completely gorgeous, with brightly colored flowers winding up the supporting columns and a huge amount of white twinkling lights dangling inside. It was like something out of a movie.

"It's so beautiful," I said in awe. "Is that what you're helping Rochelle with?"

As we came closer, I noticed my best friend was there with her family. My heart began to pick up the pace. After that, many more people stepped forward from around the corner and out of storefronts, people I hadn't noticed.

"What's going on?" I asked, growing nervous.

I had thought it was strange when he insisted that we go home to change before we went out to dinner, but I hadn't thought twice about it. He'd really found his place in Slippery Slopes this past year, but he was still set on making a good impression. I glanced down to where I'd insisted on wearing my travel slip-ons, but I had upgraded to a stretchy sundress and cardigan. I'd perfected the curly girl hair routine these last few months, so at least the curls had managed to hold up. I shook my head at myself. It didn't matter how I looked or acted, that wasn't what made me loved.

"I have a little surprise for you," Miles said, clearing his throat.

All my nerves rushed forward. I'd been hoping . . . maybe . . .

My knees felt locked as he brought me to the gazebo.

"Miles? I'm getting nervous." I chuckled.

"Don't be. This is all for you. All you have to do is be here." He squeezed my sweaty hand. He raised an eyebrow. "Seriously. It's going to be okay."

I held his gaze and felt his sincerity. I blew out a long breath through pursed lips. "Okay. It's just all a little weird."

The rest of the crowd gathered closer, and Mayor Sparks stepped forward.

"Hi, Natalie. We wanted to thank you for being the ideal representative of Slippery Slopes, New Mexico." Mayor Sparks spoke loudly for the small crowd to hear. My mouth dropped open, my hands resting against my chest, feeling my racing heart. "Not only are you a wealth of knowledge of the town's history, but you are the embodiment of all we hope to represent here. A place for those who are lost to land softly. A place to make your own family." Here she looked at Miles, whose throat bobbed on a swallow. "We are thankful for all you do. And since our attempt to gift you the tickets last summer didn't work, we wanted to present you with a key to the city."

She stepped forward to hand me an oversized, old-fashioned silver key. On one side, *Key to Slippery Slopes* was engraved. And on the other side, *Natalie Weatherby, the Heart of the Town.*

I couldn't speak, so I just nodded, chin trembling.

Slippery Slopes was a home for all those who were lost and looking for their found family.

"This is an honor. Thank you so much. Thank you for letting me be me."

Everybody clapped, and then the party started in earnest. We partied into the night and ate tacos from Tres Conejos. It was a magical evening, even if the smallest part of me felt just a fraction of disappointment, thinking the night was going to be something else.

It wasn't until much later, when Miles and I were home and I lay in bed smiling, that I confessed the truth. The events of the day had caught up, and now it was almost midnight, and I struggled to keep my eyes open.

"Are you happy?" he whispered as we lay naked and entwined.

"So happy," I said with a yawn.

"Were you surprised today?"

"Oh, yeah. I had no idea. I thought you were going to propose today," I said, my head lying on his shoulder, our hands clasped on his chest. "Not that I'm not extremely thankful for the key to the city," I added quickly.

Miles chuckled under me. "Nah. You know me. I'm not one for big public displays. Plus, Deckard was there. Wouldn't want to make the poor guy feel even worse for missing out on you."

"Please. There was no Deckard and me. We both know that. I do wish him happiness. He's a good guy."

Miles made a sound of agreement. "He'll find someone. There is a sort of magic to this town, I have to admit."

"There really is." I closed my eyes and let the nighttime start to pull me under.

"Would you have said yes?" he asked tentatively.

"I guess we will never know," I said, just to be a brat.

"That's a shame. One can't rush into these things."

I yawned again. It had been over a year, but I guess that might feel too soon to some. Not to me, I was ready from when I moved in the first week he started renting. I thought when I bought the house, he'd have asked. But it didn't matter, it would happen when it happened.

"Plus, if I were going to propose, you know I'd do it when you least expect it."

"Hmm," I said. "Sounds like you."

I felt him shift, but I didn't open my eyes.

"I'd want it to be just us two. A quiet moment. When my heart was beating so hard because it was bursting with the knowledge that it knew I had found my person, who I would love forever."

"You're so sweet," I mumbled.

"Open your eyes, for just a second more, Natalie."

I did as I was asked, with some difficulty. But when I spotted the little ring box, balanced on his chest inches from my eyes, I was wide awake again. "A moment like this, maybe?"

"Miles!" I shot up in bed.

He chuckled and pushed up too. He grabbed the box and opened it to reveal a sparkling engagement ring. "Will you marry me, Natalie?"

I rolled my eyes and shoved him lightly. "Yes. Of course."

"I wanted to ask you a hundred times, but the timing never felt right."

"I know a thing or two about that." I smiled at him, flushing as he slid the ring onto my finger. It fit perfectly.

"And you're okay I asked like this, without the town?" he asked nervously.

"Yes, Miles. This place might be where I live, but you are my home."

He let out a breath and leaned forward to kiss me. "I love you more than I ever thought I was capable of loving someone, Natalie."

"And I love you."

I didn't end up falling asleep until much later. And it was totally worth it.

**Want more Natalie and Miles? Check out a bonus scene for* All Downhill From Here *when you sign up for Piper's newsletter!*
CLICK HERE
If you are already signed up for her newsletter, all bonus scenes are linked in her newsletters.

*** But wait, there's more! If you enjoyed ALL JOKING ASIDE and want more by Piper Sheldon, read on for the first chapter of Book 1 in the Unlucky in Love trilogy, "Stranger Than Fan Fiction." An epistolary, friends-to-lovers, Romcom about a former child star with a major glow-up who starts an online friendship with his fan fiction writer across the sea. Little does she know her online pen pal is actually her celebrity crush.*

Stranger Than Fan Fiction

Two Years Ago
Charlie

I gestured to let my new housekeeper lead the way out of the dining room. Not *just* out of a sense of chivalry, but because I didn't trust her behind my back.

"The kitchen is right through here," I explained.

The older woman's sensible trainers hardly made a sound on the worn hall carpeting. *The better for sneaking around ...*

Agata had been so quiet since she arrived. Normally, I relished silence, but this felt like a form of torture. Did she have misgivings about my scandalous past? Or was she simply wondering how I'd managed this long alone?

Based on how she eyed the stack of dishes near the sink, I suspected the latter.

It had been years since I had people working for me, and as it turned out, I still found the whole experience of managing people when I couldn't manage myself incredibly uncomfortable, if not hypocritical. If Emma hadn't insisted that I hire someone to keep the ancient estate from crumbling, I might have just gone on alone forever. After all, the whole point of disappearing from a life of celebrity and into the English countryside was to avoid uncomfortable interactions at all costs.

"No dishwasher?" She sniffed, looking down her nose even though she barely reached my chest.

Did she scare me? Absolutely. I didn't like it, but dammit, I respected it.

An inoffensive light lemon smell clung to her gray frock. Her blond hair was tight in a low bun, and she had a tiny, pinched mouth.

"I plan on doing some renovations and additions over time. But for now, it's a bit rustic," I said.

I glanced away when she scrutinized me. The thing with sobriety was, as fast as everything goes to shite, it takes a hell of a lot longer to work back up to any sense of normalcy. I had intended on updating the Vicarage ages ago, but some days simply existing was chore enough.

She nodded; hands clasped in front of her. "Okay," she settled on.

The small reassurance unclenched my jaw.

"The Vicarage is a bit of a drive from the nearest town. But you can have groceries delivered. I'm assuming the agency told you about ..." I scratched the back of my neck.

"No booze," she said in her soft Polish accent.

"Right. Except in your cottage, of course. I just ask not in the main house."

She nodded firmly. "I don't drink. It's no problem."

Straight to the point and no nonsense, Agata was beginning to grow on me. Emma likely had these traits in mind when she set up this appointment with the agency's recommendation.

"I guess that's everything. Do you have any questions?" I asked.

She looked me up and down. "What you want for lunch?"

"You just got here. You don't have to—"

A hand snaked out and pinched my abdomen sharply. "Too skinny."

I flinched. That's something I'd never been accused of. "I just—"

"You don't pick. You have sausage soup." Her mouth hardly moved when she spoke, but the words felt as threatening as a yell.

Feeling more than a little frightened, I acquiesced. "Ah, that's good. Thank you."

She turned her back to me and got to moving in the small kitchen.

I looked around, feeling useless. I'd already brought her single worn suitcase to the small guest house. I knocked once on the counter. "Welp, I'll let you get settled. It's been nice meeting you. Welcome to the Vicarage, Agata."

I moved to walk away.

"It smells like boy feets in here," she said as she set a large pot on the hob.

"Ah. Right." Honesty was an admirable quality in a home-maker. "I suppose you got here in the nick of time."

She sniffed again. "My children watched you when they grow up. That space show." She looked me up and down. "You were chubby funny one."

Her kids must be grown now too. Probably close to my age. That space show she referred to was *TerraFormative*, part of a multi-billion-dollar franchise based on the science fiction books written by G.S. Sedar. The series followed three children through adolescence upon a spaceship adrift in space, looking for a new Earth. Eight solid years of my adolescence I was Freddy Finks, chubby comic relief of the Intrepid Trio. My real-life best friends Emma Flynn and Harrison Evans played my two closest comrades in trouble, Lucy Lennon and Adam Abbott, respectively.

Almost twenty years ago, over in the blink of an eye to most, and yet the thing that would always define me. I was used to these types of conversations. I kept my face blank.

"Freddy." I dropped my arm before I could scratch the back of my neck again. "Yep. That was me."

"Skinny Charlie is not so funny. You eat more. You be funny. Funny man gets wife. Or husband," she added. "I'm modern woman. I understand."

"Good. Right. I'll keep that in mind." I was hardly skinny. As I'd aged, my notable baby fat had melted off my face, but I would always be described as sturdily built—now with defined cheekbones.

Her gaze narrowed on me. "Soup will be ready in one hour. Come back. Have bread too."

"I try not to eat carbs—"

"You eat the bread."

I swallowed before I nodded, afraid to do anything but agree.

"Well, I better get back to my office to ..."

To pretend to work. I finished in my head.

She paused from taking inventory of my cabinets to give me another sharp nod.

I slunk off to my unused office. I didn't really work. Hadn't really needed to in the ten years since the show wrapped. I'd been sober three of those years thanks to therapy and rehab. My only job now was to ensure I stayed on track and didn't put the people who cared about me at risk for bystander humiliation. Each day, I spent about an hour responding to fan mail, but even that had dwindled down considerably over the years. That, reading, and working out occupied most of my time.

Maybe it wasn't an exciting existence, but it was a safe one.

It was Emma who insisted I bring in help now that I had gotten most of my life back in order. Emma was all about goals and motivations and life purpose. I didn't have the heart to tell her that simply making it day to day took so much emotional toll, there wasn't much room for anything else. I would get back there eventually, but right now, I lived tucked away safely at my home in Devon.

After rehab, I moved away from the temptations of London and bought a former vicarage. The plan was to eventually modernize the estate, but I hadn't gotten around to it yet. AA didn't recommend too many major life changes once sober, so I'd been waiting until I felt secure. Sobriety had taken more focus than I had anticipated. Employing Agata felt like a step in the right direction, another level of accountability.

It was almost time for my monthly meeting with Emma and Harrison. Their schedules were far more packed than mine, but we at least tried to arrange monthly video chats. I had dubbed those first few meetings as "proof of life," but I think seeing my face reassured Emma as much as it did me.

It was five minutes until our appointed time when they both texted to say they couldn't make the call today. Emma had got caught up in the details of arranging clean water for a town in a developing country and Harrison was working on a film bound to land him another Oscar nod. And here I was, doing absolutely nothing except getting bullied by my new homemaker.

I let out a long sigh. They weren't my keepers; they had busy lives, but this wasn't the first time I felt stuck in limbo because of my actions as the world blurred by.

I opened a tab on the internet when a wave of something crashed over me. Boredom? Listlessness? Loneliness? I fought hard to keep the indescribable emotion from pulling me under. One thing about sobriety that I wasn't prepared for was how both crucial and yet mind-numbingly boring routine would be in my life. It was better than the alternative: waking up without knowing whose bed I was in ... or what country, for that matter. This was a slow and tedious process to feel secure in myself, but how many months of monotony stretched ahead? Every day safe, but uneventful?

Agata hit the mark when she made the comment about my getting a wife. At least, she recognized my restlessness. I was lonely, but that was a whole other aspect of moderation I wasn't ready to tackle yet. Without my two best friends, who I was lucky to still have, I didn't really have anybody else to talk to. I could call my sponsor, but I didn't want a drink. I just wanted ... I didn't know, someone to talk to.

God, how pathetic.

Poor rich child star, all alone in his big country house with all his money.

I sighed again loudly and did the thing I told myself I wouldn't do any more. *One* of the things. Because what else does a retired child star do when amid a pity party? They googled themselves.

The articles about me had slowed down in the years since rehab. My publicity team had done a great job of keeping press to a minimum. The top results were old articles about England's biggest "glow up," whatever that meant. All the links led to "articles" that included countless GIFs and JPEGs of shirtless photos taken in the past few years, side by side with chubby Freddy bulging out of his *TerraFormative* flight suit.

I rested my chin in my palm as I lazily scrolled. Bored. This was pathetic. I should just close out the browser to go workout or something.

A clickbait article at the bottom of the screen caught my eye. "Top Ten Freddy Fanfics—Can't get enough of the UK's hottest former child star Charles Downing? Check out these Freddy fan favorites that take this heavenly body out of this world."

"Oh lord," I said out loud to the pun-tastic title even as I clicked the link.

I'd heard about all the fanfic that *TerraFormative* had manifested over the years. Emma, Harrison, and I had been paired in every possible combination. It was an unavoidable product of being part of one of the world's largest franchises. I'd always stayed away, feeling a new level of skeezy hearing about the various scenarios people had placed my character in. Especially with Harrison and Emma. We'd grown up together and were closer than siblings. Anything romantic was … icky.

The headline took me to a website called FanFavz. The interface was not terribly user-friendly, but after clicking around a bit, I got the gist. You could search by franchise, author, story popularity, etc. I sorted by author popularity within the *TerraFormative* world since I'd already committed to spending time in the gutter. The very first result was the story that had been mentioned in the article. In fact, the author had a few dozen "fics" under their name. The article dubbed this particular story, "Fresh Stars," "the top Freddy post-grad fantasy." It had been favorited an astounding forty *thousand* times, and comments were a never-ending gushfest, consisting mostly of emojis and lines of repeated vowels. Post-grad referred to the time after the show ended, when Freddy had graduated from the flight academy.

"Bloody hell," I mumbled. So many people out there reading a version of myself far more interesting than the one that existed. The top author on each list was someone called FreddyStan4Life.

"Regrettable username." My face contorted, leaning closer to the screen. "Who the bloody hell is Stan?"

I read the first sentence.

Then the next.

Then several chapters. The story focused on my—er, Freddy's post-flight academy life, as he worked up the ranks to become a captain of his own vessel and featured a particularly strong romance with a cyborg named Nix, who had been in the show but only briefly in season four. I'd loved that subplot when it had debuted in the show. I had approached the writers about stretching out their love story over a few more episodes but had been shot down. The writers had reminded me that Freddy's character only existed to relieve the tension when things got too heavy. But this "Fresh Stars" I read now was ... *good*. Really good.

I also couldn't help but notice that FreddyStan4Life's description of Freddy resembled me as I looked now, instead of the child I was in the series. Interesting.

It felt like only a minute had passed when a loud rap on the closed door caused me to jump in my seat.

"You come eat, Mr. Downing." Agata's soft voice was a deceptive ruse, like calling the shake of a rattlesnake as soothing as a child's rattle.

"You can call me Charlie," I shouted through the door.

"Mister Charlie, come eat."

"Can you bring me a bowl in here?" I asked.

"No. Break from computer better for your eyes." Her footsteps retreated back to the kitchen.

I sighed loudly but pushed away from my desk.

At the kitchen island, Agata shoved two warm crusty rolls on my plate and wouldn't stop staring at me until I ate them along with the soup.

The whole meal was delicious, but she side-eyed me as I shoveled bites into my mouth. I couldn't focus on anything but getting back to my computer.

"Thank you. It was fantastic," I said.

She nodded knowingly as I rushed out of the room.

I thought I knew what fan fiction was—admittedly, I

thought it was primarily an excuse to make characters have sex —but this was unlike anything I expected. The writing was compelling and thought-provoking from the first line. The world was as familiar as sliding into a worn jumper, but the new scenarios were intriguing and the additional settings captivating. It felt so familiar and yet unlike anything I'd ever read. My eyes couldn't read fast enough. My heart raced, desperate to get back to it. I missed feeling ... *excited*. About anything.

I would just read a few more chapters, just to see what happened next, and then I'd stop.

Continue reading *Stranger Than Fan Fiction...*

Acknowledgments

Hello reader! Thank you so much for being here. I was so glad to be back in Slippery Slopes and visit with all the zany characters there. And don't you worry, there is plenty more to come. I'm sure you're just as curious as I am as to who saved Deckard that day.

I loved writing this story. I had originally planned a much more intense workplace rivalry but these characters really do be doing whatever they want. Their banter was SO fun to write and I still think about Natalie and Miles all the time.

(Oh also, I don't know how many little easter eggs you were able to catch from my other books but they were there! If you were like, what is this show *Terraformative*? Don't worry, it's not technically real (much to my dismay). It's a fictional show I created in my Unlucky in Love Trilogy in which three former childhood actors and best friends navigate life and love as adults after starring in one of TV's biggest franchises of all time. So if you like my writing style, definitely check it out.)

ANYWAY. I wouldn't be here without a whole lot of people so here we go!

Thank you to Nora and Laney for always being a constant source of patient understanding when I inevitably spin out about my story. Seriously, thank you so freaking much.

Thank you so much to my amazing team of editors; Nicole, Briana, and Marla. They are all linked in the front matter of this story if you are looking for some great editors.

Thank you to my reader group Pipe's Peeps (Piper Sheldon Reader Group) - we have fun.

Thank you to the friends and family in my "real life" who know and support this career of mine. I know that I am extremely fortunate to be able to do what I do. And I will continue to do it as long as I can <3

Thank you to all the Real Human artists and creatives out there creating amazing media/entertainment in all forms, for all of us to consume and be inspired by. Art is constantly inspiring art and that can't be manufactured artificially.

Thanks to my husband who is quite literally my biggest fan even when I glare at him for breathing too loud.

Follow me on any of my socials (you'll see those linked on the next page) and shoot me a message or email me directly at pipersheldonauthor@gmail.com. I absolutely love hearing from readers. Leaving a review is hugely helpful to authors like myself. THANK YOU SO MUCH FOR READING <3

And once again, to you reading this now. I am not kidding when I tell you that I would not be able to do this without you.

THANK YOU!

About the Author

Piper Sheldon writes Contemporary Romance and Paranormal Romance. Her books are a little funny, a lotta romantic, and with just a little twist of something more. She lives with her husband, daughter, and elderly dog at home in the desert Southwest. She finds writing about herself in the third person an extreme sport in awkwardness.

Sign up for her newsletter here!
    http://pipersheldon.com/newsletter

If you are a Piper Sheldon fan, join her Facebook reader group to get all this insider info!
    Pipe's Peeps (Piper Sheldon Reader Group)

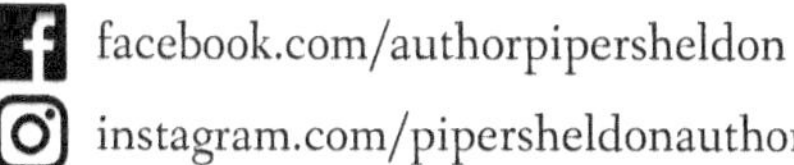

facebook.com/authorpipersheldon
instagram.com/pipersheldonauthor

Also by Piper Sheldon

Unlucky in Love Series - Contemporary Celebrity Romance

Stranger Than Fan Fiction

Better Date Than Never

Down For the Word Count

Slippery Slopes Series - Small town, Romantic Comedy

All Downhill From Here

All Joking Aside

The Unseen Series - Paranormal Romance

The Unseen

The Untouched

Cozy Creek Collection - Small Town Romance, collaborative series

Fall Shook Up

Smartypants Romance

The Scorned Women's Society - Small Town Romance

My Bare Lady

The Treble With Men

The One That I Want

Hopelessly Devoted

It Takes a Woman

The Teacher's Lounge - Small Town Romance, collaborative series

Band Together

You can find all of Piper's books at pipersheldon.com or on her author page on Amazon.

www.ingramcontent.com/pod-product-compliance
Lightning Source LLC
Chambersburg PA
CBHW020240010826

48973CB00006B/1590